Paris 1935

Destiny's Crossroads

Paul A. Myers

Published by Paul A. Myers Books
Copyright © Paul A. Myers 2011
ISBN-13: 978-0-9825960-7-4
ISBN-10: 0-9825960-7-3

Revised 2019-04-29.

Print and eBook editions available at US and international online retailers.

Send comments to myersbooks@gmail.com

Additional information at http://www.myersbooks.com

Comments on novels by Paul A. Myers

Greek Bonds and French Ladies

Love and money are both at risk in Myers' politically driven novel of intrigue and betrayal...told with humor and sophistication.
   —Kirkus Reviews

It has French charm and romance intertwined with a feeling of extravagance and elegance.
   —Jennie, Goodreads review

A Farewell in Paris

In this lively novel, Myers clearly demonstrates his familiarity with the intellectual culture of Paris in the 1920s.
   — Publishers Weekly

Few places evoke nostalgia like the City of Light in the 1920s, and Myers doesn't skimp on the literary and historical details in his latest novel.
   —Kirkus Reviews

...excellent historical perspective regarding the failed peace between the two great wars of the last century. It's the historical research that makes this book interesting.
   —Al, Goodreads review

Paris 1935: Destiny's Crossroads

...takes us into the back rooms of high-level officials, writers, and media stars in order to understand why events happened as they did...involved and intriguing, Myers' work definitely is worth reading.
   —Historical Novel Society Online Review

What were the diplomatic and political actions in France leading up to the start of WWII? What treaties and alliances in Europe set the wheels

in motion for Hitler to get Germany moving? ...the true story is the political intrigue ...
  —Barbara Ell, Goodreads review

Paris 1934: Victory in Retreat

...descriptive and thoroughly researched narrative feels true to the era; the "City of Light" shines through the page.
  —Historical Novel Society Online Review

I fell in love with this book as I was reading it. First of all I love historical fiction and the author was amazing with the plot and the details...
  —Brittany Tedder-Bixlar, Goodreads review

Vienna 1934: Betrayal at the Ballplatz

Myers' characters feel true to the era...an excellent job of making the story real due to his good research and fine storytelling. The interweaving of fact, fiction, real, and fictional people makes this book exciting and romantic.
  —Historical Novel Society Online Review

...found this story to be very informative about the pre-war situation in Europe, but especially in Austria...I found this book interesting, well written in most instances and full of intrigue, suspense, and romance.
  —Twin Two, Amazon customer review

Author

Paul A. Myers lives in Corona del Mar, California with his wife Minche. He is the author of the historical novels *A Farewell in Paris, Paris 1934: Victory in Retreat, Vienna 1934: Betrayal at the Ballplatz,* the satirical novel *Greek Bonds and French Ladies,* and the maritime history *North to California: The Spanish Voyages of Discovery 1533-1603.*

Paul A. Myers at Tuileries Gardens, Paris

Table of Contents

Contents

Epigraph

Lost Horizons

The Peace Treaties should have enabled Great Britain and France, the two countries pursuing a joint and active policy for the defense of these Treaties under the auspices of the League of Nations, to be the masters of war and peace in Europe for half a century at least.

Geneviève Tabouis
Blackmail or War
February 1938

The pages which follow are concerned with relations between allies, and either joint or single negotiations with the dictatorships whose appetites then threatened peace and later led to war. The negotiations were for the most part a record of failure, but their lessons are important.

Anthony Eden, Earl of Avon
Facing the Dictators: The Memoirs of Anthony Eden
1962

Principal Cast of Characters

Fictional

Dexter Jones – an American diplomat

Marcelle Lambert – a senior civil servant working in the premier's office

Suzanne Bardoux – a senior civil servant working in the foreign ministry

Étienne – a lecturer at Sciences Po, a prestigious university on the Left Bank

Secrétaire Général – the head of the permanent staff in the premier's office

Monsieur le Minister – a fictionalization of the finance minister

Historic characters

Geneviève Tabouis – diplomatic correspondent for a Parisian daily newspaper

André Géraud, pen name Pertinax – political correspondent for a Parisian daily newspaper

Pierre Laval – premier and foreign minister of France (and *Time* magazine's Man of the Year for 1931)

Alexis Léger – secretary-general of the foreign ministry and head of the permanent staff (later awarded the Nobel Prize for Literature in 1960 as the poet Saint-John Perse)

Anthony Eden – British minister to the League of Nations; later foreign secretary

Stanley Baldwin – British prime minister

Sir Samuel Hoare – British foreign secretary

Sir Robert Vansittart – British permanent undersecretary of the Foreign Office

Pierre-Étienne Flandin – French foreign minister from February 1936

Albert-Pierre Sarraut – French premier from February 1936

Cameo – André and Clara Malraux, Sylvia Beach, Adrienne Monnier, André and Lucy Chamson, Colonel Charles de Gaulle

Book One
The Hoare-Laval Pact

Quai d'Orsay

Friday afternoon, June 21, 1935. Dexter Jones walked up the majestic Grand Staircase of the Hôtel de Quai d'Orsay, home of the French foreign ministry, admiring the large tapestries hanging on the walls as he went. He reflected that these beautiful *objets d'art* dated from a prior century when France was the reigning power on the continent of Europe.

Reaching the second floor, Dexter continued up a less majestic stairway to the third floor. He turned and walked down a corridor in the *administration centrale*, the administrative offices of the secretary-general, the senior civil servant and permanent secretary of the ministry. He came to an open doorway and walked in. He asked the receptionist, "Is Madame Bardoux in?"

The receptionist smiled and said, "Yes." She stood up and walked over to the inner door, looked in, and whispered a few words to the prim woman sitting behind the desk. The receptionist stepped back and with her palm ushered Dexter into the office. "This way, Monsieur Jones."

Dexter walked into the office. The always-elegant Madame Bardoux rose to greet him. Out of the corner of his eye, he saw another woman sitting over in a wing chair, a pleasantly attractive lady wearing the tasteful clothes of a senior *redactrice,* or senior civil servant, the stylish black skirt, the dark stockings, the black pumps, and the starched white linen blouse of her caste. The dark hair was swept up in a chignon, elegant and functional, dark eyes glistened as she smiled at him in a professional manner. He could see that she was a woman who met men in a highly assured way—serene, and expert at creating a proper distance.

Dexter noticed the little black ribbon, the *deuil*, pinned to the woman's blouse just below the left wing tip of the collar—the badge of a widow in mourning. The little black ribbons were as ubiquitous in France in the 1930s as the graves of dead French soldiers in the grassy fields of France's eastern provinces, the epic killing grounds of the Western Front. Nevertheless, the woman, possibly in her late thirties, still seemed a little young for a war widow, he thought.

Madame Bardoux held out her hand and Dexter took it in his own, gallantly nodded and said, "Madame Bardoux."

Madame Bardoux smiled and said, "May I present Madame Lambert."

The woman stood up. Dexter could see that she was pleasingly slender and of medium height, possibly the same age as himself. Dexter silently brought his heels together, bowed slightly, and held out his hand, *"Enchanté."*

"Enchantée," replied Madame Lambert.

Dexter could see that behind the lustrous dark eyes was a deeper, more thoughtful gaze, one carefully appraising this new man standing in front of her. Dexter also saw that this woman quickly sized men up. Intriguing, thought Dexter. He idly wondered how he fared in this feminine, but highly professional, appraisal.

Madame Bardoux spoke to Madame Lambert, "Monsieur Jones is a political attaché at the American embassy."

Madame Lambert smiled in acknowledgement.

Madame Bardoux swept her hand in front of her two visitors and said, "Please, sit down." Dexter and Madame Lambert both sat down.

Madame Bardoux, speaking to Dexter, said, "Madame Lambert works at the Hôtel Matignon. She is part of the *secrétariat général du gouvernement*, what you Americans would call 'the permanent administration' that supports the office of the premier.

Madame Lambert silently nodded in agreement.

Madame Bardoux continued, "Premier Laval has served as foreign minister for the past six months. As you well know, we here at the Quai d'Orsay have supported his very imaginative ministry as he has re-fashioned France's foreign policy, very much along the lines laid out by our late foreign minister, Louis Barthou."

Dexter nodded in understanding; Barthou had been hugely energetic before being cut down in Marseilles by an assassin's bullet just nine months before.

Madame Bardoux continued, "Monsieur Laval made Italy the centerpiece of his policy to contain German Nazism. He solidly linked France with Italy in his trip to Rome last January. That of course led to the Stresa Front, the alliance between Great Britain,

France, and Italy, in April." She paused and concluded, "The cornerstone of France's foreign policy."

Dexter smiled and said to Madame Lambert, "Madame Bardoux and I were both in Rome last January when Foreign Minister Laval had his historic meetings with Mussolini."

Madame Lambert smiled in acknowledgement.

Dexter decided to interject a sharp edge to the conversation, "We at the embassy see that the British have chosen this week to announce the signing of a previously secret Naval Treaty with Germany. The accord negates another key provision of the Versailles Peace Treaty." Dexter added, almost apologetically, "The Naval Treaty would seem to put a big dent in the Stresa Front."

Madame Bardoux sighed, unable to contain her disappointment, "I cannot comment except to say that keeping Italy in the western alliance remains a keystone of French foreign policy." Then she added, "There has been talk this was Anthony Eden's doing," referring to the handsomely debonair British minister to the League of Nations, the rising young star in the aging British cabinet.

Anthony Eden

Somewhat startled by the comment, Dexter asked, "Why?"

"The rumor is that he was worried about French naval superiority over the British fleet in the Mediterranean."

Dexter's face went blank with astonishment. He mumbled, "The British were worried about French naval superiority in the Mediterranean?" Had anyone ever honestly thought French naval superiority should be a British concern since the days of Napoleon, he wondered. Seemed sort of dumb, he thought.

Then he looked at Madame Bardoux and said, "That would mean Eden has mistaken Mussolini to be Britain's adversary, not Hitler."

Madame Bardoux added in a dismissive manner, "The British worry a lot about their Mediterranean lifeline to India, apparently in a highly distorted way."

Regaining his composure, Dexter summed up, "An interesting misjudgment."

Madame Bardoux added, "Eden is rumored to be the next foreign minister. What future misjudgments might he make?"

Dexter nodded thoughtfully at this insight; a useful bit of information that he would share with his colleagues back at the embassy, who tended to be star-struck by the superbly tailored foreign secretary-in-waiting.

Madame Bardoux added, "Eden is handsome like the American movie star Errol Flynn. Very dashing."

Dexter smiled inwardly: Madame Bardoux did not mean this as a compliment.

Madame Bardoux lightly added, "The American press always loves a handsome face." Boy, the needle was out today, Dexter thought.

Dexter made a playful grimace in response to the barbed comment. Then putting a lighter tone on his next remark, Dexter suggested, "With regard to leaving France out of the treaty negotiations, you might have your London ambassador mention to the British foreign office that France has a navy, too." He smirked in self-satisfaction at this little piece of sarcasm, then flippantly added, "Tucked away in the harbor of some colony in Africa, I believe," and he turned and smiled at Madame Lambert like a prankish schoolboy.

Madame Bardoux relaxed and smiled indulgently; she had performed her task: an American diplomat, conveniently at a low level, had been informed that possibly Anthony Eden was not the wunderkind so many believed him to be.

With a slight rustle of her skirt, Madame Lambert sat forward, prim as a school mistress, and addressed Dexter, "One minor point, if I may, if your allusion was to the harbor of Mers-el-Kébir in Algeria, well, Algeria is a *departement* of France, not a colony." She sat back in her chair, a relaxed smile on her face.

Dexter's eyebrows went up, then he grinned and nodded in acknowledgement at Madame Lambert. A pleasant sensation came over him from this minor point of correction; he felt not a trace of irritation.

Dexter decided upon another sally. "The diplomatic community is quite taken with Premier Laval's widely quoted remark to the British chargé d'affaires upon hearing the news about the Anglo-German Naval Treaty, 'I may not be a gentleman, Mr. Campbell, but I most certainly would not act as you have done.'" Once again, Great Britain had gone behind France's back.

Dexter glanced sideways at Madame Lambert; she made a thin smile with what seemed a hint of approval at the premier's remark. She was not exactly a screaming headline, thought Dexter.

Dexter turned back and smiled warmly at Madame Bardoux, more as a signal of his fascination with Madame Lambert than anything else. Madame Bardoux, of course, missed nothing.

Madame Bardoux returned Dexter's smile and then looked knowingly over at Madame Lambert. Madame Lambert smiled, her face a noncommittal mask.

Deciding to move on to the next item on the agenda, Madame Bardoux placed her hands, fingers intertwined, on her desk neatly centered in front of her and in a businesslike manner continued, "Monsieur Laval has now added the duties of premier to his many responsibilities. So he has offices at both the Hôtel Matignon and here at the Quai d'Orsay. Madame Lambert and I have been charged with ensuring that the right official papers are maintained in the appropriate offices. Careful and thorough coordination is required," and she looked at Madame Lambert for confirmation.

Madame Lambert smiled, nodded in agreement, and replied with one word, "Yes." She looked at Dexter and smiled again, giving Dexter the accurate impression that one of Madame Lambert's gifts was discretion, a deep appreciation for the power of words not said.

Dexter understood. He recalled the swirl of events leading to Laval's ascension to power the previous week. A mad scramble had begun two weeks before as President Lebrun offered the premiership to one leading politician after another, each failing to muster a majority because the Chamber of Deputies would not grant "full decree powers" to meet the financial emergency driving the crisis. Finally, working through the night, the crafty peasant politician turned millionaire lawyer, Pierre Laval, cobbled together a government in President Lebrun's office just as day was breaking. Government formed, Laval then led the dead-tired ministers out of the Élysée Palace into the early morning sunrise. The press quickly named the new government the Dawn Cabinet. Sounded hopeful.

The centerpiece of the political deal was a skillfully brokered "restricted extraordinary powers" motion that would give Laval broad authority to enact by decree financial measures to stem the flight of gold from the Bank of France. But the decrees would be subject to future approval by the Chamber; accordingly the requirements of parliamentary democracy were maintained. Long-time Radical Socialist party leader Édouard Herriot provided the margin of political support; he agreed to enter the government with five other bourgeois Radical ministers. Rumor was that Herriot had assured Laval of six months continuity in the Chamber.

Madame Bardoux spoke, "Yes, as foreign minister, Monsieur Laval successfully contained Hitler. Now, as premier, he is to balance the budget."

Dexter replied, "Balancing the budget carries its own risks. It's hard to predict, but some form of deflation seems inevitable if the *franc* continues to be maintained at its current exchange rate. It is overvalued."

Madame Bardoux said, doubt in her voice, "Well, yes, but I of course do not know what the consequences of any particular financial policy will be."

"Possibly more unemployment," ventured Dexter.

Madame Bardoux winced. France was beset with difficulties.

Madame Lambert listened attentively, clearly grasping the argument, but not offering any further comment. Dexter looked at her inquiringly; she smiled at him pleasantly.

Changing the subject, Madame Bardoux asked Dexter, "What has you on our side of the river this afternoon?"

Dexter replied, "I am on my way to the Palais de la Mutualité to see the opening of the International Writers Congress. André Gide is going to make the opening remarks," speaking of the dean of French literature, a man who probably would already have his Nobel Prize if not for his well-known Communist party sympathies. Leastwise that was the way the literary rumors were traveling across the cafés of the Left Bank, thought Dexter.

Madame Lambert inquired, "André Malraux is the co-chairman. Is he going to speak tonight?"

Dexter answered, "Probably. He is the energizing force behind the convention."

Madame Lambert nodded in agreement and then ventured, "He seems to be the man to follow in Paris just now. He is the very symbol of the *écrivain engagé*"—the committed writer.

Dexter asked, "Are you interested in Malraux's work?"

Madame Lambert replied, "His books on the Far East are fascinating. The collision of revolution with colonialism. The development of the ideal of revolutionary heroism." Dexter sensed some hidden appreciation of the colonial situation in Madame Lambert's comment; possibly she had some personal experience in the French Empire. Intriguing.

Dexter nodded in agreement, "Yes, quite so. He will be giving the closing address next Tuesday evening."

Madame Lambert took in this bit of information without further comment.

Dexter rose and said, "I must be going. I don't want to keep you ladies from your work." Then he stopped, recalling the reason for his visit. "Oh, yes. You are of course invited to the American embassy for our Fourth of July reception." He stopped and swept both women up in his glance. "Both of you."

Both women rose. Madame Bardoux held out her hand. "We will be pleased to consider it." Dexter shook the outstretched hand.

He turned and held out his hand to Madame Lambert. She reached out and gave it a polite shake and smiled pleasantly at him. She made no comment on the invitation. He turned and walked out the door.

Hôtel Matignon

Late Friday afternoon, Left Bank, Hôtel Matignon, offices of the permanent secretariat to the Président du Conseil, the formal name of the office of the premier. The swarthy, dark-haired man with the black brush mustache and the white silk tie walked down the high-ceilinged hallway, his shoes making a light tapping sound as the soles hit the highly polished parquet floors. Coming to the open door of a spacious office overlooking the rear park with its long lawns and columns of trimmed trees, the man knocked lightly and stepped inside. The dark-suited man sitting behind the desk sprang to his feet and walked around the desk to greet his visitor.

"Monsieur le Premier, may I be at your service?"

The swarthy man politely replied, *"Monsieur le Secrétaire Général,* I wanted to meet your staff since we will all be working together on the most arduous tasks in the coming weeks. Paring down the public spending to balance the budget will be a severe test."

The *secrétaire général* responded, "Of course, the *service administratif* stands ready to assure the smooth functioning of the government." The *secrétaire général* smiled at the premier with an appraising glance; the premier was now a wealthy Paris lawyer, but he had started as a bumpkin from the provinces. He was admiringly referred to as the shrewdest peasant in France.

Pierre Laval during WW II

Paul A. Myers

The *secrétaire général* escorted the premier out into the hallway, "This way, Monsieur le Premier."

The *secrétaire général* nodded ahead to a receptionist and asked softly by way of inquiry for his principal assistant, "Madame Lambert?"

The woman stepped through a nearby door into an interior office and said, "Madame."

Presently, Madame Lambert stepped out of her office into the corridor, and in a moment of recognition, she smiled warmly at the premier with a look of easy friendship in her eyes.

The premier said, "Ah, Madame Lambert."

The *secrétaire général* immediately understood that the premier knew Madame Lambert, and rather well he gathered. He also knew that the premier was totally devoted to his wife and daughter, a man unknown to wander with other women. The respect for Madame Lambert would be strictly professional concluded the *secrétaire général*. Which would of course be completely consistent with everything he knew about Madame Lambert. He smiled inwardly. His wife had been trying at every social occasion for months to pry out the tiniest detail about Madame Lambert from behind her monumental discretion.

The premier turned to the *secrétaire general*. "I know Madame Lambert well from the ministry of labor."

The *secrétaire général* quickly understood. "Yes, of course." The premier had been minister of labor in 1930. With Herculean labor, he had drafted a sweeping social security program for France and through incessant lobbying of all the parties got the legislation through both houses of parliament. It was the most important law passed so far by the Third Republic.

The premier watched the *secrétaire général*, saw his mind clear, and then good-naturedly said, "In 1930, I saw that the task of passing a social insurance law had broken all governments since the Great War. Therefore, I resolved to start afresh. The people associated with the failures of the past had to go. We undertook a thorough house cleaning of the ministry of labor. Then we wrote a new social security law. With the parliament of course. Madame Lambert was of skillful assistance in our efforts." The premier smiled.

The *secrétaire général* immediately saw the threat; the senior civil service dare not obstruct the political leadership, so he mused, or the junior civil service would replace them. *Voila!* But the threat was so crudely put that he wondered what the real item on today's agenda was. He was sure he would soon find out.

9

The premier nodded at Madame Lambert. "Isn't that so, Madame Lambert?"

"Yes, Monsieur le Premier." She dipped her head in a hint of a curtsey.

"Ah, I see that you are now a *chef du bureau*, Madame Lambert?"

"No, Monsieur le Premier, I remain a *sous-chef*."

The *secrétaire général* intervened, "She has been seconded from the ministry of labor. Here she holds temporary appointment as *chef du bureau* and is paid a supplemental allowance to bring her pay up to the same level." The *secrétaire général* smiled with some self-satisfaction at the arrangement.

The premier looked at Madame Lambert. She smiled in thin acquiescence.

The premier smiled warmly at Madame Lambert's minor dissatisfaction with the arrangement. He admired her ambition, and in due time would make good use of it. The clean competence of her ambition so neatly fit into his plans. So much better than the schemes of some of the other women who tried to use their wiles, if not charms, to promote their careers. Almost always resulting in unfortunate consequences, the premier thought.

The premier turned to the *secrétaire general*. "We must keep in mind the well-deserved promotion."

The *secrétaire général* brought his heels together and bowed slightly. "Our thoughts exactly, Monsieur le Premier."

The premier nodded in approval. Then bringing Madame Lambert into his gaze, he said, "Let's go into Madame Lambert's office and talk."

Madame Lambert turned and entered her office, the premier followed, and then the *secrétaire général*, who closed the door behind them. All took a seat.

The premier began, businesslike in tone, "The government has been given the authority by the parliament to rule by decree in financial matters. A comprehensive and coordinated set of laws and regulations must be implemented by the end of July. But all the decrees must submitted to parliament when it returns in October. So the decrees must be written to exacting professional standards."

The *secrétaire général* nodded in agreement.

The premier summarized his program, "The government is striving for fiscal independence, flexibility, and for equality of sacrifice."

The *secrétaire général* focused on the words "equality of sacrifice," that would be the political issue. He understood.

The premier continued, "Since your department oversees the development and progress of all legislation, I want to see that all documents related to the implementation of the new finance program are undertaken here in your offices. You will closely work with the permanent staff of the finance ministry and other affected ministries."

The *secrétaire général* replied, "We are pleased with your confidence in our capabilities." The *secrétaire général* continued to quickly think of the angles; yes, the premier was going to hide the politics behind the professionalism of the civil service. Well, they all do that, he thought.

The premier, guessing at the thinking of the *secrétaire général*, added, "I also continue as foreign minister."

The *secrétaire général* knew that the premier had been foreign minister for the past eight months in the previous governments.

The premier continued, "We must be very professional here at the Matignon so that I can manage the politics that pounds on the front gates of the Quai d'Orsay."

The *secrétaire général* nodded his understanding: quite straightforward. Remarkably shrewd, though.

The premier moved on, "My *chef du cabinet*," and he nodded towards the other side of the building where his political staff had its offices, "will work to keep the politics of the new budget acceptable to all the political factions. Here, at the level of the premier, we are an all-party coalition."

The *secrétaire général* saw the great unspoken principle of this premiership; the government would be all-party at the domestic level, but would exercise its great powers of manipulation at the foreign policy level. The rising threat from Germany was of course the over-arching foreign policy issue. The Right wanted a closer alliance with Mussolini and Fascist Italy. The premier, as foreign minister, had earlier in the spring forged the Stresa Front with both Italy and Great Britain to just that end. The Left wanted a close alliance with Great Britain on a practical level and, on principle, collective security through the League of Nations. Others wanted to consummate the alliance with Soviet Russia, a fearsome thought to the Right, but strategically very sound.

Premier Laval watched and thought: *yes, I have been understood.*

The premier stood up; the *secrétaire général* and Madame Lambert followed. The premier said in conclusion, "Madame Lambert is quite familiar with how all of this should be done," and turning to Madame Lambert and smiling, "from our time together at the labor ministry."

The *secrétaire général*, wishing to display some initiative, nodded in agreement and added, "Madame Lambert has just returned from the Quai d'Orsay. She has established a liaison with Madame Bardoux."

The premier, a bit surprised, seemed pleased. "My compliments on your initiative, *Monsieur le Secrétaire Général.*"

The premier nodded at Madame Lambert, shook the hand of the *secrétaire général*, and then walked over to the door. The *secrétaire général* darted around the premier and opened the door; the premier returned to his offices on the first floor.

The *secrétaire général* turned and nodded at Madame Lambert to take her seat while he walked back and sat down in one of the wing chairs. He steepled his fingers together, looked over the tops of them at Madame Lambert, and said, "I did not know you knew Premier Laval so well."

Madame Lambert simply nodded; she did not feel any further comment was required since there was no personal friendship between her and the premier—all was professional. Everyone would know that except the dullest of gossips. She went on to explain, "He is a very skillful lawyer, very demanding of the professional capabilities of the senior civil service. But always very correct. He wants to get the policy exactly in alignment with what he sees as the political balance point."

The *secrétaire général* nodded in silent agreement.

Madame Lambert summed up the future working environment, "We will have long hours of work. But our professionalism will be respected."

Berlin

Berlin, early Friday evening. In the silvery twilight of a beautiful high summer day, the soft light came through tall windows from the outside garden into the spacious and darkly paneled reception room of the Reich's Chancellery. To one side stood Foreign Minister Konstantin Freiherr von Neurath taking congratulations from various notables for the successful signing earlier in the week in London of the Anglo-German Naval Treaty. The accord allowed for the significant expansion of the German navy and therefore represented another massive breach in the Versailles Treaty, the hated treaty that ended World War I but settled few of the underlying grievances. Now, German diplomacy was on the march.

One bewhiskered face asked, "Is it true the British did not consult the French before signing the treaty?"

The foreign minister smiled broadly, welcoming the question. "We do not comment on any possible divergences between London and Paris. What is important is that Berlin and London see eye-to-eye on naval issues. An exciting new development."

Another voice asked with a Prussian boom, "Is Stresa dead?"

Neurath replied with a humorously quizzical expression, "Stresa? You mean the alliance concluded in April between Great Britain, France, and Italy?"

Heads in the group nodded yes.

"Why, it barely lived!"

Laughter rippled across the group.

The Leader

Across the room in front of tall windows framed by soft blue drapes stood *Reichspräsident* and *Führer* Adolf Hitler. He was speaking to two attractive and attentive women in resplendent formal dresses, sparkling jeweled necklaces lay on soft white skin below their graceful bare shoulders. The ladies held champagne glasses in front of them. The *Führer* wore a light brown jacket with a simple Iron Cross First and Second Class below the left breast pocket, earned the hard way in bitter fighting on the Western Front. Underneath the jacket was a plain white shirt and black tie; black pants completed the unpretentious but dignified formal uniform. The *Führer* was not some bemedalled monarch strutting the stage like a peacock, rather an understanding leader of the masses, elegant in his understatement.

Hitler spoke with charm and understanding to the two ladies, "Germany is rearming exclusively for defense and the maintenance of peace."

The two women smiled in pleased agreement. He continued, "The German people, having regained their honor, may be privileged in independent equality to make their contribution towards the pacification of the world in free and open cooperation with other nations."

The two women beamed with approval at the prospect of Germany resuming its rightful place in what was sure to be the coming prosperity of nations. Hitler, looking over the shoulders of the ladies, saw a general enter the hall and quickly spoke to the two ladies, "Ah, I see General von Blomberg has arrived. I must go over and greet him." Hitler gave a small bow from the waist, stood up erect, smiled, and moved to walk away; the women murmured their thanks to him for taking the time to explain Germany's promising prospects to them.

General Werner von Blomberg, minister of defense, saw the *Führer* walk across the polished floor towards him, turned to an aide and whispered something, and then stepped away from the circle and met the *Führer* discreetly at a distance from the other guests.

Hitler approached, reached out his hand and shook General von Blomberg's in warm greeting. Then he reached his arm out and guided the general farther away from the guests while saying, "General, our diplomacy is securing Germany its rightful place among nations. This is the happiest day of my life. The London Naval Treaty may mark the beginning of an Anglo-German alliance. All Europe must stand united against the threat of Bolshevism."

General von Blomberg warmly replied, "You have accomplished more in months than the Wiemar Republic in years."

Hitler smiled in smug satisfaction, then his expression changed indicating a move to business. "When I visited your headquarters in May, we set in motion plans for a future military operation."

General von Blomberg nodded. "Yes, the reoccupation of the Rhineland by our military forces. The staff is planning the operation."

Hitler warmed, rubbing his hands together. "Good. Originally we thought 1937 would be the year. But you should plan to go earlier if the opportunity presents itself. Events are going Germany's way," and Hitler swept his glance across the gathering of guests celebrating his most recent triumph.

General von Blomberg followed Hitler's eyes and nodded in complete agreement. Hitler delivers results, he thought.

Hitler continued, "Remember, the remilitarization of the Rhineland is not aggression against France. It is just to reestablish Germany's right to maintain the security of its territory within its borders under the natural rights belonging to all sovereign nations."

General von Blomberg agreed, "The Reichswehr is sworn to that duty, *mein Führer.*"

Hitler smiled and said, "Let me not keep you from your guests," and concluded the conversation.

Palais de la Mutualité

Sunday afternoon, June 23. Dexter Jones walked out the front entrance of the apartment building on rue de Bac where he lived in the middle of Paris's Left Bank. He walked towards the river taking enjoyment in the afternoon sunlight of the warm June day. Reaching the River Seine, he turned right and walked in the shade of tall trees bordering the river towards the Latin Quarter. He passed the majestic edifice of the Institute de France. Looking beyond the walled parapet separating the walkway from the languidly flowing waters of the river below, he saw the Île de la Cité, the castle-like island dominated by the twin bell towers of Cathédrale Notre Dame. Walking further, he passed the little park in front of the Church of Saint-Julien le Pauvre. Then he turned into the warren of small Latin Quarter streets towards Place Maubert and the Palais de la Mutualité just beyond, the largest public meeting place on the Left Bank.

Inside the *grand salle* of the steamy Palais, he found the place packed to the roof with more than three thousand boisterous people attending the International Writers Congress for the Defense of Culture. The event was a major response by the European intellectual Left to the rise of Nazism in Germany. The Congress had been organized by the two Andrés: André Gide, the grand old man of French literature, and André Malraux, the charismatic young lion of revolutionary literature, the embodiment of the young committed intellectual, *trés engagé* in the slanging banter of the sidewalk cafés. Walking down an aisle, absently listening to the speaker at the podium drone on like a Moscow party functionary, Dexter saw two women walking up the aisle. Recognizing them, he smiled and said, "Madame Beach, Madame Monnier, how nice to see you here today."

Madame Beach held out her hand and said in mock disapproval, "Monsieur Jones, it is always Sylvia Beach to you. You are one of the great patrons of my bookshop," and her smile brightened into a welcoming grin.

Dexter turned to the other woman. "Madame Monnier."

Madame Monnier replied, "Adrienne." She held out her hand, adding, "Dexter, you are always so gallant."

Dexter made a small bow of his head.

16

Sylvia asked, "Dexter, why don't you join us out on the sidewalk for a breath of fresh air?"

Dexter replied, "Of course."

Out on the sidewalk, an ever-increasing throng of people, escaping from the heat and ritualistic Marxist incantations of the speaker inside, milled about. Dexter asked, "Sylvia, what do you think?"

Sylvia looked thoughtful. "Overall, the meeting is strongly Communistic," then she brightened, "but it is truly international."

Adrienne added, "That is a crucial issue that Malraux has raised: to be anti-Nazi, does one need also to be a Communist, or is the issue to be simply anti-Fascist?"

Sylvia nodded, adding, "That question vexes the Left Bank."

Dexter asked, "I got here late. What about today's speakers?"

Sylvia took on a playful tone. "Oh, I think Waldo Frank's bright orange shirt is quite in contrast to the dreamy attitude of his speech," as she described the speech of the previous speaker, a militant intellectual from New York representing the League of American Writers, a Communist front group. After outlining Frank's points, she tartly noted with an amused smile, "He of course expressed his commitment to the working class."

Dexter laughed at Sylvia's playful comment.

Adrienne shook her head in disappointment and said, "Gustav Regler took up that very point. In his address to the convention he argued that the ineptitude of Communist propaganda is the problem; the Communists in Berlin prattled on about the working class rather than engaging the feelings of the masses. The Nazis just swept to popular victory on an emotional wave. The Nazis outclass the Left at propaganda—completely."

Dexter nodded in agreement at Adrienne's insight, a finding he would share back at the embassy.

Sylvia nudged the conversation in a new direction. "Unfortunately, several important woman writers were ill and could not attend." Looking at Adrienne, she added, "And Adrienne declined to speak. So it was all quite dominated by men."

Sylvia glanced in towards the auditorium and said with great amusement, eyes twinkling, "So the men, these lions of the Left, are inside roaring away."

Dexter laughed and then said to Sylvia, "Many think, including me, that your bookstore is the geographic center of modern literature. What is the impact of all of this talk on literature?"

Sylvia smiled. "We see that new winds are blowing. For example, American literature has turned left. The leading writers—Dos Passos, Farrell, and Steinback—are portraying the struggles of the masses caught up in economic chaos, which is now an almost universal condition. Books are now judged by their commitment to social concern."

Dexter replied, "So literature is becoming part of politics."

Sylvia replied, "Here in France literature has always been more closely intertwined with politics than in America." Then Sylvia nudged Adrienne and whispered, "See, I told you, Dexter speaks some of the best French in the American embassy."

Dexter smiled and said, "Fluency is in reverse order of diplomatic rank in our embassy."

Adrienne clapped her hands together like a little girl and exclaimed, "How truly American!"

The three of them laughed. Then Dexter said in an undertone to Adrienne, "It was not always so," and then he broke into the French *patois* of the West African Equatorial colonies, speaking the lilting language of the native women in the morning marketplaces.

Truly surprised, Adrienne again clapped her hands together and said, "Truly authentic."

Astonished at Dexter's revelation, Sylvia asked, "Where did you learn to speak like that?"

Dexter replied with easy assurance, "At the wet markets in Dakar. In the morning on my way to the Consulate, I would detour through the native quarters of that beautiful coastal city."

Adrienne said, "You must come speak at my library. You will be a sensation. You have the gift of the mimic. My patrons love language in all the splendor of its diversity. You will be a hit!"

"My pleasure," and Dexter gave a small bow of acceptance.

Sylvia spoke to Dexter, "We better return to the auditorium. André Chamson is to speak next."

Dexter asked, "Do you know Chamson?"

Sylvia replied, "Of course, he is one of the Friends of Shakespeare and Company, a distinguished circle of French and American writers and patrons supporting our bookstore. André Gide was one of the

ore seats with a good view of the podium." The three
sidled down the row and took their seats.

Chamson approached the podium and Sylvia nudged Dexter and
said, "I have not seen him like this; he is pale with anger. The last
speaker must have been intolerably bad."

Adrienne added, "But look at André's determination."

Chamson launched into the day's theme, nationalism and culture,
with a determined attack on nationalism. A gifted writer, his speech
was in electrifying contrast to the doctrinaire drabness of the previous
Communist speakers who, in Dexter's opinion, spoke as if reciting
production quotas from the appendix of a five-year plan.

Dexter whispered to Sylvia, "A great political performance."

Sylvia smiled and nodded in agreement.

On the podium, Chamson, with a gathering voice, soared into a rousing conclusion "to warn our adversaries that I am their enemy because I have been French ever since France existed...Because I am linked to this soil by its cemeteries and its furrows. Because I have tried to sing them, the first of a long line of peasants who could speak only in low voices, following the rhythms and the splendor of my people."

The audience jumped to its feet and gave a clapping, thundering round of applause as Chamson walked back to his seat on the platform. Sylvia turned to Dexter and said, "We better head for the exit while we can; Adrienne and I have to get back to our shops. Business is always good after these sessions."

The next morning, in the American embassy, Dexter wrote a short report concluding that the Soviet Union's skill at organizing the conference was excellent, but that Moscow's unimaginative control of the speakers made the proceedings dull and bombastic. He stressed Adrienne's point that Nazi propaganda was highly effective at capturing the imaginations of large segments of the broad public. In the future, the Nazis could be counted on to successfully splinter public opinion in those countries where it sought influence through its skillful use of simple sloganeering.

Tuesday afternoon, June 25. Dexter Jones walked out the entrance of the American embassy into the bright evening twilight of a clear summer's day. He walked around the edge of the broad Place de la Concorde, across the Pont de la Concorde, while watching the sun set behind the magnificent Greek colonnaded façade of the Palais Bourbon, home to the Chamber of Deputies, the principal house of the French parliament. Reaching the other side of the river, the Left Bank, he turned and walked along the tree-shaded sidewalk heading towards the Palais de la Mutualité deep in the Latin Quarter. He wanted to hear André Malraux give the closing speech to the International Writers Congress for the Defense of Culture.

Approaching the front of the large building, Dexter scanned the milling crowd for any familiar faces. Suddenly, his eyebrows arched in surprise and his eyes widened in delight; there was Madame Bardoux, and, yes, besides her the intriguing Madame Lambert. He raised his hand in recognition, Madame Bardoux spotted him and leaned over and spoke to Madame Lambert, her hand outstretched to point out the approaching American diplomat. Dexter came up and shook each outstretched hand in turn, bowing his head. "Delighted you could come." Both women smiled at him pleasantly.

Dexter said, "It will be jammed inside. Malraux has captured the public's imagination." He singled out Madame Lambert with a glance; she smiled and nodded back in agreement. Dexter continued, "Let's push our way in."

Madame Bardoux said, "We'll let you lead the way."

Dexter twisted and turned inside the jam-packed auditorium clearing a path for the two women. He found an empty space along the wall near the speaker's *presidium* and waved with his hand for the women to take a space along the wall. "This is the best I can do." Both women smiled and took places against the wall; Dexter took the rearmost position.

The three listened intently to Louis Aragon, once the iconoclastic firebrand of the Surrealists, commit the apostasy of actually hewing to the party line on art. "We must come back to reality…only the proletariat and its allies can hope to achieve realism, which in their hands becomes Socialist Realism, the method of the writers of the USSR."

More party-line drivel, thought Dexter. Aragon then whipped himself into a blazing, acidic frenzy. Dexter looked towards the wall just behind the speaker's *presidium* and watched the conference co-chairman André Gide shaking his head in sad exasperation at the rant. He pointed out Gide's reaction to the two women; they turned their heads and smiled in sympathetic acknowledgement at him.

Aragon was followed by another firebrand who launched into another rant, comically brandishing a clenched fist in the final climax as a signal for applause. The audience sat motionless. The speaker looked out at the silent crowd like a mole blinking in the sunlight; the stupefied people sat in uncomprehending silence. Dexter laughed to himself. The speaker departed in a huff.

The other co-chairman, André Malraux, rose. He was regarded as the man to follow in the Thirties by Parisian intellectuals and café gossips alike, as Dexter well knew. He strode forward to the speaker's rostrum, braced himself with one hand on the table, and leaned his long body forward into the big microphone. Madame Lambert turned back and smiled at Dexter in pleased anticipation at the coming speech.

The handsome, dark-haired Malraux spoke to the political hour with eloquent phrases delivered with the assured urgency of a leading public intellectual. The staccato words rushed forth, "It is in the nature

of fascism to be nationalistic; it is our nature to be of the world."
Dexter nodded in silent agreement with the universalist message. Then,
rising above the immediate struggle, Malraux looked to the eternal
power of art, "A work of art is an object, but it is also an encounter
with time." A nice French touch, thought Dexter.

The man standing next to Dexter, nodding in approval,
whispered, "This is what we have wanted, the call to fight for a new
art." Then nodding towards a group of Communist writers, "The
Soviet writers will not understand one word of what André says."
Madame Lambert, overhearing the conversation, smiled at Dexter and
nodded in agreement.

Dexter smiled and listened to Malraux wind-up his speech, the
crowd in rapt silence. "Arts, ideas, peoples, all humanity's old dreams,
if we need them to live, they need us to live again." As Malraux
straightened up and stood back from the microphone, the crowd
erupted into ardent applause. Dexter felt that Malraux had added a
special French aura with his lofty phrases in support of the
transcendent power of art in the enduring human struggle. He didn't
get caught in the mire of ideological conflict.

Madame Bardoux and Madame Lambert straightened up, their
faces beaming approval, and vigorously clapped as Malraux walked
away from the podium. Dexter also straightened up, pulling his
shoulders off the wall, and clapped along with the women. As the
applause died down, he leaned forward and whispered to the two
women, "We better get outside ahead of the crowd." The two women
nodded in agreement. They joined the troop of people crowding their
way out towards the lobby and the sidewalk.

On the sidewalk, Dexter asked, "There's an English tea shop
down by the Église Saint-Julien-Le-Pauvre. Could I interest you in a
cup of tea?"

Madame Bardoux broke into an easy smile. "We know it well. It is
one of our secret meeting places. You have found us out!"

Dexter smiled in pleased surprise. "After you, *mesdames*."

In the gathering dusk, the three walked along the deeply shaded streets
and then past the stonewalls of the small church Saint-Julien le Pauvre.
Past the church, they crossed over to the far side of the street. Coming
up to the tea shop, they entered and walked into the wood-paneled
dining room with tables set underneath open oak beams running
crosswise on the ceiling. They seated themselves at a table near the wall

while the proprietress handed them menus and mentioned the favored teas of the day. The two women smiled, ordered tea, and whispered between themselves, settling upon fruitcakes as if they were a slightly forbidden delicacy. Dexter smiled at the proprietress and asked for the same.

Dexter asked, "What do you think of the writers' conference?"

Madame Bardoux replied, "The coming together of the Communist intellectuals with the literary Left mirrors what is going on in politics today. The Communists, the Socialists, and the Radical Socialists are all marching under the Popular Front banner on Bastille Day. Why not the writers?"

Dexter nodded in agreement, "Agreed—a cultural alliance. Are the writers following in the steps of the French government's recent agreement with Soviet Russia?"

Madame Bardoux leaned forward and spoke knowingly and with assurance, "Yes, France reaches east to the far side of Germany for alliance with Russia—a classically traditionalist policy. As foreign minister, Monsieur Laval has worked energetically to contain Hitler and Germany."

Dexter parried, "We heard that Foreign Minister Laval lunched with German air minister Hermann Goering in Warsaw on his way back from Moscow. Goering put up quite a row about Laval trying to encircle Germany. So there are real risks to the rapprochement with Soviet Russia?"

Madame Bardoux sat back a little; Dexter had got right at the most sensitive aspect of any alliance with Russia. She composed her thoughts. "Yes, Germany makes a clever diplomatic argument that France is undermining the Locarno Pact with the Russian initiative. So France tries to strengthen Locarno, and Germany says that it is violating Locarno, which is the basis of current European stability," and she added as an afterthought, "such as it is."

Dexter nodded in agreement, "We have heard from sources in Berlin that in the future Germany might use ratification of a Soviet pact as a pretext for the remilitarization of the Rhineland." Dexter understood that remilitarization of the Rhineland would force the French to confront the question of sending the French army across the border to evict the German army from the west bank of the Rhine. Dexter sighed with the knowledge that it would be a frighteningly difficult choice to contemplate. Out of his eye, he saw Madame Lambert come bolt upright.

He saw that Madame Lambert's expression had quickened; her eyes were flashing as she looked searchingly across the table at Madame Bardoux for her answer. Madame Bardoux, a little taken aback, looked at her friend, then turned and responded to Dexter, "Yes, I understand that you could have heard such speculations." Her face turned noncommittal.

Madame Lambert sat back, the meaning of Madame Bardoux's reply sinking in. A tough issue was coming.

Dexter said, "Yes, I understand. Of course, I am not prying. Our embassy has its sources." Madame Lambert looked at him and thought: yes, the Americans would have their own sources.

Madame Bardoux relaxed and smiled. "Of course." She smiled sweetly at Dexter and gave Madame Lambert a warm smile.

Dexter changed the subject. "What about Malraux's speech?"

Madame Lambert leaned forward and took the stage ever so discreetly. She looked at Dexter and said in a measured way, "Malraux made the point that the idealism of art, its individuality, must be the beacon that lights the way."

Dexter replied with a question, "Art does not follow the party line?"

Madame Lambert explained, "Artistic expression can never be confined between the bright lines of doctrine."

Dexter queried, "So art does not serve the struggle for revolutionary goals?"

Madame Lambert made a simple and ordered reply, "Doctrine sets bright lines; artistic expression always pushes outside the lines." She leaned back and smiled at Dexter. "So, no, I don't believe in Socialist Realism."

Dexter, eyes twinkling, smiled. "Last week at the convention, my friend Adrienne Monnier, the bookseller, observed that Communist propaganda is boring and dull. She argued that the Nazis are better at using propaganda aimed at exciting the working classes."

At the sound of the name "Adrienne Monnier," Madame Bardoux brightened and reentered the conversation, turning to Dexter and saying, "Why Dexter, Marcelle and I are patrons of Madame Monnier's bookstore. Do you know her friend Sylvia Beach?"

Dexter, somewhat surprised, replied, "Yes, I know both quite well. Its strange we haven't bumped into each other at one or the other bookstore."

Madame Bardoux explained, "Oh, we go to Madame Monnier's store often enough, but we are really just getting to the point where we might take on English literature in its native tongue. Madame Monnier has so much of it in good French translation."

Madame Lambert nodded in agreement.

Madame Bardoux playfully added, "Marcelle is a little unsure about being publicly seen patronizing the store that published Joyce's *Ulysses*. She would not want her colleagues to think she was talking furtive pleasures in dirty books," and Madame Bardoux laughed, nodding towards Madame Lambert's somewhat embarrassed countenance.

Dexter laughed and smiled at Madame Lambert. "There are many fine books in Sylvia's lending library in addition to Joyce's books."

Madame Lambert composed herself, getting back on top of her decorum, and replied, "Of course. I look forward to expanding my knowledge of English literature at Shakespeare and Company. Madame Monnier says Miss Beach is an excellent guide."

Madame Bardoux interjected, "Maybe Dexter can provide some suggestions?"

Madame Lambert replied, "I don't want to put him to any trouble," and she turned and smiled benignly at Dexter. Then she added, "Besides, I think building a dialogue with Miss Beach is possibly the greater part of belonging to Shakespeare and Company."

Dexter agreed, "You are quite right. She has become a great friend of mine. Hopefully you will have the same opportunity."

Madame Lambert smiled at him by way of agreement. Then she took a long sip from her cup of tea and said, "I have a demanding day at the Matignon tomorrow. I must take my departure."

Madame Bardoux turned to Dexter and said in weary agreement, "So do I. It has been delightful to talk with you Dexter, but Marcelle is right, we must be going."

Dexter stood up, "Can I escort you to the Metro?"

Standing, Madame Bardoux replied, "Yes, you are always so gallant, Dexter."

Madame Lambert nodded in agreement as she stood up.

The three walked out into the near-darkness and walked up the avenue to boulevard Saint-Germain and the Metro entrance. At the top of the stairway, they stopped and Dexter said by way of farewell, "*Mesdames*." Then with a tone of expectation, he asked, "Until July 4? At the embassy?"

Welcoming the invitation, Madame Bardoux said, "We will try. Probably late in the afternoon."

Madame Lambert made a nod of agreement.

Dexter dipped his head in farewell; the two women turned and proceeded down the stairs to train platform below.

Dexter turned and briskly walked along boulevard Saint-Germain towards his apartment, smiling, a glow of optimism to his outlook as he sensed that a romantic curiosity about a woman was starting to shape his thoughts, marshalling his emotional feelings toward some future point. Had she shared this sense, this sense of potential? He wondered.

Fourth of July

Thursday, July 4, late afternoon. Dexter stood to the side of the large reception room on the ground floor of the American embassy, the late summer sun shining through the windows from the west. He held a glass of champagne in front of him as he surveyed the crowd. It had been a long afternoon, circulating through the hundreds of Americans that had passed through the public reception. Later in the evening, there would be an invitation-only reception at the ambassador's residence on Avenue d'Iena. Fortunately, he was excused from the evening formalities; afternoon duty with the great American public was deemed sufficient sacrifice.

Two middle-aged American ladies in lovely summer dresses and large spreading hats came towards him. Dexter knew them both well; he was a frequent guest at their cocktail and dinner parties. Great occasions to keep tabs on the thinking at Guaranty Trust and other citadels of American wealth in France.

Dexter beamed and said, "Daisy, Virginia, how nice of you to visit me on duty."

Daisy, a finely figured brunette, gaily replied, "We thought you would be here. Skipping the reception at the residence tonight?"

Dexter responded, "I am quite junior. I am at my duty station."

Virginia, a bottle blond, interjected, "Don't tell me the ambassadress has left the embassy's most charming bachelor off the list?"

Dexter bantered, "Unlike you ladies, I am a million or two short of what it takes to come within social notice of the ambassadress."

The two women rolled their eyes.

Dexter continued, "I thought you two would be at the ambassador's tonight."

Daisy replied, "We will. We are out and about this afternoon. We want to wish our favorite diplomat a happy Fourth of July."

Virginia added, "No other man fills that empty chair at a dinner party quite like you, Dexter. No one."

Dexter bowed at the compliment. "The charms of the hostesses are everything."

The two women laughed; Virginia looked askance to her friend while keeping her eyes fixed on Dexter and said, "It's hard to get

Dexter over to the Right Bank in the evening lately. Think he's got something over on the Left Bank. Something French?" She turned to Daisy and winked.

Just then, looking past the shoulder of Daisy, Dexter saw Madame Bardoux and Madame Lambert slowly walk towards him, both women dressed in black skirts, white blouses, and black jackets. They had come from work.

Virginia followed his eyes and said with pleasant surprise, "Yes, I was right. Here they come."

Dexter hastily explained, "Ladies from the ministries. Part of our liaison duties."

Daisy asked, "Liaison?" She smiled. Then added provocatively, "When do I get a liaison with you?"

Dexter arched his eyebrows and said, "The ambassadress would hardly approve."

Daisy gave a little girl pout.

She was always quite cute when they went through this routine, Dexter thought. He laughed to himself; he had been told that the husbands, over drinks at the Maxim's, had a side bet over which wife would bag Dexter first.

In a flash of recognition, Virginia said, "I know the one on the right. That is Madame Bardoux of the foreign ministry. The first woman of rank in that hidebound old building."

Dexter answered, "Right you are."

Daisy, peering intently at the two French women walking towards them, asked inquiringly, "The other?"

Dexter replied, "I believe the ministry of labor."

Daisy responded in disbelief, "You believe?" Then she laughed. "I saw your eyes, Dexter."

Dexter smiled.

Dexter held out his left arm in welcome to Madame Bardoux and Madame Lambert and said, "Let me introduce you to my friends, Daisy and Virginia." The two American women beamed and held out their hands in welcome. Introductions were made all around.

Then Daisy spoke, "We must be going." Turning to the two French women, she added, "So nice to meet you." Then turning back to Dexter, she said, "You must bring your friends to our next dinner party." She turned to the two French women. "Everyone would be most interested in meeting you. Undoubtedly a fresh breeze."

Virginia nodded in agreement. "Yes, please do."

Madame Bardoux and Madame Lambert smiled in appreciation.

The two American women beamed one more big smile and turned and headed for the street outside where Daisy's car and driver were waiting.

Dexter turned to Madame Bardoux and Madame Lambert, "I am so pleased that you could come today." He nodded at the direction of the departing American ladies. "That is the more pleasant aspect of today's duties."

Madame Lambert, a touch of merriment in her eyes, smiled, "Yes." The handsome American with the charm, so rare actually, would have many admirers not interested in diplomacy, she thought. She smiled at Dexter.

Dexter looked at Madame Lambert's eyes with pleasure. He said, "I thought we could walk up rue Boissy d'Anglas. There's a small café serving the most delicious strawberries with the thickest cream…" and his voice trailed off.

Madame Bardoux brightened. "Splendid."

Madame Lambert added, genuinely pleased, "How charming."

Walking through the early evening bustle of the crowded sidewalk, Dexter and the two French women came to a small sidewalk café. Dexter pointed out a table to one side, and the three worked their way through the crowded tables. At the table, Dexter held each woman's chair in turn; each lady in turn sitting and turning an upturned face to Dexter with a polite thank you. The politeness gave Dexter a warm glow.

A waiter came over and Dexter gave the order for strawberries and cream, then turned to the two ladies. "A lemonade, perhaps?"

Madame Bardoux and Madame Lambert shook their heads in vigorous agreement.

Madame Lambert turned serious. "We enjoyed seeing the Writers Convention with you very much. Do you think solidarity between the Paris intellectuals and the Soviet Union will have a significant effect?"

Dexter replied easily, "Informally, we at the embassy believe that Paris is like the hub of a spoked wheel. There are a lot of different lines of action occurring."

Madame Lambert nodded thoughtfully in agreement.

Dexter started in, "Most likely, the question of a Russian alliance will go on the back burner. We think the question of Italy's planned aggression against Ethiopia will be the major foreign policy issue this year and into next."

Madame Bardoux asked, "Where do you think the British will go on the Italian question?"

Dexter looked directly at Madame Bardoux. "British Foreign Secretary Sir Samuel Hoare, our sources tell us, told the British cabinet two weeks ago that Italy 'places us in a most inconvenient dilemma.'"

Madame Bardoux nodded in agreement.

Madame Lambert asked pointedly, "What are the horns of this dilemma?"

Dexter replied, "Go along with Italy's conquest of Ethiopia, and destroy the basis for the League of Nations, or stand up to Italy and drive Mussolini into Hitler's arms."

Madame Lambert countered, "Last summer, Mussolini sent a hundred thousand Italian troops to the Brenner Pass to keep Hitler out of Austria. He is the only European leader to stand up to Hitler's expansionism."

Dexter sighed. "Yes, but does that mean he gets to take Ethiopia, a League of Nations member state, as his payoff? That's pretty cynical."

Madame Bardoux interjected, "Premier Laval has made keeping Italy in alliance with France and Britain central to his policy of containing Germany. Ethiopia is a small matter next to German militarism."

Madame Lambert said very evenly and gravely, "Premier Laval keeps clearly in mind that Germany is the threat to France, not Italy, not Ethiopia."

Dexter sagged a little bit; Madame Lambert obviously knew how to parse an argument for its strong points exceedingly well, he thought. He replied, "Ethiopia is the unfortunate example that tests the grand hope of an effective League of Nations."

Madame Lambert's expression changed to mild disdain.

Dexter began to make a lawyerly argument, "Two weeks ago in Britain the nationwide results of the Peace Ballot were announced. This was an unofficial referendum of the British people on the League of Nations. More people voted in this unofficial election than in the last parliamentary election—eleven-and-a-half million."

Madame Lambert asked, "And how did the island people, living in their splendid isolation, vote?"

Dexter sighed again and made a sorrowful look, "They voted overwhelming in support of the League of Nations. They want to support strong international economic sanctions to stop aggression."

Madame Lambert softened her expression but drove home her next point, "Will that keep Germany from remilitarizing the Rhineland?"

Dexter looked at her thoughtfully. "Probably not."

Dexter put down his lemonade and leaned forward towards Madame Lambert and made his point, "But Prime Minister Stanley Baldwin proclaimed that the League of Nations would be 'the sheet anchor of British policy.'"

Madame Bardoux broke in, "But it was not quite a year ago that Stanley Baldwin said that Britain's border was on the Rhine River. That seems to have gone by the boards, a firm commitment has now become, what many in France now believe, an empty platitude."

Dexter countered, "My point is that Britain is engaged on the continent in a way that it hasn't before. France should be a strong partner with Britain in making the League of Nations the strongest possible bulwark against aggression. France needs to look first and foremost to the British for alliance."

Madame Bardoux looked evenly at Dexter and said, "We, too, have sources in the British cabinet. Last January the cabinet secretly determined that the Rhineland was not a vital interest for the British."

Madame Lambert now leaned over the table towards Dexter, "Many in Paris believe the Rhineland is France's principal vital interest in containing Hitlerism. Easy access into Germany from the west through the Rhineland is what makes France a valued ally to the Poles and the Czechs in the east. It is the enticement that attracts even the Russians."

Dexter nodded in understanding agreement.

Madame Bardoux summed up, "So Premier Laval, sitting as foreign minister, sees keeping Italy in the Stresa Front as central to securing France's overriding vital interest in keeping the Rhineland demilitarized."

Dexter summed up, "It will be a dangerous tightrope to walk."

Madame Lambert made a broad smile. "There, see, we agree on something."

Dexter looked momentarily relieved and smiled. Madame Lambert noticed the relief and smiled inwardly.

The waiter, white teeth flashing, walked up with a large serving tray, which he sat down on a stand next to the table. First he sat down a dish in the middle of the table with a heaping pile of strawberries set upon a bed of green leaves.

Madame Lambert looked at Dexter and smiled. "These are not strawberries. They are wild strawberries—*fraises des bois*—much more succulent than garden strawberries."

Dexter smiled and bowed his head. "I stand corrected."

Madame Lambert smiled at him, a look of merriment in her eyes.

The waiter then set down a large crock of ice-cold cream, thick to the point of solidity. Then he placed a large plate on the table, covered it with sugar, and then proceeded to roll the strawberries in the sugar. Then with a large spoon he ladled the thick cream on top of the strawberries. With a mixing spoon and fork, the waiter kneaded the strawberries in the cream until the strawberries were bits of red in a thick sea of cream. He spooned out helpings to the dessert plates.

Madame Lambert looked at Madame Bardoux with smug delight and then nodded with grave expression and dancing brightness in her eyes at Dexter and pronounced, "Simply a wonderful choice."

Dexter picked up his spoon, waggled it at the two ladies, who then pushed their spoons into the creamy delight while Dexter followed in turn, a look of minor diplomatic triumph across his face.

Madame Bardoux then turned to Dexter. "To change the subject, last night Édouard Herriot made peace within the Radical Socialist party. He and five other Radicals will remain in the Laval cabinet to give it stability. Herriott remains as president of the party until October, when he hands it over to Édouard Daladier—the leader of the young and energetic wing of the party."

Dexter added, "Yes, Daladier wants to put some punch into the Radicals; the young and restless have been moving over to Blum and the Socialists."

Madame Lambert made the innocent observation, "Herriot got a promise that the Radicals would march behind the Tricolor in the upcoming Bastille demonstration and not get too close to their red-flag Communist brethren."

Madame Bardoux laughed. "But all three parties will be marching in a great show of unity for the Popular Front."

Dexter added, "It is rumored to be the biggest crowd in Paris since the war."

Madame Bardoux nodded in agreement and said to Dexter, "Yes, Marcelle and I will be going to watch," and she nodded at Madame Lambert. "Why don't you join us, Dexter?"

Dexter replied with pleased sincerity, "I would be delighted."

The three finished their dessert and Madame Lambert announced by way of conclusion, "I must depart. I still have some long days in front of me."

Place Malesherbes

Wednesday, July 10, Place Malesherbes, 17th arrondissement. Dexter rapidly climbed up the stair steps of the Metro station and out to the sidewalk. He stood in the middle of the bustling pedestrian traffic on the square. He looked around, saw the apartment building, and walked briskly over to the entrance. He presented himself to the concierge, who waved him towards a small *ascenseur* situated against the rear wall of the grand stairwell in the center of the building. He looked up at the curved staircases sweeping in arcs towards the upper floors.

Reaching an upper floor, Dexter got out of the *ascenseur* and walked over to a large door, looked at the brightly polished brass plaque, and then knocked. The door opened and an elderly servant led him into the drawing room. The servant said softly, "She will be with you shortly."

Dexter walked over to the tall French windows and looked out into the bright morning sunshine and the elegant Place Malesherbes below. Presently, a woman in her early forties, stylishly but simply dressed, came in and walked up to him holding out her hand in welcome. Dexter turned and smiled, casually taking in her whole presence, the brownish blond hair cut short over a handsome angular face with high cheekbones, a svelte figure, an assured smile—all the aristocratic breeding effortlessly casual, he thought. She was the niece of the two Cambron brothers, France's two most important ambassadors before and during the First World War. She had almost been bred for her current position as diplomatic correspondent for one of Paris' leading center-left newspapers, *L'Oeuvre*. The paper had a large following across the country; her writings were syndicated to other papers. She took his hand in hers, clasped her other hand over it in familiar greeting. "So nice of you to come early, Dexter. Gives us a chance to talk before the lunch guests arrive."

Dexter bowed slightly from the waist. "Madame Tabouis, always a pleasure to be invited to one of your lunches."

Genevieve Tabouis in 1938

Madame Tabouis extended her arm indicating for Dexter to take a seat; she sat down in a chair right next to it. She leaned forward and gave Dexter's knee a familiar pat. "As you can well guess, I have many good sources in Berlin, often of many years standing," and she laughed, "and an endless stream of young *provocateurs* from the German ministries ready to tell me the most amazing things just to be my new best friend."

Dexter laughed. He closely followed Madame Tabouis's daily diplomatic column. He had become close to Madame Tabouis in Rome last January on Foreign Minister Laval's triumphant visit to Rome to parley with Italian dictator Benito Mussolini. During the course of the conference, Madame Tabouis had ferreted out that Il Duce had wheedled out a promise of a "free hand" for Italy in Ethiopia from Laval. Italy was now on the verge of invading Ethiopia, an event deeply distressing to Great Britain, not the least because Great Britain suspected that France may have betrayed principle for expediency last January in Rome. Madame Tabouis had shared her information with her small circle; it was considered a rumor and not fit for publication. But the "understanding" circulated in the background, bigger than a fact, thought Dexter.

Dexter replied, "Madame Tabouis…"

She interrupted him, tapping him lightly on the knee like an aunt, "Geneviève, please."

"Geneviève, I am sure your sources in Berlin are better than mine."

"Maybe." She paused. "My German sources say that Hitler personally is orchestrating German diplomatic maneuvers."

Dexter nodded. "He is a crafty manipulator."

"Yes, he encourages Mussolini in Ethiopia knowing that it will break up the Stresa Front. Italy will eventually break from France and Great Britain. Only Hitler will stand with Mussolini on Ethiopia. Then Italy will be his. He can then pick off Austria at his leisure. So much for Laval's theory of a 'chain of allies' across Southern Europe."

Dexter had not really thought about Austria in this context; he nodded in thoughtful agreement. At some point, everyone knew, Austria was gone.

Madame Tabouis then said, "My sources in Berlin think he will run the table."

Dexter looked inquisitively at Madame Tabouis. "What do you mean?"

Madame Tabouis explained, "The secret deal with Mussolini puts distrust and distance between Paris and London. The failure to go to Ethiopia's aid makes the League of Nations the home of the empty gesture. Great Britain mentally returns to its island. When France realizes it has lost Italy, and damaged its relationship with Great Britain, she goes to the East again and agrees to ratify Laval's treaty with the Soviet Union."

Dexter silently nodded at her.

MadameTabouis continued, an edge to her voice, "The Soviet treaty was always just bait in Laval's mind to start talks with Hitler."

Dexter replied, "May be a little too clever." A safe comment, he thought, since Laval was widely believed to be too clever, too expedient.

Madame Tabouis then laid out her conclusion, "France ratifies the treaty, and Hitler then uses the treaty ratification as pretext to reoccupy the Rhineland with the German army."

Dexter asked simply, "When?"

"A couple of months before next May's general election in France."

Dexter looked at her. "And France does nothing?"

Madame Tabouis responded, "The upcoming elections create hesitancy."

Dexter asked, "And Great Britain?"

Madame Tabouis replied, "Great Britain does not commit, wants more consultation, suggests going back to Geneva. Now we can see that the admirable word 'consultation' becomes a trapdoor into which decisive action falls, never to reemerge."

Dexter nodded slowly in understanding; he could see where events were going. He raised his eyebrows to make a question mark.

She replied gravely, "The moment for action is lost."

Dexter pondered the conversation. "Indeed," he murmured, "Hitler will have run the table." He filed the conclusion away for some future report.

Madame Tabouis saw that Dexter agreed with the analysis. Therefore, she concluded, the Americans had no information to the contrary. Her Berlin sources checked out. Dexter had just provided the confirmation. She heard a knock at the door.

She smiled at Dexter. "Albert will be letting the other guests in."

Dexter stood, as did Madame Tabouis. The two walked into the foyer. Madame Tabouis cooed out a warm greeting to two distinguished gentlemen handing their hats and sticks to Albert. Dexter recognized the two as foreign ministers from Eastern Europe, undoubtedly in Paris for Bastille Day.

Another knock on the door; Albert opened the door, and some other gentlemen came in with several ladies. It will be a full table, thought Dexter.

Madame Tabouis guided a couple over to Dexter, he guessed they were in their early forties, and turning to the gentleman she said, "Jean-Paul, I want you to meet Dexter Jones. He's an American diplomat. Like you, he lives over on the Left Bank. Near the literary crowd, right Dexter?"

Dexter replied, "Correct. On rue du Bac."

The woman gazed at Dexter with dark-eyed interest.

Madame Tabouis turned to the woman, "Madeline, Dexter Jones."

She smiled warmly and said, "*Enchantée.*"

Dexter gallantly gave a small bow and answered, "*Enchanté.*"

Madame Tabouis quickly ushered the guests towards the dining room with her outstretched arms as if they were a flock of geese.

Lunch and Virtue

The guests filed into the dining room and took seats around a long table. Madame Tabouis seated Dexter to her right at the head of the table. That way she could put the two foreign ministers, one to the left, the other to the right, at the first seats on the long axis of the table. A nice point of minor protocol by Madame Tabouis, thought Dexter.

Albert went around the table and poured white wine into tall glasses. An opening course was served.

Madame Tabouis chatted with the two foreign ministers and then asked polite questions of those guests further down the table. She was quite convivial. Eyes flashing, a mischievous smile on her face, she looked down to the far end of the table and said, "Ah, Madeline, you are at what I call the 'seat of virtue.'"

The guests glanced at the woman and then looked up the table expectantly at Madame Tabouis, all faces smiling, sure that one of her famous anecdotes was coming.

Madame Tabouis did not disappoint. "Several years ago, we had a distinguished group, just like yourselves, here for dinner. Foreign Minister Barthou was seated to my right, here where my dear American friend Dexter is sitting." She was referring to Barthou, who had been killed in an assassination nine months before in Marseilles with the king of Yugoslavia.

Madame Tabouis continued, "The foreign minister, as many of you already know, loved a good many women of his own generation, and even some who were younger," and she smiled warmly down the table, "however, truth be told, he was really an inconsolable widower who lived quietly with his mother-in-law."

The guests knew of Barthou's reputation with the ladies; their expressions betrayed skepticism about the "inconsolable widower" part.

Madame Tabouis, eyes flashing, drew the listeners into her tale. "One night, here, while he was dining right at this very table, he said to me, in what was supposed to be an undertone, but which of course could be heard by the entire table, 'I have been to bed with every woman at this table, I think. But that lady over there, sitting between the fat gentleman and the young girl—I don't seem to be sure about her.'"

The guests all laughed out loud.

Madeline, sitting in the supposed seat of virtue, looked a little askance, unsure if she was being mocked. Jean-Paul, her husband, smiled sardonically, lightly amused at the idea of his wife occupying a seat of any sort of marital virtue. She smirked at him. Obviously this couple had certain understandings, Dexter thought.

Dexter smiled inwardly and then turned to Madame Tabouis and said in a soft whisper, "Geneviève, you too were one of the women at the table?"

She turned to him, eyes radiant under her soft blond hair, and batted her eyelashes coquettishly, saying, "So I was."

The two foreign ministers smiled in approving appreciation; one of them winked at Dexter. Down the table Madeline caught Dexter's eye and gave him a pleasant nod of approval and an inviting smile.

Which army will march?

Dexter walked along the sidewalk on the Right Bank of the River Seine under spreading shade trees. Sunlight from the afternoon sun sparkled on the slowly flowing waters of the river. It had been a delightful lunch, but Madame Tabouis's dark premonitions about the Rhineland nagged at his mind. Madame Tabouis was rapidly gaining the reputation as the Cassandra of European diplomatic correspondents. This, Dexter knew, brought her even more sources of inside information. In particular, she was rumored to be well connected with German dissidents. She would presume that he would include the information in his embassy reports. The American government stood informed.

But if Madame Tabouis knew this information, then so would the French government. Dexter was sure of this. But Madame Tabouis had said nothing about the French government. Since last winter in Rome, it was always the gaps in what Madame Tabouis had told him that interested Dexter—the missing pieces of the puzzle. If the Germans remilitarized the Rhineland, why the French army could just cross the border and evict them. It was allowed by the Versailles Treaty; almost demanded by it, thought Dexter. The French army had done just that in the 1920s.

Coming up towards the embassy, Dexter made a mental note of what he now thought was the big unanswered question in Europe's destiny: would the French army cross the border and evict the Germans if they tried to remilitarize the Rhineland?

Bastille Day

July 14, noon, Pont de Sully, Île Saint-Louis. Dexter stood along the balustrade of the bridge at the southeast tip of Île Saint-Louis, the small island in the middle of the River Seine. The island sits just across from the working-class districts of southeast Paris on the Right Bank. The money was downriver, mused Dexter. Crowds were streaming across the bridge from the student Latin Quarter heading for the Place de la Bastille to watch the afternoon's Popular Front parade.

It had been quite a morning. Hundreds of thousands of people had crowded onto the Champs Élysées to see the biggest military parade in Paris since the 1919 victory parade. Infantry, cavalry, artillery, sailors, marines, zoaves, spahis, and airmen, banners flying, bands blaring, had marched around the Arc de Triomphe in perfect order. After circling the Arc, the majestic procession strode down the Champs Élysées past the reviewing stand and the cheering thousands.

Overhead, roaring across the blue sky, came an astounding air parade of six hundred airplanes, squadron after squadron in perfect order. Dexter had watched all this with a group of American newsmen, several of whom remarked to him that France should not lack confidence in her ability to safeguard her own security with such magnificent military forces.

Amiably, Dexter agreed with the newsmen. Privately, he wasn't so sure. Mostly the morning had proved to him that the French knew how to put on a great parade.

Returning to the present, Dexter searched the crowds coming towards the bridge looking for Madame Bardoux and Madame Lambert. They had agreed on a noon rendezvous. There, in the crowd, he saw them and lifted his hat high above his head and waved it. He saw Madame Bardoux point towards him, a smile breaking across her face, as she pointed him out to Madame Lambert. Madame Lambert smiled and gaily waved at him in greeting. The warmth of her wave was greatly pleasing to Dexter.

The two women walked over. Both wore light summer skirts, colored blouses with wide collars, big wide-brimmed hats, and white espadrilles on their feet. Wool sweaters peeked out of the corners of their handbags. Madame Lambert wore a small black ribbon discreetly below her left collar.

Dexter broke into a grin. "You both look too delightful for a political demonstration. It should be a picnic in the Bois de Boulogne."

The two women playfully made small curtsies in polite acknowledge of the compliment.

Dexter then explained, pointing across the bridge, "We can walk up the boulevard to the Place de la Bastille. One of my embassy colleagues has rented the front room of a flat on rue du Faubourg Saint-Antoine. It's on the third floor. We can watch the parade from there."

Madame Bardoux exclaimed, "Great. The crowds today are expected to exceed two hundred thousand."

The three walked up the boulevard, jostling with the crowd, the two women pointing to this and that as they went. At the Place de la Bastille they stopped and looked at the July Column rising over one hundred and seventy feet in the air. The column marked the site where the Bastille Prison stood in 1789 when it was destroyed by a Parisian mob, the cataclysmic event setting off the French Revolution if not modern history.

Madame Lambert leaned over to Dexter and pointed towards the base of the majestic column. "There is a crypt below the column that holds many of those killed during the revolutions of 1830 and 1848. Their names are inscribed on the shaft of the column. This is a sacred place for the parties of the Left."

Dexter nodded. "You sympathize with the Left."

Madame Lambert smoothly replied, "I sympathize with liberty."

Dexter replied, "We have something in common." Then he added, pointing across the square. "This way."

The three of them turned down rue du Faubourg Saint-Antoine.

Reaching a door, Dexter knocked, and a concierge opened it. Dexter spoke to him and the man pointed them towards a stairwell. They ascended three flights of stairs and then walked through an open door into a flat were a bunch of Americans were standing in earnest conversation. Several nodded at Dexter, some of the wives smiled warmly at him, then looked at the two French women and smiled even more knowingly at him. This lightly amused Madame Lambert—of course their husbands' handsome bachelor co-worker would fascinate the wives. She smiled to herself.

Dexter introduced the two women to some people standing before tall windows, a light air wafting through from outside. Just then strains of the marching song, *L'Internationale*, came into the room. Everyone crowded around the windows looking up towards Place de la Bastille. Two taxicabs slowly entered the square, one flying a large French Tricolor, the other flying an enormous red banner.

One of the Americans pointed to a man standing atop the taxicab flying the Tricolor and said, "That's Pierre Cot, the former minister of air. He was a minister in the last Radical Socialist government."

Dexter said to his two companions, "That really shows that the bourgeoisie is joining with the working classes for a new coalition. A Radical Socialist out front."

Three men marching behind the two taxicabs came into view. Madame Bardoux said, "Look. I never thought I would see those three men marching together on Bastille Day. The Nazis have unified the Left as never before."

One of the Americans shouted at Dexter, "You know the French. Tells us who they are?"

Dexter said so that all could hear, "The one on the left is Maurice Thorenz, the Communist party chief, the man in the middle is Léon Blum of the Socialists, and the third man is former premier Édouard Daladier of the Radical Socialists."

As the three men marched past the July Column, they raised their right arms in the clenched fist anti-Fascist salute. The crowds roared their approval.

Madame Lambert said to Dexter, "The salute is really to the memory of their ancestors who stormed the Bastille to start the French Revolution a hundred and fifty years ago."

Dexter nodded in agreement.

The Americans watched as columns of workers marched in good order behind broad banners—railway men, engineers, civil servants, laborers, clerks, schoolmasters, and lawyers. As each group passed the July Column, rights arms shot up in the clenched fist salute, often accompanied by their war cry of "Down with de La Rocque," expressing their hatred for the leader of the largest of France's right-wing leagues, the Fascist-leaning Croix-de-Feu. A retired colonel, de La Rocque was scheduled to lead the right-wing demonstration later in the afternoon on the Champs Élysées.

The mighty procession passed below the open windows and the gazes of the fascinated Americans. One American commented, "What an impressive display. A real statement that the French don't want to go Fascist like the Germans."

Another American said, "Almost all the French right-wing leagues look to Mussolini and Italian fascism for inspiration. The ancestral hatred of the Germans runs too deep for any but the most deluded to believe in Hitler."

Dexter whispered to Madame Lambert, "He hasn't met the aristocracy," and chuckled.

Madame Lambert smiled in agreement. Dexter was pleased.

The crowds kept marching; Madame Lambert leaned out the window and looked down the boulevard watching the marching thousands head for Place de la Nation and the Cours de Vincennes beyond. She murmured to Madame Bardoux, "The support for the Republic is everything we could hope for."

Madame Bardoux nodded and said, "Such solidarity must be made into a foundation for peace."

Madame Lambert agreed. "Today, thousands of Popular Front supporters are taking an oath 'to give bread to the workers, work to young people, and peace to the world.'"

Dexter looked at her, affection in his eyes, and thought what a lovely sentiment. For the second time he sensed that Madame Lambert harbored sympathies for those on the revolutionary side, the anti-colonialists in their rising move for independence.

Madame Bardoux shifted her feet and sighed. "Yes, such a noble sentiment. But the national election is not until next May. I wonder if it will come too late?"

Startled by the comment, Dexter turned his gaze to Madame Bardoux and said, "You have got right at my deepest concern. It will be a long winter in Europe this year."

Both women looked at Dexter with amazement, somewhat surprised by this frank statement coming from such a discreet diplomat.

Dexter smiled at the two women and then turned and looked out the window. He was stirred by the massiveness of the march; it had to be more than a mile-and-a half long, he thought. Yes, it was an historic point.

The two women watched him and then exchanged glances between themselves. As the last of the marchers came into view, Madame Bardoux turned to Dexter. "We were wondering if you could join us for a late lunch over on Île Saint-Louis; I am to meet a friend."

With smooth assurance, Dexter replied, "Delighted."

Madame Lambert added, "We have greatly appreciated watching the parade from this vantage point." Her eyes turned and she looked up the avenue at the last of the marchers, "It is French history marching today."

Dexter pointed his arm towards the door showing the way to the two women.

The three walked up the narrow street running through the center of the little island of Île Saint-Louis, which sits in the middle of the Seine River. Tall apartment buildings along the street shaded passersby from the hot afternoon sun. They came out on a small square on the approaches to Pont Saint Louis, the small bridge leading over to the larger island of Île de Cité. The massive Cathédrale Notre Dame sat large on the other island. Dexter always preferred this view with the graceful flying arches elegantly holding up the high walls; the view from the other direction was simply of the massive bell towers, stolid and lacking in sweeping elegance, or so Dexter thought.

Dexter saw a man waving at them from under the shade of an awning at an outdoor café that looked out over the square.

Madame Bardoux said, "Oh, there is Étienne. He has a table."

They walked over, Dexter grabbed an extra chair, and held it for Madame Lambert. Madame Bardoux kissed Étienne familiarly on the cheek and whispered some little nothings into his ear. He nodded and smiled. They all sat down.

Madame Bardoux said, "Étienne, I want you to meet Dexter Jones, the man I told you about. He is an attaché at the American embassy."

Étienne stood up and reached his hand across the table; Dexter stood up and shook the outstretched hand. "Nice to meet you." Dexter noticed that where Madame Bardoux was about thirty, Étienne appeared to be in his early forties. Possibly some sort of mentor, he thought.

Étienne turned to Madame Lambert, smiled, and took her hand in a familiar clasp. "Marcelle, how nice to see you."

With cool charm, Madame Lambert replied, "Étienne."

Madame Bardoux continued the introductions, turning to Dexter. "Étienne is a lecturer at Sciences Po. He was an adviser to me there, and then…" and she let the words trail away in a small laugh and winked at Madame Lambert.

Dexter quickly understood; Sciences Po was the nickname for the Institut d'Études Politiques de Paris, the famed *Grand Établissement* that trained France's diplomatic and government elite. Madame Bardoux was a graduate, somewhat rare for a woman, Dexter knew. But more exceptionally Madame Bardoux had been the first graduate accepted into the foreign ministry at the Quai d'Orsay. And he laughed to himself as he realized that she had made a friendship along the way.

Dexter replied, "Yes, I know it well. It is right up the street, so to speak, from where I live. I live on rue du Bac."

Étienne explained, "I am a lecturer in European politics and diplomacy."

Dexter, tilting his head back and looking down his nose, interrupted, "And a former member of the diplomatic corps."

Étienne laughed. "Yes, of course."

He continued, "I was an aide to Alexis Léger," referring to the secretary-general of the Quai d'Orsay, the head of the permanent staff reporting to the foreign minister.

Étienne continued, "I knew him when he was a poet, before he became a diplomat."

Dexter understood; Léger, writing under the pen name Saint-Jean Perse, was one of France's greatest contemporary poets. And a good friend of Adrienne Monnier and Sylvia Beach, he remembered.

Étienne asked Dexter, "Suzanne tells me you are quite interested in Left Bank intellectual life," and he paused and smiled, "somewhat unusual for an American diplomat."

Madame Lambert laughed and looked with amused interest at Dexter for his answer.

Dexter responded, "Yes. But it has a practical side. We feel that if the intellectuals embrace Moscow, it makes an alliance with Russia easier to accomplish."

Étienne asked, "And do you favor an alliance with Russia?"

Dexter replied, "We support France's security needs."

Étienne nodded, now thoughtful. "Quite right."

Dexter continued, "It would offset the pro-Fascist beliefs of the Action Française," he said referring to the largest of the Far Right leagues.

Étienne replied, a slight trace of skepticism in his words, "That may not be such a bad thing. Prime Minister Laval is deeply committed to alliance with Mussolini and Italy as a check on Hitler and Germany."

Madame Bardoux now spoke, "Mussolini moved a hundred thousand Italian troops to the Brenner Pass last summer to save Austria from Hitler's putsch."

Madame Lambert nodded slightly in understanding and in seeming agreement, or so it seemed to Dexter. The French had been quite taken by Mussolini's daring challenge to Hitler. It was a well-remembered event which showed the powerful potential of maintaining an alliance with Italy. The French general staff was particularly enthusiastic.

Madame Bardoux continued, "Mussolini acted. No one else did."

Étienne nodded slowly in agreement and then added, "But Suzanne, that was a year ago. It may be growing stale now. It's hard to trust dictators."

Madame Bardoux said with sweet sarcasm, "It's hard to trust the British," in reference to Britain's having signed behind France's back the Naval Agreement with Berlin the previous month.

Étienne sighed, looked at Dexter, and shrugged his shoulders. "What can I say?"

Dexter laughed and then asked Étienne, "And what of the British?"

Étienne said, "I think the thinking is…"

Madame Bardoux interrupted and said to Dexter, "Alexis Léger believes."

Étienne nodded at Suzanne and continued, "Britain has to be France's principal ally, the foundation upon which our security rests is the *Entente Cordiale*," referring to the relationship binding Britain and France together and dating from before the First World War.

Dexter nodded and thought to himself that the missing piece was the Americans across the ocean. But he also knew that the Americans would stay missing for a long time to come.

Étienne continued, "France, in firm union with Britain, then supports collective security through the League of Nations."

Madame Bardoux added, "Foreign Minister Barthou, in one of his last acts before being killed," she said the words with great sadness, "then brought Russia into the League of Nations." She added, quite businesslike, "And Foreign Minister Laval just returned two months ago from Moscow with a signed agreement for alliance. If France can contain Germany from both the West and the East, peace can be maintained."

Dexter cut the ground out from her argument, "Then Great Britain signed the Naval Treaty with the Germans."

Madame Bardoux sighed, a trace of disgust in her voice. "Yes, that tremendously strains Anglo-French solidarity. Almost puts an end to having a common policy. What was Stresa for?"

Étienne moved to answer the question. "Laval wants to keep Italy in alliance with the western democracies against Hitler. That was what Stresa was all about."

Dexter asked, "But isn't Laval going about this wrong?"

He took a sip from his beer and then outlined his points, "He is separating France from Britain when he says that France will stand by her Latin sister in her so-called 'work of civilization' in planning aggression against Ethiopia. The entire idea behind the League of Nations is undermined. Supporting the League is Britain's number one foreign policy goal."

Madame Lambert looked at Dexter, calmly and professionally, and thought to herself that yes, the American had got straight to the heart of the issue.

Madame Bardoux spoke, in obvious sympathy to Dexter's point, "Yes," and she paused and quickly reworded her point to disguise her source, "As you yourself pointed out, the British foreign minister made that exact point to the cabinet last month. He called it 'an inconvenient dilemma.'"

Dexter remembered and said with a laugh, "Possibly we have the same source in London."

All of them laughed.

Étienne sighed. "Yes, Premier Laval may be too clever for his own good. Italy simply does not have the standing that Great Britain has."

Dexter nodded and thought to himself that once again the phrase "too clever" was used to describe Laval.

Dexter decided to shift the conversation and move to a new subject. "It was just four months ago when Hitler all but tore up the Versailles Treaty by almost quintupling the size of the German army. France failed to act."

Étienne saw the shift, shrugged, and looked at Dexter and agreed, "Yes."

Dexter moved to his conclusion. "The next step might be the remilitarization of the Rhineland by Hitler?"

Étienne again sighed. "Perhaps."

Dexter asked, "Would Britain support France in expelling German forces from the west bank of the Rhine?"

Étienne, straining to put an even tone to his voice, replied, "One would hope so."

Madame Lambert leaned back in her chair and stared evenly at Dexter. She could see the shape of Dexter's overall argument: on the diplomatic chessboard, Laval moves toward Italy, Britain moves away from France, and then Hitler pounces, using a knight to jump three spaces on the chessboard and take the Rhineland.

Madame Lambert leaned forward, putting her elbows on the table, looking directly at Dexter, and said very evenly, "The game moves on many levels."

Dexter said, "Yes, France moves towards Italy, opening up a gap with Britain, and Hitler marches into that sliver of daylight."

Madame Lambert stroked her chin in appreciation and looked evenly at Dexter; she said nothing.

Étienne moved to change the direction of the conversation. He nodded in the direction of Madame Lambert and said to Dexter, "Monsieur le Premier is completely absorbed in implementing the austerity program that was the basis of his election as premier last month." He looked at Madame Lambert for confirmation.

Madame Lambert replied, "Yes. The government is going to announce the details of the austerity program in two days. Only the final details remain to be worked out tomorrow."

Dexter looked at Madame Lambert with interest; she spoke with crisp assurance and authority about the new financial program.

Madame Bardoux shifted in her chair; Dexter sensed she was about to bring something bothersome up. She looked at Madame Lambert and said, "Étienne and I have to leave. We have another event to attend." She reached out and held one of Madame Lambert's hands in hers by way of reassurance and said, "Marcelle, I am sure Dexter will be good company."

Startled, Madame Lambert was put off balance, a look of indecision and consternation coming over her face. She was being left with this man. She looked blankly at Madame Bardoux.

Dexter, somewhat surprised, said in a low tone, "It will be all right. I also have an event to attend that I am sure you will find both fascinating and interesting up on the Champs Élysées."

Madame Lambert, regaining her composure, smiled at Dexter and said, "That will be fine." She turned and smiled at Madame Bardoux—rather thinly, thought Dexter.

Dexter and Madame Lambert walked up the wide sidewalk of the Champs Élysées, the Arc de Triomphe de l'Étoile in the distance sitting majestically at the top of the slope. In high good humor, Dexter said to Madame Lambert, "Let me introduce myself. My name is Dexter, and you?"

She turned and looked up at him, her eyes suddenly brightening, a sardonic smile lightly on her face, and laughed. "Yes, of course. Marcelle."

He smiled at her. "See, that wasn't so bad."

She laughed again.

Dexter continued, "I gather you are not a graduate of Sciences Po?"

Marcelle laughed again and then replied, "Hardly. I am a graduate from a *lycée* in Lyon. Before that convent school."

Dexter asked, "What carried you to the Hôtel Matignon?"

Marcelle, thinking back for a moment, replied, "I am very good at languages. Writing and literature have been my great interest. The French bureaucracy greatly values precise use of language."

Dexter asked, "Where did you meet Madame Bardoux?"

Marcelle replied, "Working on international labor issues. My permanent position is as a *redactrice* at the ministry of labor. I am a *sous-chef* there. I am on temporary appointment to the premier's office at the Matignon."

Dexter said, "Did you know Laval at the ministry of labor?"

"Yes," she said with a touch of finality, cutting off further inquiry.

"We," and Dexter looked at Marcelle to bring her into the embrace of this new state of togetherness, "have been invited by a journalist friend to watch the Croix-de-Feu march up the Champs Élysées. Colonel de La Rocque is to revive the flame over the Unknown Soldier at the Arc de Triomphe. We get to watch from her brother-in-law's apartment, a wealthy industrialist."

At the mention of the word "her," Marcelle's eyes lit up. "Ah, that must be Madame Tabouis," and she looked up at Dexter, her face framing the question.

"Yes." Dexter nodded.

"Ah, Madame Tata," continued Marcelle, referring to Madame Tabouis by the nickname bestowed on her by a leading Far Right journalist. She savored the sound of the name. Impishly she asked, "Does she 'Tata' to you, or do you 'Tata' to her?"

"Some of both." Dexter laughed.

Coming to the entrance of a luxurious apartment building, Dexter guided Marcelle into the foyer and spoke to the concierge. The concierge pointed towards a small *ascenseur*. Dexter and Marcelle walked over, got in, and rode the little elevator to the fourth floor, Dexter savoring the faint traces of Marcelle's perfume. Exiting, they saw the open door to an apartment and walked over. Dexter handed his hat, and Marcelle her handbag, to a maid.

Across the room, Madame Tabouis, holding a glass of champagne, was engaged in earnest conversation with several deputies. She caught sight of Dexter and her eyes brightened and she turned to the deputies. "I must go welcome Dexter. We must cultivate the Americans, you know."

She turned and walked towards Dexter and, seeing Marcelle for the first time, let her expression change from well-practiced welcome to an understanding smirk over rapidly brightening eyes. "Oh, Dexter, you have brought a friend," her voice lingering on "friend." She reached out her hand towards Marcelle.

Marcelle, highly bemused by Madame Tabouis's change in expression, shook the outstretched hand and said in her most professionally groomed manner, "*Enchantée*. Marcelle Lambert."

Dexter, always charmed by these little feminine greeting rituals, added, "Marcelle works at the ministry of labor."

Madame Tabouis glanced doubtfully at Dexter. "Your interest in labor relations must have been recently acquired?"

A look of mock chagrin came over Dexter's face. "Geneviève, I am interested in all things French."

Madame Tabouis waved to the maid to bring champagne, took a half step back, tilted back her head and looked at Marcelle, her mind searching for the missing acquaintanceship, and asked thoughtfully, "Where might we have seen you? Surely not at the ministry of labor. Haven't been there in years."

Marcelle, taking a glass of champagne from the maid, easily responded with great self-assurance, "Possibly with Madame Bardoux?"

"Yes, that is it," responded Madame Tabouis. "She is the bright new assistant to my great friend Alexis."

"You are well informed, Madame," replied Marcelle.

"Well, I am supposed to be," Madame Tabouis said, acknowledging her job as diplomatic correspondent for the Parisian daily *L'Oeuvre*. "Alexis Léger is both the conscience and competence of French foreign policy." Madame Tabouis expected no challenge to her estimation of the secretary-general of the foreign ministry.

Marcelle smiled in agreement.

Madame Tabouis glanced at Dexter and said directly to Marcelle, "I can see that Dexter is circulating in a very smart circle," and she paused, "not with his regular Right Bank sophisticates," the last word said with a sarcastic twist.

Dexter smiled at the backhanded compliment.

"Here they come," called out one of the men standing by one of the tall windows. Madame Tabouis walked over, followed by Marcelle and Dexter.

Looking out the window, they saw well-ordered ranks of veterans marching up the avenue. Out front was a large Tricolor draped with battle streamers, behind marched Colonel de La Rocque. Each veteran wore the red, white, and blue brassard of the Croix-de-Feu at his shoulder. Brass decorations hanging from colorful ribbons marched in rows across the chests of the veterans.

One of the men looking out the window sneered, "Their swan song."

Marcelle gave Dexter a questioning look; Madame Tabouis looked with interest at what Dexter might say.

"The press has been reporting that Colonel de La Rocque's bite grows steadily milder than his bark. Which is true since the public has grown tired of factionalism. Colonel de La Rocque has called for 'calm and union' in the face of the unsettled state of Europe and the grave difficulties facing the country. But the Croix-de-Feu will continue to be influential."

Madame Tabouis easily agreed with the assessment; Marcelle felt enlightened by the explanation.

Another man, watching the marching ranks stride up the avenue towards the Arc de Triomphe, remarked, "You have to admit that this is an amazing time we are living in. What miracle induces thirty thousand middle-class Frenchmen to let themselves be rounded up at the same hour and persuades them to goose-step to the Arc de Triomphe?"

Another man contradicted, "They're not goose-stepping. That's a Republican march. Let's keep our perspective. The goose-stepping is going on in Berlin, not Paris."

Dexter nodded to Marcelle. She smiled warmly at Dexter in agreement.

Another voice said, "There are at most thirty thousand marchers here. There were ten times that number marching for Popular Front today. The people of France do not want to go Fascist."

Madame Tabouis said with resignation, "I wished I could agree with that statement. But the truth is that three fourths of the French press has been gagged by the financial oligarchy—the Two Hundred Families."

Dexter said lightly, "The ratio's going up, Geneviève. It only used to be half."

Madame Tabouis quickly replied, "The Italians have come in."

Dexter laughed.

Marcelle asked, "How do the Two Hundred Families support Hitler?"

Madame Tabouis answered, "Simple. Their line is that France should not aim for a victorious peace, but at a just peace. Then they say we might be able to arrive at an amiable understanding with Hitler. Sweet reason becomes the Hemlock for the Republic," referring to the famous poison that Socrates took for his execution.

Marcelle asked, "Then might not Italy be a logical counterbalance?"

Madame Tabouis replied, "I am afraid not. Russia is the most powerful choice."

Dexter interjected, "But Laval has just returned from Moscow with an agreement with the Soviets."

Madame Tabouis countered, "They don't mean it. The Two Hundred Families scream that Bolshevism is enemy Number One."

Marcelle murmured, "Yes, that is so."

Madame Tabouis looked at the two of them rather sadly and pronounced her benediction, "And the sons shall perish because their fathers have lied."

Marcelle looked at Dexter. He looked back at her dark eyes, and, somewhat to his surprise saw that rather than being dismayed,

Marcelle's gaze took on a distant, steely determination. His fascination with Marcelle deepened.

Dexter turned back to Madame Tabouis, and with feeling, said, "If there is one person in France who speaks truth to illusion, it is you, Geneviève."

Madame Tabouis smiled weakly by way of thanks.

Marcelle caught Dexter's eyes with hers, pointing towards the center of the room. The two of them stepped away from the group. Marcelle said, "Thank you very much, Dexter, but I have a big day tomorrow. Let me take my leave. I can find my own way."

Dexter put himself forward with gentlemanly decisiveness. "Of course, but I insist on escorting you home."

Marcelle took a breath. "It's hardly necessary."

"I insist."

"I live across the river, in the outer Seventh."

"I live in the Seventh also," and he looked at her. "It will be my pleasure."

Marcelle sighed, and then responded with an edge of determination in her voice, "All right. But only to the door."

"Of course," replied Dexter.

They turned and, together, took their leave of Madame Tabouis.

In the gathering dusk of the warm summer day, Dexter and Marcelle walked across the Pont de L'Alma, from the Right Bank to the Left Bank, the silvery water of the River Seine lazily meandering down its channel.

Dexter asked, "And where do you live?"

Marcelle answered, "Oh, I live at 7 rue Monsieur. Just past the Invalides."

"Yes, I know where it is. Very nice neighborhood."

"Yes. I have an arrangement with the family that owns the flat."

"I see."

"Friends of my family."

They continued walking through the quiet Sunday evening, chatting agreeably about this and that.

Presently they turned off rue de Babylone on to rue Monsieur. They came up to two large wooden doors, brass knockers on the front, and stopped.

Marcelle said, "Here we are. Number seven," saying the street number as if it were an old friend. She reached into her handbag and pulled out a key. She put the key into the lock and turned it, the door opening slightly. She turned and faced Dexter, "It has been an informative day. Thank you."

Dexter smiled gallantly and asked with complete self-assurance, "Might we do this again?"

Marcelle took a quick breath, hesitated, and looked at Dexter with some perplexity. Then her face relaxed, her eyes softened, and she smiled. "I will be quite busy with my work. We must have the decree laws ready before the end of the month," she said summing up her busy life. Then she said, businesslike, "But I should be free at the end of the month." She smiled, her reassurance returning. "Yes, please call."

"I will."

She stepped towards him and presented her right cheek for a kiss, then the left. She stood back, smiled, and said, "Until then." She turned and went through the open door.

Dexter turned and walked down the sidewalk, a warm feeling of romantic expectation pleasantly enveloping his now very relaxed mind, a perfect end to a nice summer day.

Budget Decrees

Monday afternoon, July 15. The afternoon sun came through the windows and bathed the long room in summer sunlight. A table ran down the center of the room. The room, on the main floor of the Hôtel Matignon, overlooked the park with its long lawns stretching away into the distance. Madame Lambert, her back to the windows, walked along the table neatly boxing little piles of documents into precise stacks. Two other women, *redactrices*, trailed behind carrying extra copies of the documents. Next, Madame Lambert formed a second row of documents near the edge of the table. Now and again she would whisper instructions to one of her assistants, who would murmur, "Yes, Madame."

The *secrétaire général* poked his head through the door and watched the quiet efficiency underway. He asked, "Madame Lambert, are you ready?"

"Yes, *Monsieur le Secrétaire Général.*"

She turned to her two assistants and said, "Thank you." The two women left.

Presently Premier Laval and the finance minister with several aides came into the room.

"All is ready," said the *secrétaire général.*

Premier Laval nodded in acknowledgement and then turned to the finance minister. "Let me present Madame Lambert, our *chef de bureau.*"

The finance minister nodded by way of greeting.

Premier Laval turned to Madame Lambert and asked, "Ready?"

"Yes, Monsieur le Premier."

Premier Laval turned to the finance minister and explained, "The staff of the *administration centrale* has prepared the public announcements for each decree, which are on top of each stack. The decrees are underneath the announcements. Twenty-three decrees; twenty-three stacks."

Premier Laval looked up at Madame Lambert. "I am right in this, Madame Lambert?"

"Yes, Monsieur le Premier."

The premier continued, "The *secrétaire général* and his staff have carefully checked that the public announcements agree with the decree laws. The decree laws will be voted on by the Chamber of Deputies upon their return in October."

The premier turned to the *secrétaire general.* "Correct, *Monsieur le Secrétaire Général?*"

"Correct, Monsieur le Premier," came the reply.

The premier explained to the finance minister, "Your staff should take one set of both the public announcements and the decree laws with you. Your implementing regulations must be in strict accordance with the announcements and decrees."

The finance minister gravely nodded and looked at several of his aides, who signaled their understanding.

Premier Laval then summarized. "As you know, the cabinet will meet at the Quay d'Orsay tomorrow morning to consider the decree laws. Afterwards, a formal cabinet meeting will be held at the Élysée Palace to approve the decree laws and the President of the Republic will sign them. The announcements will be given to the press at that time."

The finance minister asked, "Do you think the cabinet will make changes?"

The premier replied, "Yes, compromise is always necessary. But they shall require only minor revision. If you change too much, the whole arrangement collapses."

The finance minister nodded.

Premier Laval then shifted the conversation. "The importance of the impartial implementation and administration of the decree laws cannot be over-emphasized."

The finance minister replied, "The ministry has already begun its work with that goal in mind."

The premier smiled and replied, "Good. In that regard, please have your ministry forward to Madame Lambert each regulation and directive required to implement the decrees as they become available."

The finance minister was somewhat startled by the premier's request.

Premier Laval soothingly added, "The entire cabinet will be reassured of the fairness and impartiality of the administration of the decree laws by the Matignon's involvement."

The finance minister nodded.

Premier Laval looked down the table at the finance ministry staff and said lightly, "It is a rare inconsistency that gets past the eye of Madame Lambert." He smiled broadly. The finance staff smiled thinly.

The premier looked around the room and concluded, "That will be all." He turned to the finance minister. "Until tomorrow."

Early the next morning in a hall paralleling the Salon de l'Horloge—the Clock Room—on the first floor of the Quai d'Orsay, Madame Lambert and Madame Bardoux arranged copies of the decrees around the immensely long cabinet table. Premier Laval came in with the *secrétaire général* at his elbow. Behind came groups of ministers chatting amongst themselves.

Turning to the *secrétaire général*, Laval said, "If you and some aides could take chairs behind me…"

The *secrétaire général* promptly replied, "Yes, Monsieur le Premier."

Laval then turned to Madame Lambert. "If you could take a chair at the other end of the room…"

Madame Lambert replied, "Yes, Monsieur le Premier."

Laval then turned to Madame Bardoux. "You best work upstairs with Secretary-General Léger for tomorrow's conference with Monsieur Avenol." Avenol was the permanent secretary of the League of Nations in Geneva. "He will have the latest developments from London for devising an arrangement with Italy about Ethiopia."

Laval then explained to the *secrétaire général* and Madame Lambert, "A satisfactory arrangement with Italy is of the greatest urgency. If next week's meeting in Geneva does not succeed, it will be a grave blow to the League of Nations."

Both the *secrétaire général* and Madame Lambert nodded in understanding. Madame Bardoux turned to leave, stopped and touched Madame Lambert on the shoulder and whispered something in her ear. Madame Lambert nodded in understanding.

The cabinet meeting began.

Towards noon, Premier Laval stood. "*Messieurs*, lunch will be served in the dining room. We will resume after lunch." The premier headed for the door leading towards the dining room followed by the cabinet ministers. After the cabinet ministers came the *secrétaire général*. Madame Lambert had a whispered conversation with him and added, "I will have lunch with Madame Bardoux." Madame Lambert walked out into the hallway leading to the staircase and went upstairs to Madame Bardoux's office.

As Madame Lambert took a chair in Madame Bardoux's office, she said, "Most of the ministers had little advance knowledge of the decrees, so the morning was taken up with presentations by various ministers on the deflation program."

Madame Bardoux asked, "Where does the meeting go from here?"

Madame Lambert replied, "The major issue is asking the low-paid government workers to take the same percentage cut as the higher paid civil servants. The Radical ministers object."

Madame Bardoux said thoughtfully, "Possibly Premier Laval has carried the concept of equality of sacrifice too far."

Madame Lambert responded, "He probably already knows that. He would want some areas where he could compromise with the Radical ministers. He seems completely assured that agreement will be reached this afternoon."

A receptionist brought in lunches and the two women ate at a small conference table in the office.

Later in the afternoon, with the discussion by the ministers continuing without decision, Premier Laval stood up and said, "*Messieurs*, let us take a break. Dinner will be served in the dining room."

Premier Laval walked around the cabinet table towards the entrance and stopped alongside Madame Lambert, the cabinet ministers backing up behind him in a jam, and said, in a voice that could be just overheard, "Madame Lambert, if you could stay this evening, we will finish tonight no matter how long it takes. Then the cabinet will adjourn to the Élysée Palace to meet with the President of the Republic. At that time, you can take the marked up copies back to the Hôtel de Matignon. The *secrétaire général* will accompany us to the Élysée; he is well connected on that side of the river."

"Yes, Monsieur le Premier," and she stood aside and watched the premier and the ministers parade through the door towards the dining room. She spoke briefly with the *secrétaire général* and then walked towards the stairway and the ascent to Madame Bardoux's office.

Entering Madame Bardoux's office, Madame Lambert smiled by way of greeting and said, "On the way to dinner, the premier stopped beside me at the doorway, stacking the cabinet up behind him like an evening traffic jam. He loudly whispered to me that the cabinet would finish tonight."

Madame Bardoux laughed. "I just wish that foreign affairs would yield so simply."

Astonished, Madame Lambert said in a rising voice, "Simply?"

"Yes, you will reach a decision. But tomorrow with the permanent secretary of the League of Nations we face the Italy dilemma again."

Madame Lambert said, now sympathetically, "Yes, I gather it is a real conundrum."

"Yes, we need to keep British support—in the last instance, they are our only real ally—and sustain the credibility and prestige of the League of Nations without driving Italy into Hitler's arms."

Madame Lambert said, almost absently, "Ethiopia hardly seems worth it."

Madame Bardoux summed up. "Yes, many believe that. But the British have become real sticklers for principle on this issue."

Madame Lambert sighed as she thought to herself that standing up to Hitler should be the principle.

The receptionist brought in two dinners and set them on the conference table. The women chatted while eating what was a very superb meal. The chef at the Quai d'Orsay was four star, thought Madame Lambert.

With midnight approaching, Premier Laval looked down the table; the ministers sat quiet. The premier stood up. "*Alors.* Very well, then. We shall go to the Élysée Palace and present the program to the President of the Republic."

Down the table heads nodded in weary agreement. The premier stood up, turned to the *secrétaire général* and said, "Please arrange to take the necessary documents for signature to the Élysée," and looking down the room at Madame Lambert and Madame Bardoux, he added, "Have Madame Lambert take the set approved by the cabinet back to the Matignon."

"Yes, Monsieur le Premier," replied the *secrétaire général.*

The premier turned, walked around the standing cabinet ministers, and towards the tall doors at the far end of the room. He smiled and winked at Madame Lambert and Madame Bardoux as he walked out. The ministers followed, a little bit more bedraggled than their now energized premier.

After the last minister departed, the *secrétaire général* came up to Madame Lambert and Madame Bardoux and said, "As you heard, I will be going with the premier. My car will take you to the Matignon and then it will take both of you ladies home."

Madame Lambert answered, "Yes, *Monsieur le Secrétaire Général.*"

The *secrétaire général* waved to several of his aides to follow with the decrees and walked out the door to the cars waiting outside.

Madame Lambert turned to Madame Bardoux. "Thank you so much for staying, Suzanne. We must be going."

Café de la Paix

Wednesday evening, July 17. Dexter walked up the boulevard des Capuchines towards Place de l'Opéra. Approaching the corner, he turned underneath the sidewalk awnings of the Café de la Paix, walked through the open front doors, and headed towards the bar. At one end, where the bar smoothly curved in a turn to meet the ornately gilded walls, sat a rumpled newsman, his fedora pushed back on his head, tie askew, nursing a drink.

Dexter sat down, nodded at the barman, and asked the newsman, "What do you hear, Phil?"

The newsman, the Paris reporter for a big New York daily, nodded at a radio sitting on the shelf behind the bar and said, "We can listen to the premier give his radio address right here, glass in hand," and then called lightly to the barman, "Right, Pierre?"

The barman smiled and said, "For our best customers, of course."

Dexter responded, "Great. You look bushed."

"Spent the day all over town talking to people inside and outside the government about the budget."

"And?"

"Everyone across the political spectrum compliments Laval on the thoroughness and completeness of his program, the scrupulous respect for the general above the particular. There's something for everyone to like about the program—and something for everyone to dislike."

"So he achieved equality of sacrifice?"

"Well, at least equality of dissatisfaction."

Dexter laughed. "What about the overall program?"

The newsman turned thoughtful. "If defending the franc is the goal, then he has succeeded far better than anyone thought possible. All day, people have remarked to me about Laval's competence."

Dexter said, "Well, that was what the Chamber of Deputies voted him to do as premier."

The newsman grunted, "That's what the Two Hundred Families wanted. Preserve wealth, put the burden of austerity on the people."

The newsman added, "But I think Laval's doing a great job fighting the wrong war very well. Your leader, President Roosevelt," and he nodded and looked at Dexter, assigning ownership of the president to the diplomat, "went the other way. He devalued the dollar forty percent against gold. Sat in his bathtub every morning and worked out the day's gold price with his treasury secretary."

Dexter smiled and nodded in agreement remembering Roosevelt's bold action.

The newsman voiced the popular opinion, "Roosevelt works for the people, not the high-hat crowd."

Dexter asked, "What do the parties of the Left think?"

The newsman looked at Dexter. "That's very interesting. Publicly they are of course opposed to the wage reductions. But they look at the sweeping powers the state has taken to regulate the economy. They love the precedent. They believe they are coming to power in next May's elections. They will use the same powers to implement their program."

Dexter was impressed with the insight and said, "So you don't think there will be big street demonstrations?"

"Not as big as people think."

Dexter took a drink and turned thoughtful and murmured, "Interesting."

The newsman knocked back his drink. "French politics is always that," and nodded at the barman for a refill.

The barman refilled the newsman's glass, then turned to the radio and switched it on. Hearing the crackle come out of the radio, other people crowded up to the bar. After a fanfare, Premier Laval began to speak. He appealed for acceptance of the program in a spirit of cooperation, that the sacrifices were necessary for the good of the nation.

The premier's voice continued in a sonorous appeal. He asked his fellow citizens to remember that other countries were watching France and that unity in facing the crisis would improve France's standing in the community of nations. Everyone listening knew he meant Germany.

The premier concluded, "If I had done nothing, I would have failed in my duty and all would have been victims of my weakness."

Dexter silently nodded in agreement and thought to himself, "Yes, victims of weakness. The big danger."

The announcer came back on; Dexter turned to the newsman. "Very impressive. He will have the country with him."

The newsman said, "For awhile."

Dexter clapped the newsman on the back, called the barman for the tab, pulled out some franc notes and left a generous tip on the tray.

Turning to the newsman, Dexter asked, "What do your sources say, Phil?"

The newsman said, "Big demonstration on the Place de l'Opéra Friday night," and the newsman nodded towards the square just beyond the windows.

Dexter replied, "Right," and stood up to leave.

The newsman called after him, "Here's a tip, Dexter. Save yourself some time. You can read about it in the papers Saturday morning."

Dexter turned back and smiled at him while giving him a farewell wave.

Quai d'Orsay

Tuesday, July 30. The slender Frenchman with the receding dark hair, handsome face, and movie-star elegant mustache, dressed in a well-tailored dark pinstripe suite, spoke softly with Madame Bardoux in the middle of one of the salon rooms on the first floor of the Quai d'Orsay. He explained, "The premier will have one of his political aides with him sitting on his left; I will sit to his right. You will be seated at the little desk and chair just behind me."

Madame Bardoux looked at the large round table centered underneath a brass chandelier in the middle of the room and at the small writing desk just behind one of the chairs.

"Yes, Monsieur le Secretary-General," she said to Alexis Léger, the permanent secretary of the French foreign ministry and her boss.

The secretary-general continued, "The British minister, Anthony Eden, and his aides will sit over there," and he pointed to the far side of the round table where the British minister for the League of Nations would sit.

Madame Bardoux nodded. An aide appeared at the doorway and signaled to Léger, who turned and said, "The delegation has arrived," and walked briskly across the room towards the reception hall.

Alexis Leger

Shortly, Premier Laval entered at the side of the debonair British minister. A half dozen aides trailed behind. Secretary-General Léger was a half step behind the premier. The men all took places at the table as indicated by the secretary-general.

Premier Laval began, "France believes that the conciliation commission should be allowed to continue its work to compose the differences between Italy and Ethiopia until the end of August."

Eden and his aides listened attentively.

Laval then drove home his point. "As was agreed by all parties last May."

Expecting the opening sally, Eden then turned to an aide, who handed him a paper. Eden started, "Let me read the British cabinet's position."

Laval nodded for Eden to continue. Eden read the declaration, a statement which was much weaker than the firm declaration he had urged the cabinet to adopt before coming to Paris."

Laval followed the argument closely. One of France's most skillful trial lawyers, he saw the weakness immediately, "Your paper brilliantly describes the dangers but offers no solution."

Eden ducked Laval's point and replied, "His Majesty's Government feels that the League Council should take up the whole Ethiopian problem Thursday in Geneva."

Laval turned thoughtful. "France's entire policy is to achieve a peaceful resolution of differences through the League of Nations."

Eden said, "Of course."

Laval set up his argument. "Nothing is to be gained by precipitating a showdown Thursday."

Eden saw his position slip away. For now, France's bargaining position was stronger than Great Britain's.

Laval moved to his argument. "The only hope for a peaceful solution of the Italo-Ethiopian quarrel lies in a determined but patient effort to seek a basis of agreement without letting the conciliation commission's efforts fail. France believes time is working toward a peaceful solution."

Eden nodded that he understood Laval's position.

Laval finished up. "That is why the August 25 deadline must be adhered to. But Thursday is only the first of August. We need patience."

Eden replied, "His Majesty's Government understands."

Laval sweetened the discussion. "France understands that Great Britain wants peaceful assurances from Italy while the commission completes its work."

Eden replied, "Yes."

Laval concluded the meeting. "Minister, we can continue our talks on the train tonight for Geneva."

Eden smiled and said, "Yes."

Laval stood up. The other men followed. All stepped around the table and shook hands and then walked towards the doorway.

Several minutes later, Secretary-General Léger returned and sat down in front of Madame Bardoux and said, "Eden is playing a weak hand. The British cabinet avoided making a firm declaration. We want to emphasize that point in the minutes."

Madame Bardoux answered, "Yes, Monsieur le Secretary-General."

The secretary-general turned thoughtful. "For your ears only, Laval's position to wait until the end of August is both strong and sensible," and then the secretary-general sighed, "but after that, he too has a weak hand. Italy is going to do what Italy wants."

Madame Bardoux asked, "And Germany?"

"They will be completely sympathetic to Italy and enjoy watching the discord among the Big Three."

Madame Bardoux nodded and then asked the central question, "What should France's policy be after August plays out."

The secretary-general summed up his long-held beliefs, "France's entire security rests with an ironclad alliance with Great Britain. Then the two work hand-in-hand to sustain the power and prestige of the League of Nations, the only real hope for continued peace in Europe. I shudder to think of France facing Germany alone."

Madame Bardoux took a quick breath; the thought of France facing Germany alone always created a physical repulsion in her stomach. She pulled her papers together and said, "Yes, the ministers come and go; Monsieur Léger stays ever-constant," and she smiled at the secretary-general. They stood up and left the room.

The Colonel

Saturday afternoon, early August. Dexter Jones sat at a small round table at an outdoor café just across the square from the splashing waters of the fountain at Place Saint-Michel. He was reading a news story about Thursday's meeting in Geneva of the Big Three at the League of Nations. It was obvious to Dexter that the French paper was treating Thursday's decisions to continue the deliberations over Ethiopia through the end of August as an important personal victory for Premier Laval, a judgment with which Dexter agreed. Always better to push a war off into the future whenever possible, he thought.

Looking up, he saw Madame Lambert walking across the square towards him. He smiled at her and she gave him a smile of recognition and a small wave. She came up and started to sit down as Dexter quickly stood and came around and held her chair for her. She looked up at him and smiled. "Thank you."

"Marcelle," he said in a singular and all-encompassing greeting.

"Dexter," she replied. Yes, she thought to herself, the meeting is really just about the two of them.

Looking at the newspaper on the table, she asked, "What is the news this afternoon?"

"Your boss, Premier Laval, has won a victory at Geneva."

"Ah, foreign affairs, that would be Suzanne's department," referring to Madame Bardoux, "At the Matignon, we continue with the budget struggle."

Picking up the paper, Dexter read from the news story, "The savior of the franc in Paris, Mr. Laval at Geneva showed himself as the keeper of peace."

Putting the paper down, Dexter said, "See, you are half the victory, Suzanne the other half. A good week's work for the premier."

"He is highly capable," she said. She shifted in her chair and asked, "What do you have planned for us today?"

"We are going to go over to the apartment of Daniel Halévy, who hosts one of Paris's more distinguished literary salons."

"Yes, I am familiar with his reputation as a publisher," and she laughed a little, "but I would think he would be too conservative for you."

"We are going to hear a young colonel talk about his new book on reforming the French army. Our military attaché recommends him highly."

"That's a departure from your Left Bank pursuits. What brings this about?" She placed her chin in the palm of her hand and looked directly at him waiting for his reply.

"If Hitler attempts to remilitarize the Rhineland, what would France's response be?"

A look of concern came across Marcelle's face. "What would it be?"

"We don't know. The French army in metropolitan France basically trains each year's new batch of national service conscripts for basic military service. It is not a fighting force," explained Dexter.

"I thought it was the largest army in Europe?"

"Only if it fully mobilizes for war."

"Like 1914?"

"Yes, like 1914."

Marcelle's face turned troubled. Of course, everyone knew what came after 1914.

Dexter relaxed a bit. "Let's go hear what the colonel has to say." They stood up.

They walked up the Quai des Grands Augustins in the shade of the apartment buildings lining the Left Bank of the river. Dexter pointed across the river to the sun-drenched façade of the Palais de Justice on the Île de la Cité murmuring, "Simply magnificent." Marcelle nodded in agreement.

They turned right onto the old stone bridge of Pont Neuf and walked towards the Right Bank. Midway across, on the Île de la Cité, they turned into a small street leading towards fashionable Place Dauphine. After a few steps, they stopped and entered an open doorway tended by a concierge. The old man pointed them up the stairway to the second floor.

Entering into the foyer through an open front door, Dexter saw an officer's kepi cap sitting on a small reception table, a set of gloves lying elegantly across the bill of the cap. Dexter nodded at Marcelle, who took in the cap and gloves and smiled. Of course, a gentleman.

They walked into the drawing room, Marcelle gazing out the tall windows at the row of green leaf-laden poplar trees lining the riverbank of the Quai de l'Horloge. Beyond were more sun-swept buildings lining the Right Bank. The buildings marched in a line down the riverfront to the Palais de Louvre.

Marcelle looked around the drawing room, taking in the darkly rich and textured paintings of Édouard Degas hanging on the walls, all set amidst elegant Second Empire furniture. Deep purple velvet seemed everywhere. An older woman wearing an elegant floor-length robe came over with a platter of refreshments. Dexter murmured, "*Bonjour*, Madame Halévy." Marcelle took a cup of tea, Dexter a glass of port.

At the head of the room stood a large, quite tall army colonel in a summer blouse and khaki slacks, the creases sword-like in their sharpness. He was standing in animated conversation with several of the guests. A real talker, Marcelle thought.

The host, Daniel Halévy, stepped forward wearing a dark, somber suit, his delicate features framed by a dark, closely trimmed beard. He stood quietly, a *grand bourgeois* standing in self-assured and nonchalant elegance, waiting until the guests quieted down. Then he opened the salon, "It is our pleasure today to welcome Lieutenant-Colonel Charles de Gaulle to speak to us about his book *Vers l'armée de métier*. He will outline his ideas towards the professional army of the future. Colonel de Gaulle is currently on the staff of the *Secrétariat Général de la Défense Nationale*, a professional planning staff serving the premier." Halévy extended his arm towards the colonel, who rose and came forward, "I present to you Colonel de Gaulle."

De Gaulle politely began, "Thank you Monsieur Halévy for inviting me to speak to this distinguished group."

Then de Gaulle launched into his talk. "Currently French national defense rests on an unswerving faith in the massive mobilization of the citizenry in times of national peril. This concept dates back to the Revolution and the *levée en masse* whereby a mass of patriotic volunteers would rise and destroy an invading army. This concept, almost sacred, binds the citizen army to the republican tradition."

De Gaulle paused and let the message sink in. He continued, "I am proposing that France form a professional corps of long-serving professional soldiers of seven divisions, mostly armored, motorized throughout. This will be an army that can bring about decision through maneuver and attack."

Again de Gaulle paused and he looked across the assemblage to see that the point was sinking in. He then pivoted on his rhetorical point. "Why?"

He paused, then provided his answer. "There has been a revolution in military strength produced in the past decades by the internal-combustion engine. This multiplication of mechanical power has revived mobility and provides motorized forces a terrible superiority over the more or less confused masses of traditional land armies. This development holds out the possibility of unforeseen, shattering results."

There were murmurings of comment among the guests. De Gaulle continued to flesh out his ideas about a professional corps of armored divisions to the audience, now held in rapt attention by his simple, but eloquent arguments. Finishing, de Gaulle said, "I will be pleased to take your questions."

One gentleman asked, "How can we talk about contemplating the offense when we have spent billions to establish the Maginot Line? Why would we be foolish enough to go beyond this barrier for I do not know what kind of adventure?"

De Gaulle smiled. "The professional corps complements the Maginot Line and in effect guarantees its effectiveness." Heads nodded in understanding.

De Gaulle continued, "As to the second question, the armored corps multiplies its firepower and shock power by maneuvering to attack the enemy in front of the barrier."

Dexter stepped forward and de Gaulle turned that large body towards him to meet the question, almost like the turret of a battleship swiveling to meet a new target, thought Marcelle.

Dexter asked, "I would like to follow up on the previous question about what a professional corps might do in front of the Maginot Line."

De Gaulle tilted his head at a thoughtful angle as a sign for Dexter to proceed.

Dexter continued, "If Hitler sent the German army across the Rhine to remilitarize the Rhineland, would a professional corps be able to advance into Germany and eject it?"

De Gaulle reared his head back and looked down and around his large nose as he smiled. "*Eh bien.* A beautiful question that answers itself." He smiled, bowing his head towards Dexter and concluding, "Monsieur."

Dexter followed up, "This could avoid a general mobilization to counter a German remilitarization in the Rhineland."

De Gaulle looked thoughtful for a moment and answered, "That of course is a political question. But a professional corps adds another credible course of action for the political leadership to consider. In short, flexibility."

Several more questions were asked; the colonel responding knowledgeably to each. With the last question, Paul Halévy stepped forward to conclude the presentation by graciously thanking Colonel de Gaulle.

Marcelle turned to Dexter. "I can only ask—where would the money come from?"

Dexter replied, "A good question. Let's discuss it over dinner. I know a nice restaurant along the river with tables underneath large spreading trees. Cool on a day like today."

Marcelle smiled. "Okay. But I have to get home early. We are working tomorrow. Premier Laval is presenting almost eighty decrees to the cabinet on Tuesday to lower the cost of living. On Friday he has invited the prefects from all the departments of France to the Quai d'Orsay to go over the new decrees. He expects a demanding administration of the new regime."

Dexter looked surprised. "That is a hugely ambitious program."

"Yes it is. But what I would expect from him. He does not shrink from a challenge."

Later that evening, with darkness setting in on the quiet street of rue Monsieur, Dexter walked Marcelle to her door. She turned and looked at him, smiled, and said, "I had a very informative time."

Dexter made a playful frown.

Marcelle laughed. "And a completely charming dinner. You are very kind."

"My pleasure. Could we meet in two Saturday's time? Sylvia Beach is having a get together at her bookshop. I am sure you would enjoy it."

Marcelle's face sharpened with obvious interest. "Yes, I would like that very much. Thank you." She presented her right cheek to Dexter for a kiss, then the left. She turned and with her key opened the door and then looked over her shoulder at Dexter. "*Au revoir.*" Then she was gone.

Finance Decrees

Thursday evening, August 8. Marcelle Lambert, bone tired, sat watching hypnotically the tall windows bordering the long meeting room in the Quai d'Orsay. To her eyes the windows were bright black mirrors reflecting back the luminous images of lights shining from crystal chandeliers hanging down over the cabinet table. Along the table sat, and sprawled, members of the cabinet. Midnight was upon them. They had been there all day discussing, and finally approving, the seventy to eighty draft decrees to complete and supplement the deflation program adopted the month before. Next week Madame Lambert would work with the ministries to organize them into exact order.

At the head of the table, Premier Laval stood solemnly giving a benediction to the evening's proceedings, "From now on the great financial danger has been set aside. Later will come a great revival of business activity if the disciplined nation responds to the effort the cabinet is pursuing without faltering and without allowing itself to be turned from its duty." He turned and headed for the doors at the far end of the meeting room. The cabinet wearily followed.

The *secrétaire général* busily came up. "Madame Lambert, I will go with the premier. My car will take you home. Can I suggest that we meet at the Matignon late tomorrow morning and we can come over to the Quai d'Orsay together?"

Madame Lambert pertly replied, *"Oui, Monsieur le Secrétaire Général."*

The *secrétaire général* hurried after the premier. Madame Lambert gathered up her papers and slowly walked to the car waiting in the courtyard.

Late the following morning, Madame Lambert was standing at a long conference table in the Hotel Matignon going over numerous piles of documents with her assistants. She had been there since early morning preparing documents for the afternoon conference. The *secrétaire général* entered and came up to her, warmly asking, "Is everything ready for this afternoon, Madame Lambert?"

"Yes, of course, *Monsieur le Secrétaire Général.*"

"Good. My car will take you," and he looked at several of her assistants, "and your assistants over to the Quai d'Orsay." He pulled a newspaper out of his pocket and motioned to the assistants to come closer and hear. "Your efforts do not go unappreciated. Look at the headlines on the newspaper," and he held it up and read, "The franc is saved." He stuffed the newspaper back in his pocket.

Madame Lambert smiled and said, "Thank you."

The *secrétaire général* departed and Madame Lambert gave final instructions to her assistants.

"Yes, Madame," they replied.

Driving through the gates of the Quai d'Orsay, Madame Lambert and her assistants peered out of the limousine's windows at the dozens of official cars crowding the courtyard. Madame Lambert explained to the astonished assistants, "All the prefects of France have been summoned by the premier to a conference on the deflation decrees, almost seventy officials from the departments."

The car pulled to a halt outside the entrance and the women got out. Guards came over to assist with the boxes of documents. Madame Lambert led her assistants into the building followed by the guards.

Inside the sumptuous Salon de l'Horloge, Madame Lambert pointed to long tables along the walls where the documents should be placed. Her assistants quickly assembled the documents in order.

Madame Lambert looked to the far end of the room, just below the fabled clock, and saw Premier Laval and several ministers. Around the room groups of prefects stood talking animatedly with each other.

Madame Lambert walked over to the tables and went over the documents with her assistants. Then she looked to the head of the room and caught the eye of the *secrétaire général* and nodded to him. She and her assistants took seats at the rear of the hall.

The *secrétaire général* strode up to the side of the lectern and shouted out in a stentorian voice across the room, "*Monsieur le Président du Conseil!*" Everyone came to his or her feet.

Premier Laval walked briskly up to the lectern; the prefects took their seats. Premier Laval thanked them for taking the time to come to Paris. Then he introduced the ministers of finance, commerce, public works, and labor standing beside him.

Premier Laval launched into an explanation of the new decrees and concluded, "It is the fate of the régime and the life of the country that are at stake."

The premier motioned for the finance minister to come forward. The finance minister explained to the prefects that interest rates were reduced from six to five percent and that the profits tax on businesses was increased from eighteen to twenty-four percent.

The finance minister stepped aside and the public works minister came forward and grandly announced that the government was providing an additional billion francs to national public works, and he paused for a dramatic second, and then said that a billion additional francs was going to the communes and departments for public works. The prefects quickly applauded, some standing and clapping loudly. Premier Laval beamed.

The other ministers came up in turn and explained additional aspects of the deflation program, many focusing on lowering prices and increasing trade.

At the end of the session Premier Laval returned to the lectern and concluded, "These decrees contain the measures demanded by the country for years. It is a long-term program which will put the franc in safety from every attack." He thanked the prefects and strode down the center of the room to the doors at the far end of the hall.

The Booksellers

Saturday, August 11. Dexter sat at a small round table deep in the shade of the *terrasse* of Les Deux Magots and watched the bustling Saturday crowd out on boulevard Saint-Germaine, the slanting sunlight of early evening putting the people into bright and lively relief. He watched as Marcelle came down the stone sidewalk scanning the tables looking for him. He waved a hand and her face brightened in recognition. She walked over. Dexter admired the light blue blouse and the fashionable navy blue skirt, a wide brown leather belt separating the two blues. Below the wing of her collar was the discreet black ribbon of the *deuil*. He stood and held her chair as she sat down.

"Thank you for inviting me. I am looking forward to this. It has been a long week."

Dexter looked at her sympathetically. "I followed the events at the Quai d'Orsay in the newspapers. Were you there till midnight?"

Marcelle nodded, then added, "And up early the next morning to organize documents for the conference with the prefects. They were almost all there."

Dexter said thoughtfully, "Yes, I saw that the prefects from Brest and Toulon had to stay at their posts and deal with riots. The workers themselves are not going quietly into Laval's age of austerity even if the union bosses in Paris are agreeable to the government program."

Marcelle replied simply, "Saving the franc was the charge the Chamber of Deputies gave to Premier Laval in June. That is his heavy task."

Dexter agreed. "Yes, he has done this better than almost all observers thought possible. If he succeeds, which seems likely, he will have proven himself the great servant of France."

Marcelle smiled a small thank you at Dexter.

Dexter moved to change the subject. "I thought we would start at La Maison des Amis des Livres, Adrienne's bookshop. I gather you already know it."

"Oh yes, both Suzanne and I belong to her lending library. We attend readings there when we can."

Dexter continued, "Afterwards I thought we would cross the street to Sylvia Beach's Shakespeare and Company. I'm told there will be a lively crowd there tonight."

A waiter brought a second wine glass and set it in front of Marcelle and poured some chilled white wine into the glass from the bottle already sitting in an iced bucket on the table.

Dexter added superfluously, "For you."

Marcelle took a sip of wine from the glass and looked inquiringly at Dexter. "And?"

Dexter continued, "Are you interested in English and American literature?"

Marcelle looked thoughtful for a minute. "Why yes. But I have been reading most of it in French translation. Adrienne has a superb collection. Both Suzanne and I want to tackle some of it in English, though. We will have our own little reading club. So we have planned to join Miss Beach's library."

Dexter finished his wine and said, "We better be going."

"Yes, of course," and Marcelle rose to stand as Dexter held her chair for her.

Turning up rue de l'Odeon in the falling light of evening, Dexter could see the front door and lights on at La Maison des Amis des Livres. Across the street, people were going in and out of Shakespeare and Company, several people engaged in lively discussion in front of the brightly lit store, the yellow light from inside falling in pools on the sidewalk outside.

Dexter held the door open and Marcelle entered La Maison and walked towards the center of the store. Adrienne Monnier saw her, stopped talking to her assistant, and came forward smiling. Seeing Dexter, she widened her smile further. "What a pleasant surprise."

Turning to Marcelle she asked, "Is Suzanne going to be with you tonight?"

"No. She is with Étienne tonight."

Looking inquiringly at Marcelle, Adrienne asked, "And you know our good friend Dexter?"

"Yes, he escorted Suzanne and me to the Writers Conference. We saw André Malraux give his closing speech. Afterwards over tea we found out we all had a shared interest in your bookshop." She turned and looked coyly at Dexter and remarked, "And since then we have shared some political discussions."

Adrienne beamed. "Yes, Dexter knows politics." Then she added in a hurried tone, "We better close up and cross the street." Adrienne said some words to her assistant and then ushered Dexter and Marcelle towards the door.

The three of them crossed the street and pushed through the door heading towards the rear of the shop and a large wooden table that served as the headquarters for the bookshop. Behind the table pasted on a wall between ceiling-high bookshelves was a poster proclaiming "The Scandal of Ulysses," the iconic book classic that Sylvia Beach had daringly published in the early 1920s. Standing by the table was Sylvia with brushed-back dark hair, touched with gray here and there, a white collared blouse, and a neat little suit coat over a plain longish skirt. She looked something like what Marcelle imagined a New England librarian to look like.

Sylvia looked up and recognized Dexter, breaking into a wide smile. "Dexter!" She looked at Marcelle, a little skeptically Marcelle thought, and then looked to Adrienne for explanation.

Adrienne gave a warm introduction. "Sylvia, this is Marcelle Lambert. She is the friend of Suzanne Bardoux's that I told you about. Like Suzanne, she is a *redactrice* at a government ministry." Adrienne looked at Marcelle for confirmation. "Correct?"

Marcelle cheerfully responded, the vagueness of the description pleasing to her, "Yes."

Sylvia's countenance relaxed and she held out her hand to Marcelle. As Marcelle shook the outstretched hand, Sylvia clapped her other hand over Marcelle's in welcoming friendship. Marcelle beamed. Sylvia said, "Yes, Suzanne works for our good friend Alexis Léger, but of course we know him as the poet Saint-John Perse." Sylvia made a small laugh. "But now his diplomatic career consumes all his time, if not his talents," and she frowned.

Sylvia turned to Dexter. "Alexis is one small ray of hope in a darkening international situation."

Dexter quickly agreed, "Certainly. He is the most realistic of, shall we say, the idealists. A master of the language of diplomacy."

Adrienne picked up on the point and added, somewhat confessionally, "Speaking of language, Suzanne told me that Marcelle is regarded as having one of the most economical and precise commands of French in the government ministries."

Dexter's whole countenance quickly sharpened as the correctness of this fresh remark sank in. Of course, he thought.

Marcelle smiled with humility but inwardly she was taken aback at this revelation from her closest friend circulating at what was almost an American cocktail party, one of the most indiscreet inventions of the modern era.

Sylvia noticed the deep reservoir of reserve behind the mask of Marcelle's pleasant demeanor.

Sylvia turned to Marcelle and asked a touch sardonically, "You know Dexter?"

"Why yes, he escorted Suzanne and me to the Writers Conference to hear André Malraux give the closing address."

Sylvia glanced sidewise at Dexter and then said to Marcelle, "Well, at least you have discriminating taste in Americans," and she laughed, "it is not always that way. With either French women or American men."

Marcelle smiled in appreciation and Sylvia caught Marcelle's assured look that said that the smooth handling of men was one of her talents. Sylvia looked a little more appraisingly at Dexter. Something more than a Saturday night adventure, she thought.

Dexter moved to lighten the conversation. "Suzanne jokes that Marcelle has not crossed the street from Adrienne's because she is afraid her friends at the ministry might think she is sneaking looks at dirty books."

Sylvia laughed. "*Ulysses* is about life, which always has it raw features. So the United States Post Office kept seizing it in the 1920s," and laughed while thinking back at the banality of the Great Protestant Republic's efforts at cultural control.

Marcelle caught her mood and mischievously asked Dexter, "As a representative of your government, why do you use the Post Office as a culture ministry."

Dexter easily answered, "We don't always. Sometimes we use the Customs Service."

Sylvia and Adrienne doubled over with laughter. Marcelle good-naturedly joined in. Marcelle said in an aside to the two women, "I am just testing his diplomatic skills."

Dexter gave a small bow from the waist.

James Joyce and Sylvia Beach with Adrienne Monnier

Marcelle added somewhat seriously, "I read Joyce's *Ulysses* in translation. Adrienne has a superb copy."

Sylvia replied, "Well, you could try it in English," and adding her own little mischief, she said, "You could read it with Dexter. He might be able to help you with some of, shall we say, the more colorful idiom."

Marcelle gave a light laugh and said, "I would hope that I am unfamiliar with some of the words, and besides," and she hesitated while her eyes darted right and left as she searched for words.

Dexter jumped in, "She would not like to give any false sense of familiarity or intimacy to her friendship with me."

Marcelle's expression lightened and she said, "Yes, exactly," and turned laughing eyes at Dexter.

Sylvia laughed and said with self-satisfaction, "See, there you are. You finish each other's sentences like an old married couple."

Marcelle's face reddened as if the words poked her in a vulnerable place. Sylvia saw the anger flash in her eyes, an anger like she used to see sometimes in her mother's eyes, the anger of a woman determined not to be hurt again. Sylvia looked sympathetically at her.

Dexter also saw the anger and decided to stand back and let it settle.

Marcelle quickly composed herself and added apologetically, "I am a widow. It has been years since I have been described as a married woman. It just startled me. Excuse me."

Adrienne moved to put the discomfort in the past and took a half-step forward and started to speak in her version of a West African French *patois*, "Dexter is a great mimic. He has promised us a performance over at La Maison des Amis des Livres. Show us Dexter."

Marcelle looked momentarily startled at hearing the West African dialect.

Dexter smoothly started to give a lilting imitation of the West African *patois* of the native women bargaining away with the fruit and vegetable sellers at the morning wet markets.

Marcelle turned towards Dexter, her face almost white in blank astonishment. Sylvia and Adrienne looked quizzically at her. Now what? they thought.

Marcelle blurted out. "When were you in Dakar?"

Dexter, a bit surprised at the suddenness of the question, answered, "I was a vice consul there between 1929 and 1931."

Marcelle, eyes looking wistfully up at the ceiling, started to recite in the same beautiful lilting French *patois* a couple of sentences describing almost forgotten trips to the morning markets. Yes, she remembered.

Adrienne and Sylvia were totally captivated by Marcelle's revelation and the beauty of her remembered conversations. The trilling of her West African French was like a songbird answering her suitor, thought Sylvia.

Dexter looked on with keen interest. An answer to something lay in the next couple of sentences, he thought.

Marcelle murmured, "I was in Dakar from 1926 to 1928."

All faces turned to her for further explanation.

Marcelle thought back, like remembering a once cherished dream, and said simply, "I went there a bride and came back a widow."

Sylvia asked, "What happened?"

"My fiancé and I were married. He had just graduated from L'École Polytechnique. He was an *ingénieur*. Our future was assured."

Adrienne nodded her head at Sylvia to reinforce the truthfulness of Marcelle's statement about L'École Polytechnique; it was the gateway to a life of distinction and prominence.

"There was just the question of his military service. He was of course posted to an elite engineering service. Scientific work."

She sighed. "The expedition, he went as surveyor, trekked way out in the desert, past the farmlands, to survey the border between the Moslem lands and the African lands. It was just a skirmish, they said, the result of a misunderstanding. They buried him out there, in the land between their God and our God."

Dexter looked at her, now plain and forlorn, a whole crushed look had swept over what moments ago to him had been one of the most self-assured women in Paris. He was struck by the change and deeply sympathetic.

Marcelle continued, "I came back to Paris. His advisers at L'École Polytechnique, who were beyond kindness, guided me towards a civil service position at the ministry of labor. Recommendations, introductions, and of course the right word to the right person."

And she said with a touch of pride, "I am still invited to tea over there. The warmth of their interest in me has been the finishing touch to my confidence all these years."

Dexter looked at her; it was a beautifully perfect explanation to the self-assured presence of this fascinating woman.

Dexter gently asked, "So your fascination with André Malraux and *Man's Fate?*"

Marcelle replied, "A little bit. I think revolutionary forces will struggle against colonialism. The rest of the world is not Europe."

Sylvia and Adrienne nodded in understanding.

Dexter said to the two booksellers, "I promised Marcelle an early evening. So we better be leaving, but Sylvia, if I could have a word with you," and he nodded towards a corner. The two stepped away from the group. Adrienne picked up the conversation with Marcelle about life in West Africa.

Dexter said in a low voice to Sylvia, "Here is an envelope. André," it was clear to Sylvia he meant Gide, "told me about the Friends of Shakespeare and Company. Here is my subscription. I, and hopefully Marcelle, will look forward to attending the readings."

Sylvia replied, "Thank you, Dexter," and she added looking over at Marcelle, "she has had, and possibly leads, a fascinating life. She has the courage of her judgment."

Dexter looked momentarily reflective, then said, "Yes." He turned and walked over to Marcelle, said goodbye to Adrienne, and took Marcelle's arm and guided her towards the door.

In the darkness walking towards rue Monsieur, Marcelle said, "You won't mind if we do not read *Ulysses* together?"

Dexter laughed, "Hardly. I am admirer of the *Odyssey.*"

"Yes, so am I. But I place *The Iliad* first. The pride of men, the fall of civilizations."

Then she turned to him, "What do you like about *The Odyssey?*"

Dexter laughed and said, "I don't want to offend you. But I was thinking about Penelope sitting at her loom working away at the never-to-be completed tapestry. Surrounded by the nettlesome suitors. Possibly you are a modern Penelope."

"Faithful and constant?"

"Oh, I am sure you are those, but I was thinking of you working tirelessly at the great unfinished task."

"So you think I work away while pining for my long lost husband?" She paused and said with businesslike finality, "Unlike Penelope, I know he is not coming back."

Dexter said sympathetically, "I know. But maybe you are keeping the suitors away."

She stayed silent for several seconds, pondering Dexter's comment, and then she replied, "I don't think so. It was always something else."

Coming up to the door at 7 rue Monsieur, she got out her key and put it in the big door lock and turned it; the door cracked open. She turned and faced Dexter. Dexter said, "Maybe someday you will tell me?"

She smiled. "Maybe."

Dexter asked, "A reception, at the end of the month on Saturday night. The staff at the weekly *Marianne* knocks back drinks at the printers on Saturday night after putting the magazine to bed. And the latest issue of *Nouvelle Revue Française* will be out."

"And you have an invitation?"

"I knock about with that crowd a bit."

"Yes, I would be delighted," and she presented her right cheek to him for a kiss, then her left. Then she grasped his right hand in both of hers. "Yes, it has been a wonderful evening, though I am afraid that maybe I said more than I should have," and she dropped his hand.

"Not at all," and he watched as she turned and went through the door. He started down the sidewalk towards home as he thought back about Dakar. It had been different for him.

The Writers

Late Saturday afternoon, August 31. Dexter sat at a small table on the *terrasse* of the bistro Les Ministres on the shady side of rue de Bac just across from the Hotel Pont Royal. The hotel's basement bar was close to the center of the Left Bank publishing district—a good place to end a day or start a night. He watched as Marcelle, smartly dressed, came down the sidewalk, saw him, and walked over. Dexter stood and held her chair as she sat down, smiling, and said, "It is nice to see you again, Dexter. What do you have planned?"

"The printer is just a couple blocks away. The final galleys of the magazine are being proofed now. It's the end of summer. Who knows who will be there tonight? Arguments about politics and culture are sure to be in the air."

Marcelle looked thoughtful. "What makes you say that?"

Dexter stood and said, "Let's go and I'll let you see for yourself."

She stood while saying, "Intriguing, but I am not sure where politics is going myself."

Dexter chimed in, "Not that you would say if you did!"

She laughed and said, "Maybe I might give a little hint."

Dexter pointed the way and the couple took off down the sidewalk, Dexter saying, "Both the Right and the Left ask the same basic question: what should France's response to the rise of Nazi Germany be?"

"And what should it be?"

Dexter replied seriously, "The Right strongly believes in an alliance with Italy. It looks to Mussolini as a model for a Rightist authoritarian government."

Marcelle asked, almost teasingly, "I thought the Royalists wanted a king?"

"In real life, some sort of strongman," he replied.

"And the Left?" asked Marcelle.

"The Left is split into two camps: one camp wants a strong alliance with Soviet Russia."

Marcelle smoothly interposed, "That is precisely what Premier Laval negotiated last May in his trip to Moscow."

Dexter responded, "Yes, but it has not been ratified. Some people think Laval is just using the treaty as bait to cut a deal with Hitler."

"A deal with Hitler might just be the solution, correct?" she said.

"If he could be counted on to keep it," replied Dexter.

"And the other camp in the Left?" asked Marcelle.

Dexter replied, "This group, which I believe includes Alexis Léger, your friend Suzanne's boss at the foreign ministry, believes that the cornerstone of French policy should be its alliance with Great Britain. France and Great Britain then present a unified front at the League of Nations in Geneva. Collective security is used to contain Germany."

"Where does Italy fit into this calculation?" asked Marcelle.

Dexter sighed and said, "Here is where it gets tricky. France wants to keep Italy in the Stresa Front and present Great Britain, France, and Italy as a unified trio against Hitler. France seems willing, how shall we say it, to accommodate Italy on Ethiopia."

Marcelle parried, "Ethiopia is a distant African country. It could have easily wound up as a European colony already if it had not been overlooked in the big land grabs of the last century."

Dexter countered, "Actually, the Ethiopians whipped the Italians at Adowa forty years ago and threw them out. It still sticks in the throat with the Italians, I guess, or Mussolini is just using it as pretext for a new imperial adventure."

Marcelle good-naturedly said, "I had better not continue or I am liable to say something."

Dexter laughed.

Marcelle now pushed forward a provocative gambit, "If Italy attacks Ethiopia, and Great Britain and France, through the League of Nations, impose sanctions, where would the United States be, Mr. Diplomat?"

Dexter looked at her bleakly, "Now I am the one who might say something."

Marcelle laughed and drove home her point, "I saw that your Congress passed a Neutrality Act last week and that President Roosevelt intends to sign it."

Dexter replied, "The American voters are very much against getting involved with what they call 'Old World quarrels.'"

Marcelle smiled, almost wickedly Dexter thought, and riposted, "Most observers think that American policy will preclude arms to Ethiopia but not industrial materials to Italy. Even-handed in principle, very one-sided in effect. One can imagine people saying that Yankee principle stands aside for the Yankee dollar."

Dexter smiled in warm appreciation at Marcelle's ability to turn his charming little lecture on European politics on its head. He smoothly replied, "Commercial interests are very powerful in the United States," and he paused and smiled at her, "as they are in France."

She looked at him, quite primly, and graded his answer, "Very good."

"Thank you, ma'am."

Dexter stopped and said, "Here we are." He held his hand out and guided Marcelle into the somewhat rundown print shop. They were greeted by the raucous noise of boisterous people drinking wine and engaged in loud conversation.

Dexter guided Marcelle into the thronging crowd, many of the writers and editors turning and giving Dexter a familiar wave and welcoming smile.

"How do you know these people?" asked Marcelle.

"I met a lot of them at the basement bar of the Hotel Pont Royal. Then I just sort of mixed in. My flat is right across the street from the hotel."

"Near the café where we met today?"

"A couple of doors down on rue du Bac."

She smiled sardonically. "Not very diplomatic."

He asked a question, "Should I be over on the Right Bank with the wealthy Americans?" Then he gave the classic Left Bank answer to his question. "I'm told that the life of the mind can't cross the Seine."

She laughed. "Ah yes, another piece of sidewalk wisdom from the habitués of the boulevard cafés on the Left Bank."

Dexter and Marcelle approached a couple and Dexter said, "André," and the man turned, "let me introduce my friend Marcelle. Marcelle, this is André Chamson and his wife, the writer Lucie Mazuric."

André Chamson extended his hand, "*Enchanté.*"

His wife extended her hand and added her greeting.

Dexter added, "Marcelle is a *redactrice* at the ministry of labor."

Marcelle glanced at Dexter with a look to say no more.

Dexter said to Marcelle, "André serves as a political aide to Édouard Daladier when he holds ministerial office. Meanwhile he edits the paper *Vendredi*," referring to the party newspaper of the Radical Socialist party.

Chamson, searching his memory, looked inquiringly at Marcelle. "Do you have business at the Matignon often?"

Marcelle sighed, looked at Dexter, and smiled. "Yes, I am on temporary assignment there."

Chamson brightened. "I see." He turned to Dexter. "We on the outside guess at policy; she," and he nodded at Marcelle, "gets to see the decisions being made that drive the events."

Lucie Mazuric was charmed by Marcelle's admission. "Someday you must write a book."

Marcelle was momentarily taken aback. "Why no. I could never do that. It would be to betray a trust."

Lucie replied, "Oh, but what intriguing things you could say. A manuscript is circulating," and she circled her head to take in the whole Left Bank publishing world, "from a young diplomat just back from Athens. Bitingly delicious."

Dexter laughed and said, "Even I have heard about that one," and he turned and said in low voice to Marcelle, "he says that the French girls in the houses in Athens told him that their 'fall,' such as it was, came from being debouched at home while the finishing touches were added at the convent."

Lucie flippantly added, "And that is just the start. In Athens they do nothing else but..."

Chamson laughed. "It will of course be a best seller."

Marcelle laughed and looked with great amusement at Dexter. "Oh, Suzanne has already told me those tales." And Marcelle, mimicking Dexter's low voice, said conspiratorially to Lucie, "She is my friend at the Quai d'Orsay."

Marcelle then said, straightening up, "I am the daughter of a good French family and," looking at Chamson, "the daughter of this French soil. I read the text of your speech at the Palais de la Mutualité last month. I loved it."

Chamson smiled at the compliment. Then Marcelle looked teasingly at Dexter. "And as for you, I was a day student at the convent. My education remains incomplete."

Dexter gave a playful frown. Chamson laughed and Lucie giggled. "Dexter has met someone fun."

Marcelle soothingly asked Lucie, "Is there such a thing as a discreet memoir?"

"None that sell!" Lucie replied.

Marcelle smiled, *"C'est parfait!"*

The cloud of smoke floated past Dexter's face and he turned to find himself standing beside André Malraux gesticulating to a small group, a cigarette dangling from his lips, a dark shock of hair across his forehead, and emphatically pronouncing, "The objective is to be anti-Fascist."

A man in the group countered, "But to be anti-Fascist you have to be Communist. Moscow leads the attack against the counter-revolutionaries."

Malraux was quick on the reply. "No. Both democracy and communism are universal. Fascism is not. Democracy can ally with one, but not the other."

Another voice agreed, "André is right. Nazism is nationalistic and particular in its hatreds against individuals."

A second voice chimed in, "The Left does not need to be all Communist. Gide said that he could be deeply internationalist while remaining deeply French." All the heads nodded in profound agreement.

Andre Malraux in 1935

Dexter reached out and took Marcelle's hand and pulled her over next to him. Malraux caught sight of Dexter out of the corner of his eye and smiled quickly in welcome. He held out his arm opening up the circle of conversationalists without missing a beat in his torrent of words. Dexter and Marcelle stepped up to the circle; Chamson and Lucie stood just behind them.

Malraux took a breath and Dexter interjected, "Let me present my friend Marcelle. She heard your concluding speech at the Writers Conference."

Malraux's eyes lit up; Marcelle held out her hand and André took it and looked deeply into her eyes with his intense stare. "What appealed to you? The art or the politics?"

Marcelle replied, "Both. I believe art illuminates politics from a perspective outside the confines of analytical debate."

Malraux smiled and looked askance at the others in the group. "Yes. Factional debate robs the Left of political momentum." Turning back to Marcelle, he asked, "How do you see art explaining politics?"

Marcelle opened the palms of her hands as if cradling an answer and started, "I was never so moved by literature, so overcome by the mix of waiting and expectation, as I was when *Man's Fate* was serialized in *Nouvelle Revue Française* in 1933. My friends and I could not wait for the next installment."

Dexter remembered Malraux's novel. It had won the Goncourt prize in 1933. He had been transfixed by the image of the ever-approaching armored train, its mournful whistle distant in the night, symbolizing the awesome power of the Nationalist forces, closing in on the doomed revolutionaries in Shanghai. Powerful images.

Malraux asked, "Your friends?"

Marcelle replied, "Yes, my co-workers in the ministry of labor and some friends at the Quai d'Orsay. We had never been so engaged by art as a tool to illuminate international politics as we were in reading your book. It was so new. And so far away. Revolutionary China. But the clash of revolution with nationalism seems to be the emerging conflict of the age."

Malraux quickly asked, "Is it the revolutionary struggle—its romantic overthrow of existing order—or its confrontation with colonialism that engages you?"

"I was in West Africa—Dakar—when I was a young woman. The exploitation of one group by another inherent in colonialism always produces a revolutionary backlash. Often given additional power by nationalism. Revolution inevitably confronts colonialism."

"Inevitably?"

"I believe so."

Malraux turned thoughtful. "That is the big issue of this century. I hope to address colonialism later this year. It has been on my mind. "

Dexter looked over at Marcelle; her insight into revolution confronting colonialism was bracingly refreshing.

Malraux quickly turned upbeat and his glance swept up the entire group. He summed up, "But right now, in 1935, we need to unify the Left in its stand against Nazism and the rise of a militaristic Germany. Anti-Fascism is the order of the day."

Heads nodded in agreement.

A voice broke in from the side. "Hey, we're moving down to Lipp's."

Malraux turned to his wife Clara. "We must be going. We must meet with Ehrenburg," referring to the Communist journalist Ilya Ehrenburg, who was sort of a Soviet ambassador to the Left Bank.

Turning to Dexter, Malraux added, nodding at Marcelle, "You must bring your friend to one of our get-togethers."

Clara smiled at Marcelle and laughed. "You see, revolution is always meeting one another. We are just up the street from Dexter."

Marcelle smiled at Clara and then André.

Out on the street, Dexter took Marcelle's hand and they started down the sidewalk. He said, "We'll go to Brasserie Lipp with the crowd. It's always fun."

Marcelle replied, "Okay, but only for one champagne cocktail. I have another big week coming up and then I go to Lyon to visit my family."

"When will you be back?"

"I should be free by the end of September."

Dexter turned thoughtful and said absently, "Good."

They followed along with the gaggle of writers, editors, wives and girl friends all heading for Saint-Germain-de-Prés. Outside Brasserie Lipp, the bright neon sign overhead, the crowd started to push through the revolving doors into the brightly lit lobby of the restaurant. One of the editors made a request; a big upstairs table had been reserved earlier in the week. The Gallimard publishing company had a standing reservation for Saturday nights at Lipp's.

As the group waited, André Chamson and his wife Lucie sidled up to Dexter and Marcelle. Lucie said to Marcelle, "I'm impressed. You had more conversation with Malraux in five minutes than most people have in five months. *Man's Fate* changed a lot of people's attitudes about what a powerful story can say about the fast-changing politics of this era. I think he's still processing its impact in his own mind."

Chamson nodded in agreement. "André really touched the younger generation. They are skeptical of the old."

Dexter added, "Yes, they have been cut off from the past by the war."

Chamson agreed, "Yes, and the revolutionaries in China feed a feverish romanticism."

Marcelle glanced over at a party of people sweeping forward to leave. Oh no, she thought. Not now. She saw the minister of finance, plump in black tie and evening attire, escorted by an elegant woman in early middle age. They were coming towards them somewhat unsteadily and followed by a small entourage. The woman had a touch of gray at her temples, a pretty face, and was rather well bejeweled, thought Marcelle.

Marcelle quickly hid behind Dexter and then, shoulders hunched down and ducking her head, she started taking small baby steps to keep Dexter between her and the departing party like a child playing hide-and-seek. Chamson looked amused and poked his finger out for his wife to watch. Lucie watched Marcelle moving backwards, head down, in childlike hiding from the departing minister.

The minister glanced over, his expression quizzical, and then his eyes went wide with astonishment. With his arm, he stopped his escort in her tracks. The minister stepped around in front of Dexter and said to Marcelle, "Ah, Madame Lambert, I see you. Peeky boo."

Marcelle stepped forward in front of Dexter and extended her hand, "Good evening, Monsieur le Minister."

The minister beamed and shook Marcelle's hand and said expansively, "I am so pleased to see that *le gouvernement* has decided to take a night off."

Marcelle stood in deep embarrassment. Chamson and Lucie looked on, highly amused.

The minister continued, "Ah, Madame la Chef de Bureau, my ministry's humble endeavors meet with your every approval, I trust," and he put a sly expression on his face, "none of those little inconsistencies that Monsieur le Premier warned of?"

Then he turned to his escort, "Comtesse, let me introduce you to Madame Lambert, leader of the petticoats at the Matignon."

The comtesse, looking askance at the rather buoyant minister, playfully held out her hand. "*Enchantée.*"

Marcelle reached for the hand quickly and gratefully in the hope that introductions would swiftly lead to departures, "The pleasure is all mine, comtesse. Monsieur le Minister of course exaggerates the humble role of our bureaucratic administration," and she looked hopefully at the minister.

The minister rocked back, unsteadily on his feet, "Oh no, comtesse...I exaggerate not...I just wanted to say hello to *la marquise*...one of the powers behind the throne."

Marcelle gently spoke up, speaking brightly, "Oh, Monsieur le Minister, remember, we are a republic."

The minister dipped his head and gravely said, "Yes, but real power is rarely in the cabinet."

Chamson silently nodded in agreement at the minister's statement.

The comtesse tugged at the minister's hand, smiled a goodbye at Marcelle, and soon had the minister walking a little unsteadily towards the door. Seeing Chamson, the minister tipped his hat, "André."

Chamson replied, "Minister."

Watching the minister and comtesse depart, Lucie asked, "Is she really a comtesse?"

Dexter laughed and with the smooth panache of a man-about-town answered, "Of course. She is rumored to be related by blood and marriage to three banks and two steelworks."

The group laughed.

Still chuckling, Chamson turned to Marcelle and poked some fun at her. "Ah, *pardon, Madame la Sous-Chef?*"

Marcelle smirked, the thwarted look of the little girl caught with the cookie coming across her face. Changing posture, she then took on a grand air and said to Chamson, "I hold a temporary appointment at the Matignon as *chef de bureau.*" She turned to Dexter and added insistently, "Only temporary."

Dexter laughed, "For the minister to compare you with Madame de Pompadour..." as Dexter made the allusion to the powerful mistress, *la marquise*, of Louis Fifteen who was said to rule France from behind the scenes in the 1750s and 1760s.

Marcelle rolled her eyes. "I will never hear the end of it." She looked at Chamson. "Besides, when André and his friends in the

Popular Front win the elections, the little *redactrice* will get sent packing back to the ministry of labor as a *sous-chef*," and she paused, "or worse."

Chamson laughed. "Marcelle, everyone on the Left is deeply impressed with the competence with which Laval has implemented the deflation program. With your detailed knowledge of the decrees and their administration, you will be in great demand."

Marcelle smiled tentatively. "You think so?"

Looking directly into her eyes, Chamson said, "That would be my expectation." Then he turned and said to Dexter, "Premier Laval is a renowned lawyer. It would figure that his *redactrices* are needle sharp." He paused and looked at Marcelle, "Correct, Marcelle?"

She sighed a sigh of resignation and said, "Yes."

The editor from *Marianne* came up and announced, "This way. Upstairs."

Marcelle turned to Dexter. "Remember, just one glass of champagne. Or I will go out of here like Monsieur le Minister."

"That might be fun."

She looked at him sharply. "I'm not the comtesse."

Dexter smiled and pointed her towards the stairs.

Later in the evening, walking towards rue Monsieur, Marcelle said to Dexter, "I have been thinking about your comments about *Odysseus*. Why do I remind you of Penelope?"

"Because you remain single after all these years."

She looked up at him. "You think I keep the suitors away so that I can continue my dead husband's service to France? That I carry the family flame, is that it?"

"Yes and no."

She snapped, "Yes and no. How diplomatic."

Dexter took a breath and explained, "Yes, I think you keep the suitors away. But not to carry a flame for a light long extinguished." He paused and then said, his voice falling to a low note, "Rather for the flame of your own ambition."

She looked up at him, giving him a very even look. There was not the slightest trace of annoyance. He could see that his argument had hit a chord of understanding if not sympathy. She replied softly, "I see."

Dexter took another breath and continued, "I know the little black ribbon helps to explain to some people why you hold the preferment in the bureaucracy that you have. It provides them a rationale for when they are passed over."

She agreed, "Yes."

Dexter continued, "But the little black ribbon also masks your own ambition."

She did not disagree. "I see."

Then she looked into his eyes and asked, "Why?"

Dexter's manner eased and he returned to his customary self-assurance, "Oh, you think that somewhere in the future that dedicated service will contribute something better to your country, your society. Every professional civil service has a few of those who, shall we say, labor under this delusion."

Marcelle turned back and looked ahead, walking forward purposively, vibrancy back in her voice. "Oh, are there any of those in the American Foreign Service?"

Dexter, catching up, looked at her and said, "Yes." Then he added, "Quite a few in fact."

She looked up at him and smiled.

Coming to 7 rue Monsieur, Dexter asked, "Marcelle, I have an invitation to use the ambassador's box at the Opéra in early in October. We could make a night of it?"

Marcelle, taken aback, stammered, "The Opéra? I couldn't. I haven't been out like that in years. A long dress? And gloves?" She looked momentarily perplexed. Then she said, "I have nothing to wear." She looked tentatively up at him. He was standing still, arms crossed, tapping his foot in mock irritation.

She eased, her expression softening, and said, "Yes, I would like that very much. I'll have to go to the very back of my closet."

Dexter brightened and briskly replied, "I'll pick you up a seven."

Marcelle turned thoughtful for a second and said, "Wait. Could you come at six? We could have a champagne cocktail here before we go. I could show you my apartment."

"I would like that very much."

Marcelle laughingly replied, "And since we will be leaving for the Opéra at seven, I can be sure of getting you back out the door."

"I always leave when a lady asks," and bowed his head in a gentlemanly nod.

"Yes, of course," she said in quick reply. She smiled at him enigmatically. She stepped forward and presented her right cheek for a kiss, then her left. She turned and put the key in the lock and opened the door. Then she was gone.

Dexter's eyes followed after her. Yes, they were of one mind, he thought. My little straight-laced revolutionary. He turned and headed back to his flat.

Quai d'Orsay

Monday morning, September 2, Quai d'Orsay. In the ornate office of the foreign minister, Pierre Laval and Alexis Léger, secretary-general at the Quai d'Orsay, stood waiting by a small conference table in front of a large fireplace. A few steps away from the conference table stood another small desk with papers on it; Madame Bardoux stood unobtrusively to one side. Presently the doors to the office opened and the usher pointed the way to the two British diplomats. They were stopping in Paris to coordinate policy with the French before traveling on to Geneva.

Anthony Eden, minister of League of Nations affairs, and Sir Robert Vansittart, permanent secretary of the British foreign office, entered the room. Warm introductions were made and the four men sat down at the small conference table. Madame Bardoux silently sat down, ready to provide any documents that Alexis Léger might summon.

Eden directly addressed Laval, "We should present a joint Anglo-French report to the League Council in Geneva."

Laval replied, "We completely agree, with the proviso that detailed terms should be left out so as not to prejudice future negotiations with Mussolini. We want to keep future bases of settlement with the Italians open."

Madame Bardoux listened and thought that Foreign Minister Laval was staying true to his twin goals of always keeping a clear road open for future talks and playing for time. Time was always the diplomat's ally, she thought. It was an article of faith with Laval, she knew.

Eden nodded in agreement. Eden then turned thoughtful and said, "British public opinion is strongly behind the Covenant and the League."

Laval nodded in sage understanding.

Then Eden put forward a feeler. "But what if war should break out? Where would France stand?"

Laval slowly responded, "*Eh, bien*. Well, France has made standing behind the Covenant and the League the cornerstone of her foreign policy since the war. So, could you give France the assurance that in the future Britain would be as firm in upholding the Covenant, here in Europe, as Britain is now in Africa?"

Madame Bardoux made a small note. "Laval puts the German question directly at the British."

Eden replied, without hesitation, "If the Covenant was upheld in this instance…our own moral obligation to assist in supporting and enforcing the Covenant in the future would be correspondingly increased."

Laval thoughtfully nodded at Eden's statement, and then replied, "That was the answer I expected. But it is not the answer to my question."

Eden looked slightly downcast and nodded at Vansittart with a knowing expression. Both British diplomats understood that the British cabinet had steadfastly refused to commit to unconditional promises about European security in the future, that is no firm promises about French security.

Madame Bardoux watched, fascinated. The British had made a statement of principle and morals; Laval had wanted a concrete assurance.

Eden continued, "Let me turn to the question of sanctions." He ran on for several sentences.

Laval replied, "Sanctions themselves might lead to war. We must go slowly here, one step at a time. And we cannot discuss a naval blockade. That would be war."

Eden nodded in understanding; no steaming the Royal Navy about in the Mediterranean, he thought.

Laval stood up. "Let us first go to Geneva and proceed with the next step. Let us maintain a common Anglo-French front while maintaining friendship with Italy."

The other men stood; Madame Bardoux rose as the men walked over towards the door. Laval escorted the two diplomats out to their limousine; Léger walked back across the room to Madame Bardoux and said, "Please prepare a set of minutes and notes. The foreign minister has kept the threat of Germany clearly in front, and he has not let the British diplomats forget that."

They both left and returned to their offices upstairs.

Geneva

Wednesday morning, September 11, Palais des Nations, Geneva, Switzerland. In the press gallery overlooking the hall of the Assembly of Nations, Geneviève Tabouis sat pencil in hand, notebook on her lap. She watched as Sir Samuel Hoare, the British foreign secretary, approached the speaker's tribune. Yes, she thought, there was the man she remembered: the neat figure, the delicate features underneath a high forehead curving back under a scanty fringe of hair. She smiled to herself: everyone's maiden aunt, it was said.

Samuel Hoare in 1930s

Into the silence of the packed hall, Sir Samuel's voice sounded clearly, his composure and self-control everything one would expect from Britain's top diplomat.

In the hall below, sitting with the French delegation, Madame Bardoux listened to Sir Samuel's opening remarks and thought, yes, here are the effusive self-congratulations that come so easily to the British these days. She listened as he said that Britain was moved by the great ideal of the League and the doctrine of collective security as the best way to secure peace.

In the gallery above, Madame Tabouis was startled by the bluntness of Sir Samuel's next statement. He said that recent events indicated that war for the sake of war was fast becoming the new motive in European politics. Yes, she said to herself, this was the great change in international politics that was developing in 1935, the desire by some nations for national self-aggrandizement above all else.

Below, Madame Bardoux waited for the innocuous loophole in Britain's support for collective security that she was sure was coming. Sir Samuel did not disappoint. "If the burden is to be borne, it must be borne collectively by all. If risks for peace are to be run, they must be run by all. The security of the many cannot be ensured solely by the efforts of a few, however powerful they may be."

Alexis Léger leaned over to Madame Bardoux and whispered, "There, by making the statement so broad and all-encompassing, he has put the almost impossible condition of unanimity in place as the controlling limitation. British diplomacy can always forestall unanimity, as it has so many times since the war."

Madame Bardoux nodded her understanding and made notes. Then she listened as Sir Samuel seemed to undercut Monsieur Léger's words, as the foreign minister concluded, "For the collective maintenance of the Covenant in its entirety, and particularly for steady and collective resistance to all acts of unprovoked aggression…the British nation…and their Government hold with firm, enduring, and universal persistence."

Léger again leaned over and whispered to Madame Bardoux, "Fine words. But what guarantees have we? The British statements lack precision."

Then Léger turned back and looked into Madame Bardoux's eyes and said with conviction, "As you go forward in your career, you will see that when circumstances get down to cases, the British skillfully argue that the general never guarantees the particular, and the particular never necessarily supports the general. The circle, lacking corners, may nevertheless become a square. Not very Cartesian." Exasperatingly un-French, thought Madame Bardoux.

Up in the gallery, Madame Tabouis wrote down the foreign minister's words. "My country will not shirk its obligations." She concluded that the British national conscience had changed slowly but surely.

Down on the floor, Léger nodded at Prime Minister Laval and whispered to Madame Bardoux, "He will be pleased. Hoare never mentioned the dreaded word 'sanctions.' Eden has not prevailed here today." Léger leaned back and listened to the final words.

As Hoare walked away from the lectern, Léger leaned over to Madame Bardoux. "The British tried to, shall we say, persuade Laval during private discussions that this would be a 'test case' and if the British did not get their way, they would lapse back into isolation. Now, Hoare has given Laval an opening to secure their public commitment to unconditional support against unprovoked aggression inside Europe. We will see."

Laval came up to Léger and nodded towards the departing Hoare. "I am afraid the British policy is for this day only and does not represent a long-term commitment." Léger nodded in understanding.

Laval turned and included Madame Bardoux in his conversation, summing up France's situation. "International morals are one thing; the interests of a country are another."

Madame Bardoux nodded in understanding: yes, she thought, the threat from Germany is France's principal foreign policy interest. To this end, Italy is a necessary ally.

Across the great hall, delegates rose and moved towards the exits. Geneviève Tabouis headed for the enormous pressroom where dozens of telephone operators sat at switchboards that connected thousands of wires with every part of the world. Anxious reporters hurried in and began to phone their stories to newspapers around the world. It was a great marvel, the international telephone system that emanated out from Geneva, thought Madame Tabouis. How could peace fail when world opinion was now so intimately linked?

In the afternoon, Madame Bardoux returned to the Assembly and sat down with the French delegates, whispering, "I want to hear the Ethiopian delegate." She looked towards the front of the vast chamber and watched as a tiny person, meek of face, dark of complexion, approached the tribune and made his plea for his country.

She was transfixed by the eloquence of the message. "We are a Christian people with very ancient traditions. Our sole aspiration is to live in peace and friendship with the whole world."

He continued, "To any insults and attacks upon her independence we will reply in the calm strength of right and law. She identifies her own person with the League of Nations itself."

The speaker next turned to the Italy's attacks on his country. "The Italian government having resolved to conquer and destroy Ethiopia begins by giving Ethiopia a bad name."

The speaker moved to confront an issue that Italy never failed to bring up. "We are reproached with slavery. Ethiopia did not invent slavery. She found it in that common fund of ancient institutions which is the heritage of the whole world. The patriarchal customs of earlier days often had a mildness and gentleness which enabled even those who were known as slaves to be better treated than those who in the modern world are described as free men though they are frequently crushed beneath the weight of mechanical life. But we understand that men must be free."

The speaker continued, speaking almost personally to the delegates, "If it is desired to confer upon Ethiopia greater well-being, that will not be brought about by war."

"The standardization of men and the uniformity of culture and civilization do not necessarily result in happiness."

Madame Bardoux hurriedly took notes; Marcelle will be fascinated by the Ethiopian delegate's speech, she thought.

The Ethiopian delegate concluded, "My nation has no fear of the light. It desires an impartial demonstration of the truth."

Simply riveting, thought Madame Bardoux. The colonialists never see the wisdom of distant peoples different from themselves. Just their own supposed superiority. Yes, Marcelle will find Ethiopia's case compelling, a voice from an ancient land speaking of the origins of future worldwide unrest and conflict. Yes, something out of Malraux.

Friday, September 13, Geneva. Pierre Laval strode up to the tribune of the Assembly of the League of Nations. He shuffled his papers and then began to speak. He quickly came to his point. "France is loyal to the Covenant. She cannot fail to carry out her obligations." Laval then gave a brief of history of France's unconditional support of the League since the war. Summing up, he said, "All our agreements with our friends and allies are now concluded through Geneva or culminate at Geneva."

Alexis Léger whispered to Madame Bardoux, "Here he seizes the opportunity presented by Hoare in his speech."

Laval deftly moved to his argument. "No country welcomed the words of the British Secretary of Sate with more satisfaction than did France. No country is better able to appreciate and to estimate the scope of such an undertaking. This partnership in responsibilities of all kinds, in all circumstance of time and place, a responsibility which is implied for the future by such a declaration, marks a date in the history of the League of Nations."

Laval then offered soothing words to Mussolini, recalling Stresa, and stressing the many efforts made at conciliation. He concluded by pointing towards the thrust of France's current approach to the mounting crisis. "The task is doubtless a difficult one, but I still do not think it is hopeless."

Laval then thanked the delegates for their attention, picked up his papers, and strode from the stage.

Pierre Laval entered the private meeting room in the Palais des Nations. The dark velvet drapes were drawn. Lamps glowed in corners of the richly appointed room. Laval came up and grasped the outstretched hand. "Sir Samuel."

Sir Samuel Hoare replied and indicated to Laval a chair at the small circular table. Laval sat down and Hoare followed, saying, "Now we can talk."

"Yes."

Sir Samuel opened, a touch apologetically. "I want to clear the ground with you and say that His Majesty's Government regrets the manner in which the Anglo-German naval pact was concluded. We would prefer that it had not happened."

Laval pleasantly responded, "Your comment is graciously received."

Sir Samuel changed tone and subject, saying, "We need to discuss the conditions under which Britain and France shall assist each other in case of aggression against one of them."

"I quite agree. Italy is of course the subject."

"Of course. Let me set forth a hypothetical case of aggression by Italy against British interests in the Mediterranean."

Laval decisively responded, "You have France's formal assurance that if the British fleet were attacked the French naval forces would come to its assistance immediately." Laval placed the gravest emphasis upon the word "immediately."

Sir Samuel listened attentively, very pleased that France would come to Britain's assistance immediately in the present case, but also understanding that France would expect Britain's immediate assistance somewhere else at some future time—a much more troubling situation for Britain. Laval was wily. The French were like that.

Laval continued, "As you know, I asked France's ambassador in London about the future British attitude in cases of aggression in Europe generally and for Austria in particular."

Sir Samuel leaned back, sighed, and became thoughtful. He responded, "Britain intends henceforward to honor the spirit and the letter of the Covenant along the lines indicated in my speech."

Laval looked on intently. "Yes?"

Sir Samuel then continued, "Austria? Little Austria sits between Italy and Germany. Currently, Italy is its protector. If that were to change, it would be difficult to see what sort of credible guarantee Britain could give. Or France for that matter. It is Italian troops at the Brenner that keep the Germans out."

Laval thought for a moment and replied, "Yes. But if Hitler grabs Austria for Germany, that would break the land chain from France through Southern Europe to our allies in the East. Czechoslovakia, Poland, and Russia would be separated from the West."

Sir Samuel hesitated and said, "A possibly regrettable development." He knew where Laval was going.

Laval put forth his point. "Keeping Italy in the Stresa Front with France and Britain is key to European peace." Laval let the words sink in, and then continued, "We may need to make large compromises on Ethiopia in Africa to safeguard peace in Europe."

Sir Samuel understood the argument—it was a good one—but he now repeated his government's position, "The British people are deeply committed to collective security through the League of Nations."

Laval nodded. Morals and principles again.

Sir Samuel thought to himself that Laval had passed up the more immediate case: re-militarization of the Rhineland. Interesting. Possibly Laval was too wedded to his "chain to the East?"

Sir Samuel returned to the present and moved to the next item on the agenda. "Soon, the Italian war machine is going to be launched at the heart of Ethiopia."

Laval nodded in agreement and then made his point, "When that happens, then the League of Nations' procedure must take its predestined course. In particular, the issue of sanctions against Italy must be carefully considered in its application."

Sir Samuel agreed. "Non-belligerent sanctions to start. Economic pressure."

Laval replied in a word, "Precisely."

Sir Samuel's shoulders sagged and he wearily replied, "Sanctions will involve difficulties too numerous to enumerate."

Laval said, "Yes. But sanctions should be applied with a view of pressuring Italy towards settlement, not war. Sanctions must not be seen as an inevitable step towards war, but towards settlement. Pressure and conciliation are two sides of the same policy."

Sir Samuel nodded.

Laval stood up saying, "I look forward to your formal reply to the question of acts of aggression in Europe."

Sir Samuel, his face tired, nodded his understanding at one more chore not to his liking. He stood up and the two men walked to the door.

Monday, September 16, rue du Cherche-Midi, Paris. Marcelle Lambert entered the small dress shop carrying a valise. An older woman came up and Marcelle asked, "I have been told by my friend Suzanne Bardoux to ask for Irène."

"Yes, Madame."

Presently an attractive young woman entered and held out her hand. "A friend of Madame Bardoux's?"

Marcelle smiled. "Yes, Marcelle Lambert," and she set the valise down and shook Irène's hand. She continued, "I have a dress with me—it's years old—and I was hoping to re-cut it into something more contemporary. I am going to the Opéra with a gentlemen next month," and she laughed, "and I haven't done that in years, so I need a dress not hopelessly out of fashion."

Irène was somewhat astonished since the woman standing before her was quite attractive. She said, "Here. Let's go into the fitting room." She showed Marcelle into a small dressing room.

Presently, Marcelle came out with the dress on. Irène looked over the silk dress with practiced eye and said, "Madame, it is a beautiful dress."

"Yes. My family have been silk merchants in Lyon for generations."

Irène walked around, now and again taking in some cloth and holding it, putting what was before her into some new vision that built on the old. Then she started in earnest, pulling cloth, pinning here and there. Marcelle watched the transformation take place in the mirror in front of her.

Marcelle said, "You work miracles."

Irène stood back, looking, and asked, "What do you think?"

Marcelle replied, "Quite nice. Let me suggest a little bit more here?"

Irène came over and tucked a little in, pinning it, and then stood back.

Marcelle tilted her head, looking intently at the image in the mirror, and smiled, "And maybe a little here?"

Irène tucked and loosened a little, and then pinned it and stepped back, and looked forward into the mirror, commenting, "Madame, you have a good eye."

Marcelle said, a little wistfully, "Once, yes."

Irène finished up. "I can have this ready for your fitting next week?"

"That will be fine," and she went into the little dressing room to remove the dress. She returned and handed the dress to Irène, thanked her, and walked back to the Matignon thinking about the work before her. The 1936 budget was going to the Council of Ministers Saturday morning for approval before being submitted to the Chamber of Deputies next month. The work was endless.

British embassy, Rome, Monday evening, September 23. Sir Eric Drummond, British ambassador, spoke to an aide outside his study, "Please have the third secretary stand by to send a cable to London. It will be ready within the hour." The aide nodded and walked down the hallway.

Sir Eric entered his study and went over to a desk busy with papers. Deeply shaded floor lamps at each end of the desk cast warm yellow pools of light. He sat down and pulled forward a pad of paper. He set a pencil down next to the pad. He leaned back and put his hands behind his head and reflected, collecting his thoughts.

Yes, he thought, the humiliation of the Italian army by the Ethiopian tribesmen at the Battle of Adowa in 1896—almost half the Italian army had been killed in one of only two defeats of white troops by Africans in the entire century—had led to frustrated colonial ambitions. Mussolini now used something that should have been forgotten as fuel to fire something new in the present that should not be occurring.

Paul A. Myers

And of course the First World War came up. Long talks today with Italian officials had brought up the black injustice of Italy having lost over a million men dead and wounded but receiving only crumbs at the Peace Conference. Crumbs, crumbs. Injustice burned deeply. And the Italians always brought up slavery in Ethiopia as an issue to justify their "civilizing mission."

Benito Mussolini in 1930s

The day had concluded with a long interview with Mussolini, who remained obstinately unyielding and stated quite clearly that he saw Germany getting stronger by the day. The blackmail was all but explicit. As for conciliation through diplomacy, Mussolini was dismissive, speaking contemptuously that Britain and France thought Italy could be bought off by giving "her a couple of deserts—one of salt, the other of stone."

Mussolini got right to his conclusion. "You will see Germany march on Vienna, the Little Entente brushed aside under a German thrust to the Bosphorus." Mussolini saw Germany as the new winner on the European chessboard.

Sir Eric sighed at the memory of the interview: Mussolini's threat was so crudely put. He reflected with deep sadness because he knew that Sir Samuel Hoare's assurances to Mussolini that Britain wanted Italy strong and secure was the correct course for Italy. The only course.

And what of the German course? Sir Eric pondered; Hitler would use the Italians like a fallen woman when the time came. They would have their way with her.

London, of course, knew all of this. Sir Eric decided on a different tack. He picked up the pencil and began his dispatch, a somber portrait of the Italian dictator, the words flowing. "One who has…condemned thousands of young Italians to painful death and millions of his countrymen to an almost animal level of existence, he seems astonishingly untroubled by the remorse of conscience. The explanation lies probably in his philosophy and creed. He believes in war as the means by which a country can be kept vigorous, young, powerful and progressive…These reasons combined have rendered him oblivious of other considerations, such as economic and financial facts, and have produced in his mind the impression that he is acting as a predestined instrument…confirms my own constant impression of a man who is the victim, not the master of his destiny."

He sat back, read the message over. Satisfied, he stood up and walked into the hall. An aide took the message down to the third secretary waiting in the offices on the ground floor. It reached Whitehall later that night.

Thursday, September 26, Quai d'Orsay. Alexis Léger came into Foreign Minister Pierre Laval's office with a message in his hand, quickly saying, "I have Sir Samuel Hoare's response and our London ambassador's comments."

Laval took the papers and read through them, commenting, "Yes, the ambassador is right. The response lacks formal precision."

He looked up at Léger. "It is what I feared. Sir Samuel's speech at Geneva represented the policy for that day only. It is not a long-term commitment upon which France can rely."

Léger nodded in understanding.

Laval turned thoughtful. "The ultimate safeguards for France are the Treaties—pieces of paper—and the Rhineland—a hard geographical fact."

Léger said, "Yes. And Britain's entente with France is crucial to both."

Laval put the papers down on his desk, tapping them with his forefinger. "But the British are saying that the unilateral violation of treaties would not necessarily occasion British support. Furthermore, they are saying that even in cases of unprovoked aggression, Britain retains its freedom of action."

Léger said, "They maintain the right to be consulted before acting."

Laval replied, "Yes, a possibly dangerous delay." Laval leaned back, his thoughts to himself: when the man in Berlin puts the pieces together, he very well might move—without consulting, without delay.

Léger summed up, "It is less than we hoped; more than we expected."

Laval nodded in agreement.

Friday, September 27, Paris. Marcelle Lambert walked down the arcaded sidewalk of the rue de Rivoli carrying a shopping valise. She turned into Angelina's Tea Room, immediately saw Suzanne Bardoux sitting at a chair in the reception area, and came up and said, "So nice we could meet for lunch."

Suzanne stood up. "Yes, so much to share."

She went over to the maitre d' and spoke briefly to him. He checked the name off his list and said, "This way, *mesdames*." The two women followed him into the dining room. The maitre d' held each woman's chair as they seated themselves.

Marcelle looked across the table. "War in Ethiopia seems imminent."

"Yes," Suzanne replied.

"What happens then?"

Suzanne said, thoughtfully, "One view is that Italy will win some early triumphs, and then run into difficulties—the Ethiopians are not without their strengths—and then some sort of settlement can be reached."

Marcelle took this in, her concerns easing somewhat. "I see."

"No one works harder for compromise and settlement than our foreign minister."

Marcelle replied, softly banging her fist down on the white linen for emphasis, "That I have confidence in."

"How is the budget?" Suzanne asked.

Marcelle crisply replied, "The 1936 budget represents a twenty percent reduction over the 1935 budget. That represented a challenge to every ministry. Constant revision, constant negotiation. The Council of Ministers approved it last Saturday morning."

"And the decrees?" asked Suzanne.

"When the Chamber votes on the budget, they are also voting on the decrees. The Finance Committee of the Chamber takes up the legislation the week after next. All or nothing."

"Do you think it will pass?"

"The budget passes or the government falls," Marcelle said.

"Falls?" gasped Suzanne. She had never thought of the budget that way.

Marcelle continued to look evenly at her, nodding to drive home the point.

Suzanne, composing her thoughts, said, "But the negotiations over Ethiopia will surely be at a critical stage then."

"Premier Laval carries very heavy burdens," Marcelle said quietly.

"The English don't make it easier for him," Suzanne added, almost absently,

The waiter brought tea and small sandwiches and put them down.

Changing subjects, Suzanne said brightly, "Tell me about the dress," and looking at the shopping valise, "and whatever else you have."

Marcelle smiled, "I must thank you for the dressmaker. Irène worked marvels with my old gown." Then she reached down and picked up the valise, pulling out a long, thin box and opening it, "Here are gloves to match."

Suzanne held them, running her hands over them, and marveled, "They are beautiful."

Then Marcelle lifted out a box, removed the lid, and pulled back some wrapping paper. "Shoes."

Suzanne took one of the shoes out of the box and rotated it for careful inspection. "Well made. Stylishly simple. Like you."

Marcelle said, "Thank you."

Suzanne looked at Marcelle, her eyebrows making question marks, "Tell me about the Opéra? And Dexter."

Marcelle leaned across the table towards Suzanne and whispered, "I will tell you everything afterwards," then smiled and added, "well, almost everything."

Suzanne laughed. "I haven't seen you like this—ever! I am so happy for you."

The two women continued eating, chit chatting, and watching the other women lunch at the tables around them, like schoolgirls.

American embassy, Saturday, October 5. Dexter walked into the ambassador's office and said, "Good morning, Mr. Ambassador."

"And a good morning to you, Dexter," the ambassador replied jovially and pointed to a chair for Dexter. "Could you give me a rundown on the Ethiopian situation. Seems the candle has gone off."

"Yes it has, Mr. Ambassador."

The ambassador's expression turned serious and thoughtful and he nodded to Dexter to begin.

Dexter started. "Ethiopia cabled the League of Nations Thursday that the Italians had bombed Adowa and that battles were in progress. Yesterday, the Italian general in East Africa proclaimed the opening of hostilities in Ethiopia."

"Was any reason given?"

"The Italian foreign ministry put out a statement that Italy was taking measures for defense in response to warlike behavior by Ethiopia."

"Any truth to it?"

"Unlikely," replied Dexter.

"And the Ethiopians?"

"Interesting. The emperor has urged his soldiers to fight the nomad war. He told them to scatter to advance to victory."

The ambassador nodded in understanding and made his own assessment. "Shrewd."

Dexter added his opinion, "The Italians may have difficulties beyond what they imagine."

The ambassador nodded in agreement and shifted the discussion. "The British?"

Dexter replied, "Prime Minister Baldwin came right out with a bold statement saying that Britain would stand by its pledge to the Covenant. He was quite clear: Britain would enforce the Covenant any time, any place, and without reference to the British interests involved."

The ambassador probed this statement. "Any conditions?"

Dexter responded, "He repeated that all members of the League must share in its responsibilities and benefits."

"Of course."

Dexter added, "And as we know, the Covenant leaves it to each member to decide if its obligations under the Covenant have in fact been invoked and how it should respond."

"Yes, the inevitable loophole."

Dexter smiled.

The ambassador then bore in. "What is going on with British policy below Baldwin's lofty declarations?"

"The British are trying to ride two horses at once. They want to stand resolutely behind collective security operating through the League against aggression. That is what is behind Baldwin's public statement—the ideal. Anthony Eden is the proponent here."

The ambassador nodded.

"The other horse is a desire for some sort of settlement with Italy over Ethiopia that keeps Italy in the anti-German coalition. That is the politics. Sir Samuel Hoare is the behind-the-scenes voice here."

"What is the weak point in the British position?"

Dexter replied, "Hoare is publicly shaking the big stick, but concealing the fact that neither he nor the British electorate are prepared to wield it."

The ambassador nodded and gathered his thoughts. "Always a dangerous game. The man in Berlin will notice."

"Surely."

"When you back down the first time, it begs the question whether or not you will stand the next time."

Dexter nodded thoughtfully in agreement. "Could set off an unfortunate chain of challenges from Berlin in the coming years as Hitler gathers strength."

"Yes," the ambassador concluded and moved on, asking Dexter, "France?"

Dexter answered, "Premier Laval is always ready to deal on Italy. He is focused on Germany. He met with Eden Thursday. Eden is concerned that Laval is too ready to negotiate with Mussolini," Dexter paused and smiled at the ambassador, "Eden used the word, we are told, 'zigzag' to describe Laval."

The ambassador smiled and then ruminated, "Yes, the British would not want a 'deal' to be seen as undercutting the ideal."

Dexter said, "Precisely."

The ambassador asked, "What has Britain so focused these days on collective security through the League?"

"In a word, airplanes."

"Airplanes?"

"Yes, Germany is within several years of having an air force capable of significant bombardment of the British Isles. That is an entirely new development in Britain's island history: they might not quite be the island they thought they were."

The ambassador stood up, signaling an end. "Thank you, Dexter. By the way, I see you are one of the guests at the Ambassador's Box at the Opéra tonight. Got something charming on your arm, have you?"

"Yes sir, quite charming."

"Have a good time. At the Opéra," and the ambassador smiled.

The Opéra

The taxi pulled up in front of 7 rue Monsieur. Dexter got out, nodded at the driver. "We'll be about an hour." The driver settled in to wait. Dexter had reserved the cab for the evening.

He approached the big double door; it was ajar and he pushed it open and walked across the stone courtyard and knocked on the front door. The door opened and Marcelle stood in the glow of light, resplendent in a long silk dress, beautifully cut revealing lovely white shoulders on which rested cascading dark hair. She said, *"Entrez."*

Dexter entered and handed her a small bouquet of flowers and a bottle of wine. She took the wine and set it on a table and said, "For later." Then she looked closely at the bouquet of flowers, looked up at Dexter with dark eyes glistening, and said, "They're lovely. Thank you."

Dexter gave a slight bow and said with great panache, "You are unimaginably lovely tonight. Sure you haven't been to the Opéra in years?"

She smiled. "No. Only a matinee now and again with some women friends."

She picked up the wine and said, "Here, let me put this away. You go into the drawing room and have a seat by the fireplace. Would a champagne cocktail be appropriate?"

"Certainly."

"I'll be right back," and she glided down the hall, the silk rustling as she went.

Dexter took a seat along the couch near the fireplace. Marcelle came back into the room holding two champagne glasses. Dexter stood up. "Great."

Then looking at Marcelle he said with customary self-confidence, "We'll have a great time tonight. I have dinner reservations after the Opéra at the Café de la Paix."

Marcelle's face fell. Seeing this, Dexter's expression clouded over.

"We can't," she said.

Dexter took a breath and said, "Marcelle, it is almost required to have dinner at the Café de la Paix after the Opéra. People will expect to see us."

She looked at him, the light smile dissolving into a smoldering look that he had never seen before. She said, "I prepared a little supper for us here. *A deux.*"

He slowly took a breath and smiled. "Of course."

A bright smile quickly lit her face, the smoldering eyes now gone like quicksilver, as she pronounced, "I thought you'd understand."

He looked at her with loving wonder.

She walked up next to him and took his free hand and squeezed it, "Let's sit down."

The taxicab pulled up in front of the Opéra House, stopped, and the driver came around and opened Dexter's door. He got out and reached back for Marcelle's hand. She slid out, smiling, and stood up. Dexter nodded at the driver. Dexter held Marcelle's hand and guided her up on the sidewalk, stopped, and turned her around in a pirouette and said, "Let me see you?"

She wore a dark navy velvet cape coming to the knee and clasped just below the throat. A soft white sweater over her shoulders just peeked out from under the cape. The cape was trimmed in soft yellow, complimenting the light sky blue of the long dress. In her hand a silk clutch purse matched the color of her dress. Dexter was simply smitten. He took her arm and they swept up the steps to the entrance of the Opéra and ascended the Grand Staircase. They walked towards the Ambassador's Box.

In the corridor behind the boxes they encountered the *secrétaire général* and his wife in full evening dress. Marcelle quickly walked up to them holding Dexter's hand and warmly said, *"Monsieur le Secrétaire Général,* let me introduce my good friend Mister Dexter Jones. He is a diplomat at the American embassy," and Marcelle turned to the wife, and smiling said, "Dexter, this is Madame…wife of the *secrétaire général."*

Dexter stepped forward and took madame's hand and bowed, *"Enchanté."*

She smiled sweetly and replied, "Oh, it is always a pleasure to meet a friend of Madame Lambert's; she seems to have so few outside of work." She nodded and smiled sweetly at Marcelle.

Marcelle smiled in reply.

The *secrétaire général* stepped forward and shook Dexter's hand. "It is a pleasure to meet a friend of Madame Lambert's. She has been so busy ever since Premier Laval came to the Matignon." He looked over at Marcelle. "Isn't that so?"

"Yes, *Monsieur le Secrétaire Général.*"

Dexter said with man-about-town assurance, "At intermission, why don't you and your wife come down to the American Ambassador's Box and have some champagne with us. Several other members of the embassy will be there. I am sure they would be pleased to meet you."

The *secrétaire général* replied, "It will be our pleasure." He smiled and guided his wife down the corridor towards the Premier's Box.

At intermission, Dexter led Marcelle out to the small reception area behind the seats where a table was covered with champagne glasses. Several bottles of champagne were cooling in buckets. A black-coated waiter stood ready to pour refreshments. Just then, the *secrétaire général* and his wife came though the door.

Dexter walked up and shook the hand of the *secrétaire général* and greeted his wife. Marcelle came up and shook her hand and asked, "Enjoying the performance?"

"Of course."

Dexter then introduced the *secrétaire général* and his wife to several other American diplomats and their wives. Dexter brought Marcelle up next to him and said to the group, "My friend Marcelle Lambert. She is a *redactrice* on temporary assignment at the Matignon. That's how she knows the *secrétaire général.* Normally she works at the ministry of labor. She's a *sous-chef* there, right dear?"

Marcelle politely responded, "Yes, a *sous-chef,*" and she looked at the *secrétaire général* with an almost accusatory look at her continued lack of permanent promotion. He smiled weakly at Marcelle in return. Women, he thought—there isn't a meek one in the species.

The wife of the *secrétaire général,* smiling more than a little mischievously, said, "Oh, Marcelle, *ma petite*, are you still doing the little *redactrice* routine about the ministry of labor?"

Marcelle smiled, made a small curtsey, "*Bien sûr,*" she cooed in mock submissiveness.

The *secrétaire général* stepped forward to smooth the waters and said to the group, "Madame Lambert knew Premier Laval at the ministry of labor. He has strong trust in the quality of her work."

The wife of the *secrétaire général* nodded in agreement. Then she said to Marcelle, "I heard that the finance minister met you at Lipp's. He was fulsome in describing your influence." She turned and took in the whole group with her glance. "I would have liked to have seen that...he said she was the power..."

Marcelle quickly pleaded, "Oh, Madame...Monsieur le Minister had had a little too much to drink."

The wife, taking the rest of her champagne at a gulp, rather haughtily continued, "He seems to know who rules the roost at the Matignon."

The *secrétaire général* winced. He quickly came over and put his arm around his wife's waist and started her for the door. "The performance is about to begin, *ma cherie*."

As she was being swept towards the door by her husband, the wife called out over her shoulder, "He called Marcelle *la marquise*." She turned to her husband, "Which Louis king was it that Madame de Pompadour controlled?"

The *secrétaire général* hurriedly said, "Fifteen."

"Oh yes, the handsome one," she exclaimed as she went through the door, waving farewell with her hand high above her head.

Dexter watched the two leave and then turned to the group, smiling, and said disarmingly, "Lipp's. Yes, it was great fun. The finance minister sparkles with wit. I am afraid it has gotten a little exaggerated in the retelling. Right dear?"

Marcelle smiled at him. "You are quite right," and then added, "dear."

The American diplomats looked knowingly at Dexter; of course Dexter's lady friend would have political position beyond appearance. The wives smiled with their deeper understanding: of course Madame Lambert would have rare abilities. As they walked back into the box, one woman said to other, "If there is a more fetching woman in France tonight, I would not believe it. *La marquise*? The finance minister undoubtedly spoke a truth."

The other woman asked, "I thought Laval was a devoted family man?"

The other answered, "He is. He is interested in power."

The other woman asked, "So Madame Lambert is interested in power?"

"So it would seem."

The other woman asked rather quizzically, "Then what does she see in Dexter?"

"I hadn't thought of that." The first woman turned her thoughts inward, then laughed. "Something to think about in the second half."

The two women turned their eyes to the stage where the curtain was going up.

The taxicab slowed to a stop outside 7 rue Monsieur. The driver jumped out and opened the door. Dexter stepped out, reached back for Marcelle's hand and guided her out to the sidewalk. She stood up on her toes and whispered in Dexter's ear, "You can let the taxi go."

"Of course."

She smiled and walked over to the big doors, put in her key, while Dexter reached around and pushed the door open.

Inside the flat, he helped her off with her cape, while she helped him out of his overcoat. She hung both in the closet and said, "Let me take you jacket." He took it off and handed it to her.

"Let's go into the dining room. Marie will have set it out."

"Marie?"

"Yes, she comes with the flat. She has been a long time with the family that owns the flat, friends of my family. She is a treasure."

"I see."

They walked into the dining room and there was a small round table with plates set out and a side table with covered dishes on it. Two small gold candlesticks held narrow white candles.

Marcelle held out her hand, beaming, and said, "*A deux.*"

She turned to Dexter and held him by the shoulders and stood on tiptoe and kissed him on the lips. She stood back and said, "I'll let you light the candles while I go get the wine."

He smiled and went over to the mantelpiece and found a match.

Marcelle came back with a bottle of wine and poured a glass for Dexter, saying, "I'll be right back. I have to get into something more comfortable," and she swept out of the room.

Dexter sat back, sipped the cool white wine, and looked around the room, the soft yellow walls, the elegant furnishings. He heard slippers coming down the hall and turned around. He stood up. She was wearing a light blue silk floor-length dressing gown, high waisted with a tied sash, and long billowing sleeves. Underneath the gown she wore a high-necked white blouse, soft and ruffled. He simply said, "Elegant."

She smiled and walked around the table. He held her chair for her, admiring the soft curve of her thigh. Then he sat down, picked up the wine bottle and poured her a glass. She picked up a serving dish and passed it to Dexter; he took a helping and passed it on to her.

With a first course on the plates, she picked up her fork and looked across the candlelight and asked, "Dakar? When did you leave?"

Dexter replied, "I left in 1931. For Washington."

Marcelle mulled this over and then continued, "You were married while you were in Dakar?"

Dexter smiled. "For a while. She left in 1930. Went back to New York. She grew up there. Loved it."

"Why?"

Dexter sat back, he hadn't thought about it in years. "Why?"

He twirled the wine in its glass, watching the candlelight reflect in the glass. "Well, Paris had been great in the 1920s. We were with a fast crowd. Fun. Then came Algiers, followed by Dakar. She saw an endless chain of out-of-the-way consular posts. Dreary."

Marcelle said, with some sympathy for the departed wife, "Yes, I could understand."

Dexter, deep in recollection, explained, "Then she realized that a culmination to my successful diplomatic career might mean an appointment as minister to Bolivia, a final posting as head of station at La Paz, in say 1955. Paris, London, never."

Marcelle smiled. "La Paz. Sounds very exotic. The beautiful Andes." Then she thought of the immense problems of war and peace coming towards them, a troubled if not tumultuous future, and said thoughtfully, "Might be charming and peaceful, a beautiful end to a career that I am afraid will be caught up in truly momentous times. Just to get to 1955…" and her voice trailed off.

Dexter saw the wisdom of her thoughts. He gazed straight into her eyes and said softly, "There's a vacant seat at that table."

"You promise?"

"I promise."

She smiled, lifted up her wine glass and clinked her rim against his, and with bright eyes and a widening smile said, "La Paz it is."

With dessert on the table, Marcelle poured small cups of coffee into little cups and passed the sugar. She said, "I have a surprise for you, I think?"

A surprise? Now? She thinks? He looked at her with something approaching puzzlement.

Marcelle continued, "Suzanne said that to trap an American man I should play American jazz on the phonograph. She gave me some American jazz records."

Dexter looked at her, then made a sweeping look around the entire room, and said, "Trap? With a phonograph record?"

She looked at him with amused dark eyes, sipping her coffee, and said, "Suzanne and Étienne are quite anxious that," and she paused and collected her words, "I may have lost my touch."

"You can tell them we will always have La Paz."

Marcelle laughed and said brightly, "We can dance a foxtrot in the other room. For them."

Dexter laughed and stood up. "Lead the way."

In the drawing room, Marcelle put a record on the phonograph and said, "It's Duke Ellington. Suzanne said you would know."

Dexter smiled. "Right she is." He held out his arms as Marcelle came into his embrace. He slowly started to move her around the floor, pushing her hair back over one of her shoulders with his hand, holding her firmly against him with the other.

He whispered into her ear, "I love you more than you can imagine. To share a future with you…" and he nuzzled her ear, kissed her temple.

She pulled him closer, moved her hips into his, pushed herself into him, kissed him on the neck and whispered, "I know. I don't know what has come over me, but I love it. Love you." And she clutched at him tighter, shoved herself into him more, her breath taking a leap. She stayed like that for several long and lingering moments. Then she pulled away, put both her hands on his chest and pushed him back, and turned him around and said, "A certain time has come."

She grabbed his hand and led him towards the hallway. She stopped and stepped around behind him and put both hands on his waist and placed the top of her head between his shoulder blades and playfully pushed him down the hallway. She released him towards the bathroom, saying, "There's a robe hanging on the back of the door. I will wait for you in my room." She darted through the door into her darkened bedroom.

Dexter came into the darkened bedroom, faint moonlight coming through the high windows to one side of the room. Marcelle lay under covers pulled up to her neck, her hair in beautiful disarray on the pillow, bright eyes watching him. He sat down on the bed, dropped the robe off his shoulders, pulled back the thick couverture and slipped into the bed.

He stretched out alongside her, with his arms he reached out and held her, feeling her body through the soft flannel nightgown. He moved his hands up and down her back, down over the curve of buttocks, along her hips. He pulled up the bottom on the nightgown, then grabbed more of it and started to push it up over her body. She wiggled her hips and then lifted her shoulders as he slipped the entire gown up and over her head.

She fell back down on her side, the length of her body brushing against his. He reached an arm around her and pulled her close against him; he ran the tips of his fingers down her spine, his fingernails rustling the ridges of her spine. He ran his nails lightly over her buttocks, edging them in here and there, and then wrapped his hand around her thigh, his fingers exploring the inner places.

She took a sudden breath, then let it out, sighed, and breathed in again and let a sound of pleasure escape from deep in her throat. She wrapped her arms around his back, her fingers digging into his back, then her nails; she breathed heavily into his ear, kissed his neck with ever-increasing rapture taking hold, carrying her off, the wonderful pleasures of her body coming back to her after a long absence.

He pulled her over on top of him, he pulled her upper legs up and out, she kissed him on the chest, he ran his hands up and down her back, then along her flanks, and then he held her waist in both of his hands and pushed her hips down his belly while he lifted himself up into her, her back arching as she bent her head up looking into the darkness above Dexter's head, not seeing anything but feeling the pleasure of consummation. Deep chords of pleasure began to keep time with the rhythm of union.

Later, in the darkness, she lay alongside him, looking at the faint moonshine coming through the glass panes in the windows high on the wall across the room, dreamy from the sensual delight. Then she felt his hands glide along her flanks and buried her head in the crook of his shoulder; she shivered with expectation as his hands came for her a second time.

In a gathering of passion, he pushed her over onto her back, bent over and kissed her, and swung his body over on top of hers. She reached down for him, then pulled one knee up, then the other, and in one smooth motion they came into union. Words flew away from her consciousness, washed away in waves of pleasure.

In the morning, a misting rain settled across Paris. Marcelle watched the soft gray light coming through the glass-paned windows; she snuggled against Dexter's chest. She savored her memories of the night before and whispered to the drowsy Dexter, "I don't think you said a word." She let her memory linger. "So nice. To go somewhere so wonderful without a word being said."

He murmured, "Uhmm."

Like a little girl she wondered out loud, "I think words just get in the way of rapture, the passion," and she paused, "and ecstasy. It's a wave washing over you. To describe it is to lose it."

He brushed some hair back from her face and looked at her.

She looked up at the ceiling and spoke, as if to herself, "In Joyce's book, and the others, the words make it all profane…base physical words…the words anchoring the experience to the profane…" and her voice drifted off into disappointment.

She turned and looked at Dexter. "But love is a large wave of emotion sweeping over you with beautiful unspoken images of beauty, a feeling completely undescribed by words…and so you feel exalted, not profaned."

Dexter now said, "The deep emotions of physical love probably were present in man's evolution eons before mankind learned to talk, or to even use the simplest of words. So the strongest emotions were always unshaped by words."

"Oh, I like your explanation. Almost like it came from the doctors in Vienna."

Dexter gave a mock frown.

"It's a wonderful insight. Can I share it with Suzanne?"

"I hope not. People might mistake me for an intellectual. My diplomatic cover is as a *bon vivant*."

She laughed. "You're secret's safe with me."

He leaned over and kissed her behind her ear and whispered, "No psychology. I simply believe beautiful women should be brought to the full potential of their enthusiasm."

Finance Commission

Tuesday morning, October 8. The *secrétaire général* came into Madame Lambert's office. "Excuse me. Premier Laval has been detained in Geneva. He remains there all week sorting out this Ethiopian imbroglio at the League of Nations. This afternoon the finance minister testifies before the Finance Commission of the Chamber of Deputies. Premier Laval was also scheduled to attend. He would like you to go, and from the gallery, take notes. He is interested in the tone and type of questions he will face when he returns. He meets with the commission next week."

"Yes, I'll go," she replied.

The *secrétaire général* added, "The premier said he wanted the report brief and to the point. He thought of you."

"Bien sûr, Monsieur le Secrétaire Général." Of course.

The finance minister sat at the table alone before the Finance Commission of the Chamber of Deputies. Madame Lambert watched from an upper gallery, seated unobtrusively in the rear.

The minister began, "The 1936 budget totals forty billion francs while a separate armament account, to be covered by a loan, will amount to six billion francs."

The deputies listened to the spending plans with a bored and absent air. The minister droned on.

In the gallery, Madame Lambert listened attentively and took notes.

After the minister concluded his presentation, the chairman opened the hearing to questions. One deputy asked, "When can we tell French business that taxes will be reduced?"

The minister replied, "At this time I see no possibility of reducing direct taxation on incomes or on business. However, we hope that the improvement in the economic situation will soon permit cuts in other taxes."

Another deputy asked, "Can you assure us that your ministry will deal leniently on tax collections for the small and average businessmen?"

The minister solemnly responded, "The government strives to be fair with regard to tax collections. We observe that tax collections this year are down twelve to fifteen percent across the board. Strictness in enforcement does not seem a problem."

"What of the public debt?" asked a third deputy.

The minister looked at his papers and then replied, "The government has borrowed five billion francs since assuming power. We have covered the deficit, extra national defense expenditures, and," and he looked at the deputies from the rural provinces, "maintained the wheat price." Several deputies nodded in understanding.

A fourth deputy asked, "How much more money does the government need to borrow?"

The minister straightened up, coughed, and gravely replied, "The government can go several more weeks without asking for loans. Possibly at that time the government will discount some treasury bonds through the Bank of France."

Most of the deputies looked thoughtful upon hearing this forecast. Not unexpected. But always a hard reminder of the stark reality that all French political questions bumped into: the need for money—there was never enough of it.

Madame Lambert wrote down what she heard. She noted which deputy asked which question. She wrote down the reactions of the others. Premier Laval would provide smooth assurances to the troubled deputies when he returned.

Finally, Madame Lambert noted that the government would require additional financing from the Bank of France. She carefully organized her thoughts: yes, this was the pressure point where the Two Hundred Families exerted their power over the Third Republic.

Looking up, Madame Lambert watched the chairman gently tap his gavel and say, "Monsieur le Minister, thank you for taking the time to inform us of the government's budget proposal." The chairman turned to the other deputies and said, "We will reconvene when the premier returns from Geneva."

The minister stood up, nodded at the chairman, and went over and spoke with his aides. The group departed.

In the gallery, Madame Lambert finished her notes. Again, she thought of the Bank of France and the Two Hundred Families. Yes, she thought—own the bank, control the government.

Rue Monsieur

Early Friday evening, October 13. Dexter walked across the stone courtyard and knocked on the door. The door opened and a middle-aged lady in a housedress bade him enter. *"Bonsoir, Monsieur."*

"Bonsoir, Madame."

Dexter stepped into the foyer and handed the woman his hat and overcoat, then his suit coat, and asked, "You must be Marie?"

The woman beamed and nodded, *"Oui, Monsieur."* With her hand she showed him into the drawing room. Dexter walked over and took a chair near the fireplace. The woman turned and went down the hallway towards the kitchen.

Footsteps came down the stairway and Marcelle entered the room and came across with her arms outstretched. Dexter stood and held out his arms and Marcelle glided into his embrace. "I have been like a girl all week. Couldn't wait for tonight." She stood on toes and kissed him, then reached around and pulled his shoulders into her chest and pushed her lips against his. She reached into his mouth with her tongue and playfully moaned, "Uhmm."

Dexter shifted one arm up around her shoulders and with the other hand cupped one of her buttocks and pulled her into him. She twisted a hip into his and let her head fall slightly the other way, her body making an elongated S shape.

After a minute, Dexter broke off and said, "Yes, the week went slower than I thought."

"Good. I like to be missed."

"I want to be with you. Always," replied Dexter.

"Uhmm...I have in mind an arrangement." She twisted out of his arms and walked over towards the mantle.

"An arrangement? You hardly seem the type for 'an arrangement'."

"Okay, I used the wrong word. With me there is no *cinq a sept*, no blue hour. No assignation and then the man running off to his other business," she pronounced. "I may be a mistress, but never a courtesan." She momentarily took on a look of self-doubt, "Or is it the other way around?"

"I never thought of you that way," and he paused, "or either way."

She gave him a demure smile and then reached onto the mantle and started to pick something up. She held up two keys on a small chain, dangling them before her eyes as she inspected them, and then turned around. She held her arm out towards Dexter, the keys hanging on the chain between her forefinger and her thumb. She wiggled them back and forth, "Keys to the house. For you...but..."

She swung the keys back and forth before Dexter's eyes, the keys making a small chiming sound as they clicked together. Marcelle continued, "But they are like wedding bells in a cathedral. They signal commitment. You take them and you are taking your vows."

"Vows?"

"Always," and she paused. "La Paz."

"*Je comprends*. I understand." Dexter cupped his right hand and held it under the keys. Marcelle dropped them into his palm. He put them in his pocket. He held out his arms and she came into his embrace and kissed him.

She held her head back from him momentarily. "Oh, yes. You are always expected for dinner. If I am not here, Marie will set it for you. I will try to call."

"And if I can't make it."

"Telephone. Marie will take the call. Let's try to be polite to one another. Our jobs are going to try to tear us apart as it is."

Dexter nodded in thoughtful understanding and said, "My pleasure, Madame."

"Shall we say, consider yourself 'committed.'"

"Not quite 'kept?'"

She smiled at him, dark eyes twinkling.

Dexter smiled. "I love you." He held her tight and kissed her deeply.

Steps could be heard coming down the hallway. Marcelle pushed away a little bit. Marie entered the room carrying a tray with plates and covered dishes on it. Marcelle looked at her and beamed, saying, "Monsieur Jones, let's call him Dexter, will be staying here. With me."

Marie smiled a warm and sincere welcome, "*Bien sûr, Madame,*" and she turned towards Dexter, "*et bienvenu à vous, Monsieur Dexter.*" She set the tray down on the table and arranged the plates and dishes and then went back to the kitchen.

Dexter went over to the mantle and got some matches and lit the candles. Marcelle poured some wine. Dexter held her chair as she sat down. As Dexter took a sip of wine, he nodded towards the bookcase and a radio. "Will your radio pickup London?"

"Sometimes."

"Let's try. Anthony Eden will be on the BBC tonight giving a report on the League of Nations to the British people."

"That will be very interesting. What do you hear? If I may ask?"

"Yes, of course. Earlier in the week…"

"Yes, I was busy covering the Finance Commission," Marcelle interjected.

"Well, the League of Nations declared that Italy was the aggressor against Ethiopia. That's a first."

Marcelle spoke, "Premier Laval said that the League Covenant was France's international law. That France would meet its obligations."

Dexter nodded in agreement. "Yes he did. He spoke well." He took a sip of wine. "Then Eden spoke. You must remember that Eden served in the trenches with the Grenadier Guards. Two of his brothers were killed in the war."

Marcelle's eyes looked at Dexter with compassion and sympathy. "I didn't know."

Dexter continued, "Eden spoke very eloquently that no effort must be spared to achieve a peaceful settlement in accordance with the Covenant."

"Dexter, I believe that is what France wants. The talk is constant that Premier Laval wants a settlement. His overriding concern is Germany."

"Yes, but now the League must move to some form of enforcement. Sanctions are difficult to implement and harder to administer," said Dexter.

"I believe France wants to avoid sanctions for now," replied Marcelle.

"Yes, so it will be interesting to hear what Eden tells the British people tonight."

Marcelle looked at the clock and said, "It should begin soon."

Dexter stood up and walked over to the radio set and turned a dial; a light flickered on. He moved the dial through the static and then caught the signal, the English words "London" and "BBC" coming through. Then they heard a voice announce, "Pleased to present...the Minister of League of Nations Affairs Anthony Eden."

Dexter sat down on the couch and stared at the radio set, transfixed. Marcelle came over and sat next to him. She took his hand in hers and placed it on her lap. She looked at the radio waiting for the words from London.

The voice of the British minister in the clipped and sonorous accent of the English high aristocracy came through the dark ether and into the warmth of the room, a modern marvel thought Marcelle. Eden explained the steps that had occurred at the League during the past week-and-a-half. Then he described the action taken by the League Steering Committee that very day to lift the arms embargo against Ethiopia while imposing an arms embargo on Italy—a step to even things up explained the British diplomat. Eden said there had been no dallying; a beginning had been made.

Eden closed his address. "I can give you this assurance, that as we have begun, so shall we go on."

Marcelle was struck by the eloquence of the words; she squeezed Dexter's hand. She looked at him, her dark eyes searching into his as if on a quest and said, "And so shall we."

Dexter squeezed her hand and leaned over and kissed her on the forehead.

Saturday evening, October 19, Geneva. Geneviève Tabouis approached the front desk of the Hotel Beaurivage, presented her card, and said, "I am expected."

"Of course, Madame," replied the desk clerk; he knew her well. He went over to the telephone and called a room, cupped the mouthpiece with his hand, and whispered a message. He placed the mouthpiece back in its cradle and looked at Madame Tabouis and said, "Momentarily."

Presently a young man, dressed in a well-tailored black jacket and striped trousers from Saville Row, almost a uniform among the young British diplomats thought Madame Tabouis, came up to her and shook her hand. "The minister will be pleased to receive you. Please follow me." They walked over to the elevator.

Madame Tabouis entered the suite, the aide took her overcoat, hat, and scarf, and she walked forward into the drawing room of the richly appointed room with cream-colored walls and long drooping satin curtains. Anthony Eden rose from a chair and walked over holding out both his hands in greeting, "How nice of you to come, Geneviève."

"So nice of you to receive me, Minister."

Eden held out his arm beckoning her to take a chair. She sat down in a comfortable armchair; he pulled up a smaller chair and sat almost directly across from her and started to talk. A bleak and depressed look came over his face as he began. "Some of the officials back at the Foreign Office in London are starting to think things over. Certain voices feel it best not to get hemmed in by too literal an interpretation of the League Covenant, particularly Article 16. They caution against an automatic response to Italian aggression."

Madame Tabouis said, "One should not have to worry about automatic action against Italy on the part of Premier Laval."

Eden smiled at the double edge of the remark. "Yes, I fear that there are many in England who are weary of the games played by French diplomacy," and the minister paused, "I fear they may be preparing a retreat at home." Then he concluded, "You know, you couldn't expect us to act alone. The French must be with us."

"All of the League nations must act in concert under the League Covenant," Madame Tabouis said. "That is the ideal, that is all of our hopes."

Eden nodded and then added, "With regard to the double game, you know my British colleagues repeat: 'You cannot trust a man whose name can be read both ways—L-A-V-A-L!'"

Madame Tabouis laughed. "They have been reading too many of my columns."

Eden laughed. Turning serious, he said, "You know, I have my heart and soul in collective security through the League. Europe must not have another war, to send the young and vibrant into such an inferno…" His words trailed off, he looked away, into the distance of time and his own painful memories.

Madame Tabouis nodded.

Eden stood up and Madame Tabouis followed. Eden held out his hand. "So nice you could come." He nodded at the young aide, who came over to escort Madame Tabouis back to the lobby.

Sunday afternoon, October 27. Dexter and Marcelle walked down the sidewalk to 44 rue du Bac and turned through the arched entranceway into a stone courtyard. Going through a door, they ascended a flight of stairs. The door to an apartment was wide open, several couples—and what Marcelle took to be the odd intellectual—were standing in a drawing room gesticulating in animated conversation. They walked in.

Dexter whispered to Marcelle, "Mostly Left Bank. André is getting his thoughts together for a speech he's making next month to the Association for the Defence of Culture. He's sharpening up his ideas."

Marcelle looked across the room and saw Clara Malraux. Clara quickly recognized Marcelle; her eyebrows flashed upwards in delight and she moved her lips with an unspoken hello. She walked over, reaching out her hand to Marcelle, smiled at Dexter, and then said to Marcelle, "So nice you could come. André will be pleased. Colonialism is on his mind."

Marcelle replied, "Great. I was fascinated by the reply André and the other intellectuals made to the Far Right's notion of the civilizing mission of the West, this idea that Italy and France are a new 'Latin Order.'"

Clara laughed. "Oh, yes, the reactionary intellectuals and their 'Manifesto for the Defence of the West.' Yes, sadly, the Action Française never sleeps. They scribble on." Then she said in a low voice, "André is going to use the concept of 'Latin Order' as a pretext to challenge the entire idea of colonialism."

"That I want to hear," said Marcelle.

"André is interested in hearing your ideas on colonialism. He thinks you have first-hand insights," Clara said to Marcelle.

"She has. She was in Dakar for several years," added Dexter.

Clara nodded and said, "The idea that there is some lofty mission behind European conquest infuriates André. The Right thinks that to civilize is to Europeanize. It's just exploitation."

Then Clara turned, a twinkle in her eye, and said to Dexter, "André said that if technical superiority implies a right of conquest, then the United States would begin colonizing Europe."

Dexter laughed. "Our businessmen go where the commerce is. But the Congress wants to stay on its side of the ocean—this time."

Marcelle said, "I agree with the colonialism part completely. The Far Right does not see Italy for what it is." Then she turned thoughtful and added, "But some of the conservative writers do see the British problem. They make the point that the British are in a righteous rage over Italy planning to send a hundred thousands soldiers to dominate Ethiopia while they are silent about Germany someday mobilizing ten million German soldiers between the Rhine and Poland for who knows what purpose."

A look of agreement swept over Clara's face. "Of course. Most of the independent thinkers on the Left want a strong alliance with Britain but desperately want to work out a solution based on collective security through the League of Nations."

"And the other members of the Left?" asked Dexter with a wry smile.

Clara looked around the room conspiratorially and turned back to Dexter. "Well, of course there is a whole cadre that believes we should all simply follow Moscow. But André believes that what is important is to be anti-fascist, not Communist."

There was a small commotion off to one side; André Malraux backed away from three intellectuals in high doctrinaire dudgeon, excusing himself with the parting words, "You don't have to be Communist. It is enough to be anti-fascist—that's the liberal intellectual way."

Approaching Dexter, Marcelle, and Clara, he blew a cloud of smoke over their heads, reached out and shook Dexter's hand, and said directly to Marcelle, "Our anti-colonialist."

André turned to Dexter. "Tell me about diplomacy and Ethiopia. Where is the League of Nations?" He folded his arms across his chest and rested his chin in his upraised palm, intently looking at Dexter for an answer.

"In a word, sanctions."

"Yes, the British are for them. What of Laval?"

"Laval is trying to slow the process down. He doesn't want a fight over principle…"

"Of course not."

Dexter continued, "Laval wants to move towards a deal."

"Hard when there's all that high-minded British idealism about."

"Precisely."

"*Alors*. Well then. As I point out to the Catholic reactionaries, after the 'Latin Order,' who and what does the West mean? England—the Protestant kingdom, or the United States—the Protestant republic?"

Turning to Marcelle, André changed his line of attack. "Which countries are adopting the modern or shall we say the Western ways? In the case of women, for instance, Muslim women in the colonies of

Morocco, Tunisia, and India are veiled. In the independent countries of Persia and Turkey, the women are not."

Marcelle was captivated; she replied, "That's it exactly. Colonialism supports the existing order, the old ways, yesterday's ruling elite, not tomorrow's revolutionaries."

André, looking up and blowing smoke towards the ceiling, exclaimed, "Exactly."

"And Mussolini?" asked Dexter.

"Mussolini? It's not conquest that made Rome," André crisply replied. "Rather it was Roman law and its guiding principles. Not war, but the regulation of war was the backbone of the *Pax Romana*. Every civilization implies the awareness of and respect for others. The reactionaries have learned nothing. Of course."

Dexter nodded in agreement. Sensing a break, Marcelle said, "Thank you for sharing your views. We just wanted to drop in." Turning to Clara, Marcelle held out her hand. "Thank you for inviting us."

"You must come again."

"We will."

André nodded, saw yet another writer across the room, arched an eyebrow in greeting like a semaphore, and he was off, wagging a trailing hand in farewell at them as he left, pushing his other hand out in front of his face towards his next encounter as a greeting, the cigarette at an upraised angle from his outstretched fingers like a pennant flying from the bow of a ship.

Friday evening, November 1, rue Monsieur. The limousine pulled up to the curb and a gendarme got out of the front passenger seat onto the pavement and walked around and opened the rear door to the saloon. Marcelle got out clutching a huge newspaper in her hand, a large handbag hanging by a strap from her shoulder. She smiled, thanked the gendarme, looked in the window and waved goodbye at the chauffeur, and walked over to the large double wood doors of her apartment. She got out her key and opened the door, turned around and waved at the gendarme, and then walked through the entrance and closed the door behind her.

In the street, the gendarme waited a moment to hear the inner door open and close. Satisfied that his charge was safely returned home, he got in the front seat of the limousine. The long black car slowly pulled away up the street, the streetlamps reflecting on the brightly polished black surfaces.

Coming into the foyer, Marcelle turned and put the large newspaper on a small table with her handbag. Dexter came in from the drawing room, kissed her on the cheek, and helped her out of her overcoat. He hung it in the closet. She handed Dexter her hat and he put it on a shelf in the closet.

"Whew, what a week." She turned and picked up the newspaper. "Let's go into the dining room and let me show what has been accomplished."

They turned and went into the dining room and sat down side-by-side at the table. Marcelle spread the newspaper out in front of her. It was a special edition of *Journal Officiel*, the official publication used by the government to print legislation, decrees, rules and other regulations. She opened it up and explained to Dexter, "It's a special edition, over three hundred pages. Over four hundred decree laws are here."

She paged through the paper and came to a separate section. "Here are the annexes; twenty-two corrections of texts already published. I and my assistants and some of the staff at the finance ministry labored on the corrections all day yesterday. That is why I was late getting home last night."

She turned and smiled at him. "I thought it best not to tell you the details."

"Understand."

"The decrees were approved Tuesday in another all day and evening session at the Quai d'Orsay. In the middle of the session Premier Laval had to leave and testify to the Foreign Affairs Commission of the Senate on the Ethiopian affair. The demands upon him are unceasing."

"Yes, the decree implementing the economic sanctions against Italy was published the same day," and Dexter patted the *Journal Officiel* lying on the table.

Marcelle nodded. "The business interests will not like that."

"So the senators seemed to say."

Marcelle continued, "President Lebrun signed all the decrees Wednesday at a special session of the Council of Ministers at the Élysée Palace. Then the real work began. Every *redacteur* and *redactrice*, officials from the finance ministry, why even the *secrétaire général* himself…"

"No?"

"Yes," she smiled and laughed, "gathered at the journal offices and we proofread and corrected all day and into the night."

"A lot of work."

"The biggest avalanche of legislation to which any country has ever yet been subjected," and she closed the newspaper.

Dexter gently interjected, "Yes, but…"

Marcelle arched an eyebrow.

"The Finance Commission of the Chamber has voted a long list of budget amendments to the 1936 budget that if accepted by Parliament would force the revision of many of the budget decrees."

Marcelle leaned back wearily. "Yes, but the Chamber gave Premier Laval an almost impossible task and he has accomplished it with great skill. He has asked to speak to the Commission next week when he gets back from Geneva. His program will stand."

"His cabinet might fall," Dexter said.

"No. That's just newspaper talk. Last Saturday Édouard Herriot was re-elected president of the Radical Socialists. The Radicals are staying with the government."

"You're sure?"

"Herriot is mayor of Lyon."

"No more need be said."

Marcelle smiled and added, "Daladier," mentioning the leader of the left-wing side of the Radical party, "thundered about the 'occult influence of the oligarchies' and called for reform of the Bank of France. He wants slogans on which to campaign for next May's elections. He got them. For now, he leaves the headaches to Premier Laval."

Dexter nodded in agreement.

There was a rustle as Marie came into the room and looked at Marcelle and asked, "Dinner?"

"Why yes." Marcelle turned to Dexter. "A glass of wine, perhaps?"

"*Bien sûr, Madame.*"

Reichs Chancellery

Thursday, November 21, Reichs Chancellery, Berlin. The long hallway led down to a spacious reception area in front of two large closed wooden doors. André François-Poncet, the French ambassador to Germany, walked down the hallway towards the doors. François-Poncet, once described as the handsomest man in France, was in late middle age a man of imposing dignity, a diplomat regarded as France's ablest ambassador. In the reception area stood the German foreign minister in a frock coat.

"Good morning, baron," said François-Poncet with easy familiarity as he shook hands with Constantin von Neurath.

"Good morning, Mister Ambassador," replied the foreign minister. The foreign minister nodded at one of the secretaries, who walked over and opened one of the big wooden doors, peeked in, and announced in a whispered voice the arrival of the dignitaries. The receptionist stood back, opened the door wider, and said, "The Führer will see you now."

The two men walked through the door and into the large office. Adolph Hitler arose from behind his desk, smiled, and held out his hand. "Good morning, Mister Ambassador." Then the Reichs Chancellor turned and said, "Good morning, Herr von Neurath." He waved his hand for all to be seated.

The Reichs Chancellor tilted his head and inquired politely of the French ambassador, "How was your recent visit to Paris?"

François-Poncet replied, "Very fine. I had long conversations with both Premier Laval and President Lebrun. They send their cordial regards."

The chancellor nodded and smiled faintly.

"They both would like to sound out grounds for mutual rapprochement."

"Germany wishes nothing less than to come to terms with France."

The French ambassador nodded while yet again his inner voice asked for the hundredth time: what would those terms be?"

"As I said after the Saar returned to Germany last spring, Germany has no further claims on France," explained Hitler.

133

The French ambassador again nodded and reflected: the big issue was the remilitarization of the Rhineland—which was of course in Germany, not France. But it was France's single most important international security concern.

"There is Locarno, Stresa, and the League of Nations," ticked off the chancellor.

"Yes, there are many opportunities for fruitful talks between our two countries," the ambassador replied.

Foreign Minister von Neurath entered the conversation. "The issue of collective security interests Germany. It could offer the possibility of Germany's return to the League of Nations."

"France would greatly encourage such a course of action."

Neurath continued as Hitler looked on, seemingly transfixed by what Neurath was about to say: "Our diplomats are much impressed by what they see at Geneva, what they call 'the British cement' by which the foundation of the League of Nations is being strengthened."

"Yes, the effectiveness of the League is being strengthened by the broad-based cooperation of all countries," answered the French ambassador.

Hitler shifted his gaze and stared with unblinking dark eyes at François-Poncet.

Neurath eased his manner and said off-handedly, "Germany is not currently a member of the League, so it would not be appropriate to comment on that which does not involve us."

"Of course," nodded the French ambassador. The Ethiopian problem works day and night to Germany's interest, he thought.

Changing the subject, Neurath said, "We view with concern some elements in France that seek to build what they call a 'chain' around Germany."

"I can assure you that France is simply trying to strengthen the bonds of peace across Europe."

"Germany does not feel that 'encirclement' improves the security situation in Europe, which ultimately is the basis for peace."

"I gather you are speaking of the Franco-Russian Pact pending ratification. France has sought out the treaty with Russia with the aim of bringing the outsider state into the European family of nations. No one is being encircled."

The three men sat silent for a moment.

The French ambassador opened a new line. "France's concern in the West is the Rhineland."

The chancellor silenced his foreign minister with a glance and turned and said to the French ambassador, "With respect to the Rhineland, Germany demands nothing less than complete equality in all matters."

François-Poncet nodded wearily and said, "I understand the problem's difficulty."

The French ambassador shifted in his chair uneasily, as if preparing to raise an unpleasant point. He opened. "Our sources indicate that at a recent party gathering in Munich there was some talk by party leaders of moderating the Nuremberg decrees. World opinion on the subject is quite different than German opinion. This would be a welcome development."

The chancellor's face froze in a mask of anger and then with renewed determination he said, "Germany's domestic policies are of no concern to 'world opinion.' We see that the newspapers in the Protestant capitals make a big racket about it. There will be no moderation of the policy towards the Jews. I would hope that Paris would not be so sensitive to Protestants and Jews."

François-Poncet stared thoughtfully at the chancellor, letting the words slowly register.

Hitler, a little nonplussed, concluded, "I thought that Premier Laval would have a better sense of realpolitik."

The Reichs Chancellor stood up signaling the end of the interview, the other two men followed. The Reichs Chancellor said nothing. The two diplomats turned and departed.

Outside the big wooden doors, the foreign minister turned and walked over to confer with one of the secretaries. Ambassador François-Poncet continued alone down the long carpeted hallway, tall and solitary. The Reichs Chancellor stood behind his desk and watched the ambassador recede into the distance with an intense, trance-like stare, his thoughts rocking between shrewd diplomatic calculation and an intense rage of hatred.

La Duchesse

Wednesday afternoon, November 27, Paris. Dexter Jones walked through the high double doors into the foyer of the elegant townhouse, the soft cream colored walls trimmed with gold gilt, dark oil paintings hanging in the spaces between tall windows, the wide interior walls resplendent with dark brown or forest green tapestries. He handed his card to a butler, who announced his name to the guests talking in small groups across the drawing room. A beautiful young woman, the hostess, glided across the carpet towards him, her hand outstretched in greeting. "Dexter, how nice of you to come."

Dexter took her hand and brought it up and made a light kiss. "Duchesse, you look younger each time I see you. What is your secret?"

"Mine? Well, many," and she pursed her lips in a light smile while her eyes took on a sly glimmer giving her a vixen-like look, a look Dexter knew she could use to devastating effect. He lingered for a moment in the embrace of a warm memory.

She watched, amusement dancing in her eyes, and then turned like a schoolgirl, her expression suddenly winsome and gay, and said to the other guests, "Look, we have an American."

Several laughed and all smiled. Many already knew Dexter. They remembered whose arm he had been on then. More smiles.

The duchesse turned back to Dexter. "Your friend Geneviève is here," and she nodded in a direction towards the windows.

Dexter's eyes followed and he saw Geneviève Tabouis holding forth with a small circle around her. Dexter smiled at the duchesse and said, "I better turn you loose to your admirers or they will plot against me." She gave a little laugh and gestured that he was free to go. Dexter walked over to the circle around Geneviève and stood at the edge.

She saw him, gave a smile, and kept right on talking to the men and women around her. "Laval is pursuing a two-faced policy. The scene we are now witnessing at Geneva is a mere comedy between Rome, Paris and London. Laval puts on a pretense about sanctions on Italy, but behind the scenes he maneuvers for the benefit of Mussolini."

136

Dexter knew the group: a vicomte, a comte, and a vicomtesse and several other titled persons of privileged status and comfortable means.

The vicomte argued strongly, "Laval is taking the only sensible course here."

Geneviève looked down her long aquiline nose at him quite skeptically. She was always the best actress at diplomatic gatherings, thought Dexter. Even real actresses deferred to her.

The vicomte continued, "France has great need of the Italian alliance." Yes, Dexter agreed with that, more or less; he understood that was the key point of Laval's overall foreign policy.

The comtesse entered the fray. "France can do without the League of Nations and certainly without Ethiopia." Dexter smiled inwardly; the comtesse had thrown the baby out with the bath water; her argument crossed into the realm of absurdity.

Geneviève countered, "My dear comtesse, I believe the League of Nations is the center of France's foreign policy. The keystone of the arch, so to speak."

The comtesse stood momentarily stupefied. Geneviève nodded politely, if not dismissively, at her and then stepped away towards Dexter. "Let's take a glass of champagne."

Dexter swept his arm towards a table set out with glasses and ice buckets. They walked over. A servant handed him a flute of champagne, which he handed to Geneviève. He took the next flute offered. Geneviève looked back at the aristocrats darkly and murmured to Dexter, "They are always one or two republics behind."

Dexter laughed. "Yes, an elegant carriage awaits to carry away their arguments."

Geneviève scowled. "I would prefer a tumbrel for their reactionary mush," referring to the heavy wooden-wheeled carts used to trundle the nobility to the guillotine during the Terror of the Revolution.

Dexter tsked, tsked. "A traitor to your own class?"

Geneviève looked up with flashing good humor in her eyes and smiled at his remark. As her smile receded, she said, "But I must tell you," a weary tone coming over her voice, "even on my own paper I find myself talking to deaf ears. The pacifists are solidly lined up behind Laval. So idealistic, so wrong."

Dexter turned his expression into a question mark.

"To think that I attached so much value to the freedom of my pen. Of what use is it—if my clear-headed colleagues…"

"Pertinax?" Dexter said in reference to the other great diplomatic columnist in Paris.

"Yes, of course," she said absently and continued, "If we are unable to incite among our compatriots protests strong enough to compel Laval to return to the true traditions of the country, then what?"

Dexter said, "You and Pertinax have great influence."

"Maybe. My own editor chides me 'You must remember Tabouis that there are many Italophiles among our readers.'" She looked at Dexter, a mischievous twinkle in her eye. "And I said, 'You mean among our stockholders.'"

Dexter laughed. "He shouldn't cross pencils with you."

Geneviève became reflective. "I believe, that if the occasion arose and I could prove Laval's duplicity, I would have public opinion with me, that I could arouse French public opinion. We could stop having these 'understandings' with dictators."

Dexter replied, "For now, Geneviève, let's see where he goes with the British. They seem the key to bringing an effective conciliation with Italy into effect."

Geneviève said, "Yes, the rumor is that Hoare and Laval are to meet in Paris with conciliation in mind. At Geneva, people asked me— 'What are they up to?'" She shrugged her shoulders.

Dexter concluded, "For now, Laval faces a vote of confidence in the Chamber of Deputies Friday night on the finance program. Will I see you there?"

"Yes."

Hoare-Laval – Maneuverings

Early afternoon, Friday, November 29, Whitehall, London. Sir Robert Vansittart came into the office of the foreign secretary, Sir Samuel Hoare. Hoare waved him into one of the chairs. "I will meet with Laval in Paris at the end of next week on my way to Geneva. Let's review our situation."

Vansittart crisply asked, "Are you prepared to go to war?"

"Of course not," replied Hoare.

"Then you have to negotiate."

"I made that exact point to our ambassador in Ethiopia. The large majority we won in the election two weeks ago," the Conservatives had won 432 seats in the November 14 elections, "showed that Great Britain is strongly behind the Government up to the point of collective economic sanctions, but it will not go an inch further. The public does not want a war with Italy."

"Drummond in Rome says that Mussolini also understands this."

"Yes," Hoare sighed. Then he took on a warning tone. "There is a point beyond which I cannot go. The prime minister has been clear."

Hoare shifted his thoughts and drummed his fingers on his desktop. "The Committee of Imperial Defense reports serious deficiencies in our military strength in the Mediterranean." The annoyance with the military was palpable.

Vansittart agreed. "It is unpardonable that we should be so handicapped particularly since it was plain to see the crisis coming. People who don't rearm force themselves by their own logic into negotiations." Almost as an afterthought he added, "As usual, the public has overlooked Germany."

"Yes, Germany, Phipps," as Hoare brought up Ambassador Edward Phipps in Berlin, "reports that Germany will expand and that the present Ethiopian imbroglio is mere child's play compared to the problems that will in some not very distant future confront His Majesty's Government."

"Yes, Phipps said earlier this week that Ethiopia was not the only pebble on the beach. Hitler is watching, waiting, rearming," warned Vansittart. Both men knew that Phipps meant the Rhineland. Both knew the Rhineland was Laval's major concern, the reason he was so eager to settle with Italy.

"But Germany is not next week's problem. Italy is," Hoare said while pondering his options. "There is an accumulation of evidence that Signor Mussolini is beginning to realize the full difficulties of his position. He may be ready to make terms. We should test the reality."

"You will find Laval very receptive to this approach. In particular he wants to avoid imposing the oil sanction on Italy at this time."

Hoare said, thinking about the future as he spoke, "Yes, keep the threat of an oil sanction out in front of Mussolini. Easy to do. The Americans are the key and they can't decide anything until mid-January when Congress returns. We have breathing space for these negotiations...with the embargo hanging over Mussolini's head he is more likely to be reasonable."

"Precisely," summed up Vansittart.

Hoare concluded, "We intend to use the next several weeks for a serious attempt to bring about a settlement."

Vansittart stood up nodding in agreement.

Hoare instructed, "It would be best, Van, if you went to Paris next week and prepared the ground."

"Yes, Minister."

Late afternoon, Friday, November 29, Paris. Geneviève Tabouis sat next to Dexter Jones in the first row of the diplomatic gallery overlooking the Chamber of Deputies. She pointed down towards the President of the Chamber sitting high above the vacant speaker's tribune and said, "President Fernand Bouisson will start the finance debate by calling on the most articulate of the opposition, former finance minister Paul Reynaud."

As they watched, short, peppery Paul Reynaud ascended to the speaker's tribune and began to speak, "We, the Netherlands and Switzerland are like beleaguered garrisons waiting for the relief army of general stabilization, which never comes, or for some miraculous intervention of a rise in world prices." The polite applause of agreement rippled across the benches.

"For four years we have practiced the policy of trying to balance our budget by economy, and each successive finance minister has announced in his turn, 'This time I have caught up with the deficit.'" Laughter spread among the deputies sitting on the benches as the truth of the joke hit home. "The government has been chasing a mirage."

Reynaud then drove home his point. "But each time the deficit has been repeated and increased, because it comes from the same cause, an overvalued money. The devaluation of the franc is the only sound and only possible solution of the present crisis. The gold bloc is dead; artificial respiration will not revive it." The deputies erupted in applause and cheers—the truth of the current malaise was spoken clearly, a truth they all knew but many feared.

Geneviève leaned over and whispered into Dexter's ear, "How many do you think applauded?"

"Oh, about seventy percent."

She nodded in agreement and smiled slyly. "We will see."

Another deputy stepped up to the tribune. "Orthodox methods of solving the present economic crisis are inadequate and outmoded. Deflation has not succeeded in any country, and why should it succeed here?"

The speaker continued his argument, "Deflation should bring down the cost of living. Here the cost of living has increased with every successive effort to deflate." Deputies murmured in assent; all understood the public frustration with rising prices.

Looking out at the seated deputies, the speaker concluded, "If any businessman had done what you have done in your efforts to balance expenditure and income, he would have been hauled into police court."

The speaker then looked over at the government bench and Premier Laval. "I do not mean to detract from your efforts. Your mission was to save the franc. That of your successors will be to save France from the economic crisis that has been produced and to save her too from the political division that has been created and that threatens the regime." The deputies gave the speaker warm applause as he returned to the benches.

Geneviève whispered to Dexter, "Now watch."

Premier Laval advanced to the tribune and made an appeal to the deputies' patriotism explaining that last summer he came to the defense of the country's interests at the behest of this very same Chamber, that he had accepted the charge only after so many others had refused. A wave of sympathy spread across the seated deputies. All knew what they had done.

Laval admitted that the tide was in the direction of devaluation. He then set up his parliamentary strategy: "It seemed to me when Mr. Reynaud was speaking that there were many devaluationists in this house. I call upon you to show yourselves by voting against the government." Some of the deputies gasped, most simply understood.

Then Laval turned to the Radical benches and paid tribute to Édouard Herriot's loyalty and that of the moderate wing of the Radical party.

Geneviève spoke to Dexter, "The Chamber is still not in a mood to face the responsibility of voting devaluation. There is no party or government ready to take the leadership. Herriot has personally ruled out forming a new government. So watch the vote. The Radicals are staying with the government."

Dexter nodded; Marcelle had already come to the same conclusion.

The clock above the benches ticked eight o'clock in the evening; the vote of confidence in the government carried 324 to 247. The defense of the franc was to continue. No devaluation.

In the ensuing tumult of congratulations, Geneviève turned to Dexter. "The Left extracted a price for its support. It wants the Far Right leagues disarmed; their guns taken away. Laval made the deal."

"When does this take place?" asked Dexter.

Geneviève replied, "Next week. Surprisingly, it seems Colonel de La Rocque of the Croix-de-Feu is amenable to this. He fears violence might lead to civil war rather than next May's election."

"Very statesmanlike," said Dexter.

"Yes, isn't it," Geneviève wryly added.

Friday, December 6. Dexter Jones worked his way down the steep steps of the diplomatic gallery overlooking the Chamber of Deputies searching for a familiar face. He spotted his friend Phil, the correspondent for the big New York daily. He walked over and sidestepped down a row of seats and plopped down. The reporter wisecracked, "So you've come to see Premier Laval save the franc, save the Republic, and save Mussolini."

Dexter laughed. "Good morning to you, too, Phil."

"What's got you here?"

"Officially. The ambassador plans to meet with Premier Laval, possibly tomorrow. He wants the latest dope."

"Unofficially?"

"Geneviève thinks something's cooking. She thinks Laval got support for the budget by promising to disarm the leagues."

"She may be right." The reporter added, "Well, I'm glad she got off her high horse and nosed around."

"She's well connected."

"Yeah, I saw her with Pertinax yesterday. Whispering no less," said the reporter, mentioning André Géraud, who wrote a well-read political column in the *Echo de Paris* under the pen name Pertinax.

"Well he's the best political reporter in France," said Dexter.

"Did you know he also writes a column for the *Daily Telegraph*. He's big in London, too."

"I was only vaguely aware of that," said Dexter. Some pieces of a possible puzzle were beginning to form in his mind.

The reporter said, "Look down at the tribune. Colonel de La Rocque's mouthpiece is about to speak," he said referring to Jean Ybarnegaray, the deputy that represented the views of the Croix-de-Feu in the Chamber.

As they watched, the Chamber seemed moved by what the conservative deputy was saying. Speaking about the armed paramilitary leagues, Ybarnegaray pleaded, "Is there anyone here who can wish that France should feel upon her face the breath of civil war?"

Deputies across the Chamber chanted, "No, no, no!"

Ybarnegaray answered, "I now speak for the Croix-de-Feu."

The deputies hushed in tense expectation.

Like a revivalist preacher, Ybarnegaray thundered out his proposal, "*Messieurs*, we are ready! We propose that everybody should be disarmed. What has the Left to say?"

The deputies all cheered, heads nodding affirmatively.

"Every bench is cheering," said the reporter, a little incredulously, "Something's going on."

Ybarnegaray continued, "Then Monsieur le Minister of the Interior, I propose that you issue at once this decree that every citizen found in the street carrying arms forbidden by law shall be immediately arrested." He then listed the punishments.

Pandemonium broke out among the deputies, delighted at the breakthrough.

The Socialist leader Léon Blum jumped to his feet to speak. "We are ready to disarm our paramilitary formations, to dissolve them, if you are."

A cry arose from the body of the Chamber. "Do you speak for the Communists?"

Surprised by the turn of the debate, the reporter turned his head towards the Communist benches and mumbled, "Let's see what that bull-necked, bull-voiced party boss says now?"

From the Far Left benches, Communist party boss Maurice Thorez stood and roared, "The Communist party associates itself with Mr. Blum's declaration in so far as its self-defense group is concerned."

Premier Laval picked up some papers and hurried to the tribune, "Here are three short bills to implement what the Chamber is about to approve, to vote for the suppression of armed politics which violates every republican tradition of our great country." Premier Laval presented the bills and then stepped down.

The debate continued, many of the deputies simply complaining why Laval and his government had taken so long to get to this day.

Premier Laval strode back to the tribune and spoke, "The government has been accused of having said nothing. I say: today, the government has acted."

The premier explained that he was soon to meet with the British on Ethiopia, a matter of the gravest import. He concluded his appeal to the deputies. "I love my country and I want to serve her. I am passionately attached to peace and want only to defend it. Tomorrow I shall have more courage with your confidence and the authority it will give me." The premier returned to the government bench.

The president of the Chamber called for the vote; the votes were tallied: 351 to 219 in favor of the government.

The reporter turned to Dexter and said, a touch of pleasure in his voice, "Geneviève was right. That was a cooked goose if I ever saw one."

Dexter looked down at the well of the Chamber as Premier Laval accepted congratulations on his second major parliamentary victory in two weeks, shaking hands all around. He heard Laval say to his colleagues, "Let's go out and eat a dozen oysters. Tomorrow I have to work for peace. I am meeting Sir Samuel Hoare."

The taxicab pulled up in front of the open gate leading into the courtyard of an *hôtel particulier* in the heart of the Sixth Arrondisement. Geneviève Tabouis alighted from the cab, paid the driver, and walked in, her long fur coat swaying with her slender hips, a tall hat pointed both to the front and rear like the prow of a clipper ship. She sailed forward serene in her confidence, the essence of her charm.

Entering the foyer, she handed her card to a butler, who called out her name. The hostess waved her hand, smiled, and came walking over. "How nice you could make it, Geneviève."

"Delighted, Madame la Marquise. Your invitation is most intriguing."

"Well, the dinner last Wednesday night at Madame Becker's was fascinating. The way you got information out of Sir Robert Vansittart. Why it's a wonder any diplomat ever speaks with you."

"The unguarded moment is my most valuable ally."

"Men used to say that about me," the marquise added, laughing, and then she continued, "Oh, my yes. I simply did not believe Van would say that it's too bad about Ethiopia, that it can't be helped." Amazement lingered in the marquise's voice.

Geneviève pulled the marquise over to one side and whispered, "Since then, I have heard that Sir Samuel Hoare is coming to Paris today to work out a preliminary agreement with Premier Laval, possibly with the back channel agreement of Mussolini, to partition Ethiopia."

The marquise gasped, "That would present the League of Nations with a virtual *fait accompli.*"

Nodding in vigorous agreement, indignation rising in her voice, Geneviève said, "Yes, the public might storm, the League might protest, and the press use all its powers of rebuke—but all to no avail. The thing would be as good as done."

"And too bad for Ethiopia," said the marquise reflectively.

"Yes, Mussolini would have put something over on the League and its most fundamental principles. The integrity of the fifty-four member states would be negated."

The marquise nodded as the full consequences of what Geneviève had just said sunk in. She turned to Geneviève. "You said you were working on an important story?"

"Yes, I only have a few gaps to fill in."

"Well, I am seating you right between the two gentlemen—just as you asked."

"Good," said Geneviève with a twinkle in her eye.

A maid appeared at the entrance to the dining room and made a wave to the marquise.

"Excuse me, Geneviève," and the marquise took several steps towards the center of the room and announced, "Luncheon will be served in the dining room."

The guests paraded towards the dining room, Geneviève right in the middle. She walked down the table peering at the placement cards, found her name, and stood behind her chair. A French diplomat came up to the chair on her right, saw her and was momentarily taken aback, like he had seen a snake. He quickly regained his composure. "Geneviève, how nice to see you again."

A British gentleman, a diplomat, came up to the chair on the left. The French diplomat quickly leaned in front of Geneviève and said to his British colleague, "Let me present Geneviève Tabouis. She is journalist," the venom barely concealed.

"Why yes, I have read your column with interest. We all do."

"Thank you for the compliment," replied Geneviève.

The French diplomat held her chair and Geneviève sat down, as did the other women at the table, followed by the gentlemen.

The butler and the maid worked their way around the table serving a crystal clear chilled white wine.

Geneviève began, looking at the British diplomat, "Why just Wednesday evening, at the house of one of my friends, we had dinner with Sir Robert Vansittart. He seemed to say it was too bad about Ethiopia but that it can't be helped."

"Well, I wouldn't know about that. I'm here in Paris working on technical details, maps and such," and he applied himself with single-minded intent to the oyster sitting in its shell on the small plate before him, working his knife and fork to separate the oyster from its shell.

Geneviève turned to the French diplomat. "My sources say that Sir Samuel Hoare is meeting with Premier Laval later today to concert a preliminary agreement before going on to Geneva."

"Yes, I read that in the papers this morning, too." The French diplomat smiled dryly.

Geneviève turned back to the British diplomat. "Maps and such, you say," as she watched him work with obvious delight at the next course, a most excellent American lobster sitting on his plate. She asked, "Is Mussolini going to try to reach the thirty-fifth degree of longitude in Ethiopia?"

The Englishman kept at his lobster, head down and diligent. Geneviève repeated the question again in French and then tried several variations in English.

The Englishman turned to her, his countenance in a broad smile, putting a big piece of lobster in his mouth, and looked at her with big

146

bright eyes. He chewed. Geneviève sighed: the old boy was in his glory. They must learn this in boarding school, she thought.

Always persistent, she turned back to her other side and started in again on the French diplomat who was now struggling with a chicken leg. He kept the knife and fork on the attack; the chicken leg began to give way. He looked up now and again under Geneviève's incessant questioning. Then Geneviève caught a glimmer in his expression, that slightly patronizing look that experts give to the unexpert when the tentative sally is so obviously the right answer.

Geneviève turned back to the table, looked across at the marquise, and let a small smile of triumph cross her face. She had what she wanted. Confirmation.

Hoare-Laval – Saturday

Saturday afternoon, December 7. In the gray afternoon, the sky threatening rain, Dexter stood in his overcoat and muffler, his arm around Marcelle's waist. She stood, prim in her overcoat, a warm winter hat on her head, holding a small overnight valise. The two of them watched the shiny black limousine come down rue Monsieur.

The limousine stopped and a gendarme got out and walked around the front of the car. Marcelle turned to Dexter, stood on tiptoe, and kissed him goodbye. "I'll let you know when I'm free. Probably by Monday at the latest." She walked around and got in the rear seat; the gendarme closed the door behind Marcelle and then got in the front seat next to the driver. The limousine slowly glided down the rain-soaked street.

Dexter watched the limousine depart. He held his chin in his hand, his fingers absently massaging the skin, and pondered. Premier Laval was meeting with the British today in the Quai d'Orsay. Normally Secretary-General Léger and his highly capable assistant Suzanne Bardoux would provide the diplomatic support. That would be normal, thought Dexter. What was Marcelle's role? He guessed she too was going to the Quai d'Orsay to provide some type of support to Premier Laval. Why? What? And what about Geneviève and Pertinax?

The limousine drove slowly down the street in one of the new neighborhoods out in the Fifteenth and pulled up in front of double wooden doors. The gendarme got out and walked towards the doors, one of which suddenly opened and a young woman came out, a scarf over her head to ward off the cold. She turned and kissed a young man goodbye and then hurried across the sidewalk towards the limousine, the gendarme just getting in front of her to open the rear door as she scurried forward. Marcelle slid over and made room for her.

"*Bonjour*, Madame Lambert."

"*Bonjour*, Sophie."

"I'm so excited. To be selected for this assignment. Do you know what we will be doing?"

"No. The premier told me to bring our best typist. That's you."

"The Quay d'Orsay. Where do we stay?"

"They have guest apartments we will stay in. Quite proper."

"This will be a new experience for me."

"Yes. I can say that the strictest confidentiality must be observed about our work, now and later. That is why I really thought about you for this assignment."

"I'm so pleased you feel that way."

"Yes, discretion and confidentiality are our biggest assets, Sophie."

"I understand."

The limousine pulled up to the sentry station outside the Quay d'Orsay and was waved into the parking lot. The gendarme got out and opened the door and insisted on carrying the women's valises into the anteroom. Inside the building, Suzanne Bardoux met them, "Good morning," and turning to Sophie she asked, "Whom do we have here?"

Madame Lambert quickly replied, "Sophie Gambier, she is my most trusted *commis*." Clerk.

"*Enchantée*, Sophie," and Madame Bardoux held out her hand.

"*Enchantée*, Madame," replied Sophie and shook hands.

"Let me show you to our apartments. This way."

The three women started up the staircase.

Saturday afternoon. Dexter sat at a table out-of-the-way at the far end of the Café de la Paix. He wondered what Marcelle was doing. Several English and French newspapers were spread out on the table before him. The Hoare-Laval talks were scheduled to begin today; that was the top story in two languages. Commentators expected something "decisive" from the meeting. The belief was that something substantial in the way of an understanding between France and Britain would break the diplomatic deadlock. Newspapers love to break deadlocks, thought Dexter.

Other stories emphasized, and Dexter nodded in agreement as he read, that the talks were only to develop a framework of understanding. The framework would then serve as the basis for further negotiations at Geneva among Italy, Ethiopia, and the League of Nations itself. France and Britain were not dictating terms. Or so they would say.

Dexter sipped his coffee and pondered; he could see that the goal of the Hoare-Laval proposals was to draw the parties—Italy and Ethiopia—into settlement discussions. The two statesmen would present "a basis" upon which further discussions might begin. Nothing would be "decided." But Dexter ruefully thought: of course I see it; I am a professional diplomat. Will the public? Will the press? They will see "a deal," he ruefully concluded, a done deal.

The practical difficulty, it seemed to Dexter, was to give an ocean port to landlocked Ethiopia in exchange for land that could be annexed to one of the adjacent Italian colonies. And make it seem fair. A hard sell to world opinion. Always a tricky game, Dexter well knew, to have some international commission go about changing borders. They would call it "rectifying" borders as if correcting some previous mistake. One party always felt shortchanged. Then came grievance, possibly a revanchist movement, a festering trouble spot on the world map. Didn't we have enough of those already from the Versailles Treaty?

He looked up and saw Geneviève Tabouis and Pertinax enter the café. He pulled up a paper and buried himself in the news, trying to appear inconspicuous. He watched as they slid into a booth at the far end of the lounge. He kept his head down and continued reading the papers. Normally, on a big news weekend like this, the two journalists would be trying to out-compete each other for a scoop, the inside angle, a unique slant on the big meeting. But then he had felt that something else had been going on with Geneviève all week. Dexter remembered the American reporter telling him that he had noticed her whispering to Pertinax. Since when did Geneviève whisper?

Dexter looked over at the barman and gave a nod. He brought over a snifter of cognac. Dexter turned to a profile article on Anthony Eden from one of American dailies published in Paris; the article would hit the parent paper in New York tomorrow. The dashing Eden, described by the Paris papers as the best-dressed diplomat in Europe, was the advocate of a new British policy of engagement on the Continent. Departing from the old ideal of splendid isolation, Eden advocated a policy where Britain played an active, leading and responsible role in assuring collective security through the League of Nations.

Dexter laid the paper down and thought: well, yes, that is just what the French had wanted from the British since the end of the war—commitment. Now that they had it, would they be able to keep it?

The picture of the well-dressed Eden stared out at Dexter from the paper. He knew that Eden was regarded as a man-in-waiting to the incumbent foreign secretary. Was it principle waiting for expediency to falter? If Hoare went down, would Eden do better? Dexter thought not. He had never seen such a tough international situation as Europe faced in 1935. He glanced down the lounge towards the two journalists. Did Geneviève understand that? He wondered.

Dexter drained his cognac, picked up the papers, and walked down the lounge, arching his eyebrows in greeting as he saw Geneviève and Pertinax. He walked over. "Good afternoon. What has you two about?"

"Our offices are just across the street," said Pertinax as he discreetly closed his notebook.

Geneviève smiled. "Nice to see you, Dexter." She turned her notebook to a blank page. "You are a long way from the embassy." Neither journalist made a hint of an invitation for Dexter to stay.

Dexter replied, "I was just returning. Need to get a cable off to Washington." He tipped his hand to his hat, turned, and walked towards the entrance.

The two journalists watched Dexter walk out of the café. Geneviève said, "Where were we?"

"You were at lunch with the marquise."

"Oh, yes, I was at the house of the Marquise de Ludre this afternoon. She seated me between the British and French experts on Ethiopia."

"What information did you get about the Italian special economic zone? That's the heart of the land swap."

"That will be the territory below eight degrees North and east of thirty-five degrees East."

"They confirmed that?"

"They indicated it by their manner."

"We'll have to nail that down before we can publish it."

"How will you do that, André?" asked Geneviève, referring to Pertinax by his first name.

"I have a source at Havas Agency," referring to the official French news agency. "Let's see what he comes up with."

"I was at the Quai d'Orsay last night. They have decreed a news blackout on all reports, even hints, about the Hoare-Laval plan. That's why I called you. This might be our chance."

"You said you were going to London tomorrow?"

"Yes, I will be staying at the Carlton."

"Call me tomorrow night at nine-thirty," said Pertinax. "We can confirm the details. We'll go with the story Monday morning."

"I'm sure we will have public opinion with us," Geneviève said as she closed her notebook, her face mirroring deep conviction in the correctness of her beliefs. She stood up and Pertinax followed. The two left the café.

Madame Lambert stood discreetly behind Secretary-General Alexis Léger and René St. Quentin, the Quai d'Orsay's expert on Ethiopia, in the center of the carpet in front of the large official desk in the office of the French foreign minister. Outside the windows, the winter darkness had set in. A formally attired usher opened the large wooden door to the office and Premier Laval stepped through, turning and extending his arm to Foreign Secretary Sir Samuel Hoare to enter the office. Next came Sir Robert Vansittart, permanent secretary of the British foreign office, then British ambassador Sir George Clerk, and finally Maurice Peterson, the British expert on Ethiopia.

Premier Laval said, "Gentlemen, I believe you all know one another." The premier nodded in the direction of Madame Lambert and said, "Madame Lambert is on the permanent staff at the Matignon and will assist us with paperwork." The men all nodded a greeting at Madame Lambert.

"Let us go into my study for our meeting. It is warm and comfortable," and the premier pointed with his hand to an open door at the far side of the official office. The men trooped in, Madame Lambert following. She took up a chair at a small desk just behind the premier and Alexis Léger.

Premier Laval prefaced the talks, a minor trace of irritation in his voice. "Signor Mussolini's speech to the Italian Chamber this morning did not seem to signal the conciliatory posture that the Italian ambassador has been assuring me is the Italian government's intent."

Sir Samuel Hoare listened to this declaration with polite interest while Sir Robert Vansittart displayed a "what-did-you-expect" look.

Laval then opened the meeting more formally. "This afternoon our two governments should come to agreement on determining the bases that might be proposed to the two parties for a friendly settlement of the Italo-Ethiopian dispute. Our experts have shown the way," and Laval nodded at Peterson and St. Quentin.

Léger spoke, "We must continually stress that these are bases of discussion between Italy, Ethiopia, and the League of Nations. Not dictates from Paris and London." Heads all around the table nodded.

Vansittart interjected, "There can be no question of publishing these formulas."

"Agreed," replied Laval. "We must stress that the formulas, though not published, are preliminary and tentative."

Vansittart changed topics. "The oil sanction is scheduled for action Thursday at Geneva."

Laval replied, "An oil embargo could lead to dramatic and unforeseen consequences. It would be better to conciliate before applying sanctions. Sanctions are deeply unpopular in France. I dislike this talk of a fixed date."

Hoare now entered the conversation, nodding agreeably. "As long as negotiations are fruitful, everyone would understand the wisdom of a delay in the oil sanction."

Laval looked at Hoare hopefully. Laval was pretty sure he could get Mussolini to make the right gesture.

Hoare said, "Then, we should get some serious signal from Mussolini before Thursday. His Majesty's Government is not disposed to ask for a postponement of Thursday's meeting in Geneva of the Sanctions Committee without it."

Laval replied, "Then time is of the essence. I am sure Mussolini is ready to negotiate. To give a meaningful signal."

Hoare responded, "Good, with that in mind, I have decided to put off going to Switzerland tonight. I will stay in Paris tomorrow and we can complete our talks."

Laval smiled. "Excellent. Let's leave drafting a communiqué on today's meeting to *Messieurs* Vansittart and Léger."

"I quite agree." Hoare turned to Vansittart and said, "We want to stress the complete agreement between our two governments for continuation of the policy of close collaboration. We don't want to let the press find any daylight between the two governments on this."

Madame Lambert carefully wrote this down, capturing the exact words in their sequence.

Laval silently nodded in agreement. He was close to achieving with the British what no other French minister had achieved since the war—strong agreement.

Léger leaned forward. "I believe we want to stress in the communiqué that this meeting is not taking any position on implementing the oil sanction at Thursday's meeting."

Vansittart looked at his French compatriot and nodded in agreement. "Yes. Let Rome understand they must make a positive step."

Hoare nodded his assent and added, summing up the British position, "London is very concerned that any proposals do not give the appearance of rewarding aggression." All present knew that Anthony Eden was in London at the foreign office that weekend. He was a concern.

Laval looked inward and gave a faint smile of appreciation for Hoare's situation, if not predicament. Then he stood up and the others followed. Laval turned to Léger. "Monsieur le Secretary, to your capable hands." He nodded and then smiled a "thank you" to Madame Lambert.

Léger turned to Vansittart. "Let us go over to Madame Lambert's office and work on the communiqué. She has a typist who can prepare the communiqué. It is just on the other side of foreign minister's official office."

The two men walked out with Madame Lambert picking up her papers and following.

Madame Lambert and Sophie stood at the rear of one of the Quai d'Orsay's beautiful meeting rooms. In the front of the room, Sir Robert Vansittart and Alexis Léger took questions from the reporters seated in rows of chairs before them. To one side stood Suzanne Bardoux, holding extra copies of the communiqué.

A reporter, an American from a big New York daily—Madame Lambert recognized Dexter's friend Phil—looked over his notes, glanced again at the communiqué, and asked, "One more thing. There's no mention of the German situation in the communiqué. Is that an oversight or intentional?" The reporter was disbelieving that top French and British diplomats could meet and not talk about Germany.

Vansittart answered in his beautifully modulated upper crust voice, itself dismissive to the street English of the New York reporter, "One thing at a time is plenty" He smiled.

The reporter came back. "So at tomorrow's meeting the ministers and their advisers will discuss how slowly to apply the 'strangle hold' on Italy?"

Vansittart winced and said, "You Americans—'strangle hold'— really now."

The American shot back. "Those are Mussolini's words, not mine."

Vansittart quickly took a verbal step backwards. "Right you are."

Léger moved forward to end the press conference. "Madame Bardoux can take any other inquiries you might have."

The reporters stood up and headed for the door; deadlines were waiting. Madame Bardoux smiled as she watched them leave.

Madame Bardoux came back to where Madame Lambert and Sophie were standing. "Thank you for your patience."

Sophie exclaimed, eyes wide, "That was fascinating." She turned to Madame Lambert, "And Madame, the way you worked with *Messieurs* Vansittart and Léger on the communiqué. And in two languages, too."

Madame Lambert smiled. "Thank you. That is what we are trained to do."

Madame Bardoux said, "Good news. Monsieur Léger has arranged for us to have dinner in his private dining room. This way."

A formally attired waiter met the three ladies at the entrance to the small private dining room near the secretary-general's office. He ushered them in and held their chairs as each took her seat in turn.

Madame Lambert turned to Madame Bardoux and said, "The American reporter from New York is one of Dexter's friends."

Madame Bardoux replied, a wistful tone in her voice, "He has a knack for taking official words and putting them back into his questions and then sending them forth to the podium in ways which, shall we say, are inconvenient to the overall message the government is trying to put forth. The Americans seem obsessively fact conscious."

Madame Lambert laughed and then said somewhat ruefully, "Dexter keeps hold of the inconvenient fact for what seems forever. Doesn't let it go."

Madame Bardoux now turned wistful. "There are a lot of inconvenient facts this weekend."

Madame Lambert nodded in silent understanding.

Madame Bardoux moved to change the subject; she turned to Sophie and politely inquired, "And you, my dear, you seem young to be a *commis* at the Matignon?"

Sophie enthused, "Yes. My ministry seconded me there. I keep hoping to sit for the *concours* to become a *redactrice*, or at least get on the list. But the budget cuts keep pushing the exam off into the future. The ministry felt that time at the Matignon would help my future promotion."

Madame Lambert added, "Sophie has her *bac* from a *lycée* outside of Paris."

Sophie said, almost apologetically, "I would have continued, but the depression and my younger sisters' educations…"

Madame Bardoux quickly cut in sympathetically. "Yes, I understand. But the Matignon itself is a *grande école*."

A waiter began placing small plates with appetizers in front of each woman. Another held a bottle of chilled white wine for Madame Bardoux's inspection and she nodded in affirmation at the choice. "Excellent."

She turned and smiled at Madame Lambert and Sophie as the wine was poured. Then she picked up her glass and held it out in salute. "To your future promotion, Madame Gambier."

Sophie beamed at the approval of the two older women.

Hoare-Laval – Sunday

Sunday morning, December 8. The limousines brought the British delegation to the front steps of the ceremonial entrance to the Quai d'Orsay. Premier Laval and Secretary-General Léger stood on the steps in welcome. Once inside, walking down the hallway towards the foreign minister's office, Premier Laval said to Foreign Secretary Hoare, "Let's leave the experts to their work. We will keep our session small and focused on the overall agreement."

Hoare looked over at Permanent Secretary Vansittart, who nodded in acquiescence.

Léger stepped back and directed the French and British experts and their aides into a separate conference room.

Laval escorted Hoare into his official office, stopped, and said, pointing towards Madame Lambert and Madame Bardoux standing by his large desk, "Madame Lambert from yesterday. She has a typist nearby to help us with the draft agreement. Madame Bardoux, who I am sure you know is Monsieur Léger's assistant, can assist with drafting the communiqué."

Hoare replied briskly, "Excellent. Hopefully I will be off for Switzerland this evening and the settlement will be off to London." He smiled a warm good morning to Madame Lambert and Madame Bardoux.

Laval guided Hoare towards his study; Vansittart and Léger followed. Madame Lambert and Madame Bardoux came after the men and discreetly took their seats at a small table behind Léger.

Laval opened the discussion. "We must strive today for a real unity of view and intention between our two countries."

Heads nodded in agreement.

Hoare spoke, "The arrangement must be a judicious mixture of an exchange of territory and the conferring of economic concessions."

Laval then set forth his first position. "The exchange of territories should be the northern province currently occupied by the Italian army for a corridor to a seaport for Ethiopia."

Léger added, "The remainder of the exchange should be explained as a rectification of the borders to the east along the Danakil frontier and to the south along the Ogaden frontier."

Vansittart entered the conversation. "The corridor to the sea must be emphasized in the communiqué. World opinion must believe that landlocked Ethiopia is gaining something of value from the exchange."

Laval agreed. "The key element of a diplomatic solution is to give Ethiopia access to the sea." Then he shifted in his chair uneasily and said, "Now for the hard part. We need a zone to the south and east for Italian economic expansion. That has been Mussolini's argument to the Italian people, if not the world."

Hoare leaned forward and looked at Laval directly. "His Majesty's Government can never consent to Italian sovereignty in fact. The sovereignty must remain with the emperor of Ethiopia. That must be made clear."

Laval sighed. That would be a big sticking point with Mussolini, he knew.

Léger came in on an optimistic note. "We propose a chartered Italian company to administer the exclusive Italian rights to economic expansion in the zone."

Vansittart looked skeptically at Léger and then added, "We need to go further. There needs to be a formal plan of assistance under the auspices of the League in the Special Economic Zone. The principal adviser must be appointed by the League and report to the emperor. Among other things he would look out for the social welfare of the indigenous peoples."

Léger listened intently. "No problem."

Hoare now turned to Léger. "I want the entire matter of the Economic Zone to be in the League's hands, not Britain's."

Laval spoke softly, "I agree."

Hoare then turned to Laval. "The bases for an agreement are in place. Just as important is how the agreement is presented to the parties."

Laval nodded. "Mussolini is ready to negotiate."

Hoare straightened up. "What has been discussed here requires approval from the British cabinet before going forward."

Laval said, "Of course."

Vansittart spoke, "When we get the agreement drafted, we will have Peterson immediately leave for London with a copy. The cabinet can discuss it tomorrow afternoon, the evening at the latest."

Laval, his mind moving ahead to the next step, said, "On Tuesday we can have both the French and British ambassadors communicate directly with Mussolini, on identical terms, the outline of the proposals. This step must be strictly confidential."

Vansittart said, "In that case, the following day we will have the French and British ministers in Addis Ababa present the proposals to Emperor Haile Selassie as a basis for conciliation under the League Committee."

Hoare looked thoughtful. "There might be some difficulty with the cabinet on this. It's not fair play to speak with Mussolini first and Emperor Selassie second."

Vansittart spoke, "Possibly we can arrange something informally," and he looked over at Léger, "through the Quai d'Orsay."

Laval looked thoughtful and stroked his chin. "Yes, our expert, Monsieur St. Quentin, might be of assistance here."

Laval, feeling the substance of things was settled, stood up. "Gentlemen, let us go to our dining room for lunch. After lunch we can draft the documents." The other men stood up; Madame Lambert and Madame Bardoux arose. The men trooped out.

Madame Bardoux said, "Let's go get Sophie and we can go to Monsieur Léger's dining room for lunch."

Madame Lambert said, "With pleasure."

Early evening darkness was settling in outside the window of the small office in the Quai d'Orsay where Madame Lambert was sitting at a desk while Premier Laval stood by her side. Both were intently looking down at the most recent draft of the agreement the premier was working on with Foreign Secretary Hoare. In the corner of the office, Sophie sat at a typing desk looking expectantly at the other two, awaiting instructions.

"The foreign secretary keeps fiddling with the language," the premier complained. "What do you think?" he asked.

"The foreign secretary keeps marking up the language describing the terms of the Special Economic Zone," replied Madame Lambert. "This issue has been bothering the British all day. Possibly you could add language 'subject to such arrangements as will be developed by the League Committee in Geneva.' That moves the final resolution to Geneva, which is where I believe the British are trying to move the issue."

"Why, I believe you are right."

Madame Lambert took the draft, made an annotation on the page, and handed the sheet to Sophie. "Could you re-type just this one page?"

"*Bien sûr,* Madame.*"

Laval stood patiently while Sophie typed the page. She pulled it out of her typewriter and handed it to Madame Lambert, who carefully read through the draft and then compared it to the annotated draft. Satisfied, she handed the finished page to Premier Laval, who inserted it into the four-page agreement. Madame Lambert inserted carbon copies into the second and third sets of the document. She handed these to Premier Laval, too.

"Thank you. Let me review these with the foreign secretary," and he turned on his heel and left.

Several minutes later, Premier Laval returned, a smile on his face. He showed the final pages of all three sets to Madame Lambert. "See?"

Madame Lambert saw the neat initials "S.H." and "P.L." on each final page.

"Come on ladies. Let's go find the others. I am sure they have the communiqué done by now. Then we can have the press conference and be done with the matter."

Again Madame Lambert and Sophie stood at the rear of the large meeting room being used for press briefings. In the front they could see Madame Bardoux handing out copies of the communiqué to the reporters. Premier Laval and Foreign Secretary Hoare stood front and center, flanked on either side by Secretary-General Léger and Permanent Undersecretary Vansittart.

A reporter asked a question about the specific provisions agreed to as part of the agreement. Hoare took one step forward. "There can be no question at present of publishing these formulae. The British Government has not yet been informed of them and once its agreement has been received it will be necessary to submit them to the consideration of the interested Governments and to discussion by the League of Nations."

"We have worked together with the same anxiety to reach as rapidly as possible a peaceful and honorable solution."

Looking over at Laval, Hoare concluded, "We are both satisfied with the result which we have reached."

Vansittart stepped forward and added, "With that in mind, Maurice Peterson has already left for London with a copy of the agreement for consideration by the cabinet." Vansittart took a step back.

Hoare then returned to the subject of specific details, "I would urge members of the press to abstain from guessing or trying to discover what this basis of settlement might be. Its details are of no importance except to the people immediately concerned—that is to say, in the first place, the Italians and Ethiopians."

Vansittart stepped forward and added, "And the League of Nations. Remember, Premier Laval and Foreign Minister Hoare have in the present instance been acting as agents for the League, which body has charged them with the task of seeking an amicable solution. The governments of France and Britain are not proposing a specific settlement."

Hoare nodded in vigorous agreement.

Léger now added his voice, "We do not want the chance of an honorable peace to be compromised by the excitement of public opinion reacting to false surmises." The reporters mumbled to themselves; they hated it when the world of officialdom tried to draft them into a conspiracy of silence, always for some high-minded reason.

Another reporter asked about possible differences in approach between the French and British governments. Laval now stepped forward and spoke briskly, heavily emphasizing the words "complete solidarity." He repeated it several times in different contexts. The reporters seemed to grasp the point.

A reporter directed another question at Laval. "What do you think Mussolini will do?"

Laval, speaking in a hypothetical way, implied that if he were in Mussolini's place "he would accept the basis of settlement that is proposed and be glad to do so." The reporters sensed Laval felt a breakthrough was coming.

The American reporter from New York stood up, scanned his notes, and said, "In brief, it comes down to this—between now and Thursday Mussolini will have time to reflect on the joint Anglo-French proposals as a basis of settlement. If by then his reply is not encouraging, the League Committee will extend sanctions to include an embargo on oil, coal and iron." The reporter looked up. The four officials on the dais looked directly at him and said nothing. The reporter smiled. He had his conclusion: sanctions might be a live issue on Thursday.

Next, the reporter from the *Times* of London stood and asked Hoare for his assessment. Hoare calmly replied, "I am neither optimistic nor pessimistic. I only hope there is as sincere a desire for a settlement and peace as is claimed by everyone. For ourselves and for the French I can say that desire is very deep and very sincere."

The reporter from New York, who had remained standing, looked to the officials on the dais and asked a question as a means of summarizing the situation, "So once more the answer is up to Mussolini." No one moved to contradict the reporter.

Madame Bardoux stepped forward. "That will conclude the briefing. If you have further questions, you may contact our press office or the British embassy. Good night."

As the reporters departed, Premier Laval walked over and shook Hoare's hand while clapping him on the back. "Now we're finished with Italy."

Sunday evening, December 8, London. In the dining room of the Carlton Hotel, underneath spreading crystal chandeliers, sat some older women draped in light-colored evening gowns. Other women, still blessed with the slenderness of youth, were elegantly sheathed in dark *couture*. The ladies chatted with men dressed in black-tie dinner jackets. The round tables were draped with thick white tablecloths on which bone-white china dinnerware glistened. Some men self-importantly made serious points, others, possibly more important, lightly joked, while women spoke with amused little laughs; a tinkle of gaiety hovered in the air.

Geneviève Tabouis, dining with friends, was making a serious point: "If the peoples of Europe lose confidence in the League and its authority to insure the peace, then the joint solidarity between Britain and France loses its leverage point." Heads at the table nodded in agreement. Geneviève always broke the table taboo of no politics at dinner, or leastwise not until coffee.

Geneviève continued with emphatic sincerity, "That is the danger in the so called 'deal' that is being negotiated in Paris." The English heads nodded in agreement: the French were always maneuvering some deal, always a little greasy around the edges.

One of the men cleared his throat to speak. "This head-long rush to the oil sanction carries risks, too. Don't want to wind up like July 1914 with soldiers marching over the paper treaties. Sanctions, like principles, have to be applied with great care to the circumstances." Heads around the table nodded in wise agreement.

Geneviève quickly replied, "Yes, but the little countries at the League are watching. Selling out a little country sets a bad precedent." Again, heads nodded in agreement. Dilemmas everywhere.

Glancing down at her watch, Geneviève saw that it was nine-thirty. She set her napkin on the table before her, leaned forward, and said, "Excuse me. I have to leave for a while. Continue. I will be back for coffee."

Geneviève went up to her room and picked up the telephone and called Paris. The line clicked and a voice came on. "Yes?"

"Good evening," replied Geneviève. No need to say more. Other ears might be on the line.

In Paris, a sigh of relief. "Not exactly as we thought. An outlet to the sea. Some occupied territory to the occupier. Corrections of the frontiers east and southeast. The large zone indicated by the north latitude and the east longitude is to be a special zone with a monopoly of economic development under a chartered company. League supervision."

Geneviève wrote this down in her notebook. "How good is the source?"

"Good, but he doesn't have the actual document."

"Are you running with the story?"

"Yes, tomorrow morning. Paris and London."

"I'll telephone mine in from here."

"Good. See you in Paris later in the week." The line clicked dead.

Geneviève placed the telephone in its cradle. She went over and sat at the desk. She took the pencil draft of tomorrow's column and read it through, correcting here and there, making additions in other places, lining out a few sentences. She read it through again. She wanted it simple and direct. She made some more changes. Satisfied, she walked back over and picked up the telephone.

At the offices of *L'Oeuvre* the night editor came on. "Yes?"

"It's Geneviève. Here's tomorrow's story. It's big. I'd run it page one."

"Your wish is my command. Here's a stenographer." The editor handed the telephone to an assistant.

The editor sat back in his chair. Yes, everyone knew the British foreign secretary was meeting with Laval at the Quai d'Orsay. Everyone knew there was a press blackout. The paper breaking the news would sell papers by the thousands in the morning. He could hear the shouts of the newsboys now. He smiled.

Hoare-Laval – The Storm

Monday morning, December 9, London. Anthony Eden sat at his dining table, drinking breakfast tea and thinking about the dispatches he had received Sunday about Saturday's meeting. He was uneasy. He wondered how many cooks were stirring the broth in Paris.

He thought to himself that a firm policy would compel Mussolini to negotiate for terms which the emperor of Ethiopia would accept, such as those already discussed at Geneva. This would immeasurably increase the League's authority, the truly important goal. It would also be a salutary warning to Hitler. Why can't Laval see that?

The door opened and the butler ushered Maurice Peterson into the dining room; Anthony Eden set down his cup and rose. He walked around and shook Peterson's hand and said, "What do you have for me?"

"The agreement," and he handed the document to Eden.

"In French, no English translation?"

"No, Minister."

Eden read through the document while standing. "These terms go beyond any which you had been authorized to accept last week."

"I did not suppose that you would like them."

"Yes, quite. How did Hoare come to sign these? Can you provide any further illumination?"

"I was not in the room when final terms were worked out. I was working on the communiqué."

Eden looked astonished. "Yes, I see," he said with dismay in his voice.

"I believe that I could have obtained considerably better terms if I had been given more latitude last week," Peterson said in a tone of polite insistence.

"Undoubtedly true. Thank you, Peterson. The cabinet will meet tonight."

"Minister…"

"Yes."

"Substantially correct accounts of the terms are in two French newspapers in Paris this morning and the *Daily Telegraph*."

Eden's eyebrows went up. "Very well. Stand by at the foreign office. Undoubtedly we will communicate the results of tonight's cabinet meeting to Paris."

Monday evening, 10 Downing Street, London. The prime minister, Stanley Baldwin, opened the cabinet meeting. "You all know how difficult the situation is. The early and unauthorized release of some of the terms, which by the way are doubly inaccurate in some important respects, makes going forward doubly difficult." Yes, the terms would look worse than they were, if that was possible some of the ministers thought—ruefully.

Baldwin turned the discussion over to Eden. Eden presented and explained the proposals, concluding, "Some features of the proposals are likely to prove very distasteful to some members of the League." An undertone of agreement rumbled around the table; heads nodded in understanding.

Eden then made his main point. "We must insist that the proposals go to Italy and Ethiopia at the same time. One cannot be favored before the other." Heads nodded vigorously in agreement. Eden looked over at an official taking notes; the resolution was entered in the minutes.

Baldwin then offered his concluding resolution. "To support the policy of the Secretary of State for Foreign Affairs as set forth in his Memorandum."

Eden looked around the table and added the corollary, "As to the Memorandum, it should be forwarded to the League as soon as possible, and we should emphasize, for possible modification and support."

Voices around the table said emphatically, "By all means, get it to Geneva. Modifications, by all means." Heads nodded approval.

Baldwin concluded the meeting.

Tuesday morning, rue Monsieur. There was knock on the front door. Marie opened it and a small man in a big overcoat with a large workingman's cap pulled down to his ears handed over a half dozen newspapers. "Monsieur Jones asked these be delivered."

Marie thanked the man; he ran the kiosk around the corner. She carried the papers into the dining room.

"Ah, the morning papers. Let's see."

Sipping her coffee, Marcelle said, "Dear, everyone in Paris can tell you that the threat of real war in the Mediterranean recedes. The proposed Hoare-Laval settlement ends the danger."

"There are people in Paris who say this is rewarding the aggressor."

"Yes, your friend Geneviève and her little band of idealists."

"There's a whole island of them across the Channel."

"The British have gotten a firm commitment from France to back a settlement through the League of Nations, a settlement acceptable to all parties. It is in Geneva's hands now. The island people should be pleased."

"The agreement has to get to Geneva. It's not there yet."

"Just a matter of time."

Dexter smiled at her while scanning the papers. "Here it is. In the American daily. They get the same wires that go to New York."

He looked across the table at Marcelle and began to read, "African peace plan stirs ire in London. Commons storm likely today as it is admitted Hoare exceeded authority. Betrayal enrages Eden. Those are just the headlines."

"Eden again." She scowled.

Dexter turned earnest and continued to read, "According to this explanation, the rights of Ethiopia go into the dustbin, and Britain and France for the sake of escaping from an immediate difficulty take the risk of destroying the League and letting Germany in the near future do to Austria and Hungary what Italy is allowed to do to Ethiopia."

Marcelle, a pained look on her face, started in. "Not to be the headmistress, but…Hoare-Laval are just tentative proposals. The agreement will belong solely to the League. It will be its triumph. Will Italy get everything it wants? No. The world community will have successfully pushed back. Collective security will have a success, not perfect, but something of some substance. The principle can then be more strongly applied the next time. In Europe, possibly."

Dexter reached his hand across the table and took hers in his, "As well said as can be." He looked into her eyes with serious affection, real pride at her understanding, the fortitude of her resolve.

Tuesday evening, House of Commons, London. Prime Minister Stanley Baldwin sat at the government bench, Anthony Eden at his side. Baldwin said in a low voice, "The article in the *Times* this morning has created a sense of anger and betrayal." Eden nodded in the direction of the Opposition benches. "Attlee will make us out as hypocrites."

At the head of the hall, the speaker intoned, "The prime minister." Baldwin stood up and took several steps forward to the Government's speaking desk. He made his introduction and opening remarks, stressing that "Britain would insist on a settlement acceptable to the League, Italy and Ethiopia."

He concluded his remarks, "We are going on with exactly the same policy we have been pursuing. Mr. Eden is going to Geneva tomorrow and we shall know very shortly what the reactions may be to the course that we have been pursuing."

Then he reminded the House that he understood the morning news reports in the *Times* to be inaccurate. He stepped back and sat down.

The leader of the Opposition, Mr. Clement Attlee approached the Opposition podium. After his critique of the government policy, he raised the critical issue: "It is a matter which has been subject of a General Election. We understand that the proposals overthrow the whole position of the existing League system in order to settle this question." He stepped back and took his seat at the Opposition bench.

Eden stepped up to the Government podium. "This is only the first step in a long and complicated enterprise...only a beginning." He looked down at his papers and then up to the Opposition benches, "We are not seeking to impose terms on anybody...Let's face the facts. If Italy, Ethiopia, and the League accept discussion on the basis of the suggestions which have been made in Paris, there is nobody here that is going to say 'no,' even if some of those proposals may not be particularly appealing to us."

Eden explained in more detail three general principles involved in the proposals and then concluded his speech, "I ask for latitude and confidence in the task ...for the discharge of which, I trust, all parties will seek to bring me aid." He stepped back and took his place on the Government bench.

Prime Minister Baldwin stepped forward to close the debate, "I have seldom spoken with greater regret, for my lips are not yet unsealed, and were these troubles over I would make a case and I would guarantee that no man would go into the lobby against us."

Baldwin concluded portentously, "I do not believe that there is anyone in this country who wants war."

Baldwin knew the speech would quiet the storm until such time later in the week the actual agreement circulated in Geneva. But the riddle remained: how far could the League push sanctions before getting war? Baldwin was set on pursuing the trickiest of political strategies: a dual policy.

Thursday, December 13, Geneva. In the horseshoe-shaped League Hall, all eyes were on Anthony Eden as he strode to the speaker's podium to address the Sanctions Committee overseeing the Italo-Ethiopian peace efforts.

The British minister began, "Great Britain proposes that the League of Nations Council hear a full statement of the Hoare-Laval peace plan next Wednesday and determine as and when it sees fit what course it would wish to pursue in the light of the situation thus created."

Looking out at the delegates in the closed session, Eden explained, "I emphasize that as far as His Majesty's Government is concerned we will not only readily accept the judgment of our colleagues but will continue to use our best efforts to further the two objectives which have been constantly before us in this dispute—restoration of peace and maintenance of the League's authority."

One of the small power delegates from Eastern Europe whispered to a colleague, "He's going back to a simple restatement of British policy towards the League. He is not championing the British cabinet's current initiative. We backed the sanctions too soon. The British are cutting the ground out from under us."

Eden further explained, "The proposals now put forward are neither definitive nor sacrosanct…Indeed, we would cordially welcome any suggestions for their improvement." The delegates murmured amongst themselves, some observing, "The British are divided…London stands behind Hoare, Geneva with Eden."

Over among the French delegates, Édouard Herriot, minister of state in Laval's cabinet and president of the Radical Socialist party, now a restless bedmate in Laval's coalition, sat listening. He spoke to a colleague, "Incredible, Eden seems to be asking for a disavowal of his own government's proposals." Herriot mused that Laval was being left out on a limb. He looked over as Laval rose and went to the speaker's podium.

Laval began to speak by explaining it was the League that had asked Britain and France to undertake settlement discussions. The delegates simply listened; everyone already knew that. He moved to support Eden while also putting distance between himself and his own proposals:

"We propose to communicate them very shortly to the Council of the League. Our task will then be at an end and it will be for the League itself to decide what is to be done. We are at least confident it will appreciate the loyalty of the effort, which, I say again, has no other purpose than to hasten a settlement within the League itself of a dispute the prolongation of which weighs heavily on the world."

Herriot whispered to his colleague, "Pierre always prefers to work in the shadows, not the public forum. He will return to the back rooms."

With Eden's proposal accepted, the delegates stood up and headed for the exits. The small power diplomat whispered to a colleague on the way out, "The oil sanction was not mentioned today."

Friday evening, December 13, Geneva. The New York reporter picked up the published copy of the Hoare-Laval peace plan at the press center and went over to a desk and started to read.

Yes, he thought, Geneviève and Pertinax had been correct Monday morning—mostly. Almost half of Ethiopia was given to the Italians as a special economic zone but supposedly under the "sovereignty" of Ethiopia. Who was going to believe that fairy tale? The reporter laughed to himself. He gave his own answer: a few ministers on the government bench in the House of Commons? He shook his head in wonderment.

The reporter looked at his notes. Today, Ethiopia had told the League that the plan was simply giving land to the aggressor "pending future annexation." The Ethiopians went on to denounce "secret negotiations." Undoubtedly they would garner worldwide sympathy if not support, thought the reporter.

He started to write his dispatch to New York.

Saturday morning, December 14, rue Monsieur. A knock at the street door carried into the dining room; Dexter jumped up and went into the courtyard and opened the large wooden door. The man from the kiosk handed him a bunch of papers and tipped his hand to his cap, "Monsieur."

"Thank you," Dexter replied. He had already paid the man handsomely yesterday for this morning's errand.

Dexter walked back into the dining room and set the papers down on the table. Marcelle took one and scanned the front page. Standing, Dexter searched through the papers and found the Paris edition of the big New York daily. He set it down next to his coffee cup, sat down, and began to read a long article about last night's debate in the Chamber of Deputies.

"Here we go, Cot declared," Dexter said in reference to the Pierre Cot, a leading speaker for the Radical Socialist party, "that the position of France must conform to the traditional policy of fidelity to the League of Nations. We want peace, but it must an honorable peace for all. What a disgrace and shame it is to see France propose a project which leads to conferring a reward on the aggressor of yesterday and of tomorrow and in effect to a new 'partition of Poland.'" Everyone would know that Cot spoke for Édouard Herriot.

Dexter also knew that Poland had historically been divided up between Russia and Germany during the ebbs and flows of Central European history. France had always tried to champion an independent Poland, most recently in the early 1920s against a Bolshevik invasion. He remembered from last summer's talk that Colonel de Gaulle had served there. An interesting example: partition of Poland. Almost sounded prophetic. But then Poland was always getting divided up.

Marcelle tartly rejoined, "Monsieur Cot obviously picked up his language by reading the *London Times* this week."

"Yes, he is echoing British public sentiment."

"Monsieur Cot is gallantly supporting a principle; he is appealing to great ideals."

"Public opinion is shaping today's foreign policy decisions with a force it has never had before," Dexter ventured, a little tentatively; he knew what was coming.

"Premier Laval has his eye on Hitler and the Rhineland. They are not principles, they are not ideals—but they are there. Ready to pounce. Ethiopia is a sideshow. Some arrangement must be worked out."

"I do agree with that."

Marcelle smiled at him.

Dexter continued, "Here, the story quotes members of the Left as saying they do not want to overthrow Monsieur Laval, but just let him fall."

"Of course. The budget has not been passed yet, nor the bill outlawing armed political leagues and the right-wing militias. The Senate will not vote final approval until sometime in January."

"You're right. The Center and Left will keep Premier Laval in power awhile longer. But Laval is being maintained by a large negative political power. No other faction wants to form a government right before a general election."

Marcelle glanced down at a copy of *Action Française*, the leading Far Right newspaper, lying on the table and asked, "What does the Right Wing say?"

"Well, they are continuing their line that sanctions mean war with Italy."

"They should be pleased with Premier Laval's many efforts to avoid the oil sanction."

"They are never pleased with republican government. They have published a list of hundred-and-forty deputies who they say support sanctions against Italy. They call them 'murderers of peace, murderers of France.' And of course, they really have it in for Léon Blum," mentioning the Jewish leader of the Socialist party. "They call him the 'old semitic camel' and other names."

"Yes, the Dreyfus affair will live on with the Catholic reactionaries forever."

"It's more than that now. The *Action Française* cries 'We are not available for the Jewish Crusade' and that Herriot's Radical Socialists are guided by 'obscure powers' and dominated by 'millionaires without a fatherland.'"

"Well, yes, and who might they be?" she asked rhetorically. "The difficulty with this hysteria is that across the Rhine is Adolph Hitler. They are doing his work."

Nodding, Dexter moved on to the next point, "They're really upset that the paramilitary militias are being outlawed. Laval really surprised them."

"They should be worried about the change in the press law that went with it. Crimes of incitement have been transferred to tough magistrates, not indulgent juries." She looked across the table at Dexter, her expression putting an end to the discussion, and she concluded, "I must be off soon. The budget calls."

"Can you tell me about it?"

"Yes, Premier Laval has been voted special powers. Ordinary procedure calls for the Chamber to discuss the budget chapter by chapter, to vote on it article by article. This can take weeks, if not months. The special powers should allow the votes to be undertaken next week."

"That will be unprecedented."

"Yes, and we must have the first chapters ready to go Monday morning."

"Does it balance?"

"Yes it does. Except there are extra expenditures for military defense in a special fund being financed by defense bonds discounted by the Banque de France."

"Your favorite, the Banque de France."

"Yes, the Banque de France…maker and breaker of governments. Sort of like an epithet in a Greek epic poem…mighty Zeus, hurler of thunderbolts."

Dexter smiled, "In America, Roosevelt threw a bridle over the banks two years ago."

Marcelle stood up, eyes twinkling, "Mighty Roosevelt, bridler of banks."

Dexter laughed as he stood up, "I'll walk you to the Matignon and then go on to the embassy."

Tuesday, December 17, Paris. In the Palais Bourbon, the deputies sat in their semi-circular amphitheater waiting for Premier Laval to give his speech in defense of his foreign policy. Many of the deputies looked over to the seats near the government benches at Édouard Herriot, minister of state in Laval's government. He was the keystone in Laval's coalition with the majority Radical Socialist party.

Two days before Herriot, speaking as president of the Radical Socialist party, outlined a three-point statement of principle on foreign policy that supported conciliation, required any settlement to be acceptable to the League, and a process of acceptance by Italy and Ethiopia that did not involve imposing a settlement on the weaker party. The speech was widely understood to mean that Herriot and the Radicals thought peace at any price, and especially at the price of Ethiopian territory, was not sound policy.

The deputies understood that French public opinion had swung, like that of the public in Britain, strongly behind the concept that there must be no rewarding of the aggressor and no injustice to the victim.

Laval stood and strode to the tribune. He laid the pages of his speech before him and started by explaining France's respect for the

League Covenant and how, when the Ethiopian war started, the government had promptly moved to put into motion the system of collective security.

Then he got to the heart of the difference between his position and the position of the pro-sanction faction in the British government, "But sanctions do not constitute the only means of stopping hostilities. It is also in conformity with the letter and the spirit of the Covenant to seek a friendly settlement, that is to say, a peaceful solution, as soon as possible."

He then explained how France and Great Britain had supported the imposition of non-military sanctions step-by-step, concluding, "We did everything possible to prevent what might have provoked an extension of the Italo-Ethiopian conflict into Europe." This was the nightmare that haunted the two top leaders of the British and French governments, two men who desperately understood their peoples did not want another war. They would speak of solution, rarely of principle, never of ideals.

Laval continued a thoughtful exposition of the events surrounding the Hoare-Laval pact and concluded, "To avoid the risk of extension of the war, I have preferred, and I declare it with a full sense of my responsibility, to propose formulas that may lead us, if they are accepted by the interested governments, to a peaceful solution of the conflict, which will be honorable and just if it carries the seal of the League of Nations."

As Laval descended from the tribune, more than half the Chamber gave him warm applause. Reporters noted that Herriot sat with his arms folded across his chest.

Later in the debate, a leading Radical Socialist said, to loud applause, "It must not be believed that French opinion will accept a partition of Ethiopia to the profit of the Italy, the aggressor."

Still later as passionate tides of opinion swept over the Chamber, Laval went to the tribune to answer critics, receiving resounding applause from his supporters as he went. In the galleries, some women joined in the hand clapping; they quickly found themselves admonished by an attendant to behave themselves. Fernand Bouisson, president of the Chamber, addressed a stern rebuke to the galleries. The ladies assumed a chastened silence. Nevertheless, peace had its very enthusiastic supporters.

Laval and his government carried the motion 304 votes to 252; his majorities were narrowing. There were smiles in the galleries.

Facing the Commons

Wednesday, December 18, London. The American reporter, the London correspondent for a big New York daily, was simply stunned—a spokesman had come out of the cabinet meeting and announced that Sir Samuel Hoare had resigned. Before the meeting, the reporter was given to understand that Sir Samuel was to deliver the government's case the following day in support of the peace proposals in the House of Commons, proposals that he himself had co-authored with French Premier Laval ten days ago in Paris.

Now the cabinet had decided to condemn the proposals. Even more dramatically, Prime Minister Stanley Baldwin would personally deliver the condemnation in opposition to the Labor party's motion of censure.

However, tomorrow Sir Samuel would still speak, the reporter discovered, but as a private member from a backbench, in a personal statement outlining his participation in the Hoare-Laval proposals.

What had happened? The reporter buttonholed cabinet members as they appeared. The story tumbled out: the cabinet had simply revolted at Sir Samuel's proposed speech as it was explained to them. He took notes.

Then the reporter spoke with cabinet aides over in the corners and moved among his colleagues, swapping information. Another story emerged: that day a powerful cabal of senior members had formed against Sir Samuel, fueled by discontent among young Conservative members. A plot was hatched at the Carlton Club, long-time bastion of the parliamentary establishment. The club's backrooms had spawned many a parliamentary coup over the past century or two. A resolution demanding an expression of regret about the Paris negotiations emerged. Confronted by the dissidents, Prime Minister Stanley Baldwin was forced to ask the foreign secretary for changes to tomorrow's speech to the House of Commons.

Sir Samuel refused pointblank. Instead, he brought a letter of resignation with him to the cabinet meeting. At the meeting, he explained to his cabinet colleagues that he was not about to change the speech to express regret at what he had done in Paris. The cabinet members in turn explained to the foreign secretary that Sir Samuel's proposals were in conflict with the recent general election and that the government would come perilously close to falling on a motion of censure. Sir Samuel tendered his resignation.

The reporter went to a vacant writing desk, quickly rewrote his story, and headed for the wireless office.

Thursday, December 19, London. The Prince of Wales approached his seat in the gallery overlooking the hall of the House of Commons, reaching out and shaking hands with lords and ambassadors, giving greetings with his big toothy grin, the winsome Windsor charm at full wattage. He took his seat; the ambassadors and lords sat down. All knew one of the great dramatic moments of modern parliamentary history was at hand.

Below, Prime Minister Stanley Baldwin and Sir Samuel Hoare entered the chamber, cheers rising from the Conservative side of the House. The prime minister took his position at the government bench. Sir Samuel Hoare walked past the government bench and mounted the steps to a third-tier bench, the other members squeezing down to make room for the now private member who was once foreign secretary.

The day's proceedings began and were quickly disposed. The speaker called, "Sir Samuel Hoare." Long tradition allows a retiring cabinet minister to state his own case to the House when circumstances force him out of government.

Sir Samuel stepped forward and outlined the Paris proposals, explaining their reasonableness. He went on to say that he had been driven by an "obsession" that Italy might attack Great Britain. He expressed his great dread that such a war would likely lead to a general European war, a "conflagration" he called it.

He described the lack of cooperation among the European powers to enforce restraint on the aggressor. "You cannot have one-hundred percent peace if you have only five percent of the cooperation that goes to making it."

Hoare drove home the point. "Not a ship, not a machine, not a gun has been moved by any other member state." The members understood. The British had moved their fleet in response to Italian aggression, the French had done nothing.

Sitting in the press gallery, the New York reporter listened intently and then found himself spellbound as Hoare continued:

"I have been terrified with the thought—I speak very frankly to the House—that we might lead Ethiopia on to think that the League could do more for them than it can do, that in the end we should find a terrible moment of disillusionment in which it may be that Ethiopia would be destroyed as an independent state…"

"I could not help thinking of the past, in which…we have given all our sympathies to some threatened or downtrodden race, but because we had been unable to implement and give effect to those sympathies, all that we had done was to encourage them, with the result that in the end their fate was worse than it would have been without our sympathy."

The reporter wrote all this down, thinking that like great art, these eloquent words carried the gift of prophecy, a warning of the terrible risks incurred when cheap assurances are tossed onto the playing table of world politics.

As to Ethiopia, Hoare said that peace could come by either negotiation or surrender. He preferred negotiation. He acknowledged that for now negotiation had failed but he gave a clear opinion that eventually peace would have to be negotiated according to the main principles implied in the Hoare-Laval plan.

He closed. "I say to this House that I cannot honestly recant—and I sincerely believe that the course that I took was the only course that was possible under the circumstances." Hoare turned and returned to his bench, his great dignity magnified by the prophetic truth of the words he had spoken.

The leader of the Opposition, Clement Attlee, rose and offered the motion of censure, a now formalistic ritual. He launched a rhetorical attack on the government. "If it was right for the foreign minister to resign, the whole government should resign. Not only the honor of this country is involved in these proposals to give half of Ethiopia to Italy, but the honor of the prime minister himself."

The government now offered up an amendment on which the real vote of confidence would turn, a motion disowning the Hoare-Laval proposals but sustaining the government's continued efforts to find peace at Geneva through the League of Nations.

Conservative supporters rose and spoke in strong defense, one cabinet member making the point that Germany was the real issue. At the end, Stanley Baldwin closed for the government, admitting error that the proposals had gone too far and that the government did not have "that volume of popular opinion which it is necessary to have in a democracy behind the Government in a matter so important as this."

The government carried the vote. The New York reporter watching from the press gallery quickly descended to the lobbies to hear comments. One Conservative eminence said, "Hoare says, 'I have done nothing wrong and I resign,' and Baldwin says, 'I have done everything wrong and I do not resign.'"

Writing this down in his pad, and without looking up, the reporter asked a question with a statement, "Hoare has the sympathy and respect. Baldwin gained the votes."

The Conservative sighed and said, "Yes, that is the way these affairs are designed to work."

The reporter made an inward smile and turned to another Conservative grandee standing in the circle, a veteran of many cabinets in the past, and asked, "The prime minister?"

The old man stood a little more erect, glanced off into the distance of his memories, and then looked at the reporter, "Neither the prime minister nor the foreign minister spoke of principles or ideals. They, looking over the heads of their countrymen to the far horizons, saw the horror of war and moved in the real interests of their people."

An English reporter asked, "Did Laval in Paris move in the real interests of his people?"

The grandee raised a skeptical eyebrow and shrugged. The reporters all laughed. The grandee, thinking better of it, turned thoughtful and said, sympathetically in French, "*Peut-être.*" Perhaps.

Sunday, December 22, Sandringham House, rural England. The limousines brought the official party up the drive, past the broad lawns, to the front steps leading into the large country house owned by the royal family. In the bitter cold, the officials got out of the limousines and hurried up the steps and into the warmth of the grand edifice. Entering a large meeting room, the Privy Council met under the auspices of King George V. Anthony Eden stepped forward, took the oath of office as foreign secretary, received the seals of office, and "kissed hands" with the monarch on his appointment. Congratulations were made all around. The king invited Eden for a private audience.

In a smaller, warmer room, the aged and now quite frail king sat down and Eden took a chair just across. The king, coughing now and again somewhat painfully, spoke understandingly of the difficulties Eden had inherited, adding, "I am very interested in foreign affairs and in the appointment of ambassadors. Please keep me fully informed. We shall give you all that help that we can."

The king grew reflective and spoke of his last meeting with Sir Samuel Hoare when he had come to surrender the seals. "I told him that the Hoare-Laval proposals had been a blunder." The king explained that a train could not go full steam in one direction, and then without warning change direction without somebody coming off the rails. Eden thought how true. He also recollected in his own mind that at an earlier audience the king had spoken to him with vehemence about the importance he attached to good relations with Italy. Yes, Eden thought, the problem with dual policies—sometimes they come off the tracks. Even for a king.

The king continued, amusement in his voice, "I said to your predecessor: 'You know what they're all saying, no more coals to Newcastle, no more Hoares to Paris.' The fellow didn't even laugh." Eden smiled and gave a light chuckle to the chestnut going around the upper crust clubs in London.

Facing the Chamber

Friday, December 27, Paris. Dexter Jones walked down the crowded sidewalks of rue de l'Université towards the Palais Bourbon, home of the Chamber of Deputies. The street was jammed with motorcars, the police worked to keep groups of people moving. Dexter showed his diplomatic pass at a police cordon, walked past groups of Mobile Guards guarding the approaches, and entered the building, heading upstairs to the diplomatic gallery. The gallery was already packed; Dexter stood at the rear.

President of the Chamber Fernand Bouisson announced, "The President of the Council."

Pierre Laval walked to the tribune and began. "It was at my request that the Chamber open today this debate on foreign policy." He briefly summarized the Hoare-Laval proposals, noting, "I have reminded you that it was in conformity with the principles and the spirit of the League Covenant."

The premier set forth the standard upon which the debate should turn, "The essential question before us is to know whether the policy I have pursued is in conformity or not with the interests of my country. That is the only question which has to be examined by the French Chamber."

He explained in further detail the proposals he and Sir Samuel Hoare had worked out, "Our proposals, which have been judged excessive, seemed reasonable to us...Sir Samuel Hoare explained them in the House of Commons in moving language, with a dignity which did him honor and which compelled the admiration even of those who had judged us most harshly." Laval concluded movingly, "He defended our common work."

The premier next turned to the all-important future. "What will happen tomorrow? We agree that the Paris proposals are dead, but the way of conciliation remains open."

Dexter thought that there was another alternative: the war could simply grind on and Hitler would opportunistically pick up the broken pieces from the crumbling Stresa front.

Laval concluded and returned to the government bench to listen to the debate.

Léon Blum strode forward to the tribune to open the attack for the Opposition, arguing that Laval continued to threaten France with a false alternative: his policy or war.

Blum loftily proclaimed, "Peace depends upon equal rights between nations and on their mutual support of one another. Today, a collective system was showing its power for the first time, but instead of rejoicing at this and at the attitude of Great Britain, the government had shown sympathy for the aggressor and has given cause to suspect that it was unfaithful to the Covenant."

Blum continued, somewhat more tiresomely than Dexter thought necessary, and then concluded with deeply personal attacks on Laval, attacks uncharacteristic of parliamentary debate:

"You have proceeded in the great affairs of the world as we have seen you proceed here, every day in petty affairs and petty dealings. You tried to give and at the same time to take. You have tried to play both ends against the middle…what is deplorable is this: insensitive to the nobility and power of great and disinterested things, you have reduced them to the scale of your petty means.

"And that is how, with your petty mistakes, you have succeeded in accumulating a great disaster."

After several more speakers, Paul Reynaud, highly respected and a former supporter of the government, came forward. Reynaud assured the Chamber that the nation which France had to fear was not Italy but Germany, and that the nation whose support she needed most was Great Britain. Dexter agreed, so far.

Reynaud asked, "What chance had Europe of escaping war?"

He answered his own question, "The textbook of German youth is still *Mein Kampf* in which Herr Hitler said that Germany must ensure the neutrality of Great Britain in order to have France at her mercy. The movement in favor of the League and of collective security in Great Britain is a godsend for France."

Reynaud argued that the failure of the Hoare-Laval proposals was such a godsend because it renewed popular support in Great Britain in favor of the League and of collective security. Dexter felt the argument contrived: failure rarely had a silver lining in international politics.

Reynaud then added a pleasing touch for his listeners, "The problem of peace has been solved by the victory of a French idea," referring to France's championship of the creation of the League of Nations after the world war.

He concluded, "France has to choose today between Italy, the breaker of the Covenant, and Great Britain, the guardian of the Covenant."

With the clock approaching ten o'clock in the evening, the president of the Chamber adjourned the session to the following day. Dexter walked out past the police cordons and started towards rue Monsieur in the chill winter evening. In his view, none of the Opposition speakers had dealt with the world the way it was, but as they wished to see it.

Dexter crossed the courtyard and opened the front door. Marcelle smiled, kissed him welcome, and took his overcoat and muffler, adding, "We have warm coffee and cognac in the drawing room for the weary warrior. Something to eat?"

"Both, thank you."

"How is the debate proceeding?"

"If the vote were held today, the premier would lose."

Marcelle smiled and said matter-of-factly, "Tomorrow will be another day." They entered the drawing room and took seats near the crackling fireplace. She handed him a large crystal goblet partially filled with cognac.

"Uhmm," he purred as he took a long swallow.

He turned and looked at Marcelle, businesslike, "Laval opened with a clear declaration that the way forward was conciliation. None of the Opposition heard him. But it is the only good option on the table. Besides, the time is ripe."

Marcelle looked a little perplexed. "Why is the time ripe?"

"Italy is in a 'black period.' On the northern front, four Ethiopian armies under the leadership of some of their great warrior chieftains closed with the Italians. They inflicted severe and bloody casualties on the Italians. The warriors attacked the Italian tanks with bare hands and pulled the Italians out."

Dexter took a swallow of his cognac and looked at Marcelle, "Then they beheaded them."

Marcelle took this calmly. "I see."

Dexter added, "The warriors put the other Italians to flight, sending them running back towards their own territory."

"So?"

"Now is the time to offer Mussolini a face-saving way out of the quagmire. He'll take it. But only Laval seems to see the opportunity."

"Why?"

"Everyone else speaks of principles, ideals, or," and Dexter said disbelievingly, "honor."

"Yes, Premier Laval said that morals were one thing, but a country's interests were another," recalled Marcelle.

"Quite so."

Marcelle came over and sat beside him and stroked his hair, caressed his neck, and said, "Let's go to bed. Tomorrow will be another day. The premier is very persistent and the Opposition is not yet ready to turn him out, no one wants to form a government and be held accountable for a budget that slashes spending."

Dexter said, "Yes, Laval's austerity plan will carry the Popular Front to victory in the May elections. The country hates the budget. But they should all stand behind their country so that Germany can't pick up a cheap trick in the Rhineland."

Marcelle looked serious for a moment. "That is my unanswered question in this dilemma. What is right for France? And will the politicians see it?"

Dexter pushed his way through the crowded aisle of the diplomatic gallery in the Palais Bourbon. He saw Phil, the New York reporter, who waved him over to a seat he had been saving for Dexter.

"Come to see the grand finale?"

"You bet."

"The circus continues, the clowns from the Opposition will entertain us. Then Laval mounts his defense."

The last of the Opposition speakers was concluding, again personally attacking Laval by calling the premier "the Louis Eleven of the suburbs, plodding along and hoping to accomplish big deeds by means of little tricks." Laughter erupted from the Left benches; all were confident in victory.

Dexter turned his gaze towards President of the Chamber Bouisson, who announced Premier Laval, *Messieurs*, the President of the Council."

Laval walked forward carrying a thick file of papers with him, which he set down on the tribune in front of him. He began, after a brief explanation, "I asked myself what crime I might have committed against the country and against peace."

He looked over at the Left benches. "What you have been doing is to accuse me of my politics."

The deputies all across the Chamber grew silent and listened intently. Laval was always a fascination.

First, Laval explained that he had never given a free hand to Italy to attack Ethiopia in his meeting with Mussolini in Rome the previous January. To the contrary, he argued, at each and every turn he had warned the Italian government it had everything to gain by conciliation.

As for the agreements made with Great Britain, he had supported the ally at every key point throughout the summer and fall. He lifted and turned over document after document, enumerating the secret agreements made between the French and British armies, navies, and air forces, the meetings between their general staffs. Paper after paper was turned over on the tribune.

Laval looked out across the Chamber, holding the memoranda in his hands. "These notes were exchanged at my request, in the course of carrying out my promises of last September to the British."

He paused, then turned to the Left benches and hurled his words at them. "What did you take me for?"

Applause started on the Right benches, moved to the center, and then a smattering from the Left benches.

Phil leaned over and whispered to Dexter, "He's won."

Laval continued, growing ever more relaxed and serene, and then concluded, "I am done...I have been premier only since last June. I have not asked for anything. You have given me difficult tasks."

Applause broke out across the right and center of the Chamber as they remembered Laval's many accomplishments. He continued, "With the help of my colleagues, all of my colleagues," there were coarse shouts from some deputies over on the Left, and Laval turned and looked at them and reaffirmed, "yes, all of my colleagues. We have been able to defend the franc, and if the vote the Chamber is about to cast permits it, the budget will be voted on in two days."

The premier wrapped up. "Gentlemen, the entire orientation of French foreign policy hangs in the balance. You are the representatives of the country and its responsible lawmakers. Choose!"

As Laval walked back to the government bench, applause redoubled across the Chamber, shouts of "Bravo" echoed in the room, and deputies stepped forward and shook his hand and clapped him on the back. When calm returned, President Bouisson read the order of the day upon which the government had asked a vote of confidence. It carried 283 to 261, the narrowest margin yet; nevertheless a victory. The government would continue into the new year.

Phil leaned over to Dexter, almost shouting to be heard above the din. "The best fighting speech of his career."

Dexter replied, "Yes, very cool, courageous even."

Dinner Party

December 31, 1935. Paris. Dexter and Marcelle, bundled up in overcoats, scarves, and hats against the winter cold, walked down darkened rue de l'Universitié past the big closed doors leading into Gallimard Publishing and past the big closed doors leading into Sciences Po. They turned on a small residential street and walked up half a block to an apartment building and knocked on a large wooden door. The door groaned open, the hinges creaking in the frozen night, under the hand of an elderly concierge. Dexter whispered a name and the old woman pointed them towards the third floor landing, "*Deuxième étage.*"

Knocking on the apartment door, it quickly opened and Suzanne Bardoux smiled warmly. "*Entrez.*"

Étienne came up and eagerly shook hands. "Come into the drawing room. Turns out our other guests have met you before," and he gave Dexter a devilish smile. Marcelle watched this male bonhomie skeptically but with more than a little interest at what the coded exchange might signal.

Étienne led them into the drawing room and as Marcelle recognized the other couple, Étienne added, "Marcelle, you remember Madeline?"

Marcelle smiled to herself and thought that, of course, this revelation would answer some questions and raise a host of others.

Madeline rose from the couch and held out her hand to Marcelle. "So nice to see you again, Marcelle."

Marcelle stepped forward and kissed her on both cheeks. "Yes, it has been some time, hasn't it?"

Étienne introduced the man. "Dexter, this is Jean-Paul. He lectures at École Normale Supérieure, naming the distinguished school for France's ruling elite. "He's a *normalien* himself, of course," indicating that he was also a graduate of the school.

Dexter shook the hand and looked at Étienne sidewise and said, "Of course."

Jean-Paul smiled and said, "We met at Madame Tabouis's. Lunch, I believe."

186

Dexter said, "Yes, I remember it well." He turned to the woman and said with a mock frown, "Madeline, how could I ever forget?"

Madeline smiled, batting an eyelash, and said, "Your riposte to Geneviève was rapier-like. It was quite gallant of you. Rescuing me like that."

Marcelle watched this with amused expectation; she immediately understood Madeline's interest in Dexter. This was going to be a fun evening, watching him wiggle out of this, and she laughed to herself.

Étienne said, "Please be seated."

Suzanne said, "Let me bring some wine."

Jean-Paul, with great flair, recounted the anecdote about Foreign Minister Barthou at Madame Tabouis's lunch the previous summer.

Étienne said to Suzanne with an arched eyebrow, "Foreign Minister Barthou was always very considerate of you?"

Suzanne laughed. "I was much too young. I believe Madame Tabouis would have been considered 'young' for him. Besides I was in the Quai d'Orsay. I believe his conquests were of the drawing room."

Étienne smiled like a professor grading a prized student's answer. "Very good."

Suzanne turned to Marcelle. "You are lucky to be working for Premier Laval." She turned to the group and expanded, "Everyone knows that when it comes to sexual intrigue, Premier Laval and Madame Lambert walk as saints."

Madeline gasped at this, barely getting her wine down, astonished, but she now saw her opening. "Marcelle, are you continuing saintly?"

Marcelle laughed and looked at Madeline sweetly. "Less so than before."

Madeline let her face turn momentarily crestfallen with disappointment; Marcelle had a hold on Dexter. Watching the realization cross Madeline's mind, Marcelle smiled in small triumph.

Gazing at her friend Marcelle, Suzanne savored the moment, then said, "Let us go into the dining room for dinner."

At the table, Étienne continued the conversation, looking at Marcelle. "Yes, we were wondering over the years just what interests Marcelle might have."

Marcelle looked evenly at him, raised her wine glass, took a sip, and said nothing. Suzanne sort of laughed. Disciplined.

Dexter said, in a rather flip way, "Duty, perhaps?"

Marcelle quickly looked at him, not smiling. There were places not to go, her expression said.

Étienne watched and leaned back, stroked his chin, and looked across the table, saying, "Dexter is onto something." Then he looked very evenly at Marcelle under arched eyebrows and said, "I think Dexter is right."

Marcelle looked at him and made a slight nod; she was not going to dispute the point.

Étienne smiled broadly at everyone at the table and said, "*Alors.*" We continue.

As one course moved to another, Jean-Paul shifted the conversation and asked Dexter, "You speak French like a native?"

Dexter replied, "I went to *lycée* here in Paris. Then the war started, and I had to leave in 1914."

Étienne asked, "Then where did you go?"

"Oh, I went home to Connecticut."

Suzanne asked, "What is Connecticut like?"

Dexter replied, "Oh, it is sort of like the south of England. Grassy and nice."

Jean-Paul continued, "And did you finish your schooling?"

Marcelle spoke up, "Oh, yes, he attended prep school. That is like one of those English public schools."

Madeline's fascination took a leap, "Like an English public school?" She smiled waspishly and looked directly at Dexter, "That is where the boys learn, how shall we say—*to play*—with other boys." She leaned forward towards Dexter and with great intent pronounced, "You must tell us all. Hold back nothing. Details."

Marcelle roared with laughter and looked at Dexter, "Your admirer calls."

Dexter took a sip of wine and began to explain, "It is not like that. In America boys are raised to like women."

Suzanne broke in, "Raised to like?" She frowned and turned to Étienne, "Are French boys raised," and she paused, "*to like* women?"

Étienne, with great aplomb, took on the tone of a teacher, and very pedantically said, "Like? No, they are raised to respect women. It is assumed that they naturally enough like girls, who of course eventually become women."

Everyone laughed.

Madeline took another sip of wine—she was on her third or fourth glass—and said rather dreamily to Dexter, "You must tell me more about the prep school *tête-à-tête*, possibly some afternoon we could meet?"

Dexter quickly replied, "At a café."

Jean-Paul gently said to Madeline, "But Dexter belongs to Marcelle."

Madeline looked at him and said, "I know. But if Marcelle should tire of Dexter…"

Marcelle leaned back and looked at the ceiling, smiling.

Jean-Paul said in a soothing voice, "Madeline, for as long as we have known Marcelle, she has always been constant." And he looked over at Marcelle and said with some certainty, "And so she will continue."

Marcelle nodded in polite agreement.

Madeline moved on, "But Marcel and Suzanne and I are like sisters…and sisters share."

Jean-Paul, looking at the others with an amused smile, said, "No, Madeline, they don't share husbands."

Madeline said, "But Étienne and Dexter are not husbands," and she sat up and brightened, saying, "Yes, they should get married. Then they would be husbands." She then sat up ever more straight, and primly clasped her hands on the table in front of her, and pronounced, "And everyone knows that husbands are the common property of the women of France."

The dinner guests all laughed.

Jean-Paul nodded in an approving way and said, "In this *arrondisement*, perhaps. In France, no." Then he said in a low voice to Madeline, "I think Marcelle makes husbands take a secret vow."

Madeline's eyes went wide. "A secret vow?"

Dexter broke in. "Then there is the threat of death."

Madeline gasped, "Death?"

Marcelle looked heavenward and rolled her eyes.

Suddenly, small explosions were heard outside, bright flashes of light reflected on the windowpanes from fireworks down by the river. The conversation stopped, glasses were raised, and all at the table joined in, "*Bonne année!*" The New Year had arrived.

A half hour later, Marcelle said, "We must be going."

Jean-Paul said, "Would you like to share a cab with us?"

Marcelle said, "Oh, no. Dexter only lives two blocks away."

Suzanne said, quizzically, "You're staying at Dexter's tonight?"

Marcelle said, "Yes," and turned to Dexter, "What was the American word you said I could use?"

189

Dexter whispered.

Marcelle said, "Oh, yes, 'slumming.' We're slumming at the bachelor's apartment tonight. No maid."

She turned to Dexter, "What was the other idiom?"

Dexter whispered again.

Marcelle smiled, "Oh, yes, 'roughing it.' Mark Twain."

Everyone laughed and shook hands around.

Outside, Dexter took Marcelle's hand and they started to walk down the sidewalk in the frozen darkness. Marcelle looked up at Dexter, "Dexter, you know that Madeline means it."

Dexter stopped, turned Marcelle towards him, cupped her face in his gloved hands, and said with great assurance, "They *all* mean it."

She laughed, "I love you."

He kissed her, and they continued walking, savoring their happiness together.

American Embassy

Monday, January 6, 1936. American embassy. Dexter walked up to the open entrance to the ambassador's office and gently rapped on the large oak door with his knuckles and stepped inside.

"Dexter, why come in," said the ambassador as he stood and held out his hand.

"Good afternoon, Mister Ambassador," replied Dexter as he shook the outstretched hand.

"Sit down. Now tell me what you think about the Hoare-Laval affair. Things went to Hell-in-a-handbasket, in what, three weeks?"

"Yes sir." Dexter gathered his thoughts and continued, "The Hoare-Laval proposals were very sound. In fact they still are. Mussolini needs a way out of the Ethiopian fighting."

"You don't think he can win?"

"Oh, he can probably win—eventually, and at great cost. He would much prefer a deal."

"Why won't he get it?"

"In a word, Eden."

"Yes, a young man," the ambassador mused about the thirty-eight-year-old foreign secretary, "wants to show his stuff. Validate the ideal of collective security, use Italy to show that the League of Nations works."

"Something like that."

"And the French?"

"Laval would like to go back to Mussolini and conciliate. Do whatever it takes."

"What's stopping him?"

"The Radical Socialists are melting away. Once the budget is passed and the law outlawing armed political leagues signed, the government will probably fall."

"When?"

"Later in the month."

"Do the Radical Socialists think that Hitler is going to send a bouquet of flowers to a new interim French government?"

"They can't see the reality of Germany. The glare from high principles and the glow of great ideals blinds them."

"Bayonets in the Rhineland, I would think."

"Quite probable, sir."

"What was the big error here, the lesson to be learned?"

"Neither the British nor the French prepared public opinion for the importance of negotiations, that talk could lead to a path away from war."

The ambassador leaned forward towards his desk, clasped his hands in front of him, and looked at Dexter, preparing to give his instructions. "Dexter, I would like you to prepare a report," and he looked mischievously at Dexter, "for your friends back in Washington." Dexter smiled; Dexter's backchannel to Washington was their little unspoken understanding.

"Use Hoare-Laval to discuss how critical issues need to be managed in international forums in the future, how our diplomats should proceed, the frameworks that the policymakers need to work out."

"Yes sir."

"Oh, Dexter, I believe you were at the Paris Peace Conference?"

"Yes, sir. I was almost the youngest lieutenant in the army. I arrived after the Armistice." Dexter paused and looked into the distance, wistfully, and muttered, "Thank God."

The ambassador said softly, "Of course." Pershing had driven the American divisions into the German lines like a sledgehammer that summer and fall of 1918.

Dexter resumed, "I was sent to the Hotel Crillon, the American headquarters. They quickly packed me and some other lieutenants off to another hotel where we worked on maps. Austro-Hungary, Palestine and Syria, Afghanistan, and then the creation of what became Iraq. We joked it meant British Oil in Mesopotamia in Arabic."

The ambassador laughed. "How true."

"The Peace Treaty is the infernal machine that has been grinding up international cooperation ever since—so much discontent, so much injustice, so much grievance. So yes, I and some of the younger men in Washington are interested in developing new approaches to international organizations and better peace treaties."

"Dexter, you and your friends must do better—*next time.*"

"Yes sir."

The two men rose and the ambassador walked him to the door, his arm around the younger man's shoulders.

Tuesday evening, January 21, Quai d'Orsay. In the private living quarters of the premier, Pierre Laval packed his bags for yet another trip to Geneva, what he knew might be his last chance to work for conciliation of the Italo-Ethiopian war at the League of Nations. The telephone rang. Madame Laval picked it up; she turned to her husband, "It's Herriot. He is sure to tell you that he is resigning."

Laval took the phone and arranged a meeting in one of the drawing rooms with the elder statesman of the Radical Socialist party. There, Herriot retracted his promise to accept the extension of the Chamber that had been the basis of forming the coalition cabinet the previous June. The government would fall.

Three days later, having returned from his last meetings at Geneva, Laval wrote a letter of resignation for the cabinet. He went over to the offices of the *administration centrale* to have typed copies made. The *secrétaire général* was not there; he went to Madame Lambert's office, gently knocked on the door and entered. Madame Lambert promptly stood.

"Madame, here is the letter of resignation of the cabinet for President Lebrun. Could you have typed copies prepared?"

Madame Lambert replied, "Right away." She took the handwritten sheet, went outside, and handed it to one of her assistants with whispered instructions. She returned to her office. Premier Laval motioned with his hand for her to take her seat. Then he sat in one of the wing chairs.

"I will wait for the letter."

"We are sorry to see this come to pass."

"Yes, it would have been better to wait for the general election and let the people change the government."

Madame Lambert nodded in silent agreement.

The premier continued, "At Geneva, I am afraid, it will be all sanctions. There is a way forward with conciliation, a path towards peace, but it is a bendy road and takes perseverance to stay on it. But the rewards would be many." He sighed and looked slightly forlorn.

Madame Lambert ventured, "The British have abandoned the dual policy?"

"Yes. For now."

Madame Lambert added sympathetically, "A dual policy is always hard to pursue."

"Yes," the premier sighed, "but at this level, the level where Sir Samuel Hoare and Stanley Baldwin and I work, it is always a dual policy, in almost every sphere. There is never a single clear course for a head of government. Only in the newspapers," and he gave a low laugh.

Madame Lambert smiled and said, "I see."

"Yes, and I wanted you to know and understand that. It will help you in your future work, your service to France."

"Thank you, Monsieur le Premier."

The assistant came in with typed copies. Madame Lambert read them over, checked them against the handwritten draft, looked up and smiled and said to the premier, "Here they are."

"Thank you, Madame," and he took them and walked out of the office.

Before going across the river to the Élysée Palace to hand in the resignation of the cabinet to President Lebrun—the ninety-ninth cabinet resignation of the Third Republic—the premier held a press conference.

Standing before the reporters, he said, "The franc, which I was appointed to defend, is intact. The budget, reduced by one-fifth, has passed."

He concluded, "During the last few months, in the foreign field grave difficulties appeared. Peace was maintained; our obligations to the League were carried out; our friendships and alliances were kept intact; the independence of our foreign policy was assured and reinforced. That is our record." He turned and left heading for the limousine waiting to take him across the river.

Geneviève Tabouis sat and finished her notes. Relieved that Laval, the conservative nemesis, had finally fallen, she wondered whether Laval's many maneuverings on what seemed Mussolini's behalf would sow seeds of distrust among the British. Would Britain be quick to come to France's aid in the event of a future aggression? Surely Britain would come to France's aid if the Rhineland were challenged.

BOOK TWO
The Rhineland Crisis

New Government – Old Troubles

Saturday, February 1, 1936. In the cold winter evening, Dexter held open the door to Café de Flore, the elegant bistro on boulevard Saint-Germain de Prés, and Marcelle walked in. Dexter mumbled a question to the maitre d' and he nodded upstairs. The two of them turned to their left and Dexter followed Marcelle up a tightly turning stairway to the second floor. A quick look and they spotted Suzanne Bardoux and Étienne sitting at a table. They walked over. Étienne stood and shook hands with Marcelle and Dexter. All sat down.

"*Alors*," Étienne began. "A new government. Confirmed by a 361-165 majority, the largest yet in this parliament. Surprisingly, deputies on the Left cheered Sarraut. Blum said nice things." Albert-Pierre Sarrault was the new Radical Socialist premier.

A waiter came up and poured white wine for Dexter and Marcelle. Dexter murmured, "*Merci.*"

Dexter took a sip and said to Étienne, "I would like a rundown on what you think of the new government."

"Sarraut has put together a solidly centrist Radical Socialist government. The majority will carry through to the elections."

Marcelle silently nodded her agreement.

Étienne continued, "The powerful center is augmented by two wings, an almost daring innovation—with strong ministerial representation from both the Right and the Left. Thus, the large majority."

Dexter nodded thoughtfully; he had not really heard these insights before. He asked, "Foreign policy?"

Étienne glanced at Suzanne, then Marcelle. He looked with amused resignation at Dexter, "Here we are, you and me, sitting between two of the most informed people in Paris, and we know nothing. And you ask me?" He laughed.

Dexter smiled. "They won't talk, but you will."

Étienne took on his professorial tone. "As to the new foreign minister, Flandin declared flatly that he had never been in disagreement with Laval on foreign policy. He said he would continue with these policies." Pierre-Étienne Flandin was the new foreign minister, a politician from one of the conservative parties.

Marcelle said, "That is the only practical way forward. With Italy, conciliation or continued war in Ethiopia."

Suzanne nodded in agreement.

Dexter turned and asked Suzanne about the new foreign minister, "What do you think of Flandin?"

Suzanne paused for a second, she was of course not going to really say anything. "Oh, he is everyone's idea of a *grand bourgeoisie.* He is more country gentleman than the English. Dresses like an Englishman. Speaks excellent English."

Dexter quoted a story going around, "Is it true he has his personal laundry done in London?"

Suzanne put her nose up in the air and replied, "He should get along quite nicely with Anthony Eden."

Dexter laughed—Anthony Eden was not one of Suzanne's favorite people.

Étienne looked at Suzanne and Dexter like school children. He put the conversation back on a serious track, "There is talk going around that leaving the Italians simply bogged down in Ethiopia serves British interests quite well. Italy cannot be a threat to the British in the Mediterranean if they are struggling through the sands of East Africa."

Dexter turned serious and nodded in understanding. "We've heard similar talk."

Marcelle interrupted, "Not to break up your reverie, but it is Hitler on the other side of the Rhine that should be the issue."

"Why Marcelle, there has hardly been any mention of Hitler at all in the newspapers," Dexter chided with the look of an innocent on his face.

She looked at him with the exasperated hopelessness of a fed-up mother.

Étienne soothing said, "You are quite right, Marcelle. Flandin raised the issue with Anthony Eden earlier this week, between trumpets and ceremonies," alluding to the many meetings and ceremonies that attended the burial of King George V in London the previous week.

Dexter said, "Yes, the Rhineland seems to be something of a muddle."

Suzanne perked up and looked at him intently.

Dexter, looking at Suzanne, continued, "I read the papers carefully. The French want to be sure in advance just what the British will do. But Flandin mentioned nothing about any military collaboration on plans by the two countries' military staffs."

Then Dexter really stared deeply into Suzanne's eyes and drove home his conclusion. "But certainly nothing like joint military cooperation is contemplated by the British." He read the agreement in Suzanne's expression.

Dexter relaxed and then he looked again at Suzanne with a thoughtful gaze, both Étienne and Marcelle following the pantomime closely. "Neither the French nor British government think remilitarization of the Rhineland is imminent." Disbelief at Dexter's statement was written all over Suzanne's face, Marcelle noticed.

Étienne said, matter-of-factly, "The Chamber is to take up the Franco-Russian pact next week." He looked at Marcelle and said, "Some observers think that could trigger a German march into the Rhineland." Marcelle's expression didn't change; she said nothing.

Dexter looked at her; he understood—both women turned nervous as cats when the word Rhineland was mentioned. They knew.

The waiter came up carrying a big tray covered with dinner dishes, delicious aromas wafting into the air. As the waiter expertly laid the dishes on the table, Étienne asked Marcelle, "By the way, how is the Matignon?"

"Pleasant."

"And the new premier? Is he pleasant, too?"

"The *secrétaire général* and I met with Monsieur Sarraut. As you know, Monsieur le Minister…continues at the Finance Ministry…"

Étienne nodded in understanding, "Money maintains its privilege."

Marcelle smiled and continued, "Monsieur le premier requested that the *secrétaire général* and I continue our close collaboration with the finance ministry."

"Yes, this budget should deliver a resounding victory to the Popular Front in the May elections," Étienne added.

"Is Sarraut simply being sacrificed by the Radicals to ensure the May victory?" asked Dexter.

Étienne smiled knowingly. "He will be taken care of. I would call him a housekeeper, something of a concierge if you will."

Dexter didn't even smile but went straight to his point. "Laval was both premier and foreign minister. In this government, two different men hold the two jobs. Is there a weakness that comes from divided responsibility?"

Suzanne looked at Dexter stunned: she had not quite thought of the new administration from that angle. She replied to Dexter,

"Foreign Minister Flandin is a former premier. Foreign policy is in capable hands," but her voice trailed off in doubt.

Marcelle caught the doubt in Suzanne's voice.

Dexter crisply replied, "But the premier controls the military, the ultimate response to a Rhineland crisis."

Étienne looked towards the ceiling and asked, "Does he?"

Marcelle saw the point: Laval had complete control of the French government at a point of crisis. Not now.

Dexter added, "Hitler has an eye for the tiniest cracks in his adversaries' positions. He is a gifted conspirator."

Étienne said, voice falling, "Not much of a parliamentarian?"

Dexter looked at him. "No."

Étienne looked at Marcelle and with a skeptical gaze repeated, "Pleasant?"

She looked evenly at him and said nothing.

Suzanne looked at Marcelle, then at the two men, a sense of unease in her manner, "My understanding," and she hesitated and looked at Marcelle. Marcelle nodded imperceptibly. Suzanne continued, "Last year, the French ambassador in Berlin delivered a personal message from Premier Laval to Hitler and Neurath that if the Reich were to reoccupy the demilitarized zone without negotiation, France would be compelled to take the most serious measures."

The two men looked at her intently; this diplomatic demarche had never even been rumored in the press.

Suzanne solemnly added, "The message was repeated at the end of December."

Étienne looked at Dexter. Both men understood: Laval had clearly seen the danger of Nazi adventurism in the Rhineland in the wake of the Hoare-Laval imbroglio. He had moved decisively to confront the threat.

Suzanne continued, "So people whisper at the Quai d'Orsay: does the fall of Premier Laval mean the fall of the policy, the evaporation of the credibility of the deterrent?"

Dexter looked at Suzanne and nodded in thoughtful agreement: once again a question for history—would a nation's resolve turn on the determination of a single man? Laval, whatever his faults, was always quick and decisive.

Marcelle looked at Dexter and slowly nodded with a sad look that said now you see what I mean. Dexter signaled his understanding with an eyebrow.

The waiter stood back and spread his hands; the dinner was ready. Étienne smiled at him and said, "*Merci.*" The waiter departed.

"*Alors,*" said Étienne, "where were we? Oh yes, Dexter was going to tell us about being taught how to like women in the American prep school."

The two women laughed.

Thursday, February 6. Secretary-General Alexis Léger walked into the foreign minister's office in the Quai d'Orsay followed by his aide Suzanne Bardoux. The new foreign minister, Pierre-Étienne Flandin, rose to greet them and then waved them into chairs.

Pierre-Etienne Flandin in 1914

The foreign minister opened the conversation, "I am beginning to have just one preoccupation: the Rhineland. The stream of warnings continues."

The secretary-general responded, "We have thoroughly studied the situation. We can outline three scenarios."

The foreign secretary nodded. "Let's have them."

Madame Bardoux handed a memorandum to the foreign minister.

The secretary-general explained, "In the first case, if Germany announces an intent to militarize the zone, we claim a breach of the Versailles Peace Treaty and take the issue to the League of Nations.

The second case is similar. Here Germany denounces the treaty provisions. France then takes the issue to the League of Nations."

The foreign secretary nodded his understanding at these obvious alternatives.

Léger then moved to the real issue, "If the German military enters the Rhineland, that would be a hostile act. France would inform the League."

The foreign minister looked gravely at the secretary-general. "What then?"

Léger answered, "France would be free to take such military measures as appeared necessary. No treaty limits France's ability to take independent action."

Flandin asked, "Any qualifications?"

Léger replied, "France ought not to take military action without an understanding in advance with London."

Flandin sighed. "Yes, the one thing I can never quite get out of the British." He looked at Madame Bardoux and by way of self-justification said, "Neither could Laval."

Flandin then turned businesslike and outlined his plan of action, "I am meeting with the ministers of War, Navy, and Air on Saturday. Afterwards the Council of Ministers meets. I am recommending the demilitarized zone not be subordinated to any outside condition. The French government will assume complete responsibility for any decisions it might make."

Léger nodded in complete understanding.

Flandin concluded, "France must be seen as firm. I will make these resolutions public the following week. We must do this before the Chamber takes up the Franco-Russian Pact."

Léger added, "Very sound. Strong continuity of policy."

The foreign minister stood; the other two followed.

Thursday, February 13. The large touring car crawled along in traffic on rue de L'Universitié on the Left Bank. In the rear seat, snuggled up in a long fur coat, Geneviève Tabouis fretted about being late for lunch with one of her dearest friends, a feminist editor of long standing.

"I can't get through," the chauffeur called from the front seat.

Madame Tabouis peered out and saw the rowdy procession of right-wing marchers, some students, others simply ruffians from the Camelots du Roi. All were followers of the Action Française. The angry crowd was marching up boulevard Saint Germain in a funeral procession for Jacques Bainville, a writer for the group's rabidly anti-Left and anti-Semitic newspaper.

"Isn't that Monsieur Blum's car ahead?" asked the chauffeur.

"Yes," replied Madame Tabouis as she watched the car ahead slowly proceed. She could see that Georges Monnet, a Socialist deputy, was driving. Madame Monnet appeared to be in the rear seat with Blum.

As she watched, a cry went out from one of the marchers, "There's Blum!" A crowd of ruffians descended on the car, surrounding it and rocking it. A short, stocky youth in a leather coat tore off the license plate and used it as a weapon to break the windows. Shattered glass flew inside the car. Madame Monnet moved to protect the 64-year old Socialist leader, placing herself over his lap.

The ruffians tore open the door and dragged the bleeding Blum out of the car. Madame Tabouis could see his head covered with blood, his broad brimmed floppy black hat knocked off in the melee. Blum staggered down the sidewalk.

"Madame," the chauffeur cried out, "They're trying to assassinate Monsieur Blum."

Gaping in astonishment, Madame Tabouis saw some men working on a house open the gate and let Blum into a courtyard and then promptly slam the gate shut on the shouting pursuers.

Madame Tabouis exclaimed, "They're bent on killing him."

The chauffeur exclaimed, "Here come the police."

"Thank God," said Madame Tabouis with a heavy sigh of relief. She peered out into the crowds, her interests piqued: there was a bystander filming the entire episode with a small handheld movie camera. As she watched, a policeman came up to the cameraman and spoke with him. The cameraman nodded agreeably, the policeman handed the man a receipt and took the camera.

After several minutes, an ambulance got through the traffic and a heavily bandaged Blum was led out and put in the rear with several attendants. The ambulance drove off.

Madame Tabouis leaned forward and said to the chauffeur, "The Palais Bourbon is just ahead. Take me to the Chamber of Deputies." She leaned back and thought. The law passed just weeks ago outlawing the armed leagues also carried heavy penalties for incitement to riot. Would the government enforce this sanction against the Action Française? Just the month before, Charles Maurras had called for death to Blum and over a hundred other deputies for supporting sanctions against Italy. As always, Maurras couched his attack with vicious Jew baiting.

Late in the afternoon, Madame Tabouis came out of the Chamber of Deputies and stood on the sidewalk, holding her long fur coat close against the winter cold. Her car slowly came up the street and stopped. A policeman graciously opened the door for her. She had watched this afternoon as Premier Sarraut promised the deputies that not only those who took a direct part in the outrage but those who "have prepared and premeditated these incessant provocations to assassination would be harshly dealt with."

Sarraut was also minister of interior; he could make good on his promises. Madame Tabouis had watched as he walked out of the Chamber to order a police raid on the headquarters of Action Française. Sarraut had seemed uncharacteristically decisive today, thought Madame Tabouis.

As the car pulled away, Madame Tabouis leaned forward, "Across the river. To the Cours la Reine," mentioning the broad boulevard running along the Right Bank of the Seine. "I want to go to Duchesse de Cosse Brissac's reception," speaking of the young daughter of one of France's wealthiest industrialists. Madame Tabouis always enjoyed "Thursdays" with the charming young duchesse and her wide circle of friends—senators, deputies, aristocrats, foreign princesses, and members of France's oldest families, nearly all of whom were intimate friends of Madame Tabouis's distinguished family.

Arriving on the second floor of the grand townhouse, Madame Tabouis was announced. She walked into the salon and took the young duchesse's hand in both of hers and bade a warm hello. Madame Tabouis looked around the large room where clusters of people were talking, the attempted assassination creating an intense buzz among the guests.

Madame Tabouis walked over towards a group in the corner as one gentleman, justifying the assault, pronounced, "André of Compagnie du Nord saw the whole thing. Blum was giving the Communist salute. This was more than the crowd could stand and they fell upon him."

Not bothering to contradict this "eyewitness" account, Madame Tabouis asked, "Does anyone know how Blum is?"

"Who cares?" came a reply. "It's a pity they didn't kill the swine. Then we'd be rid his reforms," a major concern among the moneyed class.

A young princess in the group added, "And be rid of his warmongering." The young ladies by her side complimented her on her spirit, oblivious to the irony of describing one of France's leading pacifists as a warmonger. Madame Tabouis smiled indulgently.

A well-known writer came up and, amid a flutter of expectation from the young society women, spoke, "All our troubles are due to the fact that the Republic was born of hate. Only the monarchy can grasp the whole of France in its embrace." The lovely creatures were delighted at the wisdom. Visions of grand balls held under glittering chandeliers danced in their imaginations. Yes, by all means, the Royalists.

Another young man, known to be "too close" to Berlin in Madame Tabouis's estimation, said, "If France goes ahead with the Franco-Russian pact, it means war! This pact is the greatest obstacle in the way of our coming to an understanding with Hitler and Mussolini. If we encourage it, we are committing a crime." He was doing his work rather well, thought Madame Tabouis, and to a good reception.

Another gentleman, looking sternly at Madame Tabouis—she was known to be on good terms with Russian diplomats in Geneva—said, "Could anything be more absurd than the idea of our going to war to help Russia?"

Madame Tabouis, realizing the small circle was socially distinguished but politically unsophisticated, dryly replied, "If we do not set about resisting Hitler, he will soon have all of Europe." Understanding that illusion was the basis of aristocratic sentiment, Madame Tabouis nodded at the group and took her departure. As she descended the beautiful white marble staircase, she ruminated: only events shatter illusion, never argument. She tapped the marble handrail with her knuckles. Events it will be.

Plotting Begins

Tuesday, February 18, Berlin. Foreign minister Constantin von Neurath entered through the massive doors into the inner sanctum of the Reichs Chancellery—the office of Adolph Hitler. The Führer stood and shook his foreign minister's hand. "What have we from London?"

"Count Otto von Bismarck met with the head of the Central Europe section of the foreign office. He followed up on Ambassador von Hoesch's talks that indicated the British were interested in 'stabilizing conditions' in Europe."

The Führer nodded in understanding. His diplomats were developing excellent information.

"The British official, shall we say, over spoke. The British are drawing up a 'working agreement' to find common ground between Britain and Germany without discussing this with France. They feel once common ground is established, the French can be brought along."

The Führer asked, "What of the British cabinet?"

"The British are going to rearm on the one hand and they want an understanding with Germany on the other."

The Führer thought out loud. "While they rearm, they will want to avoid war."

"Count von Bismarck was told that one of Eden's guiding principles is to cultivate friendly relations with Germany."

The Führer asked, "And the British posture on the Rhineland?"

"We carefully scrutinized Eden's answer to that very question in the House of Commons last week. Very legalistic, lacking in conviction."

Neurath watched Hitler's expression carefully. The Führer had an instinct for such things, thought Neurath. Hitler's decision was forming.

After a moment, Neurath added, "They desperately want an air agreement."

The Führer concluded, "Good. We will know what to offer the British when the time comes."

Neurath changed subjects. "Tomorrow Ambassador von Hassell will be here from Rome. He has news of promising developments."

The Führer stood. "Good." Neurath departed.

Wednesday, February 19. The secretary opened the door to the Führer's study. Ambassador Ulrich von Hassell walked in, followed by Foreign Minister von Neurath. Adolph Hitler stood and shook the ambassador's hand. "I have been following your reports from Rome most closely." He turned and waved the two men into their chairs.

The Führer nodded at Hassell to begin.

"Italy has reoriented its policy with regard to Austria. Mussolini expresses little interest in Austria. Weakness has changed Mussolini. He understands that Germany and Austria are closely linked in language and thought."

Hitler interjected, "German sovereignty must follow German blood."

"Yes, but we want to be careful of a ruse. Mussolini may want to embroil Germany in Austria to distract the League from his difficulties in Ethiopia. It would be a risk to look on Italy as a trustworthy ally."

Hitler nodded in obvious appreciation and added, "Here time is on our side. Our plan will unfold." He leaned back in his chair and looked into the distance and savored his thoughts: the Rhineland, Austria, the Sudentenland Germans, Danzig. All in time.

Hassell and Neurath watched, careful not to disturb Hitler's thoughts.

The Führer quickly returned to the present and asked, "How will Mussolini react to an initiative in the Rhineland?"

Hassell replied, "In my view, based on very close observation of Mussolini and the Italian foreign ministry, the Italians will not react to a German movement into the Rhineland. Nor will they cooperate with Britain and France. That has gone cold."

The Führer nodded and indicated for Hassell to continue.

"As I told the foreign minister," and Hassell nodded at Neurath, "there need be no haste with respect to the Rhineland; there will be plenty of opportunities to abolish the demilitarized zone."

Hitler leaned forward and politely and firmly disagreed. "The longer the demilitarized zone remains intact, the more inviolable it becomes. If Italy succeeds in Ethiopia, British attitudes will stiffen. No, passivity is not a policy. Attack is better."

Hassell was impressed with the resolve and decisiveness of the Führer.

Hitler continued, "When the French parliament ratifies the Franco-Soviet pact, the time will never be better."

Neurath entered the conversation and explained to Hassell, "At the same time as the soldiers march, the Führer will offer a comprehensive peace plan to the European nations: a new demilitarized zone on both sides of the frontier, a pact to defend the independence of Holland and Belgium, a limited air pact to the British, a nonaggression pact with France, a Four-Power pact including Italy covering Western Europe."

Hassell listened to Neurath; not only would German soldiers march, but German foreign policy would be on the march as never before. The ambassador turned and looked at Hitler and thought: yes, it was a masterstroke.

Neurath looked at Hitler for a moment and then said to Hassell, "Ambassador von Hoesch in London has proposed that the Führer announce as part of the comprehensive peace plan that Germany will return to the League of Nations. The British are much interested in Germany returning to Geneva."

Hassell smiled and nodded in agreement.

Hitler said, rather absently, "By all means, a return to the League. For the British."

Saturday, an evening in February, Paris. In the cold of a winter evening, Dexter and Marcelle walked up rue de l'Odéon with other guests towards the bright lights shining out of the windows of Shakespeare and Company, Sylvia Beach's bookshop.

Dexter said, "This is the debut reading of Friends of Shakespeare and Company. All of literary Paris will be here tonight."

"Why now?" asked Marcelle.

"The Depression has been hard on the English-language bookshop. The American and English tourists aren't here. Many of the expatriates have gone home. The big glamour puss, Hemingway, and the other famous American writers are gone. James Joyce's books are being commercially published in America now, not smuggled in under brownpaper wrappers."

"So the Protestants can admire the depravity of the Irish Catholics from the comfort of their reading chairs."

"Exactly," laughed Dexter. "But the real news is that the French literary world is stepping in. They dearly love Sylvia. Somewhat to their surprise, I think, it is giving new life to their own literary establishment which recently has been riven by political conflict."

They moved through the door, removed their overcoats and held them in their arms. Dexter pointed to some empty folding chairs towards the back of the room. Marcelle whispered and pointed, awestruck, "There he is!" Sitting up front was James Joyce, black eyepatch over one eye, the bushy iron gray hair brushed back. "Look," and Marcelle pointed to a picture just above the small fireplace, "he looks just like his photograph. Remarkable. And look, there's Gide," she said, pointing at André Gide sitting behind a small wooden table just in front of the rectangular marble fireplace. Dozens of photographs of famous authors stared down at the dean of French letters from the wall behind him.

Marcelle turned to Dexter. "Oh, thank you for bringing me here tonight."

"My pleasure," he said, and then catching the eye of a person sitting near Joyce, Dexter waved and whispered to Marcelle, "There's André Chamson. And his wife Lucie."

Marcelle smiled and waved at Lucie. "She's so much fun."

Dexter pointed Marcelle towards a chair. "We better sit down."

Sylvia Beach strode to the front of the room and said, "*Messieurs et mesdames, bon soir.*" She continued with a few remarks and then said, "André Gide. He is going to read to us from his unpublished novel *Geneviève.*"

"It better be a dark tale," said Marcelle with mock disdain.

Dexter smiled.

Gide began reading in a clear and precise voice, grabbing the audience's attention and never letting it go. The audience followed with rapt attention minute after minute as Gide read, the austerity and energy of the elocution itself an object of art. Finishing, the audience burst into a long round of applause. People began to stand.

Dexter and Marcelle stood. Adrienne Monnier came up, telling all around her, "His voice moves through a text with the timbre and an authority that awaken a world." She shook Dexter's hand and then reached out and hugged Marcelle.

André Chamson and Lucie came up. Chamson shook Dexter's hand. "Following events?"

"Reading your editorials in *Vendredi,*" referring to the leading Radical Socialist newspaper that Chamson edited.

Chamson laughed. "You would be better informed speaking with your—is she now—fianceé."

"Almost," replied Dexter.

Adrienne looked at Chamson. "Ah, Paris's best political writer is here."

Chamson looked at her. "I think not. I think the best writer is standing there," and he nodded at Marcelle to Adrienne's astonishment. "She is the one that turned the phrase that brought the British foreign secretary to agreement at the Quai d'Orsay last December."

Dexter looked at Marcelle utterly astonished. Chamson looked at him and thought: he didn't know?

Marcelle's eyes flashed and she looked at Chamson searchingly. Adrienne stepped back; she had seen this fire before. What would the charming little volcano do now?

Lucie stepped forward and took Marcelle's forearm in her hands, "Now, now, that came straight from Laval's *chef du cabinet*. At someone's salon after the Laval government fell. It's not a state secret anymore." And then she looked wickedly at Marcelle. "But it is in everyone's diary!"

Marcelle's expression eased; she smiled a thank you at Lucie. She had been afraid that Suzanne Bardoux had leaked the confidence. But it had just been a politician.

Marcelle spoke apologetically to Chamson, "I had been afraid there might have been a betrayal of a confidence by someone on the professional staff. Only a handful were present."

Chamson understood and reassuringly replied, "No. Nothing like that at all." He thought how much he really admired Marcelle's discretion. Not even Dexter knew.

Sylvia Beach came up and clapped Dexter on the back. "I am so glad you could come," and turning to Marcelle, "and I am always so pleased to see you." She turned to Chamson and Lucie. "Oh, I think André's reading went off beautifully!" Everyone nodded in agreement. "It's a flash of light amongst storm clouds gathering." Again, heads nodded.

Monday, February 24. Secretary-General Léger, followed by Madame Bardoux, entered the foreign minister's office. He rose to greet them. All sat down.

Foreign Minister Flandin began, "I want to record my conversations with the Minister of War on the Rhineland." He turned to Madame Bardoux, "If you could take notes?" She nodded and opened her notebook.

"Two weeks ago, Minister of War General Joseph Maurin told me that the military would respond to a German move in a restrained way to avoid provoking a conflict." Flandin gave Léger a bleak look. "The army would man the border fortresses, move troops into the border zone—all on our side of the border—and guard lines of communication and await further political decisions."

Looking at Léger, he continued, "I told General Maurin that he had to prepare the military response now, that we needed a strategy to discourage Germany. I asked General Maurin for a more, shall we say, 'illuminating' response." Flandin smiled weakly.

"Then last week the General Staff let it be known that if Germany reoccupied the Rhineland, possibly Britain could be prevailed upon to enter a new Franco-Belgium-British alliance backed up by military accords. They prefer a new military alliance to keeping the Rhineland demilitarized."

Léger interjected, "That completely ignores our interests in East Europe. If the Germans remilitarize the Rhineland, the countries of East Europe will believe their alliance with France is worthless."

Flandin agreed. "Properly so."

Madame Bardoux hurriedly wrote this down in her notebook.

Flandin said, "Today, I got a further 'clarification.' General Maurin sees German reoccupation of the Rhineland," and the foreign minister took on a bitter tone, "as a chance to obtain new government credits for the military."

Léger took this is in with a touch of resignation. Indeed, the French military had been a separate kingdom ever since the war, unreachable by ordinary diplomacy.

Flandin concluded, "No counterstroke is contemplated. No thought of how to intimidate the Germans has been considered. No plans to force a German withdrawal."

Léger said, "A failure to even plan. Without a plan, the cabinet cannot debate a course of action. No plan, no action."

Flandin slowly nodded. "The Council of Ministers meets next Thursday. The Rhineland is on the top of the agenda."

The foreign minister stood. The other two rose. Flandin said to Madame Bardoux in conclusion, "Please see that I get a copy of your memorandum."

Thursday, February 27, London. Ambassador Leopold von Hoesch entered the ornate office of the British foreign secretary in Whitehall. Anthony Eden came around from behind his large desk and shook the ambassador's hand and bade him take a seat.

"Minister, my government wonders if any further progress relative to your internal discussions has developed?"

"Yes, we want to strengthen our relations with Germany."

"Berlin is concerned about efforts to encircle Germany."

Eden vigorously responded, "We deny any intent to encircle Germany."

Hoesch nodded in understanding. "As we speak, in Paris they are debating ratifying the Franco-Russian Pact, which proposes to do just that."

Coldly, Eden replied, "We have little interest in the Franco-Russian Pact."

Hoesch smiled inwardly; the interview was going swimmingly well. He continued, "What steps might move the process of improving relations between our two countries forward?"

Eden smiled warmly, "Yes, my government is anxious to pursue talks about an air pact."

"The Ethiopian war poses difficulties."

With determination Eden replied, "Difficulties are to be overcome. I will see Foreign Minister Flandin in Geneva next week. When I return to London, I will inform you fully of developments."

Hoesch smiled and said, "That would be most helpful. I will discuss further with Berlin a possible air pact."

Eden stood and came around the desk and escorted Hoesch to the door.

Monday morning, March 2, Berlin. Adolph Hitler sat at the head of the large oaken conference table in the Bendlerstrasse, the army headquarters. Along the walls were large maps of Europe. On the wall behind the chancellor was a large map of western Germany, the Rhineland. A line of bright red yarn snaked down the map from the North Sea to the Swiss border about fifty kilometers east of the Rhine river—the hated demarcation line to the demilitarized zone. Of all the indignities of the Versailles Peace Treaty, this was the provision most hated by the Reichswehr, the German army.

The bright red line glared at the general staff, day after day, year after year. To the west of the red line along the Rhine, the heart of western Germany, were the ancient German cities of Mainz, Frankfurt, Coblenz, Cologne, and Dusseldorf, beautiful cities without their army garrisons. This was where the Germany army traditionally maintained its watch on the Rhine.

To one side of Hitler at the long table sat Field Marshal Werner von Blomberg, minister of war. Down each side of the table sat officers in field gray uniforms, bright red collar insignia with gold embroidery setting the generals off from the colonels.

Hitler began the conference. "I am instructing Field Marshal von Blomberg to issue operational orders for the reoccupation of the Rhineland. The soldiers march Saturday morning, March 7."

The officers had been expecting this. Nevertheless, they were conservative, conscientious about risks. General Werner von Fritsch, head of the army, replied, somewhat hesitantly, "I would like to state again my reservations that negotiation might be the best way forward because our army is not ready to meet the French army in combat."

Hitler nodded in acknowledgement.

General Ludwig Beck, chief of the general staff, warned, "We would be unable to successfully defend against the obvious counterstroke, a French retaliatory attack."

Hitler leaned back in his chair, took on a relaxed air, and looked down the conference table. "Gentlemen, I am sorry to tell you that your information is all wrong. If you believe that the French army would start a campaign, you are much mistaken. Let me tell you that France won't move an inch, and that we can get going without the least fear. In fact, you needn't serve out any ammunition to your troops because they won't need to fire a single shot."

General von Fritsch asked, "But suppose France were to launch an attack?"

Hitler laughed. "If France takes any countermeasures on the evening of our entry into the Rhineland, I will commit suicide and you can give the order to withdraw."

Several of the generals down the table smiled. The Führer knew something they did not; of that they were sure.

Hitler stood. "France will not act." He bade the generals farewell and departed.

212

Monday afternoon, March 2, Geneva. Foreign Secretary Eden entered the well-appointed meeting room off the Hall of the League of Nations and walked up and shook Foreign Minister Pierre Flandin's hand. The two men sat down.

Flandin moved briskly to the point. "We are concerned that moving forward with the oil sanction will cause Italy to abandon the League, drop out of Stresa, forget about the Locarno Treaty, and even worse move towards Germany. Nothing could be more perilous for France." Warnings about the Rhineland had been streaming into the Quai d'Orsay for weeks.

Eden smoothly moved to his points; he was very concerned about diplomatic precedents. "If the League were not to move forward on the oil sanction, then we would be allowing the aggressor state to choose its own sanctions. Protection of principle is involved here."

Flandin paused, inwardly exasperated: protection of the Rhineland was what was important. The British just don't see the real threat—Germany.

Flandin countered, "France would like to propose a further peace appeal before applying the oil sanction. France feels that time is late and the oil sanction will not be effective in improving Ethiopia's situation." Britain seemed to be disregarding the impending Italian victory, thought Flandin.

Eden replied, "Of course, His Majesty's Government will be pleased to give you several days to call for immediate negotiations between Italy and Ethiopia."

Flandin smiled and nodded in agreement. One small victory.

Having given something up, Eden replied, a touch of sternness in his voice, "But it is my duty to tell you that the British cabinet has decided in favor of the oil sanction."

Flandin replied with a noncommittal, "I understand." Eden had played his card. Now it was his turn. He gathered his thoughts and spoke decisively, "It is my duty to tell you that the French cabinet has formulated its Rhineland policy."

Eden looked startled; he had rather thought the Rhineland was not on today's agenda.

Flandin laid out the basis of French policy. "The French government does not intend to take isolated action separate from Locarno and Stresa."

Eden nodded and thought: good, a British veto on any French action was still in place.

Flandin described France's proposed course of action if Germany were to march, "In case of a breech, France will report it immediately to England, Belgium, and Italy with a view towards concerting a common response pursuant to the Covenant of the League of Nations."

Eden listened: good, the pause for consultation was still in place. A pause is almost as good as a veto.

Flandin then moved to his most important point. "But while talking to our partners, France reserves the right to take all necessary measures, including those of a military character, which France deems necessary."

Eden looked sharply at Flandin: military measures? That would put action before talk. Would involve generals and such. Always dangerous. Not very diplomatic.

Flandin then played his trump card. "Before France would feel comfortable moving forward with an oil sanction on Italy, France must be sure of Britain's support on the Rhineland, even if it means just France and Britain responding without the other treaty partners. France must be able to count on Britain's support."

Eden collected his thoughts. "Yes, of course. This is a matter upon which I must consult my cabinet colleagues. I will do so promptly upon my return to London Thursday."

Flandin made a thin smile: Eden would not stop the French from deferring action on the oil sanction this week. He had put something bigger and more immediate on Eden's plate.

Flandin stood up, as did Eden. The two men shook hands and walked towards the door. Flandin had achieved a minor triumph.

Thursday, March 5, London. At Number 10 Downing Street, the British ministers sat around the long cabinet table. Anthony Eden stood up and began his report on the proceedings at Geneva. He explained that he had announced the British cabinet's support for the oil sanction. He described French concern that an oil sanction against Italy would lead Mussolini towards Germany. Italy might stay neutral if Germany militarily reoccupied the Rhineland.

Various cabinet ministers took up a discussion about what the consequences of Italy opting out of Locarno might be. Eden stood listening.

Eden finally spoke, "If Italy opts out, Britain is still obligated to France under Locarno."

The prime minister, Stanley Baldwin, now spoke to the larger issue, "The British people see the Rhineland as a much more doubtful cause than Ethiopia. The Rhineland is inside Germany's borders and part of their country. So stationing one's own army on one's own territory seems normal to the average Englishman."

Eden nodded in agreement and then made an oblique point, "We must rebuild our alliance with France and keep Locarno alive as the most effective deterrent to Hitler in the future."

Down the table, heads nodded: a well-made point.

More discussion followed. Baldwin then summed up, "The reality is that neither France nor Britain is in any position to take effective military action against Germany."

Heads slowly nodded, others sighed.

Eden stepped forward and authoritatively put forth his alternative. "We should take the initiative with Germany. I would ask the cabinet's authority to approach Germany on an air pact. Germany might raise the Rhineland issue and at that point we could draw the French into the talks. Possibly settle the issue." Several of the ministers looked quietly at Eden: yes, clever, go behind France's back in the guise of helping France.

Baldwin called for the cabinet to back Eden's proposal. Yes, by all means take the initiative with the Germans. Discuss an air pact.

Thursday evening, March 5, Place Malesherbes, Paris. At eleven o'clock at night the telephone rang in the study of the apartment of Geneviève Tabouis. She picked up the phone, heard the clicks and static—a long distance call. A voice came on the phone that she immediately recognized; she quickly wrote down on her pad "the diplomat," a code word in her notebooks.

The voice, speaking urgently into the mouthpiece, said, "Madame Tabouis, the reoccupation of the Rhineland will take place in two days. That is definite. You must print this news immediately to avoid catastrophe."

"Yes. This has been expected. But now?"

"The German people, and also circles in the Reichswehr, are praying that France will act. Hitler has had terrible quarrels with his generals. The German troops are badly equipped, and they have orders to retreat at the first sign of resistance on the part of France. Hitler believes that France will not act."

"He may be right," replied Madame Tabouis.

"He has staked everything on that. If France resists, it will mean his personal ruin, and the end of Nazism!"

Madame Tabouis replied, "I will get it in the morning paper." The line went dead.

Friday morning, rue Monsieur. Dexter opened *L'Oeuvre* and quickly found Geneviève Tabouis's column. He read it, giving a low whistle. "Whew, Geneviève has really done it."

Marcelle looked up. "What's she up to? Selling state secrets?"

Dexter looked at her with a smile. "Yes, but they're German state secrets. She's spilling secrets from Berlin. She says the Germans will reoccupy the Rhineland tomorrow."

Marcelle looked astonished. "Tomorrow?" Marcelle felt that if the French government knew this was coming, then somehow she would have noticed unusual activity yesterday at the Matignon—hurried meetings, comings and goings, a bustle of activity." She looked at Dexter. "How would she know?"

"Her specialty is the deepest secrets in both Paris—as you've seen—and in Berlin. No one else has sources so deep in the German ministries."

Marcelle grabbed the paper and read through the story and said, "She calls her source a diplomat stationed in Berlin. How would a diplomat know what's going on inside the top of the Third Reich."

"Most of us suspect her real sources are Germans high up in the ministries, not foreign diplomats. She doesn't want to tip her sources."

Marcelle said, "I see. What do you think, if I may ask?"

Dexter replied, "I think the Germans will reoccupy the Rhineland, if not tomorrow, then soon. As to the rest, I think the Nazis have had an absolute grip on the German state ever since the Night of the Long Knives in 1934. It's too late for one setback to topple the regime."

"And France?"

Dexter looked evenly at Marcelle, "I don't think the French army will advance across the border."

Marcelle looked very evenly at Dexter. "I see." She pondered Dexter's statement for a moment. "That was the point of Colonel de Gaulle's talk last summer?"

Dexter nodded.

Friday, March 6, Whitehall, London. Anthony Eden looked down at the note on his desk: Chancellor Hitler was going to address the Reichstag tomorrow at noon. Not really surprising. The Foreign Affairs Commission of the French Senate had voted for ratification of the Franco-Russian pact on Wednesday. Some sort of response from the German government was expected, possibly a denunciation of the demilitarized zone in the Rhineland.

There was a knock on the door and it began to open. Eden stood up. An aide ushered Ambassador von Hoesch into the darkly paneled office. The foreign secretary walked around his desk and shook the ambassador's hand and motioned him towards a chair.

Returning to his chair, Eden briskly began, "With regard to your inquiry whether we have concrete proposals, I can now say that His Majesty's Government believes it opportune to open serious discussion on an air pact. We would hope you would bring that up with the chancellor."

"Chancellor Hitler has no objection in principle to an air pact."

"Good. I suggest we proceed through diplomatic channels to agree on principles."

Hoesch nodded in understanding. Eden continued, "Britain has no intent to encircle Germany. Britain's wish is for relations based on confidence with Germany. To that end, Germany's return to the League would be most welcome."

Hoesch smiled inwardly; Hitler's plan involved just such an announcement—at his suggestion. Hoesch let Eden continue, then Hoesch said, "A messenger from Berlin is on his way. I will have an important communication to deliver tomorrow morning. Could we meet at 10 o'clock?"

"By all means," replied Eden. Possibly events were developing faster than previously thought. He stood up signaling an end to the interview.

Soldiers March

Saturday morning, March 7, London. Ambassador von Hoesch was escorted into the foreign secretary's office at ten o'clock in the morning. Anthony Eden rose and motioned the ambassador to a chair. Eden leaned back in his chair and looked noncommittally at the ambassador.

Hoesch cleared his throat and said, "I have a communication from Berlin. I am afraid that the first part will not be to your liking." He looked at Eden. Eden nodded his head to continue. "But the later portions contain an offer of greater importance than has been made at any time in recent history." Eden looked mildly interested.

Hoesch began reading, "France has replied to the repeated friendly offers and peaceful assurances made by Germany by infringing the Rhine Pact through a military alliance with the Soviet Union exclusively directed against Germany."

Eden listened thoughtfully. Yes, this was all quite predictable since the French Chamber of Deputies ratified the Franco-Russian pact.

Eden kept listening as the ambassador read, "The German government has today restored its full and unrestricted sovereignty in the demilitarized zone of the Rhineland." Eden presumed that German troops were marching into the Rhineland as the ambassador was reading. That was the normal way with dictatorships, he thought.

Hoesch continued, "These measures are purely defensive in character." Of course, thought Eden. The ambassador continued reading, "Now that Germany's equality of rights has been finally attained, the chief reason for Germany's withdrawal from the League of Nations has been removed. Therefore, Germany is ready to reenter the League of Nations."

Eden thought: yes, there's the bait. It will play well with the European publics. Eden now addressed the ambassador, "This is a unilateral repudiation of the Locarno Treaty."

The ambassador responded, "The Franco-Russian pact was the violation of the Locarno."

"Italy, France, and Belgium are unlikely to see it that way."

"Yes, we have a difference."

Paul A. Myers

Eden agreed and continued, "His Majesty's Government will give careful consideration to the offers in the latter part of your memorandum since Germany's attitude towards the League is most important."

Hoesch, on an upbeat note, said, "Chancellor Hitler wants to respond to the views frequently expressed by Prime Minister Baldwin and yourself in your speeches. Germany is willing to share in a policy of collective security through the League. And of course, we are ready to open talks on an air pact."

Eden sighed to himself and thought that the Germans' gambit had been well thought out. Neurath was competent. Eden stood up, "Thank you Mister Ambassador. Could you hold yourself in readiness for further discussion over the next few days."

The ambassador replied in a subdued and polite manner, "Of course." Inside his head, the voice of analysis told him the British would not move. Another voice shouted at him: you have a triumph! The recommendations you made to the Chancellor Hitler have been completely born out by events.

As the ambassador turned to leave, he said casually, "Oh yes, a few small detachments of the German army are moving into the zone today."

Eden smiled weakly. Of course.

Saturday morning, March 7, rue Monsieur. The telephone rang. Marcelle stood up and walked into the foyer and picked up both the earpiece and mouthpiece. "Madame Lambert here." She listened, then replied, "Yes, I will be ready." She put the phone down and walked into the dining room and said to Dexter, "I have to leave. Work."

"I will escort you."

"That won't be necessary. They are sending a car."

He nodded and smiled inwardly. She had a positive gift for saying little.

Several minutes later, the two of them stood on the sidewalk of rue Monsieur in the cold wintry morning. They watched silently as the government limousine came down the street and stopped. A gendarme got out and came around and opened the door. "Madame Lambert." She got in.

As the limousine pulled away, the gendarme turned around from the front seat and said, "There is an attaché case there. I was told to

219

give it to you. You are to take it with you." Marcelle did not ask where they were going.

She looked out the window of the limousine and pondered her thoughts. Yes, most likely Madame Tabouis was right. She watched as they crossed Pont Alexandre III, the cold gray waters of the Seine flowing desultorily down the stone-lined channel.

Arriving in front of the ministry of the interior, the limousine stopped, the gendarme got out and opened the door, and escorted Marcelle up to the sentry box outside the imposing edifice. A guard escorted her into the building. An aide came up and met her, "The fifth floor. You have the attaché case?" He nodded as he saw it.

On the fifth floor the aide escorted her down to a guarded door. Premier Sarraut also held the portfolio of minister of the interior. It was this office in which he customarily worked. Madame Lambert was familiar with it as she frequently brought papers to and from the Matignon during the past several weeks.

As Madame Lambert entered the office, Premier Sarraut stood, as did Foreign Minister Flandin. The premier said, "Good morning, Madame Lambert."

She replied, "Good morning, *messieurs*." She noticed both men seemed unusually resolved, determined looks on their faces."

The premier said, "We would like you to sit over there," and he pointed to a small desk in the corner, "and take notes of the meeting about to take place."

Madame Lambert replied, "Yes, Monsieur le Premier," and she turned and faced Flandin, "Monsieur le Minister."

Sarraut explained to her, "The Germans are reported to have moved into the Rhineland this morning. Minister of Defense General Maurin and Chief of the General Staff General Gamelin will be here shortly with several other ministers to discuss how best to respond."

"Yes, Monsieur le Premier." She understood what was wanted and walked over and sat down.

Presently the door opened and several men came in, one in the uniform of a French general. She stood up. Several of the men nodded a greeting to her. Hands were shaken all around and then the men sat down at a small conference table in the middle of the room. Madame Lambert sat.

Premier Sarraut moved to set a decisive tone. "What does the army propose to do?"

General Gamelin, taking on an almost professorial air, said, "The army requests your permission to take the first measures of precaution."

Sarraut's expression opened into astonishment.

General Gamelin continued, "We will recall soldiers on leave and start moving up reinforcements by road to the border defenses. We will prepare to move more by rail," and the general paused and added parenthetically, "if needed."

Sarraut was floored. He looked at the two generals. "That's all!"

The generals sat silent.

Sarraut asked, "I asked you to study how to make a series of small but rapid advances into German territory for just such a case as we face this morning. You have not mentioned one thing about any offensive operation."

One of the other ministers interjected, "I would like to see you in Mainz as soon as possible," mentioning the German city on the Rhine that was the French headquarters in the 1920s.

General Gamelin now came into his own. "Ah, that is another affair. I would like nothing better. But you must give me the means."

Sarraut asked incredulously, "Means?"

"Yes, a general mobilization. The *couverture*, a mobilization of a million men in eight days."

The civilian ministers all looked at one another—aghast. A general mobilization seven weeks before a general election?

The premier took a different tack. "If we act alone against Germany, without allies, what will be the outlook?"

General Gamelin began an explanation, concluding, "In a long war the superiority of the Germans in numbers and industrial capacity would play a strong part."

The civilian ministers looked at one another: a long war that the Germans might well win. For some time, they had all known and feared this truth, a truth that had grown huge this Saturday morning.

Premier Sarraut stood and adjourned the meeting without taking any decisions. Foreign Minister Flandin approached him and said, "I must return to the Quai d'Orsay and confer with the foreign ambassadors." He turned on his heel and left. The two generals and the other minister followed.

Premier Sarraut walked over to Madame Lambert, "Stay seated. Complete your work and prepare one copy, and one copy only, and deliver it to me personally." He looked out through the windows into the gray winter sky and then turned to her and said, "Do not repeat what you saw here today." The disappointment and scorn in his voice was unmistakable.

She nodded in deep understanding. "Yes, Monsieur le Premier."

Late Saturday morning, March 7, London. The door to the foreign secretary's office opened and Ambassador Charles Corbin of France entered. Anthony Eden was standing in front of his desk and he stepped forward and warmly shook the ambassador's hand, "My dear Ambassador Corbin, we have much to talk about. The German action this morning is most deplorable." He waved the ambassador over to a chair and walked around and took his seat behind the desk.

The French ambassador began, "The Rhineland operation is possibly a flagrant violation of Locarno."

Eden composed himself. "We are proposing a meeting of the Locarno powers in Paris on Tuesday with that in mind."

The Germans would be dug in by Tuesday. The ambassador pressed forward, searching for some indication of Britain's policy, "Surely you have some views on the German action?"

Eden crisply replied, "I am consulting with the cabinet Monday morning. After which I shall be able to talk freely and frankly with France." A clear message: no action was to be taken over the weekend.

The ambassador sank back in his chair. "I see."

What the French government had feared: Britain had no policy in place. Except to consult.

Eden replied, "I am sure you have seen the German memorandum." The ambassador nodded yes. Eden earnestly continued, "Even a hasty reading indicates several important points for consultation between our governments. First, a new nonaggression pact among France, Belgium, Germany, all guaranteed by Britain and Italy."

Ambassador Corbin looked at Eden without comment. The British were going for the bait.

Undaunted by the ambassador's expression, Eden continued, "And there's Germany's proposed return to the League of Nations. We should not leave that unconsidered."

The Germans knew which bait to use, thought Ambassador Corbin. He could see that Eden was interested in the negotiation of new arrangements, not enforcement of existing treaties. Eden was simply not looking at the menace posed by the remilitarization of the Rhineland.

Eden summed up, "I am confident that the French government will not do anything to render the situation more difficult. A calm and steady examination of the situation is required."

The ambassador nodded that he had heard. As the French had feared, consultation had become the mechanism for nonaction.

Eden looked at the ambassador sympathetically and said, "We must not close our eyes to the significant offer the Germans have laid on the table. Public opinion in both our countries will demand careful consideration. The man in the street will find the proposal irresistibly attractive."

Ambassador Corbin sighed inwardly: yes, neither the British nor French publics want to risk a war with Germany. But there was a larger perspective. He sat back and reflected: last week in Geneva, Eden was "in high principle" to immediately apply the oil sanction against Italy, not to let the Italian dictator chose his sanction. At the weekend, the German dictator can launch his aggression without fear of consequence. So, principle only applies in the easy situations. Again, the ambassador sighed inwardly: as always. Oh well, now Eden will have to retreat on sanctions for Italy; a beautiful principle made irrelevant by events.

Late Saturday morning, March 7, east of Cologne, Germany. The colonel stood tall and erect as he watched his gray-uniformed soldiers dismount from the trucks while others disembarked from railroad cars that had just pulled into the siding beside the large field. The regiment had crossed the border at daybreak, some traveling by truck, most by train. The colonel watched the operation unfold flawlessly; the German army was the most skilled railway army in the world.

As the colonel looked on, the sergeants and sergeants major formed the men into platoons, companies, and battalions. Officers moved among the men, checking final dispositions. As each company was called to attention, a careful inspection by sergeants major and officers was undertaken. Ammunition pouches checked, rifle actions opened at present arms and inspected.

Presently, the three battalions of the regiment were formed up. The battalion commanders came forward and reported. The regimental sergeant major came forward and reported to the colonel, "Herr colonel, ammunition pouches are empty, rifles clear. There is not one round of ammunition in the regiment."

The colonel replied, "Good." The sergeant major saluted and turned on his heel.

The three battalion commanders stood before the colonel. The colonel spoke, "We must have absolute route discipline on the march into Cologne. The eyes of Germany, the eyes of the world, will be upon us. The men must not give way to provocation."

The battalion commanders clicked heels and replied as one, "Yes, Herr colonel."

The regimental commander continued, "The first battalion will continue across the river bridge, meet transportation on the other side, and deploy along the western border. The other two battalions will remain in Cologne." The colonel paused, then said to the expectant battalion commanders, "The City fathers undoubtedly want to welcome the soldiers. Give the men leave." The colonel smiled inwardly: undoubtedly the girls of the city in their enthusiasm would also like to express their gratitude. He savored the thought; in fact there was an invitation in his map case from a baroness—a sweet lilac scent, he recalled.

Returning to the present, the colonel turned to a fourth officer, the drum major for the regimental band. "The band will lead the way." The officer clicked his heels and saluted.

The colonel spoke to the battalion commanders, "In Cologne, General von Kluge will take the salute."

As the colonel took one last sweeping look at the assembled regiment, a groom brought over a beautiful chestnut horse. "I will ride at the head of the regiment. Dismissed." The colonel mounted his horse in one graceful arc.

The colonel looked forward, over the heads of the regimental band marching in front of him, over the tops of the flags of the color guard, towards the reviewing stand half a kilometer ahead on one side of Cathedral Square, the huge central square of the city of Cologne situated in front of the majestic twin spires of the cathedral. From the top of the spires came the magnificent peeling of huge bells, deeply pitched and sonorous. The colonel stood in his stirrups and turned around and looked back over his regiment. The battalion commanders were mounted on their horses on one side of the column, the company commanders mounted on the other side of the marching soldiers. The colonel stood taller in his stirrups, squinted. All was in order. He scowled at the battalion commanders. He turned around and sat easy on his horse.

As he watched, the color guard entered the square and the municipal band of Cologne, drawn up on one side of the plaza, thundered out the German national anthem, *Deutschland Uber Alles*. At that moment, the regimental band caught the beat in unison and thundered out its response. The crowds went into a frenzy of cheering.

The colonel rose in his stirrups and turned and looked back over the regiment. Young women were bursting through the police lines and festooning the soldiers with flowers, others pouring champagne over their heads. The soldiers were at least keeping in step, all that could be expected, the colonel thought. The colonel made a faint nod to the battalion commanders and turned around and sat on his horse.

As the color guard passed the reviewing stand, the flags dipped, heads snapped right, General von Kluge saluted. The color guard continued, the regimental band, brass blaring, passed the reviewing stand.

The colonel's horse now came abreast the reviewing stand; the colonel sat ramrod straight in his saddle, half turned and faced the reviewing stand and saluted General von Kluge. The general returned the salute. The colonel dropped his salute, turned back and sat back on his saddle and looked resolutely forward. On all sides of the square thousands of onlookers clapped and cheered. The colonel continued looking directly ahead. He listened carefully; he could hear the crescendo of clapping and cheering as each battalion commander passed the reviewing stand and saluted.

As the colonel rode out the far side of the square, watching the adoring crowds, he thought what a fitting tribute this day was, a celebration of the beginning of the great expansion of the German army under the inspired leadership of the Führer: company commanders would become battalion commanders, battalion commanders would advance to regiments, and regimental commanders would command divisions. Yes, a great day for Germany, he thought.

The colonel looked to his left; the massive steel girders of the bridge over the Rhine glistened in the sunshine. The first battalion would soon be marching across. Trains were waiting to carry the battalion west to the border with France. Would the French come across the border?

Sunday morning, March 8, rue Monsieur. Marie brought in a large pot of coffee made American style. She poured a full cup for Dexter, who looked up from the newspaper and said, "Thank you." Marcelle stayed head down in her newspaper completely absorbed.

Dexter spoke across the table, "Not to interrupt. Here, the French general elections are set for April 26 and May 3."

Marcelle looked up, tapping the headline about the German march into the Rhineland, "Somehow I think the two events are connected."

"Most certainly," replied Dexter. "However, the Paris papers say that Chancellor Hitler's denunciation of the Locarno Treaty yesterday in Berlin was received by the French public calmly, no sign of panic."

Dexter remembered yesterday afternoon. He was having lunch at Les Deux Magots when the newsboys started running up and down the sidewalk with the early editions shouting, "German troops are entering the Rhineland." The papers were read with excitement, Dexter recalled. He had listened to the comments by the passersby, which could be summed up: "Let us hope, at least, that this does not mean war."

Marcelle looked up and sighed. "War is the one thought the French public does not want to hear."

Dexter nodded in understanding. "Nor the British."

Marcelle, summarizing from her paper, said, "The chairman of the Chamber's Foreign Affairs Commission thinks that the practical consequence will be to strengthen Franco-British solidarity."

Dexter said absently, "Maybe." He read from his paper, "Here, the paper *Petit Parisien* says world opinion ought to be made to understand what the demilitarized Rhineland zone means for France. It is a question on which France cannot waver. If the Reich is allowed to construct a concrete wall along her frontier which could halt a French attack, it would mean we are leaving Germany free to direct aggression to the East without any danger of interference from France."

Marcelle looked at Dexter, "That is precisely the point that Suzanne makes. The eastern alliances with Czechoslovakia and Poland lose all practical value."

"But you get a stronger relationship with Great Britain," ventured Dexter in a statement that ended softly as a question.

Marcelle looked at him, her expression changing to disdain. He flashed his eyebrows.

Turning back to her paper, she said, "Here is Pertinax, Geneviève's friend, saying we hope that Baldwin and the British cabinet will understand that the interests of France and Britain and the interests of Europe demand action. Moreover, we hope they will remember that Britain to a great extent carries the moral responsibility for the Locarno Treaty. And let us hope that the Locarno powers meet next Monday on the request of the French foreign minister and that there will be no divergence of views between the French and the British."

Dexter said, "There you have it: a Locarno meeting on Monday followed by France presenting a formal complaint to the League of Nations on Tuesday."

Marcelle gently said, "Yes, Pertinax speaks loftily of moral responsibilities. He has very noble aspirations. Makes Geneviève look pragmatic."

Dexter gave a skeptical shrug.

Marcelle continued, "Hitler sized up public opinion in France and Great Britain pretty well. Allied diplomats talk; German soldiers march."

Dexter took a breath and nodded. Then he added, "Yes, Hitler is offering twenty-five year nonaggression pacts all around. Like candy."

Marcelle lobbed the conversation back across the table. "Oh yes, here the paper says that Hitler offers to return to the League of Nations. Suzanne said to expect that. It is for the British, she said. What do you think?"

Dexter raised his eyebrows. "Let the German wolf in among the sheep?"

Marcelle smiled.

Dexter opened another paper. "Here's the news from Britain. Anthony Eden told the French ambassador yesterday that the French government should study the German offer and avoid hasty action. Then he drove to Chequers, the prime minister's country estate, and met with Stanley Baldwin. Baldwin declined to call a special cabinet meeting Sunday in favor of staying with Monday's cabinet meeting. He wants to avoid any appearance of panic."

Marcelle asked, "Doesn't sound like the Rhine is Great Britain's border anymore, does it? What does it all mean?"

Dexter summed it up for her, "No support for any military action by the French."

Marcelle looked at him very evenly; she did not nod her head. She remained still. She knows something, thought Dexter. Better not ask.

Dexter took a long sip of coffee and moved the conversation in a new direction, his home turf, the diplomatic chessboard. "There is one more thing. Hitler's timing relative to Mussolini is perfect. He has in a singular fashion paved the way forward for the Italians to finish their conquest of Ethiopia without further interference."

Marcelle nodded at the insight. She looked at Dexter: yes, the diplomat sees the future moves on the chessboard. He is good at that. She took pride in her observation about him. She smiled and took a sip of her coffee, her mind turning over the morning's developments.

Dexter silently watched Marcelle compose and organize her thoughts. Yes, a very well ordered mind was her big strength. And discretion.

Diplomats Gather

Monday morning, March 9, London. The cabinet ministers sat around the long table, many of them pointing at the morning's editorial in *The Times* entitled "A Chance to Rebuild." Fingers traced out the main points, concerned voices whispered worried comments. The editorial agreed that there had been a breech of a treaty that "the more sensationally minded" could call an act of aggression.

Tapping the page, one minister whispered to another, "I don't think we have any sensationally minded people at the table this morning."

The other minister looked down the table skeptically at the empty chair which would soon be occupied by Foreign Secretary Anthony Eden. "It's one thing to stand on principle with the Italians and go on about sanctions," and he cleared his throat, "but it is altogether something different with the Germans."

"Quite so."

"Yes, the German troops are simply reoccupying their own territory. The *Times* points out that it is hardly an invasion that carries 'fire and sword' into a neighbor's territory."

"Quite so."

"And then there are the reactions in the City," referring to the large number of financial transactions with Germany undertaken by British financiers.

"Quite so."

There was a rustle of movement and Prime Minister Stanley Baldwin and Anthony Eden entered the room. Eden walked over and took his seat. Baldwin remained standing and turned to his colleagues and said, "Before the foreign secretary addresses the present crisis, I want to say that I do not think there is any support among the British public for military action."

A loud murmur of agreement arose from the table.

Baldwin concluded, "Britain is not in a state to go to war."

Sounds of agreement rose from the table, "Quite right, prime minister."

The prime minister concluded, "We need time for our rearmament program to proceed."

With heads nodding in agreement, Baldwin sat down. Eden stood and addressed his colleagues, "Foreign Minister Flandin has assured me that France will take no isolated action."

The ministers took in this statement with a collective sense of relief. Keep the crisis diplomatic.

"The French government wants the Locarno powers to meet in Paris Tuesday and then bring the matter before the League of Nations on Thursday."

The ministers' heads all nodded in understanding agreement. Time was being bought. Good.

Eden continued, "Condemnation of Germany's action by the League is inevitable."

The ministers all understood the obviousness of this step. An unfortunate necessity. But what would follow?

Eden answered the unspoken question, "The following steps would be economic and financial sanctions."

Murmurings of disagreement at the word 'sanctions' arose from the table. Eden let the dissents percolate among the ministers.

Eden soothingly said, "Follow-on actions will be a subject for further discussion."

The ministers understood. Good. Give the French a taste of their own tardiness on the sanctions issue. Delay.

Eden shifted his stance and moved to the proactive. "The Germans have made an interesting set of proposals. It would be in our interest to conclude as far-reaching and enduring a settlement as we can while Herr Hitler is in the mood to do so. In particular, Germany's return to the League is the most important; it should be explored."

The ministers listened attentively.

Eden then spoke to the immediate difficulty, "Yesterday, both French Foreign Minister Flandin and Premier Sarraut declared that France would not negotiate with Germany until there were deeds, not words, of Germany's respect for international law."

Yes, the ministers had all read the declarations. Principle again. Britain wants to talk about new arrangements; France wants to enforce old treaties.

On an upbeat note, Eden continued, "In our coming discussions with the French, we will stress the importance of testing the German's good faith."

The ministers understood. Of course, there would be a lot to talk about, a lot of meetings. Always a good thing in diplomacy.

Eden then picked up a piece of paper, a draft of his speech to be delivered to the House of Commons later that day. "Let me read from today's speech," he said, "The transition from a bad past to a better future…"

The ministers listened. Eden continued, "If peace is to be secured there is a manifest duty to rebuild. It is in that spirit that we must approach the new proposals of the German chancellor. His Majesty's Government will examine them clear-sightedly and objectively…"

One minister approvingly tapped the headline of the *Times'* editorial "A Chance to Rebuild" and smiled at his colleague. The colleague returned the smile. Prolonged negotiations. The way forward.

Eden concluded, "No opportunity must be missed which offers any hope of amelioration." More talk. Good.

Most of the ministers nodded in determined agreement. Show the damn French. Britain wants a lasting peace in Europe.

At the far end, one minister, skepticism washing across his face, looked with his eyes across the table and into the eyes of a sympathetic colleague. Both ministers thought Berlin would see the speech for the triumph that it was.

The prime minister adjourned the meeting.

Saturday, March 14, Savoy Hotel, London. In Geneviève Tabouis's hotel room diplomats and newspapermen stood shoulder-to-shoulder and face-to-face furiously discussing the week's events in London—the League of Nations Council had been meeting in London all week and additional sessions had been rolled over to the following week. Standing amidst a gaggle of European diplomats Geneviève pounded out her points with Gallic intensity, "Even the British Laborites are anti-French. Pierre Laval has done his work well by wooing Il Duce. The British feel France betrayed Ethiopia. Why stand up for us now against the Germans in the Rhineland, they ask? France is alone."

Heads bobbed in agreement and in three different languages the men surrounding Geneviève shouted "yes."

A Russian diplomat pushed in. "But Geneviève, our foreign minister, Comrade Litvinov, has supported the French."

Geneviève retorted, "Yes, and so have all the small countries. But have you seen all the cars on the streets of London festooned with placards saying 'Germany wants Peace. Let France come to terms. Let us have Peace!"

Heads nodded in agreement. British public opinion was everywhere for peace. London bristled with anti-French feeling.

Geneviève turned to the men and said, "Excuse me for just a moment. I have to call my story into Paris." She stepped away and pushed her way into a small bedroom off the drawing room. She closed the door, went over and pulled her notebook out of her handbag, and sat down on the bed and picked up the telephone.

Reaching the night editor, she spoke into the mouthpiece, "The moment we arrived in London we realized that the first mistake made by the French was to have come at all...Treaties, pacts, solemn oaths—all these things seem to matter little to the British...our experts can scarcely believe that the men who are confronting them now are the same Englishmen who, a few days ago, were demanding, in the name of international law, the application of sanctions against Italy!"

She caught her breath and continued, indignation coursing through her dispatch, "If it might be necessary to overlook the violation of treaties committed by the Reich, Mr. Baldwin seems perfectly ready to do so...I have a strong feeling...it is his present purpose to present the Council of the League with a German peace offer which will counterbalance the violation of the Locarno treaty by the Rhineland remilitarization." She finished up, a curt goodbye registering her disgust, and set the phone down.

Geneviève opened the bedroom door and pushed her way back towards the small circle of diplomats with whom she had been talking, and without missing a beat, launched right back in. "Flandin," speaking of the French foreign minister, "has played his cards very badly."

Heads nodded in eager anticipation, eyes went wide, they all knew that Geneviève was the niece of two of France's greatest ambassadors. She was a hard grader.

Geneviève continued, "Flandin has not represented the true interests of his country. He prefers to be the spokesman of the appeasers and the financiers. They don't appreciate the German threat."

A voice with an accent from the south and east of Europe asked, "What do you think will happen, Madame Tabouis?"

"Flandin will settle for a condemnation of Germany by the League. And some sort of assurance that the British will come to France's aid if Germany attacks across the border. Like Eden said last week."

"Is there a catch?" asked a diplomat from one of the Low Countries.

Geneviève said, "Eden will assure the cabinet that the assurance does not guarantee any new obligation."

"Yes, with the English, an assurance is never a guarantee," sighed the diplomat in a Flemish accent.

"So we have just seen," observed Geneviève.

All the heads nodded in agreement; Geneviève always said the truth with the sting of wasp.

Sunday, March 15, Luxembourg Gardens, Paris. In the late afternoon, Dexter and Marcelle strolled down the shaded walkway, the last rays of sunlight filtering through the tree limbs, the gravel crunching under their shoes.

Marcelle said, "Foreign Minister Flandin has been in London all week."

Dexter ruminated, "Yes, and British public opinion has mounted to a fever-pitch in favor of peace. No military action."

"So?"

Dexter replied, "Tomorrow the League Council meets in London. A ritual condemnation."

"Ritual?"

"Yes, ritual."

"Like the plebiscite Hitler has called for in Germany at the end of the month?"

"No. The League condemnation will ring hollow. The Germany election will be the roar of the new Germany."

"Let's go home and have a cup of tea."

"Calvados?"

She laughed. "The roar of the old Dexter!"

Standing at the sideboard in the dining room, Dexter poured some Calvados into a rounded glass snifter, the light from the small chandelier sparkling on the sides of the glass. Marcelle walked in holding a mug of hot tea. In a downcast voice she said softly, "May be it would be better to be sent back to the ministry of labor?"

"Nonsense. The Popular Front is going to win a landslide. Chamson is right. The new government will want your expertise. They want to move fast."

Her face brightened. "You think so?"

"Of course," he said confidently. Then he took on a reflective tone, "I think for me, for us, it would be better if you went back to the ministry of labor. We could quietly get married."

She looked at him warmly. "Married?" she said distantly. "That would be nice."

"You are saying yes?"

"Someday," she said. "You know that."

"The way things are going with Germany, I would be in a position to protect you."

"Protect me?"

"Yes, if the Germans come—and they will come the next time—I could be assured of getting you out."

"Out?"

"To somewhere safe."

She set her tea down and turned and faced him directly, "Dexter, I think the French people have a right to expect senior officials of the civil service to stay. The politicians go this way and that with the political winds; that is their function. But the permanent staff serves the people of France; the sinew and the continuity of the state. Forty million French people can't all go to America."

Dexter said, "Very brave sentiment. But you should leave the heroics to the French generals."

Marcelle's face instantly clouded. She shifted and put one well-poised foot in front of the other, she turned slightly and stood in a position of grim determination, her face turned cold, and she said sharply, "I am not a French general," the contempt and disdain rising in her voice.

Surprised, Dexter looked at her with blank astonishment. He had simply meant to comfort her. He said softly, "No, of course you're not." It dawned on him. He now knew—she had been in the room. She had known all week.

She watched him. She saw a flash of understanding cross his face. She softened her expression and said, "I still expect to be your wife in La Paz. After my service to France."

Dexter smiled, "I know."

She smiled at him gently and then with a certain firmness asked, "Did you really expect any other answer from me?"

He shook his head slowly—no.

He set his glass down and walked over to her and, to her complete surprise, in one quick movement swept one arm under her

234

legs and the other behind her back and lifted her up in front of him. Her legs kicked in a flutter of delight and she shrieked in amazement, "Dexter, what are you doing?"

He held her and looked down into her eyes, "I'm taking my bride to the bedroom." He bent his head down and kissed her, her bright brown eyes glistening in expectation.

"Bride?"

"Bride, there's no law against married civil servants."

"Soon?"

"Soon," and he started down the hall, her arms wrapped around his neck.

"And tonight?"

"Love—no words."

"Waves?"

He bent over and kissed her.

Saturday, March 21, Paris. Charles Maurras, the aging editor of the *Action Française*, stood in the well of the courtroom. The judge spoke, "Justice is far removed from politics. The court has previously found you guilty of incitation to murder under the Newspaper Law of 1881."

The judge looked down at the unperturbed defendant, who quietly waited for what he expected would be his political martyrdom. The judge read from the sheet of paper, "The court sentences you to four months' imprisonment and fines you one hundred francs."

The bailiff came to escort the prisoner from the courtroom.

Saturday, March 21, Dover, England. Geneviève Tabouis stood at the rail of the steamer pulling away from Dover harbor for Calais, France. She looked back at the white cliffs. She was wrapped in a long fox fur coat, a large black hat firmly pinned to her upswept coiffure, a big handbag on her arm. Around her stood a bunch of men in thick overcoats with big dark hats squashed down on their heads.

Geneviève spoke to several gathered near her, "I was struck by the British foreign office's obstinate refusal to understand that the basic interests of the democracies were at stake now that the dictators were gaining in power."

A man said, "Possibly they cannot understand what they are helpless to stop."

Geneviève nodded silently at the insight. "Helpless to stop" was not a state she ever willingly accepted.

She sighed and said, "Yes, France has lost her high place in the world, ceding it step by step to Germany."

The men listened. None of them would ever say that out loud.

With a deep sense of resignation, Geneviève continued, "At the last session of the League Council, I felt humiliated before the German correspondents. They were unable to conceal their satisfaction in the turn of events. As I passed their seats, they made disagreeable remarks about the politics for which I stand." She paused for a moment, then added, "That morning was a disagreeable first, but probably not the last."

One of the men, a deputy close to Flandin, moved to an upbeat note, "The foreign minister is bringing back an agreement from Great Britain about a guarantee in case of attack, an agreement for the British and French general staffs to consult."

Geneviève nodded in understanding: the French press and much of the public would be pleased, overlooking the smallness of the gesture. Once again large hopes had ended with small accomplishments.

The deputy gave his summation of London, "Granted, Tabouis! Let us assume that we are in an inferior position now and will henceforth have to take orders from Ten Downing Street," mentioning the office of the British prime minister, "You yourself have said many times that there is a better understanding of foreign affairs at Ten Downing Street than at the Quai d'Orsay. It could be worse."

Geneviève listened silently. She looked at the deputy with sorrowful understanding.

Next to Geneviève a man moved to speak, a senior minister of long standing on the Left. "The tragedy lies not in our taking second place," Geneviève turned and looked closely at him, "but in the uncertainty as to how long England will be able to maintain herself, as well as us, in a firm position in face of the war-threat blackmail carried on by Hitler and Mussolini!"

Geneviève silently nodded at the wisdom of what the minister had just said. She nodded at the other men. All agreed. All understood a troubled future was coming. Germany had run the table.

Sunday, March 22, Breslau, Germany. A sea of faces looked towards the speaker's stand. In front stood a phalanx of brown-shirted storm troopers and black-uniformed SS troops. Dignitaries were six deep across the stage. This was the largest campaign rally to be held before the following Sunday's plebiscite on Chancellor Adolph Hitler's leadership of resurgent Germany.

A roar went up as the crowd saw the bareheaded, dark-haired chancellor advance across the stage towards the lectern. The applause mounted into a rolling thunder. The chancellor held out his arms for the crowd to quiet down. The noise slowly subsided.

He began, "I have therefore done my best to reestablish the honor of the German people not only domestically but also in foreign affairs. In these three years the resurrection of the German people has succeeded so completely that one seeks in vain for a comparison in history. Let those who follow me judge whether I have succeeded in these years in bettering the position of the German people in the eyes of the world," and he paused, "or whether I have failed to do so."

The crowd broke into applause; the chancellor quickly held out his arms to quiet them so he could finish his point. "In all these three years no word has been spoken in Germany that threatens another nation."

The crowd applauded and began to chorus, "Heil Hitler." The chancellor stood back and listened for a moment; then he stepped forward and held his arms straight out while looking down with his head, a minor show of humility in the face of the massive approval of the German people.

The chancellor looked up. "The Versailles treaty cannot serve as a foundation for a new era of peace…Germany bases its reorganization upon equal rights and therewith the assumption of equal duties."

The crowd applauded in polite agreement.

Hitler, voice rising, arms spread out before the audience, moved to his closing, "The peoples of Europe must find a new relation to each other, some new form must be created…this new order must be set up under the words: reason and logic, understanding and mutual consideration. They," and he paused to let the word sink in, "make a mistake who think that over the entrance to this new order there can stand the word "Versailles."

The audience looked on with rapt attention, completely silent. It was coming.

Then with a swirl of his head, his forelock brushed back, his arms outstretched forward in a triumphant "V," the Führer of all the German people thundered, "Versailles, that would not be the foundation stone of the new order, but its gravestone!"

The crowd erupted in a frenzy of applause and cheering, the unspeakable ecstasy of a triumphant new destiny just over the horizon, an unshaped vision in the imagination of every foot-stomping, hand-clapping person standing in the broad square.

Ambassador's Reception

Saturday, April 18, Paris. In the early evening darkness, the taxi stopped and started as a throng of limousines and taxicabs snaked its way up Avenue d'Iéna towards the American ambassador's residence at Number 2. Dexter sat in the rear seat quite relaxed and said to Marcelle, "One encouraging comment for you. In London there is now an undercurrent in Parliament that the Baldwin cabinet should have had the courage of its convictions and proceeded with the Hoare-Laval process. It was only meant as a start."

Marcelle said, rather evenly but with an absent air, "Yes, the advantages come into sharp relief against the backdrop of lost opportunities."

Dexter leaned back and listened to the tune *Tout va très bien, Madame la Marquise* (All is just fine, Madame la Marquise) coming from the great new innovation, the car radio. He smiled; the song was everywhere these days. He began to hum along. The song told a story of a vacationing marquise calling her caretaker, who starts describing to the marquise a series of cascading misfortunes befalling her country estate, each misfortune followed by the reassuring words that "all is just fine." The last verse describes the chateau burning down followed by the ever-reassuring chorus.

Marcelle smiled and listened with a contented smile on her face. She knew Dexter thought the song described the arc of France's foreign policy, which she agreed had been an ever-cascading series of misfortunes. She also felt that the flippant song described how quickly the privileged elites of Paris had gotten over the German reoccupation of the Rhineland. They had resumed in just a matter of weeks their mindless pursuit of this year's vacuous social season, a wonderland of balls and soirées. Like tonight, she harrumphed to herself.

The taxi pulled up to a curb, a doorman came forward and opened the door, and Dexter stepped out and then reached back for Marcelle. He held her hand as she set one high-heeled shoe out on the asphalt and then the other. She had a lovely cream-colored stole trimmed with dark foxtail around her shoulders. She held a small clutch purse in her left hand while holding the stole clasped in front of her. They walked over to the entranceway and into the foyer. A maid came up and took Marcelle's stole and hat and handed Dexter a claim check. He handed her his hat, stick, and topcoat.

Dexter took Marcelle's arm and they swept forward into the large drawing room. Dexter said, "It's what they call an informal reception. No announcing of names and such. Less formality. You get to the champagne straightaway."

Marcelle laughed: the insights of an aging junior diplomat.

A waiter came over with a tray of champagne glasses, looked at Marcelle. "Madame?"

"Yes, please."

Dexter nodded affirmatively and the waiter handed him a second glass. Across the room, Dexter spotted Daisy and Virginia beautifully gowned and their prosperously stolid husbands, black ties standing above starched white shirtfronts. He said to Marcelle, "Come on. Duty calls. You've met the ladies before. Now the gentlemen."

She saw the two American ladies from last year's Fourth of July reception. She presumed the men were the husband bankers. As they walked across the room, she saw out of the corner of her eye the American ambassador and his wife standing over in the center near a large fireplace. The wife had a beautiful sash across a grandmotherly bosom ending in an ample midriff that dropped into a dress of ever-wider flounces nicely arranged. Marcelle was impressed with the bright blue trim on the pale green dress. Yes, there was an artistry combined with shrewd business acumen for the couturiers who made and sold these dresses to the aging doyennes of society. She smiled to herself. Irène had just re-cut one of her old silk dresses into something long and elegant for tonight. She was a treasure.

Seeing Dexter and Marcelle approach, Daisy exclaimed, "Ah, a diplomat for the ambassador's reception." Turning to Marcelle, she held her hand. "So nice to see you again."

Dexter held out his hand to Daisy's husband and said, "Henry, may I present my fiancée Marcelle." Marcelle held out her hand.

The husband shook her hand and turned sidewise to the other man and said, "John, I lost another bet."

Marcelle looked askance at John and turned and held out her hand to him and cooed sweetly, "I heard about the first bet. What was the second?"

Dexter looked startled. Marcelle turned to him and laying on the sugar, eyes twinkling, said, "The first one traveled the corridors of the Quai d'Orsay," and she paused and said with an edge, "dear."

Startled, Henry put his hand to his mouth and said, "Oops!"

Daisy rolled her eyes and scolded him with her expression.

John stepped forward to push the conversation towards a safer shore. "Here, let me see your left hand." Marcelle held out her left hand. John took it in his own and held it up, admiring the beautiful diamond ring on the ring finger. He showed the hand around. "See?" Daisy and Virginia looked on with true admiration.

Marcelle said, "It belonged to Dexter's grandmother." Daisy and Virginia were truly impressed.

John bowed his head towards Marcelle and said, "That's the second bet." He explained to Marcelle with some seriousness, "It's so rare for a man so skilled, at shall we say the first bet," and he nodded at Dexter, "to fall for the second bet. But I see why," he gallantly added and kissed her hand.

Marcelle smiled warmly at him.

Henry turned to Dexter. "You really need to come speak to the American club. Dreadful about the Rhineland business. But why did the Frogs ever sign a pact with the Bolshies?" referring to the Franco-Russian pact that was the ostensible cause the Germans gave for marching into the Rhineland.

John chimed in, "Hitler said Communism was enemy number one. Surely we can all agree on that. He's put Germany back to work."

Dexter said, good naturedly, "Yes, I have been neglecting my duties. I will come speak to the American club." Turning to John, he said, "The Bolshies, as you so affectionately call them, are two thousand miles to the east. The Nazis are barely two hundred miles from Paris. Remember 1914?"

"Yes," he mumbled, "but what does it all mean? Next week the French are going to vote. The Socialists are expected to win big. Then we'll have a Bolshie right here in Paris. In the Matignon," and he looked at Marcelle. He knew where she worked.

Dexter knew from experience that a light laugh was the right tonic for this situation. So he laughed and explained, "Blum," referring to the leader of the Socialists, "took the Socialists out of the Communist International in 1920. He's the best bulwark against a workers' uprising there is. A new French government may be able to turn around the French economy. Keep the money in your bank safe."

John nodded with some understanding. "Well, it's sure the Radicals haven't done it."

Dexter nodded in agreement. Daisy broke in, lightly saying to Marcelle, "Yes, the Rhineland business was simply dreadful. Threatened to upset the entire spring social season." Marcelle gave a quick look of sympathetic concern to Daisy. Dexter was impressed with the sincerity of the insincerity.

Virginia quickly added, "But it got right back on track. Why the Rothschilds had one glittering affair after another. Next month the horses will be upon us…and then the automobiles," she said referring to the horse races at Longchamps and elegant automobile shows held in the Bois de Boulogne.

Marcelle smiled in agreement. "Yes, Tout-Paris lives in a world of its own delight." Dexter laughed to himself; that's the way Suzanne and Marcelle would describe Anthony Eden.

Over in front of the fireplace, the ambassadress turned to her husband between wellwishers and said, with barely concealed curiosity, "There's Dexter. With his new ladyfriend. I hear she's a real marquise."

The ambassador good-humouredly replied, "I think that's just a nickname."

"Oh, no. I am sure. She's a marquise." The ambassadress continued to look at Marcelle with great interest. "She doesn't seem to have very many jewels for a marquise?"

"Rather pretty, though," said the ambassador.

"There. One of the men is looking at the ring on her hand."

"Oh, I am told by the social secretary that Dexter got engaged," said the ambassador.

"Engaged?" A look of perplexity came over the ambassadress's face. "Why I didn't take Dexter for a climber."

She turned and looked at her husband and asked earnestly, "I thought you said Dexter came from a good family."

"He does."

"Does he need money?" the ambassadress asked, her face clouded with concern. "Maybe that's where the jewels went?"

"Oh, no. His grandparents settled a small trust on him when he joined the Foreign Service. The grandfather was at Gray Brothers Harrison and Company. It's still in New York. Doing rather well, I hear. Well connected to Roosevelt."

"Then where did the jewels go?" The mystery simply confounded her.

The ambassador snuggled up to his wife and whispered, "Into your imagination."

"Oh, you're so sweet," she beamed. "Tonight you get a big hug and a warm kiss."

"My dreams will be fulfilled," answered the ambassador as he watched Dexter and Marcelle walk over towards them.

Dexter came up, nodded at the ambassador, and said to his wife, "Madame, may I present my fiancée, Marcelle Lambert."

"Oh, how delighted I am. We have heard so much about you," and she giggled.

The ambassador started to hum and whistle *Tout va très bien, Madame la Marquise,* his eyes looking upwards at the ceiling like an innocent schoolboy.

Marcelle quickly shot him a sharp glance and then looked back at the ambassadress, "You have?"

The ambassadress eagerly asked, "Are you really a marquise?"

Marcelle threw her head back and laughed and looked at the ambassador with great good humor. He's really just an old boy, she thought.

"No, I am not," Marcelle pleasingly answered.

"You are not related to the three banks and two steelworks?"

Marcelle laughed again, "No, that is the comtesse."

The ambassador quit humming and smoothly intervened, "Why yes. We all heard about your evening at Lipp's last fall."

Marcelle smiled and explained, "The comtesse was with Monsieur le Minister…"

The ambassadress brightened, "That of course explains it." Money was always on the arm of an important minister.

Marcelle added, "At the Matignon, I wear a black skirt, dark stockings, and a starched linen blouse. Not quite a maid. But close. A *redactrice*."

The ambassador smiled and said with insightful shrewdness, "Marquise has a certain ring of truth to it." Of course in today's world, real influence would unobtrusively wear a black skirt and starched linen blouse.

Marcelle laughed and looked into his eyes. "Oh, yes, we are a great couple. Rumors travel the corridors of the Quai d'Orsay about him while nicknames about me echo down the halls of the embassy." She held out her hand to the ambassador, who swept it up and gallantly gave it a kiss.

Marcelle looked at Dexter and then turned to the ambassador. "I can assure you the rumors about my influence are greatly exaggerated." She arched an eyebrow towards Dexter and said, "About him, I'm not so sure."

The ambassador laughed and hugged his wife. She looked at Marcelle and said with wonderful sincerity, "Someone has a beautiful daughter-in-law coming."

Hôtel Matignon

May, 1936. The man briskly walked down the hallway, stopped outside the door of the *secrétaire général,* and gently rapped on the open door. The *secrétaire général* stood up and said, "Come in." He held out his arm to one of the waiting chairs. "Ah, Monsieur Moch, congratulations on your appointment as the new secretary-general at the Matignon."

The man deferentially tipped his head and replied, "And congratulations on your appointment at the Élysée Palace. The President of the Republic will be well served."

The *secrétaire général* replied with a certain abashedness, "Thank you."

Moch added, "Your wife must be pleased."

The *secrétaire général* looked thoughtful and smiled, "Beyond measure. She is very attached to the ceremonial."

The *secrétaire général* folded his hands on the desk in front of him and came to the point of business, "We here in the *administration centrale* stand ready to support the orderly transfer of responsibilities."

"Yes, let's speak about that," replied Moch.

The *secrétaire général* gave a small tour de horizon of the organization and concluded, "You will find our *chef de bureau,* Madame Lambert, to be highly competent and efficient."

"Yes, so we have heard," Moch replied, noncommittally.

The *secrétaire général* cleared his throat and proceeded to bring up a personnel matter of minor delicacy, "With regard to Madame Lambert, she holds permanent rank as a *sous-chef* at the ministry of labor. They have consented to her permanent promotion to *chef de bureau* subject to the new administration's approval," and the *secrétaire général* nodded in Moch's direction.

Moch said evenly, without commitment, "Yes, of course."

The *secrétaire général* continued, "They very much would like to have her back," and he paused, "after completing the transition here at the Matignon, of course. We presume you want to use your own people in key positions."

"Yes, for the most part that is true," said Moch.

The *secrétaire général* was finding Moch a bit more reticent on this promotion matter than he would have liked. He looked inquiringly at Moch, his expression making the question.

Moch shifted in his chair and said, "Yes, we want to smooth the way. I will forward to you this afternoon a letter of approval for the promotion. I will leave in your capable hands the coordination with the ministry of labor."

The *secrétaire général* beamed and replied, "Madame Lambert will be greatly pleased." He paused for a moment's reflection and said, "We are having a small reception here Friday evening for her and her fiancé; they are getting married Monday and taking a two-week honeymoon. She will be back well before the change in administrations."

Moch listened, a minor disappointment seeming to cloud his expression, the *secrétaire général* thought. Moch said tentatively, "Yes, we heard she was engaged to an American diplomat." The statement hung as a question.

The *secrétaire général* replied, "Yes, a junior attaché. But there is a sense among our people, confidentially, that he is well connected to important people high up in the American State Department. He seems to have some sort of parallel role here in Paris."

Moch looked inwardly thoughtful and said, "Yes, so it would appear." He had read a detailed report from the embassy in Washington. There were elements in the American government thinking about Europe's future; they had men in Europe.

The *secrétaire général* thought to himself that Moch might possibly know more than he was letting on. He was after all a graduate of L'École Polytechnique; he must be quite smart, possibly capable.

Moch stood up and the *secrétaire général* came around his desk to escort the visitor out. Moch said, "Possibly I could come to the reception Friday evening? It would be a pleasure to meet Madame Lambert."

"Why yes, of course." The *secrétaire général* smiled.

The telephone rang in Dexter's office. He picked it up, "Dexter Jones here." He listened to the caller and wrote down some notes, "The new secretary-general at the Matignon…"

Dexter continued listening, periodically speaking into the mouthpiece, "Yes, I understand. No. Shorten the honeymoon? To the contrary, she will be very pleased. A change of plans? No, Saturday would be fine. No, I won't tell her. Other announcements…we will look forward to Friday evening."

Dexter hung up the phone and leaned back in his chair. He thought about what he had just heard. He smiled. Then he looked at his watch; he had an appointment. Time to leave.

As Dexter approached the entrance to Café de la Paix, he saw Geneviève Tabouis standing just outside waiting for him. He came up and said, "Geneviève, so nice we could meet."

He held the door open as they entered; Dexter nodded at the maitre d' who escorted them to a table along the windows overlooking the Place de la Opéra.

Geneviève started right in, "Ethiopia has been a terrible disappointment."

Dexter responded sympathetically, "Yes." The Italian armies had taken the capital Addis Ababa in what Mussolini had hailed as "The March of the Iron Will." Emperor Selassie had abandoned the capital and left Africa on a British warship for exile. Ethiopia had been vanquished.

A waiter brought two chilled glasses of white wine and set them down on the table.

Geneviève continued, "Anthony," she said referring to Anthony Eden, "made the case for collective security and the League as well as one could hope."

"Yes, but at the end of the day force has to stand behind guarantees. One of the English MPs said that a dictator who was not afraid of losing his head would always win against politicians who are afraid of losing their seats."

Geneviève slowly nodded in agreement.

Dexter continued, "Eden resolutely defends principle and policy; the sanctions against Italy remain in place. However, the chance to bring Italy back into alliance with France and Great Britain diminishes by the day. The strategic cost is great."

Again, Geneviève nodded in agreement, "Time is working in favor of the dictators."

Dexter nodded in silent agreement.

Geneviève brightened. "There is a rumor you are getting married."

Dexter smiled, "The rumor will be confirmed shortly. A small ceremony. I will send a messenger with an invitation to you shortly."

She raised her glass of wine and clinked glasses with Dexter, "*À votre santé.*"

Dexter smiled warmly.

Parc of Hotel Matignon

Friday evening. Dexter and Marcelle stood together in a small reception room in the Matignon that overlooked the spacious lawns and columns of trees marching away into the sunset. They were sipping champagne from crystal glasses. He wore a dark gray pinstripe suit, white shirt, and a soft red tie, giving him something of a festive air, different from the dour diplomatic dress of everyday duty. Marcelle stood, poised, heels together, in a dark blue suit, the skirt coming just two inches below the knee, dark stockings, and black high-heeled shoes. She wore a dark maroon silk blouse and a pearl brooch just below her left collar tip. Fashionable and subdued. Her hair was down, but beautifully coiffed.

Suzanne Bardoux tugged at Étienne's sleeve and whispered in his ear, "And you were worried that she had lost her wiles. She is radiant tonight," and gave a small laugh.

Then Suzanne looked over at the new secretary-general and whispered again to Étienne, "There's Jules Moch. He's Léon Blum's new secretary-general. I hear he has a charter to completely reorganize the staff services. The Popular Front has a big agenda."

Étienne whispered back, "And he is looking at Marcelle. He seems to like what he sees."

Suzanne laughed. "What man wouldn't!"

Étienne laughed. "Yes, but I think his admiration is professional."

Suzanne looked at him with consternation. "Yes, you would think that." She took a sip from her champagne glass.

The *secrétaire général* stepped forward, cleared his throat to get the guests' attention, and said, "We, *le gouvernment*, are pleased this evening to announce Madame Lambert's permanent promotion to *chef de bureau*. Both the new administration," and the *secrétaire général* nodded at Jules Moch, "and the ministry of labor have approved this long-merited promotion." The *secrétaire général* turned towards Marcelle and raised his glass, "Madame Lambert."

The other guests raised their glasses in turn and called out in turn, "*À votre santé.*"

Dexter leaned over and kissed Marcelle on the cheek, "See dear. You were not forgotten."

Marcelle beamed and looked at the *secrétaire général* and graciously said, "Thank you." She turned to the wife of the *secrétaire général* and beamed. "Thank you so much for your encouragement and support, Madame."

The wife smiled pleasingly at Marcelle and said with great sincerity, "Your efforts have contributed greatly to my husband's promotion to the Élysée Palace. We are of course grateful," and she hugged her husband's arm. There would be the state visits, the dinners, no more of this drudgery about budgets.

The *secrétaire général* stepped forward and said, "The new secretary-general to the premier, Monsieur Jules Moch, would like to say a few words," and he stepped back.

Moch stepped forward, "We congratulate Madame Lambert on her promotion," and he smiled warmly at Marcelle and then looked at her very directly, "and I think we have some good news and possibly some not-so-good news." He looked around at the guests and let the words settle in.

Moch looked at Dexter and said, "I, of course, discussed some of this with her fiancé," and he let the words trail off.

Suzanne gave Étienne a very concerned look; this was not the way to start off with Marcelle.

Marcelle quickly turned and gave Dexter a sharp, hard glance. He smiled at her encouragingly and mouthed silently that all was OK. Suzanne watched and her concerns ebbed. Dexter pointed to Marcelle to listen to the new secretary-general. Marcelle turned her attention back to Moch.

Moch looked at Marcelle and said, "We are not really looking at a transition. We have spoken with the ministry of labor. They have reluctantly, very reluctantly I might say," and the secretary-general looked around at the guests to drive home the point, "given their consent to Madame Lambert's continued appointment to the premier's office here at the Matignon."

Marcelle looked at Moch with interest, then turned and looked inquiringly at Dexter, who nodded to her to keep looking at Moch. More was to come.

Moch smiled, warmly for the first time the *secrétaire général* noticed, and said, "We have another temporary appointment for you, Madame Lambert. We are appointing you *directrix de administration* of the *administration centrale* here at the Matignon.

Suzanne Bardoux gleefully clapped her hands and looked triumphantly at Étienne.

A very pleased look came over Marcelle's face but her quick mind wondered about the not-so-good news; another shoe was to drop.

Moch said, "We would really like you to take up your new duties a week from Monday. Your fiancé said that this would most likely meet with your approval."

Marcelle looked at Dexter and smiled at him. He really did know her.

Marcelle turned back and graciously said to Moch, "It would be my greatest pleasure. This is a wonderful appointment."

The *secrétaire général* now stepped forward again. "We have used our influence with the administration of the Seventh Arrondisement, modest as it is," and he chuckled at the laughter, "to have your marriage ceremony moved up to tomorrow afternoon."

Then the *secrétaire général* turned to Dexter. "We have heard that your diplomatic tour has been extended to 1939?"

"Yes, it has," replied Dexter.

The *secrétaire général* thought for a moment and looked at Dexter and said, "Possibly when you come up for reassignment, the French government will be able to find a suitable posting for Madame Lambert. And she can accompany you."

"That would be quite generous," replied Dexter.

Moch's face clouded over with minor annoyance, he cleared his throat, "Yes, of course," and he stopped and fumbled for words, "however, in the future," and he paused as he let the uncertainty of a troubled future settle into the guests' minds, "reasons of state could possibly intervene. In that case, senior officials would have to stay at their posts."

Marcelle looked at him and nodded her thoughtful approval at what he had said. She said, "Yes. I completely understand. I would not expect less."

Undaunted, the *secrétaire général* continued, looking at Dexter, "In that case, why since the French government gets along so well with the American State Department, I am sure we could arrange a posting for you as, say," and he paused and thought, "a visitor at the École de Guerre or as a lecturer at one of the *grandes écoles.*"

Dexter beamed and smiled at Étienne while vigorously tapping his chest with school boyish pride and said, "We'll be colleagues."

Étienne laughed and raised his champagne glass in playful salute.

The *secrétaire général* basked in the glow of warm cheer that his suggestion set off.

Marcelle stepped forward, nodded politely at the *secrétaire général,* then turned and stood in front of Dexter. She looked over her shoulder at the guests and pronounced, "I think not."

Dexter looked down at her, his expression turning inquisitive.

She looked up at him, warmly and affectionately. Then she turned and stood halfway facing the guests and said, "I think that by 1939 even the Americans," and she paused and let the words sink in. Then she repeated, "Even the Americans will be advancing the ablest men to the front rank."

Suzanne and Étienne laughed in agreement. The others nodded as understanding dawned. Moch stroked his chin in thoughtful consideration and thought: a wise insight. He liked her insouciance, often the companion of high intelligence, he mused.

She turned back and stood in front of Dexter and reached up and played with the knot of his tie. She looked up at him with the deepest love he had ever seen in her eyes. With her back turned to the guests, she said for all to hear, "I love you."

Then she turned her head around and looked over her shoulder and said, "And I am going to support him wherever he is, wherever he goes."

She turned and again looked up at him, the adoration in her eyes staying constant as the expression on her face changed to one of steely, even determination, the look he had come to see as the mirror to her inner self.

"Even if I can't be there with him."

End

Paris 1935

On Reflection – Some Words

Hoare-Laval

Everyone could now see that the Hoare-Laval Agreement was a very shrewd, farseeing agreement which could have saved the Negus of Abyssinia from ruin before his army was destroyed.

> Winston S. Churchill, *Times*, May 9, 1936

If (1) settlement by compromise is to be vetoed in the name of League principles, and (2) the League is unable to make these principles prevail, our last state will be worse than our first. We shall have lost the advantages of ordinary diplomacy, and gained none of the benefits of the new order.

> Veteran journalist J.A. Spender, *Times,* May 12, 1936

We are all agreed now that the best chance of stopping Hitler was when he sent his troops into the Rhineland; and that we failed. I know you think that the last chance was at Munich. I disagree. The last chance was at Stresa. Austria, not Czechoslovakia, was the essential bastion of Central Europe.

Only one power could have saved Austria and that was Italy. We could have had Italy. But the price was Abyssinia [Ethiopia]. It was well worth paying; and believe me, it would have been a benefit, not harm, to the Abyssinians.

> Pierre Laval, conversation with British parliamentarian Robert Boothby, March 1940.

In rejecting the Hoare-Laval pact, the British people put moral considerations, considerations of honor, above the national interest. History rarely records this as wise policy.

> J. Kenneth Brody, *The Avoidable War*, 2000.

The Rhineland

If the French had marched into the Rhineland, we would have had to withdraw with our tails between our legs, for the military resources at our disposal would have been fully inadequate for even a moderate resistance...A retreat on our part would have spelled collapse...The forty-eight hours after the march into the Rhineland were the most nerve-wracking in my life."

Adolph Hitler, from Paul Schmidt, *Hitler's Interpreter*, quoted from William Shire's *The Nightmare Years: 1930-1940*, 1984.

Would Hitler have retreated before a French riposte in the Rhineland? Historians today are not so sure. "We now know, one of the most eminent has concluded, that Hitler would at least have tried to fight—he was quite mad enough for that."

The stakes were overwhelming and Hitler's determination and conviction are well known...At all events, he was not put to the test.

Brody, *The Avoidable War*, 2000.

Since the challenge of March 7, 1936, the entire structure of 1919 had been collapsing; the edifice of Versailles was now just a historical memory. It was a terrible blow to French policy and also to British policy, though this would only become apparent later. The 'gathering storm' was absolutely certain after March 1936.

Maurice Baumont, *The Origins of the Second World War, 1978*, quoted from Brody, *The Avoidable War*.

The Principals

Not long after his resignation as Foreign Secretary, Sir Samuel Hoare returned to the Cabinet as First Lord of the Admiralty...he was a member of the Big Four that under Chamberlain dominated government. In wartime he served usefully as Ambassador to Spain. A grateful government rewarded his services to the state with a peerage and as Viscount Templewood, he lived elegantly and devoted himself to literature and sport.

Brody, *The Avoidable War*, 2000.

For his role in the Pétain government [Laval was prime minister during much of the German occupation of France 1940-44] he was promptly indicted on the day of victory. His trial was less a judicial proceeding than a calculated act of vengeance.

Paul A. Myers

The trial opened on October 4, 1945. Judgment of death was rendered on October 10 and the execution set for October 15. Laval bore all this with immense courage and spiritual grace.

Brody, *The Avoidable War*, 2000.

The officer raised his saber. Laval cried "Vive la France." The saber was lowered, the volley exploded…From throughout the prison came raucous cries: "Assassins, assassins. Vive Laval."

Brody, *The Trial of Pierre Laval*, 2010.

Some Sources

Books

Bernier, Olivier. *Fireworks at Dusk: Paris in the Thirties.* Boston, 1993.

Brody, J. Kenneth. *The Avoidable War: Pierre Laval & the Politics of Reality 1935-1936 Vol 2.* New Brunswick NJ and London, 2000.

_____. *The Trial of Pierre Laval: Defining Treason, Collaboration, and Patriotism in World War II France.* New Brunswick NJ and London, 2010.

Cate, Curtis. *André Malraux.* New York, 1995.

Chambrun, René de. *Pierre Laval: Traitor or Patriot?* New York, 1984.

Colton, Joel. *Léon Blum: Humanist in Politics.* New York, 1966.

Doughty, Robert A. *De Gaulle's Concept of a Mobile, Professional Army: Genesis of French Defeat?* Monograph, Army War College, Carlisle Barracks PA, January 1974.

Fitch, Noel Riley. *Sylvia Beach and the Lost Generation.* New York, 1983.

Horne, Alistair. *La Belle France: A Short History.* New York, 2005.

Huddleston, Sisley. *Paris Salons Cafés Studios.* Philadelphia and London, 1928.

Hussey, Andrew. *Paris: The Secret History.* New York, 2006.

Lottman, Herbert R. *The Left Bank: Writers, Artists, and Politics from the Popular Front to the Cold War.* Chicago, 1982.

Madsen, Axel. *Malraux: A Biography.* New York, 1976.

Pertinax. *The Gravediggers of France.* New York, 1944.

Schuker, Stephen A. *France and the Remilitarization of the Rhineland, 1936.* JSTOR, *French Historical Studies,* Vol. 14, No. 3. (Spring, 1986), pp. 299-338.

Shirer, William L. *The Nightmare Years: 1930-1940.* Boston, 1984.

_____. *The Collapse of the Third Republic.* New York, 1969.

Tabouis, Geneviève. *Blackmail or War.* London, 1938.

_____. *They Called Me Cassandra.* New York, 1942.

Weber, Eugen. *Action Francaise.* Stanford, 1962.

_____. *The Hollow Years: France in the 1930s.* New York, 1994.

Newspapers and Periodicals

New York Times (Internet archives). Numerous news articles from 1935-36 generally datelined Paris, Berlin, or London. Paris correspondent P.J. Phipps in particular.

Times of London (Internet archives). Numerous news articles from 1935-36 generally datelined Paris, France, or London.

Time (Internet archives). Articles from 1935-36 datelined Paris, France, or Germany.

Note: The residence at 7 rue Monsieur was where English writer Nancy Mitford lived from 1947 until 1967.

Note: The song *Tout va très bien, Madame la Marquise* can be heard and seen with English subtitles at YouTube, as can other songs and anthems mentioned in the novel.

List of Illustrations

Cover Image

"Café de la Paix à Paris," Konstantin Korovin, 1939, Wikipedia Foundation license, photographic reproduction/image is in the public domain in US and elsewhere due to copyright expiration.

Interior images

Anthony Eden, Google Images, Slingshot.com, image in public domain.

Pierre Laval, during World War II, WikiCommons, image in public domain.

Sir Samuel Hoare, 1930s, WikiCommons, image in public domain because it is a work of the US federal government.

Geneviève Tabouis, approximately 1938, low resolution image scanned from cover of her book *Blackmail or War,* London, 1938, image is in public domain because copyright in the United States has expired or was never filed.

Alexis Léger, WikiCommons, image is in public domain.

Sylvia Beach with James Joyce and Adrienne Monnier, Paris 1920, WikiCommons, image is in the public domain in the United States.

André Malraux, 1935, WikiCommons, low resolution image qualifies for fair use under US copyright law.

\#\#\#

www.ingramcontent.com/pod-product-compliance
Lightning Source LLC
Chambersburg PA
CBHW071133170626
46809CB00002B/595